The NOTORIOUS BRIDEGROOM

BOOK YOUR PLACE ON OUR WEBSITE AND MAKE THE READING CONNECTION!

We've created a customized website just for our very special readers, where you can get the inside scoop on everything that's going on with Zebra, Pinnacle and Kensington books.

When you come online, you'll have the exciting opportunity to:

- View covers of upcoming books
- Read sample chapters
- Learn about our future publishing schedule (listed by publication month *and author*)
- Find out when your favorite authors will be visiting a city near you
- Search for and order backlist books from our online catalog
- Check out author bios and background information
- Send e-mail to your favorite authors
- Meet the Kensington staff online
- Join us in weekly chats with authors, readers and other guests
- Get writing guidelines
- AND MUCH MORE!

Visit our website at
http://www.kensingtonbooks.com

The NOTORIOUS BRIDEGROOM

Kit Donner

ZEBRA BOOKS
Kensington Publishing Corp.
http://www.kensingtonbooks.com

Chapter 1

Winchelsea
Southeast England
Spring 1803

Patience Mandeley considered the wisdom of her plan, and determined that either she was very courageous, believed in guardian angels, or was quite tetched in the head. At the moment, she leaned toward the latter. But what else could she do? She could think of no other way to save her younger brother Rupert from treason charges.

"Miss Patience, quit woolgathering, and let us be off to the fair," her companion of two days, Colette, told her, smiling. "Time enough to worry about your new position later."

Patience started, suddenly awakened from her reverie. She slowly rose, gathered her bonnet and matching shawl, and followed her friend out the door of the inn. *Her plan had to work.* There wasn't much time to help Rupert before the magistrate found him.

Against her better judgment, Colette had convinced her to enjoy Winchelsea's Mop Fair before they began their work in the morning. Colette, attired in a black walking dress with light gray mantle, and Patience in deep blue with a light blue cashmere shawl, strolled down the main street joining the other fairgoers.

Patience kept watch for her brother, who might be lurking in the shadows of the lively crowd. She had to get word to him about her plan that would save him.

The twilight hours of the fair cast a dusky rose on the street choked full of locals, travelers, merchants, and farmers. Most of the noisy rumble headed toward the market square, where a bonfire blazed merrily near rows of oxen on spits wafting a delicious aroma to the hungry crowd.

The women made their way to the merchants' tents, hearing the vendors shouting over each other to entice their customers with exotic perfume from the Far East, bright-colored linen, or a sweet orange. The Annual Mop Fair brought a variety of folk from several miles around who looked forward to this spring event. Crowded streets slowed the ladies' walk as Patience searched and worried about her younger brother and his troubles.

Examining the softest of silks and delicious gingerbread occupied the ladies for a time until they heard a loud voice halloing the multitude to the Wild Beast show. The crowd surged forward, pulling Colette in its wake. Patience started after her friend but stopped suddenly.

Someone tugged on her skirts. "Lady, can ye help me find Bella?" a pitiful little voice asked.

Startled, Patience glanced down to find a forlorn small child with tear-stained cheeks, clutching a wooden doll. Four or five at the most, the girl peered at Patience from beneath her tattered gray day cap. She looked to be a sweet tyke, dressed in a faded blue frock, well-worn shoes, with long, disheveled gold curls bobbing down her back. Patience was always lost when it came to children and animals, and the little girl caught at her heart.

"Hello, little one. What's your name?" Patience inquired, removing a handkerchief from her reticule. She knelt down, and after wetting a corner of the lacy white square, she rubbed at the child's dirty face and wiped away her tears.

"Me name's Sally, and I need to find me Aunt Bella. Do ye think she's lost too?" the girl sniffled.

Patience smiled. "No, your aunt must be very worried and looking everywhere for you." Confident they would find the child's relative somewhere nearby, she tucked the handkerchief in her sleeve and held out her hand. "Come, let us see if we can find her," she told the small girl as they walked together toward the bonfire.

"What's yer name?" the little girl asked, her head cocked to look up at Patience.

Patience hesitated before revealing the name she had chosen for this masquerade. It simply wouldn't do for anyone to learn Patience's true identity. Looking down at the small child, she told her, "Patience Grundy." She noticed Sally clutched something to her chest. "Is that your doll?"

Sally's eyes opened wide and an innocent smile hinted at missing teeth. "Me baby is Jane. See here, Miss Grundy," she said as she held her unclothed wooden doll for Patience to get a closer look at four sticks and a wooden ball for a head.

Patience's eyes widened in consternation. "Does your doll have any clothes?"

"I couldn't find any." Sally shrugged her thin shoulders. "Someday, I'll ha' a baby with lots of clothes and hair. But me aunt says I ha' to be a good girl. But I'm always a good girl." She frowned, obviously confused by adult logic.

They reached the boisterous crowd in the square who were enjoying the fiddle music, shared ale, and succulent dripping roast pig and oxen meat. But though Patience examined the merrymakers intently, no one appeared to be looking for lost kin. The tiny little hand in hers firmed her determination.

She was about to ask Sally to describe her aunt, when they reached the fiery pier surrounded by those seeking warmth on this damp spring night. Just as Patience released the little girl's hand briefly to adjust her bonnet, a foxed young man pushed past them and knocked Sally toward the flames.

Patience uttered a shriek and lunged for Sally but a gentleman nearby proved faster. He grabbed the child before she could feel the heat's sting. As the stranger lifted the child up and away from the blaze, Sally squealed in delight.

Breathless with relief, Patience watched the gentleman set the child down safely and told her, "You must be more careful, little one."

His concerned voice invoked a warm smile of gratitude from Patience. Before she could express her appreciation, a young man interrupted them, handing a black cane with a gold tip to Sally's rescuer.

"Lord Londringham, you dropped your cane, over there." The pale, pleasant-featured man gestured over his shoulder to the firepit.

"Thank you, I had forgotten it."

Patience dropped her jaw.

It was he, Lord Londringham, her new employer—and her enemy. What was he doing at the fair? Patience had assumed that nobility would have no interest in local events. She was obviously proved wrong.

Once in his household as the new still-room maid, she would need to try to be inconspicuous if she was to complete her mission. Given her purpose, she wanted to spend as little time as possible with him this night.

The earl, dressed in black, returned his attention to Patience with a quick nod. "If you'll forgive these circumstances, I am

Lord Londringham. Madam, you should watch your daughter more closely. She could have been seriously injured." Censure was implicit in his tone and manner.

Still shaken by his presence, Patience could only manage to sputter indignantly, "I . . . I assure you, sir, I *am* in the habit of taking care of those in my custody, but a man—"

"Where's Jane?" Sally cried, effectively suspending Patience's defense.

Lord Londringham looked inquiringly at Patience.

"Her doll," she responded flatly as the child tugged on Patience's skirts.

With a quick look around, the earl spotted the ravaged wood figure by the fire. He picked it up and showed it to the child.

"Was this your doll?" he asked. At Sally's sad nod and trembling lower lip, the earl told her gently, "She could not be rescued, but might your mama allow me to purchase you a new doll?" He raised his eyebrows at Patience, his gaze inscrutable.

Patience stared in amazement, her lips dry at his intense stare. The man was a chameleon, either gentle and soft-spoken or an arrogant toad. He really should tread the boards with his talent, she thought. He was certainly handsome enough, with dark brown hair, penetrating blue eyes, a lean face, and square jaw. Oh, but she was becoming distracted. She must keep her mind on her plan. Nothing else mattered.

"Madam, do I have your permission?" He threw the charred remnants of the doll back into the fire and turned to Patience for acquiescence.

His dark face impassive, she knew why he made such a good spy. She blinked in confusion. What had he just said? Something about her *daughter*? "Oh, but—" belatedly she began to explain.

"Of course ye may, right *Mama*?" Sally smiled innocently up at Patience, who raised her eyebrows and dropped her jaw. The little minx wanted to pass off Patience as her mama in order to get a new doll.

She hesitated to admonish the child, then well aware the earl stood nearby quietly watching, told the little girl sweetly, "Sally, I told you I would buy you a doll. And we really must not detain this kind gentleman any further. Remember, we must search for Aunt Bella."

His smooth voice disrupted her thoughts, startling her. "Perhaps I could assist you in purchasing a doll for the child *and* your search for Aunt Bella."

Patience put a hand to her head. How ever was she to endure his company, even for one moment? He was not truly considering *joining* them. Did he not have any spy work to do?

She hid her trembling hands in her skirts' pockets. Being so close to the one who was possibly guilty of causing harm to her brother, she had to bite her lip to stop from pronouncing him the rogue she knew him to be. Before Patience could reply negatively, Sally answered for her, running to his side.

"Oh, please, me lord. I would really love a new doll. E'en though I'll miss Jane. And ye can help us find Aunt Bella too." Her sweet supplication would have felled Goliath faster than David's stone.

Patience watched in surprise as he bent down toward Sally.

"Then we are agreed." When the earl smiled at Sally, Patience saw the child's face light up.

"Oh, yes, please, sir," Sally whispered, then turned to Patience with a smug look. "Coming, *Mama*?"

Patience uttered, "Of course, sweetheart" through gritted teeth while following the little lamb leading the big bad wolf off to find a doll. Patience was beginning to believe Sally didn't even have an aunt.

Surely this evening was getting a bit out of hand. Resolved

to once more control the events, Patience hurried after Sally and the earl, noting they had already exchanged names. She had to admire the undivided attention the earl showed the child. But she was not fooled. She knew the man would have helped sell Joseph to the merchants. Her brother James's sermons not forgotten.

After the little girl had tried repeatedly to pronounce his last name without success, she announced decidedly, "I'll call ye 'Mr. Long.'"

The earl threw Patience in a panic when he turned his dark blue study in her direction. "Might I know your name, madam? Surely I cannot call you 'Mama.'"

She knew his smile was deceptively pleasant for Sally.

Sally cut in. "Me mama's name is Miss Grundy."

Trying to remember her "new" last name and hearing the word "mama" in the same sentence disconcerted Patience but not as much as the earl's thorough scrutiny of her before inquiring, "Should that not be *Mrs.* Grundy?" in a low voice that sent warm sparks to her cheeks.

Mortified, her mouth dropped open before she quickly recovered. "Of course. My husband died, soon after we married." She wet her lips in despair. That didn't sound right. "Sally is really my stepdaughter." *Yes, much better,* she thought. She really needed to be rid of his presence and to regain her composure.

Thankfully, he chose not to pursue further inquiry. "Mrs. Grundy, what does Aunt Bella look like?"

"Look like?" Patience asked distractedly, trying to think of an answer.

He chuckled softly, causing her to stare at the softening of his features. "Yes, Aunt Bella. Surely you know what the woman looks like?"

Shoulders back, she bluffed her way into a response. "She's rather difficult to describe, rather ordinary."

Desperate, Patience searched the crowd looking for anyone who could pass as Sally's aunt. She determined to carry Sally if necessary into the crowd, hoping to lose the earl and his interest in them behind.

She spotted a middle-aged woman in black and pointed to her. "Sally, I think I see Aunt Bella over there. Come along, dear."

But the child frowned in confusion. "But, Mama, that's not Aunt Bella." Suddenly, the sound of the merry-go-round caught Sally's attention, and immediately dolls and aunts became yesterday's candy. She pulled at the earl's arm. "Can we go on the merry? Oh, please! Please, Mr. Long?" Sally pleaded.

"I don't see why not, as long as your mama approves," he told her, looking back at Patience a few steps behind them.

She stared at him in bewilderment and found herself nodding. She should have been content to have the opportunity to study her enemy this closely, but could not quite reconcile this man with the image of the purveyor of evil. But what did she really know of him? Unnerved, she could not suppress a shiver.

Unfortunately, the earl must have seen her tremble, for he immediately removed his coat and placed it around her shoulders. "It is certainly a chilly night after the recent rainfall. Let us take the little one on a ride. Then we will look for Aunt Bella."

Sally and the earl walked over to the ride, while Patience followed slowly, enveloped in a musky cocoon of warmth in his greatcoat. His strong, clean scent disturbed her, and she knew not why. It worried her. The sooner she discovered proof of the earl's guilt, Rupert could be free of the treason charges, and they would see the last of this devious man.

At the merry-go-round, Lord Londringham handed coins to the proprietor and lifted Sally onto the wooden platform, already crowded with other children arguing over who would have the best chargers. Sally eagerly climbed onto a small brown pony and turned to look at the earl with a smile.

As Patience dug deep into her pocket for her lucky onyx stone, she watched the child, aware that her ordeal of pretense had only just begun. When she turned to look for Colette, she suddenly felt strong hands at her waist easily lifting her onto the brightly painted horse beside Sally.

She heard him whisper in her ear, "Thought you might also enjoy a ride."

It all happened so quickly, his touch, his whisper, then he was gone. On her gray-and-yellow wooden charger, Patience sputtered like a candle at the end of its wick, for she had no notion of taking a ride. But before she could climb down, the carousel jerked into motion. With a firm hold on her horse's pole, she shook her head at the man's audacity. Next time, she would certainly be ready for him. She hoped.

Her contemplation was cut short when she heard Sally's peals of glee as they spun around and around. Thankfully, Patience's charger was wooden, given her fear of horses. But after a few more revolutions, she was ready to exchange her seat for solid ground, while Sally protested her ride had ended much too soon.

The earl stood ready to help them down from the platform, a package tucked under his arm. He plucked Sally down first, then reached for Patience, who tensed, feeling his sinewy hands about her waist. The heat of his touch ignited a strange warmth in her belly and a flush across her cheeks. She did not have to look up to know he watched her as she clung to his hard forearms in an effort to regain her balance.

Finally, when able to stand without his assistance—he seemed oddly reluctant to let her go—she told him succinctly, "Sir, the next time, I will advise you if I wish to take a ride."

She must remember to keep her wits about her, and her feet firmly planted on the ground when dealing with the man.

"Mrs. Grundy, I sincerely hope you do," he returned pleasantly.

The gleam in his eyes confused her, and she quickly looked away, finding her bonnet needed adjustment again.

"Oh, that was fun! Shall we try again?" Sally cried, as she spun in circles, her arms flung out as if to fly.

"No, little lady, we shall find your aunt," Patience stated firmly.

Her authoritative tone brought the child to a slow halt. A grin suddenly lit Sally's face as she spied another amusement. "A puppet show! Let's see the puppets!" She grabbed the earl's hand and began to pull him in the direction of the little curtained box where a group of children were laughing at the antics of *Simple and Master Simon,* a comedy about a hopeless servant and his hard-to-please master.

Patience sighed and reluctantly followed her companions, suddenly suspicious that both Sally and the earl enjoyed themselves at her expense. She saw the earl purchase the child an orange from a merchant, but declined when one was offered to her.

"Really, Mrs. Grundy, that disapproving look on your face surprises me. Do you not like to see your daughter, your *stepdaughter* enjoy herself?"

Startled, she blinked up at the earl, standing a little too close for her own peace of mind. She swallowed. Hard. "Yes, I only worry about finding her aunt. And it is growing quite late. Surely we must be keeping you from something or someone?" She watched his guarded expression carefully.

He pulled out his watch. "Yes, I am due to meet someone. But they shall wait." He returned the watch to his pocket and leaned idly on his cane, seeming to mask his predatory nature. "I believe you are unfamiliar to Winchelsea. Where is home?"

Alert, she replied, "A good two-day journey from here, my lord."

Watching the performance, he asked her, "And what brings you to Winchelsea? A new position? A suitor?"

Patience turned to stare at his hard profile, then quickly focused on the show when he glanced her way. *Think quickly. I must think quickly.* "Ah, visiting. Yes, visiting my cousin for a short while."

Preventing anything further along this line of inquisition, she smiled brightly. "And where is the woman for your arm?" Her question edged in flirtation, hoping to distract him. She observed him intently, waiting for his answer.

When he shifted his stance to face her, his smile almost charmed her. "Madam, fate has not seen fit to provide me with a wife, and I must take my pleasure like this evening when it is afforded me."

Patience blushed, wondering if he lingered a little too long over the word "pleasure." She remarked hurriedly, "You seem to enjoy children, you must wish for your own."

His blue gaze grew deeper as he gave her an amusing smile. "First a wife, then children. Are you quite sure this is not some kind of proposal, Mrs. Grundy?"

Horrified at his pronouncement, albeit in jest, she clasped her hands to her now-scarlet face. "My lord, I intended no such liberty."

He laughed at her expression, then, as if he remembered something, said softly, "I almost wish—"

Sally interjected, "Please, I want to see the tigers and unicorns and . . . and ponies!" as they left the puppets for the Wild Beast show.

Wearily, Patience told her, "Ponies, my dear girl, are not

wild beasts, and I do not believe there are any unicorns around here."

"Where've ye been, Sally?" a thunderous voice commanded from high above.

Startled, they looked up to find a tiny woman clad in a sparkling bright-red dress climbing down the ladder from a tightrope. She hurried over to Sally, who stood subdued by Patience's side.

"Where ye been? Answer me! Ye should ha' been back over an hour ago," the woman scolded, with a jerk on the child's thin arm.

At first, Patience could only stare at the scarlet-clad woman who must be Sally's aunt. An acrobat? Small wonder they could not find her on the ground.

Lord Londringham stepped forward. "Madam, we have been searching for you for some time. Do not be harsh with the child. She only wanted to enjoy the fair." His intercedence acted like cold water on a fire, and the aunt's anger slowly died.

The little woman stared in surprise at the earl. "Sir, I do beg ye pardon. I hope me gel hasn't caused trouble."

The whiny voice grated on Patience's frazzled nerves, and she told Sally's aunt, "Little Sally was no trouble at all. We were only concerned we would be unable to find you."

"Well, ye did, and I'm much obliged. I'll take care of her now," her aunt ordered, giving a second glance to the gentleman in front of her.

Quiet during the reunion with her aunt, Sally now gazed up at Lord Londringham. "I never had near so much fun before. Thank ye, Mr. Long, for the orange and the rides and the puppets and everythin'." Her voice floated sweetly up to him.

Patience watched as the earl knelt stiffly beside the little girl. "You are welcome, child, and I did not forget. For you." He offered her the brown-wrapped package he carried under his arm.

The child eagerly ripped open the paper and discovered a pretty wooden doll dressed as a shepherdess, with long flaxen hair, rosy cheeks, and holding a tiny crooked staff.

Sally looked in awe at her present and then at the earl. "Oh, thank ye, sir. I'll take good care of her." Her small face turned pale, and she leaned forward to whisper in his ear.

The earl nodded and rose to a stand, his eyes unwavering on Patience.

Hesitantly, Sally approached Patience, who sank to her knees. "I'm sorry about pretendin' ye was me mama. I did want the doll. I guess I wanted a mama too. I hope yer not too mad."

Patience smiled at the child's honesty. "I am not mad, but lying is seldom rewarded, except perhaps this time."

Sally nodded before smudging a shy kiss on Patience's cheek.

"C'mon. Ye be 'nuff trouble for three children."

The woman's brusque coldness chilled Patience's warm heart. She wished that there was something more she could do for the child.

When the woman would have dragged Sally off, Patience called, "Please wait." She quickly slipped the earl's coat from her shoulders and offered it to him with a short nod. "I must go. Thank you for your kindness. I know Sally truly enjoyed herself."

She turned to leave, but a firm hand on her thin sleeve prevented her. "And Mrs. Grundy? Did she enjoy herself as well?"

His face again in the shadows, somehow she felt her answer to be important to him.

"Of course. You . . . you proved an amusing as well as

considerate companion." She thought her praise high, in view of the circumstances.

His smile widened to a grin. "I suppose the same can be said for Gulliver."

"Gulliver?" She knew she should not have asked.

"My dog."

While studying her flushed face, he raised her hand and softly kissed her glove, his warmth penetrating through to her skin.

"*Mrs.* Grundy, you do interest me, a great deal. I'm confident that we will meet again," he told her and bid her good evening with a touch to his beaver hat.

Patience froze looking after him. His sentiments seemed ominous. Perhaps they would meet again, right before he was hung for treason.

Sally interrupted her troubling thoughts, tugging on her hand for attention. Looking at Sally's aunt's suspicious countenance, Patience was aware she needed to explain a few things to the little woman. A few bob, and she gained the aunt's silence.

After matters were finally remedied, and Bella had taken Sally home, Patience could search for Colette. Since most of the fairgoers had wandered into the night, only a small handful of people remained near the dying bonfire. To her relief, she soon found Colette at the square, looking for her too. They strolled back to their lodgings, along with the rest of a tired crowd. Patience could only hope her disguise as a still-room maid in Lord Londringham's house would hold up to scrutiny after this night.

Back at Paddock Green, Bryce lay awake for a long time reflecting on the sweet countenance of one Mrs. Grundy. He knew Grundy was not her last name. Who could she be? He wished he had inquired as to the cousin's surname.

The bright flames of the bonfire around Mrs. Grundy had created a vivid aura against her soft brown hair. He remembered the tiger-lights sparkling in her lovely hazel eyes, and the warm look she unknowingly had sent him when he had given the child a new doll. He rose from the bed to walk over to the chair where he had laid his coat. He could still smell her lavender perfume on it. And a faint odor of peppermint.

The lark awakened him outside his window with the morning light pouring onto his bed in uneven lines. He had not slept this deeply in months, and it took him a few minutes to realize the cause.

No nightmares. It was because of her. Mrs. Grundy. He knew little about her, but sure as the world held hope and regrets, he would find her again. Unfortunately, he had to find his stepbrother's murderer before he could enjoy her tempting pleasure.

Chapter 2

A man of middle years with a long, thin face, Viscount Carstairs slowly drained the last drops of beer from his tankard and contemplated the inside of the familiar Bear's Wit tavern with half-masted eyes, yet again wishing for a good fellow to whom he could boast of his ingenious plan. But this late on the starless and windy night, anyone still awake was no doubt about the Devil's work. He grinned at the thought. He wanted to crow that by tomorrow morning he would be rich and a long way from England.

"We need to talk." The soft-spoken voice startled the older man, not yet in his cups.

The viscount looked up suspiciously to spy his young cousin. The lone candle on the table flickered, briefly lighting the pale, drawn face of the young man, obviously wearied from a long journey. "Rupert, my boy. What do you here? Did you not get my note? You are wanted for treason. It is not safe for you," he told him under his breath. Then Carstairs smelled it: the odor of the hunted. "You look all in. Beer will straighten your back."

A quick shout brought the innkeeper and another tankard. When he protested about wanting to close for the night, the viscount silenced him with a few more coins in the man's pocket.

Rupert took a long drain from his cup before he replied in an undertone, "I know. I have spent the last two days avoiding a press-gang who wanted to throw me on a blockade ship and the constable's men who seek to hang me. I do not remember my last meal or soft bed. Please, you have got to help me." He paused. "I'm tired of running."

His weary brown eyes unmistakably betrayed fear and hunger of a man no longer a boy. Worry lines had replaced laugh lines in the young man's suddenly old face. He took another draught of the watered-down liquid before him. "Tell me, Peter, why in bloody hell does the constable believe *I* am selling secrets to the French?"

Carstairs narrowed his eyes as the boy settled uncomfortably onto the hard chair. He chose his next words carefully. "I was as shocked as you when I heard the news. Perhaps you met some untrustworthy chaps during your stay with me, and they gave your name to the constable in order to save their own."

Rupert's eyes widened in dismay. "But I was with *you*. The only blokes I met were *your* friends."

"Yes, and I am afraid even I do not trust everyone within my acquaintance. I did try on your behalf to defend you. I told the constable you were only my relative come for a visit, and being of true English stock could not possibly be guilty of treason." He raised his hands and shrugged. "But alas, he maintains he has proof of greater conviction than the weight of my words."

Rupert, resting his head in his hands, looked up to catch his cousin's last words. "Proof? What proof?" he sputtered.

Carstairs heaved a sigh. He needed more time to think. "Rupert, listen to me. Your running away from the authorities only convinces them of your guilt. Stay tonight with me and tomorrow we will visit my solicitor. I am sure he will find a way out of this coil, he's very clever."

"But what about Lord Londringham? Have they not caught him yet? You told me he is the man they seek."

"Yes, well, unfortunately, Londringham is still unfamiliar with the inside of a gaol. He has been very clever, that man, clever enough to cover his tracks."

"I suppose an earl is better at eluding justice than a mere baronet's brother."

"Come now, not so gloomy. We shall take you home and let Mrs. Keene make up a bed for you. Tomorrow, we will see to everything." The viscount rose and started toward the door, calling over his shoulder, "My horse is outside, you can ride behind me."

Rupert caught up with him, his step livelier with restored optimism. "Thank you, Cousin, for your kindness. I am sorry to be such a nuisance. You see, the family is in a state over me, especially my sister."

"Naturally. Let us discuss this more tomorrow."

When they arrived back at Loganmoor, Carstairs's estate, the housekeeper gave him a filling repast and then led the exhausted young man to his bed.

Alone in his study, the viscount's smile faded and annoyance hardened his rough countenance. Rupert's reappearance proved a lump in the pudding, but would not disrupt his neatly arranged plans to be on a ship for America in the morning.

Assuring himself of his deft handling of his young cousin's affairs, he began to gather his important papers to take with him. And the Devil took his due.

The new morning dawned bright for Rupert. Confident that his troubles would soon be over, he whistled as he dressed, eager to grab his fate by the tail. He trotted down the stairs, aware of the household sounds of clanging pots, clinking silver, and servants' voices—the normal morning routine.

On his way to breakfast, he noticed that the French doors leading from the viscount's study to the balcony were open, and he ventured inside. The smile drained from his lips as he viewed the study in shock: papers strewn on the floor, books toppled from their shelves, a disaster.

Then he saw him. Lord Carstairs lay face-down on the floor, dried blood staining the Oriental carpet beneath his body. Rupert knelt down and rolled the prone figure over, confirming what he already knew. The vacant death stare told the gruesome story.

Horrified, he rose and continued to stare at the body, shaking his head. Who had killed his cousin, and why? Would he be next? Now he had no one to help him.

"Murderer!" screamed the housemaid.

In deep thought, he didn't realize anyone was nearby. He frowned, looking at the young girl before he stumbled toward her, holding out his hand, but she threw up her hands and ran shrieking for help. Soon footsteps and anxious voices echoed in the hall.

After quickly considering his options, Rupert decided to flee and plan his defense from a safer distance than prison. He ran through the balcony archway onto the garden steps. Barely pausing, he bent to retrieve a shoe buckle glistening in the early dew, then raced out into the mist-dampened morning.

The carriage tilted and swayed over the bumpy, dusty road from Winchelsea. On their trip to Paddock Green, their new place of employment, Colette and Patience discussed Patience's plan.

Colette shook her head in resignation. "I still cannot

understand why you believe the earl is responsible for your brother's plight."

Patience studied the Sussex landscape of rolling hills in distraction before looking over at her friend and tucking a loose strand of hair back under her mobcap.

"Both my brother and our cousin Lord Carstairs are convinced it is the earl who is selling information to French agents, and that he has informed against Rupert to throw suspicion from himself. Our cousin says even the constable has his men watching the earl."

Colette pounced on Patience's remark. "There, you see. If the constable's men have yet to convict the earl, why ever do you believe you can succeed where they have failed?"

"Perhaps because I have more at stake," she replied softly.

"This could be very dangerous."

Patience nodded. "I know," and added more cheerily, "I feel so fortunate that I met you on the post chaise. It has been nice to have a friend to confide in. Without your entrée into his household, I would still be thinking of some way to have the earl arrested." She still marveled her luck in meeting a young woman her age traveling from Storrington to Winchelsea. With their dark brown hair and hazel eyes, many of the other passengers thought them sisters.

Colette replied in her lilting French accent. "I hope we both do not live to regret your masquerade as a still-room maid. You, the sister of a baronet." She waved her hand. "La, you English girls are much more adventurous than we French counterparts. I am happy being a simple lady's maid to the countess."

Shrugging, Patience returned to watching out the window, and wondered what the next few days or months would bring. The carriage rocked past workers planting in the fields and foot travelers on their journey home from the fair. Ripened to nature's glory, the spring splendor of the

countryside unraveled along the ribbon of road bedecked
with new grass and budding trees.

Even the brilliant landscape could not help Patience
forget her purpose. But for the horrible picture of Rupert
swinging from Tyburn, she would have had the carriage turn
around and head back to Winchelsea. Palms moist, she
smoothed down her apron over her light gray dress, presum-
ing it would be suitable for her position as a still-room maid.
The mobcap and spectacles she hoped would prove a fine
disguise from the earl, especially after their unexpected
meeting last night.

At last, the post chaise creaked through massive iron
gates, signaling the journey's near end. Patience stared out
the window, her mouth agape. Majestic sycamore trees stood
along both sides of the carriageway in welcome. The newly
green-carpeted lawns stretched for miles in early-spring
beauty dotted with a sprinkling of mischievous dandelions.

When their carriage bumped over the stone bridge and
she saw Paddock Green, fear returned to mock her courage
and moisten her brow. Approaching from the east, the house
of gray stone loomed on the horizon, dark and imposing, its
castle spires nobly reaching toward the sky. She surmised
grimly that the house had probably been designed to suit a
king but more likely entertained n'er-do-wells, thieves, and
homeless spirits, given the earl's rumored cohorts.

Upon closer view, Patience saw the stone turrets and gar-
goyles, perched ready to pounce on curious travelers, intrigued architects, or new servants. The tracery on the
windows, the lacy parapets, and the unguarded battlements
led her to wonder if the earl hid a mad wife behind the
dormer attic windows. Her whimsy was no doubt attributa-
ble to Mrs. Radcliffe's novels. Certainly Paddock Green,
with its Gothic structure amidst a verdant panorama, created

a dramatic setting for the mysterious man who played dangerous games and bought dolls for little girls.

Left at the servants' entrance, Colette and Patience waited an answer to their knock. A thin, older woman, who had seen the glory of her days past, opened the door wearing an unpleasant frown making her features even less attractive. A cap placed carelessly on her head held fewer gray strands than had initially been arranged. A greasy dirty apron belied her position as the cook, and her face told a tale of having known more regrets than smiles, given her wizened look.

She stared sullenly at the young women before allowing them entrance into the kitchen, a cavernous room with a long pine worktable occupying the place of honor in the center. Since no windows lined the stone walls, the skylight granted the kitchen its only illumination. Sweet bread smells scented the stifling air.

The woman shuffled around them and muttered, "Ye must be the still-room maid and lady's maid. We were told to expect ye. The one what's the lady's maid is to go to the first floor to meet the countess. There's the steps. The other is to see Mrs. Knockersmith, our housekeeper, in her rooms."

The cook returned to kneading bread with nary a glance in their direction again.

Colette gathered her belongings and headed for the stairs while Patience waited to be shown to the housekeeper. At the far end of the table, Patience noticed a young boy with large brown eyes in a small round face, whose thick brown hair needed a good brushing. He was dressed in mussied livery, and half-heartedly plucking a chicken and blowing the feathers in the air.

"Lem, show the still-room maid Mrs. Knockersmith's quarters," the cook instructed over her shoulder.

The little boy stared suspiciously at Patience before he

shrugged, then rose to head out the far door, not waiting for her to follow him.

Patience met her new overseer, Mrs. Knockersmith, a kindly woman in her sixth or seventh decade, in the housekeeper's rooms where they discussed Patience's duties and uniform. Afterward, the little footboy showed her to her small attic bedroom. Alone again, wondering how Colette fared, Patience sat on one of the narrow beds and bit her lip in contemplation. She had no idea what to expect when she saw the earl again. How long would she need to play this part?

With a long sigh, she soon returned to the kitchen in a uniform that had once belonged to another maid, which, unfortunately, fit as well as a squirrel would fit in a snakeskin. The bodice pulled across her bosom and the drab dress hung a few inches from the floor. Obviously the previous owner of this uniform must have been a flat-bosomed midget. Patience knew she would need to use a needle and thread to save her dignity, when she had the time.

Hiding her shaking hands in her pockets, she found her lucky onyx and rubbed it. It usually brought her good luck. Her throat dry, she would have given her shoes for a cool glass of water. Would she pass muster?

Mrs. Knockersmith met her in the kitchen where she showed Patience to the distilling room and the pantry. Patience then spent the better part of the day distilling simple waters by placing plants in the cold still to dry them, capturing their fine-flavored spirits. A tedious process for not a large return, but it kept her too busy to think about what her next step would be. As she worked, a light mint scent filled the air.

Later that night, lying in bed and rubbing her sore arms, Patience thought about how to get into the earl's study. That seemed the likeliest place to start.

* * *

The next morning when Patience arrived in the kitchen, she saw no signs of Mrs. Knockersmith, only Mr. Gibbs, the butler, whom she had met at the Mop Fair. He held his hand in a bucket on the table, swearing under his breath.

"You, girl. The earl needs his tea, and I've just burned my hand. Go deliver it," he ordered, indicating the tray on the nearby table. "When you are finished, return to the kitchen."

Patience widened her eyes, then frowned. This could be her chance, but she hadn't been hired to serve. Would she make a muck of it? *Steady, girl.* "Of course, Mr. Gibbs. Ah, one moment. Where is the earl's study?" She offered a game smile.

Irritatedly he directed her toward the back of the house, and she headed to the lion's den, the china cups and saucers chinking in her wake. As she approached the closed doors, she winked three times for luck, straightened her shoulders, and knocked loudly.

Outside the door, she could hear the murmur of voices, which halted at her knock. Her heart beat a little faster as she balanced the tray and waited.

At the word "Enter," Patience took a deep breath and wet her dry lips before opening the door. She had to blink several times to adjust to the dimly lit room and to locate the occupants. Silence reigned briefly when she entered the room, but the men soon took up where they had left off. Lord Londringham reclined in his chair behind his massive desk and gestured to a table in front of his companion, who sat comfortably in a wing chair nearby.

She set the tray on the table and began to pour the tea, her spectacles and mobcap firmly in place.

The earl's friend told him, "I would like to accompany you to Carstairs's estate tomorrow morning. There must be some piece of evidence we might uncover which will lead us to his murderer."

Murderer? Patience could barely breathe. The cup in her

hand shook. Was her cousin, dead? The man's next words confirmed her fears.

"With any luck. You know, I believe his murder was not totally unexpected. What do you think of this young Mandeley having murdered him?"

Her eyes widened in alarm, her breath held in desperate suspense. *They suspected Rupert of Lord Carstairs's murder?* In infinite horror, she gulped and dropped the china sugar pot onto the table with a crash. The noise immediately awakened her stupor.

Startled, both men looked her way, then resumed talking. Patience quickly cleaned up the mess, reminding herself that she must go on, no matter the worry that threatened to paralyze her thoughts.

A few harried minutes later, Lord Londringham told her, "No sugar or milk for me."

Cup and saucer in hand, she warily approached his desk and placed his tea in front of him, half-expecting him to jump from his chair when he recognized her as the woman from the fair. But although she stared as long as she dared at his granite-carved face, he merely glanced impersonally at her before returning his attention to the papers before him.

His friend continued, "Damn difficult to know. It certainly does not do the chap well that he fled with the skirts of dawn. But what possible motive could his cousin have? I checked with a solicitor in the village who states that a distant relative of Carstairs on his mother's side will inherit." He leaned back in his chair after instructing Patience that he required sugar.

Londringham sipped his tea before replying, "Indeed. What motive? It is a piece of unfortunate business, especially when I nearly had Carstairs in my sights." He looked over at Patience, who stood near the tea table, and dismissed her.

A brief curtsy and she reluctantly left the room,

disappointed she would not hear more. She had to learn what he knew. Perhaps the earl, himself, had killed Carstairs and tried to misdirect his friend to her brother. On an impulse, she cracked the door, hoping to hear a gem of information. Surely, here in the shadows, no one could find her.

The earl's friend began, "Yes, Carstairs was . . ."

Just then she heard steps and a woman's voice above her on the staircase. She rushed across the hall into what she hoped was an empty parlor. Heart pounding, she swiped her sweaty palms on her apron, her hands clasped the cool doorknob.

Inside the quiet parlor, she listened at the door and heard more voices and footsteps. Precious minutes ticked by until suddenly everything resumed its normal tomblike silence.

Cautiously, she peeled open the door and peeked up and down the hall. No one. She scurried back across the hall to the study door, still slightly ajar. Leaning her ear close to the opening, Patience heard the earl's voice.

"Meet me in my rooms tonight. I should be back after eleven."

She did not hear the reply because the young footboy, Lem, beckoned her from the vestibule. "Miss," he called insistently.

Patience hurried down the hall to meet the little boy. "What is it?" she asked him.

He pointed toward the kitchen. "It's Mr. Gibbs. 'e's been looking for you. 'e 'as more work for you."

The minute he relayed his message, the lad shot out of the house like a cannon, probably in an effort to avoid work or the butler. She glanced once more at the study doors, sighed, and headed toward the kitchen. Already she was busy planning how to be in the earl's bedchamber when he met with his friend tonight.

Chapter 3

The sun's dying scarlet rays washed across the sky after Patience's second day as Paddock Green's newest still-room maid. She stretched her weary arms above her head, stiff from polishing the last looking glass with wine spirits, then added whiting for a final shine.

Finished earlier than expected, Patience had helped rub and sift sugar for cake, although the cook complained that Patience's cake dough could be used as cannon fodder to shoot at the unsuspecting French enemy. Perhaps next time she could remember to add the yeast, the cook hinted scornfully.

But Patience's mind was not on baking a better cake. Like Pandora with the key to her box, she wanted to unearth the earl's secrets in his locked study; it had been secured, no doubt, to keep out prying still-room maids.

After she helped Lem cut the cotton tops off the candles and change the lamp oil, Mrs. Knockersmith sent her to bed with a warning to be up earlier than the sun. Patience wearily climbed the stairs, scratching her head through her large mobcap.

Lord Londringham, a subject never very far from her mind. What kind of a man was he? He was certainly guilty of espionage, but murder? She shivered as if ghostly hands had reached out to her from the grave. Biting her lip, she realized resignedly that she would have to get much closer to the earl if she wanted to discover the answers she sought.

Although the hour grew late, Patience decided to take a quick nap before attempting her first foray into spying. She had thought about it all afternoon and planned to eavesdrop on the earl and the captain when they met tonight in the earl's rooms. With any luck, she could secure evidence to be used against the earl.

Once safely inside her maid's room in the attic, Patience threw off her mobcap and spectacles, and in relief, unbuttoned the maid's uniform before pulling on her thin blue lawn nightdress. She unpinned her hair, then combed the thick strands through her fingers, as she massaged away the slight pain from the cap and pins. She promptly curled into a ball and closed her eyes. *Just for a few minutes,* she promised herself.

An hour later Patience awakened, slowly, then jolted into a sitting position. It all came winging back to her on a cry.

Tonight. The earl's room.

A glance at the clock showed almost half-past eleven. She grabbed a pale blue wrap and slipped quietly out the door, not giving herself pause for failure, and winked three times for luck before hastening toward the stairs.

Patience thought her frantic breathing would awaken the dead. Lips dry and hands trembling, her bare feet whispered across the moonbeam-lit wooden floor as she ran down the hallway. She prayed the shadows would hide her as she hugged the cool walls on her descent to the second floor, forcing her cowardly feet forward step-by-step.

When the longcase clock in the Grand Hall began to chime, she stopped to take quick, shallow breaths, keenly listening for any sleepless companions in the night.

What if she was too late? What if the earl had not returned yet? Too late for a change of heart. A spur of righteousness lit her heels and with frantic archangels beating in her heart, Patience began her secret advance toward the enemy. As she crept down the long corridor in the west wing, she noted the ornate pillars standing sentinel outside every other door down the hallway, which would provide a perfect refuge if needed.

Luckily, nothing disturbed the night. Wax candles nestled in their wall sconces flickered from the slight breeze through the open window at the end of the hallway. The dim light slightly illuminated the path to the earl's door.

Stealthily she continued on, her palms dampened, as she moved closer, four doors, then three doors away. Not far from his suite of rooms, she could see a light under his door. Was success near at hand or was disappointment about to send her scurrying back to bed? On tiptoe, she crossed the hallway to his door to listen.

All quiet. At the point of deciding whether to wish for better luck tomorrow, someone made the choice for her. Heavy footsteps thudded on the stairs heading her way. The only escape available was a nearby door. She fervently hoped she had done something good lately to warrant an unoccupied room and a place to hide.

Patience sprang for the door, jerked it open, and then almost slammed it shut, her nightdress and robe flying about her ankles. She pressed her back to the door, holding her mouth with one hand to muffle her breathing. Thankfully, no indignant person leapt from the large tester bed. She leaned against the door and listened as the footsteps continued past her door and the earl's rooms. Who could that have been? If it was the captain, why had he not stopped?

Putting a hand to her heart to calm herself, Patience peered into the room, her eyes adjusting to the moonlight laced faintly through the window. She slowly and cautiously circled a long chaise longue in the darkened room while holding out her left hand to guide herself to the wall, which she thought must adjoin the earl's room.

She leaned an ear to the silk damask wall and with her senses tuned for sound, she strained to hear. A moment passed and then another. She held her breath and waited. Nothing. Were the walls too thick for the convenience of eavesdroppers or would-be spies?

If only she had not fallen asleep. She shook her head and sighed, regret as unfamiliar to her as poverty to a king.

Patience straightened up with an idea. Perhaps the captain had not yet arrived for their rendezvous?

A puff of wind just then wafted a ribbon of white curtains into the room. The upper housemaid must have forgotten to close the window.

The window. Might she be able to hear something if the earl's windows remained open? Not willing to give up yet, she hurried across the room. In her haste, she stubbed her toe on a small chest at the end of the bed. A knuckle in her mouth helped to stifle a moan as she rubbed her sore toe while hopping on one foot. *Clumsy must be my middle name.*

Had anyone heard the noise? After a few uneasy minutes and no one barged into the room, she sat on the chest in relief, her toe still throbbing.

All remained quiet, though she did not want to examine exactly how long her luck or the silence would last. Her heart might give out before then. At last, when she felt she could move safely, she limped to the window and drew aside the white curtains. Clouds paraded past the moon, dulling its white light. The night offered damp possibilities as Patience contemplated her next move.

When she stuck her head out the window, she discovered the earl's windows were still open. Her moment of glee was cut short quicker than wind to a flame upon realizing the distance seemed too great to scale.

She perched on the windowsill, her nightdress and wrap smoothed underneath her, her toes curling against the cold stone, her chin resting on her hand.

Disappointing. It was times like these that Patience Letitia Mandeley had no idea what she was doing. She was not normally the adventurous type, but she had to do something to help Rupert.

Patience gazed across the sprawling lawn and neatly trimmed gardens of the estate and contemplated her situation. Perhaps the distance to the earl's window was not as far as it seemed. She looked below and spied a stone balustrade running the entire length of the house. The balustrade appeared to be about two feet in width. *Strong enough to stand on?* There was only one way to find out.

She grasped her nightdress and wrap closer to her body, and with a deep breath she precariously crawled out the window onto the ledge a few feet beneath her. For a fearful minute, her feet dangled in the air as her toes sought purchase on the narrow shelf. Her luck held as her feet touched the hard, cold surface.

She held the window ledge in a firm grasp and tested the balustrade. It appeared to hold, even though it was designed more for an ornamental purpose than a functional one.

Her cheeks felt warm from her exertions as she tried to still her shaking hands. Reluctantly, she released her slippery grasp from the windowsill and slid her hands down the rough stone wall. Between both windows there was nothing to hold on to but the uneven surface of rough stone. Eyes closed, she carefully maneuvered her body around so that her back fit snugly against the stone wall.

She stopped to reward her efforts and regain her fortitude,

if not her courage. The ground appeared exceedingly far away, and it would take only one slip—

She made up her mind to concentrate on the ledge and not look beyond it. Grasping the raspy edges of the stones blindly with touch as her only guide, Patience started to walk sideways along the side of the house. The distance was farther than she had initially determined, but by a tentative step-and-slide crawl she felt her way over to the earl's windows.

A chair scraping the floor stopped her progress. *What was happening? Was there anyone with the earl?* Her heart pounded in her ears, and she suddenly felt quite ill.

This is too dangerous. I shall never make a spy. Torn between retreat and advance, Patience abruptly had a more pressing concern and realized this is where luck deserted her to the elements. While she had been concentrating on her progress, the moon's light had diminished and the breeze had picked up.

Was that a wet drop on my nose? Please let it not be rain. Three plops landed on top of her head, convincing her this prayer would go unanswered. A gentle hushing heralded the drizzle. *Perhaps it will only last a few minutes.* At about the time she was soaked to the skin, Patience had decided that whatever the earl had to discuss with his friend could wait to be discovered another day.

Bryce stretched out his legs before the fireplace snapping and sputtering to its death. The room had become quite warm, so warm that he had earlier discarded his shirt and wore only breeches. With a half-empty glass in his hand, he leaned more comfortably into his velvet wing chair.

Their trip to Winchelsea had proved unproductive. Normally reliable informants had nothing to report about the French spy's location or his new meeting place. The only interesting tidbit gleaned was a rumor that the spy might be a woman. *Could it be the same—no, she must still be in France.* He shook his head. Probably the good pint of ale he had paid the man had embellished his story.

Tonight seemed like a fine night to waste at the bottom of a bottle. He did not eagerly anticipate his visitor, due any moment, which contributed to his imbibing. With his right thigh pulsing a dull pain, his mood grew as foul as the weather had become. The wind taunted the last bright sparks as he rubbed his leg. He didn't want to remember the night of Edward's murder, and the French bullet torn into his own leg trying to bring his brother's body home.

The floor-length curtains flag-waved from across the room while the quiet rain lullabied the night's peaceful stillness. Admiring the fiery contents in his brandy glass, the brilliant color reminded him of a beautiful young woman.

I wonder where she is. Mrs., or, more likely, Miss, Grundy.

She was all goodness. He wanted to wrap himself in her goodness to forget for awhile. *Forget about the woman responsible for his brother's murder. If only he could return to France.* But Secretary Hobart expected a report soon of the sea fencibles stationed in Kent to protect the shoreline that he had been assigned the task of overseeing. With resignation, he knew he had to finish this mission before beginning his own.

Bryce sighed and flexed his shoulders, then rose to pour himself another drink. Returning to his chair, he moved it farther away from the heat still emanating from the fireplace.

What in blazes? He noticed something blue blowing across the window opening. Obviously not his curtains, which, upon closer inspection, he realized were deep red.

Intrigued, he cautiously approached the opened window. He rested his left hip on the sill, leaned out, and looked over to his right. What he saw amazed him and immediately removed any lingering effects of the liquor.

A young woman, very wet, with eyes closed, clutched the side of his house. The edges of her nightdress blew teasingly toward him. *Whatever was a young woman doing outside his window? And why did she seem somehow familiar?* Could she be spying on him?

Without hesitation, he leveraged his hip across the ledge and reached out his hand toward her while grasping the side of the window with a firm hand.

Softly he called to her, "Don't be afraid. Step toward me and grab my hand. I will pull you through the window."

The woman's eyes fluttered open in shock. She paused and studied his outstretched hand before lifting one trembling pale hand from its anchor to the house and trustingly placed it into his. Immediately, he tightened his grip around her fragile hand and drew her gently toward him, murmuring soft encouragements.

She managed the last few steps to his window in a wet shuffle until he could grasp her narrow waist. In one smooth movement, he pulled the woman against his chest and carried her through the window onto safer ground.

Or that is what he would have believed. When he felt her cool, wet body against his, rationality escaped him. Before he had time to reflect on the desire hardening his body, the uneven weight of her high in his arms awkwardly knocked them to the ground. She landed on top of him with a *whoosh,* momentarily taking his breath away. Wet strands of sweet-smelling hair slapped his cheek as lovely hazel eyes in an ashen face gazed down at him in terror. She gaped at him as she braced her weight on both sides of his head, while the rest of her body pressed intimately against his.

"You." The word pushed from his lips in an incredulous whisper. He could not help but stare.

This was her. Mrs. Grundy or Miss Grundy or whoever. *What was she doing here?* Her mouth opened as if to say something, but caught off guard by her familiar countenance and the very right feel of her supple body pressed against his, Bryce responded by raising his hand to her head and bringing her lips gently to meet his, his other hand holding her tightly against him. He would get the answers from her, but first his body willed his mind to forget for a moment. There would be plenty of time.

Strangely, she offered no protest, and he wasted no time examining his motives or his good luck, only pleased with this wet nymph's response to his ardency.

Her soft, pliant lips quivered as he wooed her mouth in tender exploration. His tongue licked smooth caresses over her mouth in light persuasion until she allowed him entrance into the sweetest haven he had ever tasted.

He groaned at her innocent acceptance of his tongue. With his other arm still wrapped around her waist, he pulled her down until her breasts pressed intimately against his wet chest and the rest of her damp body lay more firmly anchored in the harbor of his legs. This woman had aroused him in a matter of seconds. His body responded to her sweetly rounded hips beneath his hand, and her peaked nipples against his chest tortured his sanity.

Caught in a dream of wanting and blood-pulsing, fiery desire, he easily circled her slim waist and rubbed his aroused manhood against her feminine heat, wondering if she ached as much as he did.

A knock on the door caught the entranced couple off guard, and Bryce heard the countess call out.

"Bryce? Are you in there?"

Chapter 4

His hands tightened on the young woman's hips upon hearing Isabella, reluctant to let her go, yet not wanting his ex-mistress to find her here in his arms. A brief hesitation, then his wet companion rolled out of his surprised arms onto the hard floor with a thump. Her action immediately cooled his heated senses.

With no further delay, he rose onto his good knee and deftly raised himself off the floor. In his haste, he did not risk another look at the young woman, but hurried across the room to the unlocked door to prevent Isabella from entering.

Too late. She burst into the room in a manner which suggested no amount of bars or locks could have prevented her. Her azure-blue silk dressing gown hissed around her silk slippers as she pushed past him.

"*Mon chéri,* you know I do not like waiting. And it has been so long since you have made love to me," she told him reprovingly, with red lips pouting.

He closed his eyes and muttered a groan. He did not turn around but waited for her anticipated reaction.

"Bryce, how could you? You are quite careless," her cool voice adding to the chill in the air.

Ironically, she had just reminded him of how warm he had been. Puzzled, he turned to find the countess gliding to the open window. No trace of the damp sprite remained. She had simply vanished.

Suddenly a fearful thought occurred to him. *Had she escaped the way she'd arrived?* In a few strides, he reached the window, but Isabella had already closed it.

"This rain has *certainment* soaked the curtains. What a dilemma! You should have shut these windows earlier," she chided him. She faced him with a sly smile painted on her lips. "*Mon amour,* I could not stop thinking about your invitation," she purred.

He brushed her aside and yanked open the casement windows. A quick glance to the left and down allowed him to breathe again. She had not left by the window. The only other exit was the door to his valet's room, which had a door to the hallway. Desperately, he tried to think of a way to get rid of Isabella as he shut the windows again.

Isabella's long arms curled around his waist as she pressed her full breasts against his back, then stepped away and walked in front of him. "Bryce, why are you wet? Were you standing at the window letting the rain soak you?"

"Ah, yes, I thought I saw something outside, so I leaned out to see what it was."

"I can dry you. Come to bed. I have what you need." Her searching hands efficiently found his aroused member, still hard with the memory of another woman. "And you have what I want."

Bryce removed her hands from him. *This was a foolish idea. It had been from the beginning.* She had been amusing a few years ago, but when he returned last November, she had insisted on accompanying him home. She thought he needed her. She was wrong. He had not had a need for her in a long time.

However, Providence had played a hand in the arrangements by bringing the countess's cousin Alain Sansouche, a suspected French spy, with her to Paddock Green. And while Sansouche was under the same roof, it would be easier for Bryce to observe him.

Keeping Isabella at arm's length while he continued with his plans to locate the ring of French spies had proven to be a nuisance these past few months. Obviously not undone by his lack of encouragement, she pressed her hands to his chest and raised her head to seal a wet, inviting kiss on his lips.

The kiss, vastly different from the one with his wet nymph, triggered Bryce to his senses. Where the nymph's kiss had broken through his despair, Isabella's felt cold and manipulative. He'd tasted youthful, redeeming innocence and wanted a second course of the vision that had dropped into his arms.

Intent on his comparison, he realized too late the countess had pulled him to the bed. He watched her dispassionately as if he was in the audience and not a participant of the show as she reached up and slowly untied the only ribbon holding her dressing gown together. She lay back on the bed waiting for her temptation to work as it had done before.

The temptation she sold was hard not to buy. Long, thick blond hair draped over one milky-white shoulder, her tall, full body shone pale against the black canvas of the rich marble counterpane. Honeyed nipples pouted for attention.

But another woman occupied his mind. A woman he had held briefly and would remember for a lifetime. He reached across Isabella's white body and gathered her dressing gown together, securing the ends with their tiny blue ribbons.

"I think perhaps you should leave," he said, his voice quiet.

"But why do you turn me away? I thought you wanted me. *You* asked me here tonight." She pursed her bright lips, then rose indignantly from the bed in displeasure over his rejection. Because of his plans, he needed her in his home and cast about for a worthy excuse for his behavior.

"Please forgive me, Isabella. My leg rather pains me this evening."

Bright blue eyes grew concerned, and she threw herself into his arms. "Why ever did you not tell me? Perhaps I could stay and rub it? Would it not feel better?"

Her cloying perfume nearly suffocated him. He easily detached her ivylike arms from around his neck and showed her to the door. "Thank you, no. I need to rest."

"Bryce, do you not realize I love you? I believe you once cared for me." She dared a hand on his arm, her gaze searching his face, almost looking as if she remembered how to cry.

He removed her hand gently before responding. "Isabella, you do me no service in your love for me. I have told you that before."

"I will not give up hope, *mon cher*." Isabella, with a tiny smile on her face, lifted her chin and sailed through the door, taking her still-intact pride with her.

Bryce sighed in relief and quickly closed the door to begin his search for the wet young woman. Where could she be? He looked under the bed, then in his valet's room, hoping she might have hidden there waiting for him, her lithe body still flush with the heat of their embrace.

But his search proved fruitless. He then exhausted most of the house and did not rest until he had looked into every darkened corner for a splash of dark hair and willing full lips.

Finally, reluctantly, he accepted that she was gone. Left him without a promise to return or proof she even existed. He wandered back to his rooms and threw himself on the bed.

Had he only dreamed her? Had he really held her sweet form in his arms? When sleep finally arrived, his body and soul sought sanctuary from his regular nightmares with thoughts of Mrs. Grundy. Was she his savior or his nemesis?

* * *

Safely back in her room, door locked, Patience fumbled with the sleeves of her damp nightdress. In her haste, she ripped the seam at the wrist, causing her to mutter an oath. She threw aside the nightdress and wrap and then buttoned herself into a long linen shirt before crawling into bed. She gathered the bedcovers up to her neck, but the shivering would not stop.

She knew it was only a matter of time before he uncovered her disguise. Maybe not tonight, but soon, if she didn't use more sense. Would he suspect she was one of the new maids? She could only pray he would have no cause to look further than the first two floors, and hoped that her venture would have no ill affect on her health. Thankfully, her guardian angel had seen her through this little escapade.

Suddenly, Patience sat up. She had not taken her lucky onyx with her. Yes, that must be the reason why fortune had deserted her.

With a tired shake of her head, she settled back onto her small, lumpy bed. Although she'd intended to put the night from her mind, when she closed her eyes, the past hour replayed itself like a nightmare. Or possibly more like a lovely dream, as if his lordship was not her enemy but her lover.

Back on the ledge, she had already decided to return to the other bedroom when the earl held out his hand to her. Panicked, her mind went daft. His voice rang in the wet night loud and yet gentle, compelling her to trust him to save her. Her hand held in his firm grasp, she knew he would not let her fall.

After he had carried her through the window, she remembered a fright so great that if he'd asked her what she was doing out there, she would have confessed her deception.

Everything had happened so quickly that before she realized it, she had landed on top of his warm, hard body.

Stunned at being discovered, Patience allowed this stranger to press a kiss on her unsuspecting lips. She had never been kissed in such a way that numbing fear could dissolve into sweet, mind-robbing pleasure. She heaved a sigh. He had tasted of rain and fire and—she licked her lips—brandy.

Patience shuddered, thinking how close she'd come to becoming unmasked. If not for her quick action of rolling right under the bed and over to the far side, she would still be in the earl's room trying to explain why she happened to be standing outside his window in the pouring rain.

Before she had crawled through the opposite door, she had taken a quick peek across the room and saw the earl embrace a woman. Probably his mistress that the servants had mentioned earlier. She was amazed that the earl could so easily trade one woman for another. But if what she suspected of him to be true, his Don Juan nature was yet another sly trick in his basket of spy misdeeds.

With the earl and countess absorbed in each other, it had seemed a perfect time to exit. She went through a small study, which she disappointingly had no time to explore, to the hall door, nearly safe. As if the French were after her, she flew down the hallway and up to the attic, hoping no one was up and about to see her flight.

Secured in her tiny room, she'd deliberated over whether she was thankful or disappointed that the countess had arrived when she did. *What was the matter with her?* Of course she was thankful, ever so grateful that his seduction had ended when it did. She chose not to pursue musings on what might have happened if the countess had not made an appearance. *Oh, how could she have let herself be cozened by him?*

True, he was handsome when he smiled, and he might kiss as if he could set her world on fire, but she, Patience Leticia Mandeley, would have none of it. She vowed not to let him near her again when her emotions were unguarded.

She would be more careful in the future. This spy business certainly would take some practice.

Oh, the earl was a devious one. I will just have to watch him more closely next time. Since he was a spy, he probably knew all sorts of ploys to make people talk. Convinced that she would yet prove to be a worthy opponent in his game, she drifted off to sleep, still reproaching herself for vividly remembering the earl's kiss and finding pleasure in it.

Chapter 5

Patience scowled into her small looking glass on the shelf. Shadows under her eyes heightened her translucent skin. Admittedly, she was a bit tired from her adventure last evening, but then she always had difficulty rising in the morning. When she'd dragged her protesting body from bed and washed, she felt fit to face the beckoning day and the unsuspecting earl.

Brother James often said a righteous cause has the strength of angels behind it, but Patience thought she could have used a little more help from above. With a shrug, she turned to look for her ivory combs to capture her unruly hair. Only one could be found. She searched the small room and saw no sign of the missing comb. The pair had been her mother's, and she hated losing one.

Slowly sinking onto the bed, Patience believed she may have worn them last night on her ill-planned trip to the earl's room. If she wanted it back, there simply was no recourse but to search his room. The thought of entering his bedchambers again so soon made her apprehensive. When would it be safe to venture back into the enemy's lair? Only when she was absolutely certain the earl was nowhere nearby.

Ready to work, Patience entered the kitchen, wondering how she could learn the earl's whereabouts, since she wanted to explore his study. Although the housekeeper was not about, the old cook, Melenroy, told Patience that she was to see to the storeroom and organize it. With a heavy sigh, Patience headed downstairs in the direction the cook pointed, determined to be the fastest organizer Mrs. Knockersmith had ever hired.

Bryce spent a few hours reviewing crop rotations with his land steward, then mounted Defiance and headed for Viscount Carstairs's estate, with Captain Keegan Kilkennen by his side. The captain's ship would be undergoing repairs for the next week, and Bryce wanted Keegan's opinion on the viscount's murder. They planned to meet the constable at Carstairs's home to discuss it.

"You seem preoccupied, my friend," Keegan remarked as they trotted side by side over the rolling verdant meadow. Their horses' hooves left fresh imprints on the soft, rain-dampened ground. "What causes the frown? This murder business or a woman?" he teased.

Bryce returned a grin. "Truthfully, a bit of both." Although he should concentrate on Carstairs's murder, Mrs. Grundy haunted his thoughts. Where had she come from? Why and how had she entered his home? Where was she now? And what was her real name? Whatever her purpose, he wanted her not to be a part of the deceptive world of spying.

Keegan pressed Bryce further. "Tell me it is not the countess who brings that look to your face. Why do you allow her and that scurvy cousin of hers to remain at Paddock Green?"

His grin broadening into a smile, Bryce shook his head. "You certainly harbor little love for Isabella. Actually, I consider it my duty to the king to keep them under my roof. I do not trust Sansouche, and he can be easily followed from here on his midnight jaunts through the countryside. We almost caught him and his cohorts in Little Shepherd's Cemetery a few nights past. The next time, we will succeed. The problem is holding the countess at bay. If I send her to London, her cousin would go with her."

Keegan blew a low whistle after Bryce's explanation. "So that is your game. You think Sansouche is the French spy."

"Actually, I think Sansouche is in league with the spy, but he's not their leader. I had Red Tattoo on his trail, but lately my valet has been working on another matter."

With raised brows, Keegan asked, "Yes?"

It was not until both men slowed their mounts to cross the narrow, rambling brook which adjoined Londringham's and Carstairs's estates that Bryce replied, "Red has been looking for a young woman that I met at the fair as well as the young Rupert Mandeley. He may know something about his cousin's murder, but unfortunately, the boy seems to have disappeared without a trace."

Keegan mused, "A girl, a murder, and French spies. Must keep Red busy. Where is he now?"

"He traveled to Storrington to visit the young man's family. I expect his return any day, hopefully with good news." Conversation was postponed as they hied their horses up the circular driveway.

Carstairs's butler greeted the men at the door and ushered them into the front parlor where the local constable, Lyle Cavendish, awaited them. Bright sunlight from the windows that aligned the east wall lit the dark-wainscoted room.

Cavendish's small eyes blinked behind his thick spectacles as he squirmed his pudgy body further into the small chair. His bushy black moustache seemed to cover most of his countenance except for the thick brows that framed his small, pale face.

Bryce nodded to his friend. "Mr. Cavendish, this is my associate, Captain Keegan Kilkennen. I asked him to accompany me today. Your note indicated that you have suspicions that Carstairs may have been selling secrets to the French. What accounts for this?"

Cavendish rubbed his hands together and replied in his earnest Yorkshire accent, "Yes, I believe the viscount was working with our enemy. Connecting the pieces to the puzzle, I recently learned that Carstairs had lost funds at a rather rapid pace for several months. Then suddenly, his situation changes, and he has money to spare. Even his lawyer cannot explain the viscount's recent wealth. Apparently, the man trusted no one and was extremely secretive."

Keegan leaned against a nearby desk. "And who might you think killed him? His French benefactors would have wanted to keep him alive for his information. Do you think his cousin, this young Mandeley fellow, had anything to do with his murder?"

Drumming his fat fingers on the arm of his chair, Cavendish intoned, "Too soon to say. The maid declares she saw the young man standing over the body. That's all we have. No motive, no murder weapon, nothing. But it certainly does look serious for the young man. His disappearance has only increased the opinion of guilt most have about him."

"It is not Mandeley."

Cavendish and Keegan glanced over at Bryce upon hearing his surprising conviction.

The captain frowned and confronted his friend. "How did you come to this conclusion?"

Bryce slowly progressed around the large study, studying the objects and furniture as if seeking answers and seemingly uninterested in the conversation when he looked up and said thoughtfully, "It is my job to know people and where their loyalties lie. I have been thinking about the night

I met Rupert Mandeley at a local family's soiree. We spoke only briefly, but he seemed like an eager, jovial chap and very wet behind the ears."

He held up his hand to halt any encroaching argument. "Not in Carstairs's league. If we find the motive behind the murder, we shall find our assassin. However, I certainly would like to find the Mandeley boy. I think he could tell us something."

The constable's eyes squeezed tight, listening to Londringham's pronouncement. He moved his jaw from side to side, then decided, "Londringham. You could be right. However, we may indeed find that behind the innocence of youth lies a deceitful heart."

Bryce's only response was a lift of an arched brow.

They spent the better part of the morning interviewing the house staff and searching for answers in the shambles of the study. But they found no motive for the murder or clues to the murderer's identity. Reviewing documents left on Carstairs's desk, Bryce noticed Cavendish absentmindedly spinning the large globe on its stand near the windows.

Remembering something Carstairs had once said, Bryce hurried over to the stand and stopped its movement. His hands expertly skimmed over the smooth circumference as the other men watched in amazement. At the bottom of the globe, his forefinger felt a tiny metal hook. He pulled the hook and a document fell to the floor.

Bryce bent down and scooped the rolled paper into his hand. A quick glance at the unfurled scroll was all he needed. "This is what he wanted."

"Who?" Keegan asked, peering over Bryce's shoulder.

"The murderer. It is a map marked with weak joints of our battlements along the coast. I saw a similar document in Hobart's offices. This map could help the French determine where best to land their troops in an invasion." He paused thoughtfully. "Carstairs's death must have something to do with the French spies in our midst. If Carstairs was feeding information to the French, that would account for his sudden wealth, but not his murder."

All three men stared at the document in the earl's hands, wondering what vital information Carstairs might have passed on to the French. Although Cavendish wanted to claim the paper as evidence, Bryce persuaded the constable to allow him to keep it for awhile. It might prove useful in catching a spy or two, he jested.

Later, after dinner, Bryce relaxed in the library on the settee near the fireplace, wincing unconsciously at the pain in his right thigh. He thought very little about his injury and too much of a deeper wound he allowed no one to see. Just one of the many casualties of last November. Revenge held him tighter than a spiderweb holds a fly. He was a captive of that night and would never be free until he had caught Edward's murderer.

Soon. Soon, he'd find the French spies. Then he could return to France and search for the Frenchwoman spy.

He turned his mind to Carstairs's murder. Although he and the constable were convinced that the viscount had been in league with the French spies, they were not entirely sure what other Englishmen might be enjoying heavier pockets in exchange for military information. And then there was the matter of the countess's cousin, Alain Sansouche.

In the past month, the Frenchman had acted extremely re-spectable, with not one whiff of any peculiar or suspicious actions.

Further contemplation was interrupted when, under half-closed lids, he watched Keegan, Isabella, and Sansouche stroll into the library. Isabella immediately disengaged herself from her cousin and glided across the room to sit by Bryce's side, leaning very close to him, the deep cut of her ruby-red gown displaying her assets.

"Bryce, *mon cher,* you should have heard the charming story Alain told about his trip across the Channel. It was very dangerous. They nearly capsized twice and were shot at by the English! Is that not exciting?"

The subject of the countess's discourse stood near the fireplace. "My cousin believes my journey more amusing than it truly was. Londringham, I have not had an opportunity to extend to you my appreciation that you permit me to stay here with my cousin."

Bryce noticed the Frenchman's smile did not reach all the corners of his face, but he acknowledged Sansouche with a slight nod.

Bloody hell, where is my port? He smiled grimly to himself—though his thirst was more for revenge, he'd have to settle for libation. Nothing would satisfy him but a Frenchwoman's head on a plate or a pretty green-eyed vixen in his bed. No sense in letting that thought distract him. He was amazed how often he did think of Mrs. Grundy, even with Isabella practically sitting on his lap.

Thankfully, he noted the footman had arrived with the sought-after port.

"Shall we have a game of cards, anyone?" Isabella's suggestion caused everyone to turn to her. "We need four players and there are exactly four people in the room. Whist? Bridge? Alain, yes?"

"Your servant, madam," he responded.

The countess next turned to Bryce, who had stood and walked to the sideboard and poured a glass of port. "And you, my lord? Shall we count you in?"

Bryce stared into his port as if the opaque color could tell him something. When he realized they were waiting expectantly, he looked up and smiled apologetically. "Cards? I think not." His response brooked no opposition.

"Captain, would you . . . ?" Isabella looked across the room to Keegan, who studied several leather-bound books on the wall-length bookcases.

He took a long swallow before replying, "Not interested in games with any Frenchies."

The countess raised her chin perceptibly. "You Irish are beneath the lowest servants. You are so vulgar and unimaginative, no culture, no fashion. Whatever do you have in your dreadful little country?" She shared a chuckle with her cousin.

The captain strode over to the settee. Bryce recognized his friend's dark expression, which had frightened many a lazy sailor and loosened a few tongues. Keegan rested a hand on the arm of the settee and leaned down mere inches from her face. "The Irish, mum, enjoy the finest stout, the fastest horseflesh, and the rarest women, none of which I am sure the frog-eating Frenchmen have ever seen."

Keegan's insolent answer stunned the woman into what Bryce knew was a rare speechlessness. The captain sauntered back over to the bookcase and drained his glass with one swallow.

Bryce watched as Isabella's face turned red with anger, her blue eyes small slits of spitting venom. He would have to remind his friend to curb his tongue around the countess. They mixed together like Whigs and Tories.

In obvious exasperation with the Irishman, Isabella spilled her drink on the front of her dress and jumped up, sputtering. Sansouche appeared at her side immediately.

"*Ma chérie,* it is truly insignificant. Calm yourself and let us see if your maid might be able to save it." He soothed and calmed her while escorting her to the door.

At their absence, Keegan smacked his hands together. "What delightful events conspired to rid us of her presence."

Before he could continue, they heard it. *Click.* Followed by a smooth rolling. The wall behind Bryce's desk disappeared and Red Tattoo, Bryce's valet, walked into the room. A ruddy face to match his red hair and a thin scar along the side of his face and neck, Red looked more like a smuggler than a valet, especially given his filthy appearance. "Ready for my report, my lord. I waited for the French witch and her cousin to leave and thought the air clear."

After locking the library room door Bryce gestured to a nearby chair. "Yes, I am most anxious to learn of your progress."

"It's like this. I went to that place, Storrington, you sent me to and had me a look around. Spoke to the neighbors, even the boy's family at a place called Susetta Fields. Sounds French to me."

Bryce waved him on. "Yes, and do they know where their missing brother is?"

"No, their lips were closed tighter than a nun's legs. I told them as how the boy owed me money from a card game, and I was meaning to see he came through with it. The one brother blathered on about being his brother's keeper and such. Couldn't follow it much. One of the other fellows offered to show me his garden of rutabagas, but before I could find out more, the older one threw me out!" Indignation showed plainly on his face.

"So his family either does not know where young Mandeley is or they are not saying," Bryce said.

"That's the way I'd tell it, my lord."

"And the girl?"

"Sorry, no luck there. No one in Winchelsea remembered a girl like that. There are some what say she may have only been here for the Mop Fair and got a job elsewhere."

Bryce rubbed his brow and responded thoughtfully, "Yes, hired at the Mop Fair. I had thought—no matter. But I believe she is still around here. We should be able to determine from the locals who hired her. Can you continue that business?"

Red Tattoo smiled. "I shall deliver her and that Mandeley fellow to you on a silver tray."

Bryce grinned. Red Tattoo, his friend and valet, had overwhelming confidence in his own abilities, most of which was justified. Often were the times that Bryce was glad to have Red watch out for him.

Keegan told Bryce with a wry smile, "This woman must mean something to you."

Shrugging indifferently, he replied, "Perhaps. I think she might lead to fairly interesting answers."

Another long day passed quietly, too quietly. Patience sat in the servants' hall alone finishing her dinner, thinking about events of earlier in the day. She had seen the earl only once in the morning after his return from an early-morning ride when he stopped to talk with Mr. Gibbs at the front door. From an open window, she had studied him unnoticed, objectively, she thought, belying the fast pace of her heart.

His thick brown hair touched his collar. He wore no coat, and his white sleeves were rolled up to reveal tanned, strong forearms. His hands rested casually on his hips. She remembered those strong hands that had warmed her skin. She shook her head. It simply wouldn't do to remember that night, she admonished herself.

He had a lean, hard look about him, and seemed as if he were never truly at rest, with a compelling countenance warmed by the sun, no doubt attracting many women.

Not that it mattered to Patience, of course. She imagined

how disappointed all of his conquests would be when they learned he was a traitor to his country.

When he'd headed back toward the stables, she could not keep her eyes off his formidable, muscled form, outlined in revealing buffed breeches. He strode with an easy assurance and yet lightly, almost as if he knew someone watched him. She'd suppressed a shiver that swirled up her spine, and returned to the required task of mixing white vitriol and sugar for boot polish.

As usual her thoughts were not far from the man who had drawn her and her brother into this little drama of his.

Patience left the servants' hall and climbed the stairs to the kitchen, which she found empty. Dinner long over, the clock would soon strike ten. The earl and his friends enjoyed libations in the drawing room. Melenroy reclined in her worn seat by the fireplace, snoring while probably dreaming of more tasteless dishes to cook. It had been three days since beginning her still-room maid adventure. Her patience was growing as short as brother James's sermons were long.

Just then, Lem burst through the kitchen door, glanced around, and ran over to her side. "Miss, I 'ear something. It's a whinin' sound. I think it's comin' from behind the stables. Come with me and see what it is."

"Did you ask Lucky about it, Lem?"

"Oh, Lucky can't 'elp, 'e's asleep in 'is cups. Ye got to help me. It may be bad."

As always, Patience found his little round, lively face hard to ignore. "Show me where you heard the noise."

The back door slammed behind them as they ran outside swinging a lantern, the half moon hidden in the shadow of the clouds. They swiftly ventured across the lawn, colored black in the night, to the stables.

Crickets hummed softly in the unseasonably warm night as the sound of the waves rushing to shore haunted the darkness, even at this distance. A perfect night for a stroll, but a more pressing concern made them quicken their steps.

As Patience and Lem rounded the stables they paused to listen for a noise out of place in the country air. By and by, Patience began to believe what Lem had heard was an owl or perhaps a lost sheep.

"There it is!" he shouted exuberantly.

Indeed, a howl that sounded like an animal in pain split the calm night. A second cry pinpointed the noise. It came from the copse of woods sitting back on a slight slope from the stables.

They raced toward the noise, and at the edge of the woods, they found him. Gulliver, the earl's greyhound. Patience placed the lantern nearby and saw immediately that the quaking animal's front paw was caught in a rabbit trap. Using pressure, with Lem's help she gently pulled open the trap and released the dog's paw, her hands inked with blood. Patience bristled over the injustice and pain to the animal. Poaching had long been a crime proven mostly unstoppable.

Lem crouched by Patience as she tended to the weak animal, petting Gulliver's sleek coat with devotedness. "'e's such a nice dog. Why did 'e 'ave to get 'urt?" Patience heard the tears in Lem's voice.

"I don't know, Lem. But he'll be fine, we'll take care of him," she rushed to assure him.

"The master will be quite angry at the poacher what set this trap," he said solemnly.

Patience nodded. "Lem, go quick and ask Lucky to bring a cart to carry Gulliver back to the stables."

Eager to do his part, Lem flew across the expanse of meadow to the stables while she remained behind to comfort Gulliver. She pulled a handkerchief out of her pocket and wrapped the wound several times to staunch the bleeding. All the while she murmured soothing words to the shaking dog as she stroked his soft fur over and over.

Not long after, Lem and Lucky returned with a cart. The three of them carefully lifted the squirming animal onto the cart and turned toward the stables, with Lucky pulling the cart behind him in a zigzag pattern, given his slightly foxed state. Patience and Lem followed close behind; Gulliver's eyes never left Patience.

Once safely in the stables, Lucky and Patience worked to create a poultice for the dog. The night air must have helped wake Lucky because as Patience held the greyhound's head in her lap, the groomsman was lucid enough to apply the thick mixture of water and bruised linseed, and rewrapped the dog's paw with a clean bandage. Eager to help, Lem provided water, which Gulliver lapped up.

The three of them sat on the floor of the stables and watched over their patient for a time.

Needing to stretch her tired muscles, and confident that Lucky and Lem would see to Gulliver, Patience rose and wandered out of the stables, wanting more than anything to pull off her uncomfortable disguise.

She stopped abruptly when she heard the sound of horses' hooves pounding down the lane. Puzzled, she looked back to the trees which lined the road and caught a glimmer of a light from a lantern.

Could the earl have an appointment this evening? This might be important. Perhaps if she stayed in the shelter of the trees, she could avoid detection. Surely his lordship was about to betray his hand.

Chapter 6

Stars dotted the night sky, forming a quiltlike pattern over slumbering angels whilst mortal men fought their battle below. Where had that poetic nonsense originated from? Bryce wiped the slight moisture from his brow. He wanted to take off his coat but couldn't. Not when he expected a visitor.

Here in the woods near his home, he planned for any unforeseen events, fingering the steel of his pistol warming in his hand. He had no idea why the French spy had chosen this location, but did not question it. He thought of Keegan back at the house, who was annoyed that he was not invited to this party of two.

But Bryce could take no chances. If the spy thought a trap lay in store for him, all his plans would be for naught.

Shadowy trees shook their leaves in conversation. Strange popping and crackling noises filled the air from a frenzy of animals embarking on their nightly activities. Bryce had relied on Red to arrange this rendezvous, and his valet had not disappointed before.

Finally, after these months of cat-and-mouse games, his mission seemed to be nearing completion. Resting lightly against a large waist-high boulder, he prepared himself to meet perhaps Carstairs's murderer or Sansouche. He did not know whom to expect, but vowed to unmask a villain this night.

Periodically he flashed his oil lantern toward the road in signal to his prey. A glance at the darkened house assured him all occupants were abed.

Suddenly, a whisper of wind rustled his senses, warning him of someone's approach. Soft, muffled horse's hooves rhythmically padded across the forest bed. His horse, Defiance, moved restlessly nearby.

He quickly reviewed his "turncoat" plan. Bryce hoped to convince the spy that he would be willing to trade his country's secrets for a handsome purse. And in the process Bryce hoped to learn who led the nest of spies here on the coast, and, more importantly, the date of the planned French invasion. He had to convince the spy he was one of them in order to accomplish his plan.

A gruff, raspy voice disturbed the dead of night. "My lord, this is indeed a victory for France. I would have you show your face and proof of your loyalty to our cause." The spy slowly approached the clearing on horseback; a black mask and black greatcoat cloaked the rider's identity.

Bryce leaned an elbow on the rock. "You ask for trust but you remain atop your horse and with a mask? Can we not meet face to face, eye to eye?"

"If we were civil men, I would have been asked to your study and not to the woods." The black stallion remained steady beneath tightly controlled reins.

"Ah, then we must not be civil men. Let us not waste our time. Our meeting here was for your safety, not mine." Bryce's words were cool and dispassionate.

A snicker behind the mask. "My safety? Your concern is touching. My contact tells me you are anxious to take Carstairs's place. Why the hurry? After all, he is dead." The throaty voice breathed smugness.

Bryce's jaw tightened, but he offered no riposte.

The masked spy continued, "Although many might wish to join our forces, all do not serve. Why should I consider you?"

"You already have, your presence implies that. Before I tell you what I have to offer, I would like to know if I deal with a second or Napoleon's own man." Brow furrowed, Bryce stared at the figure, trying to discover any clues to his identity. The lantern at his feet helped little to discern any distinguishable features. But he was certain the rider was not Sansouche.

"Due to your worthy status"—the masked rider dipped his head in mock honor—"I thought to meet you myself. I know much of you and believe not that you wish to change sides. What can you offer me that might change my mind?"

Bryce controlled the urge to knock the pompous ass off his horse. He sauntered closer. "Do your sources tell you that I have the locations of all England's military army settlements along the coast? Of which I am looking for a buyer. Is this enough proof?"

He reached his hand up to his coat but his actions stalled.

"My bullet will be between your eyes before your next breath."

Patience settled comfortably into a tree with knotted vines draping old and young branches. The earl and his friend met a few yards away, but through the foliage it proved difficult to see very well. The wind blowing and the night suddenly noisy, she even had difficulty following their conversation. She dared move no closer without being caught.

A few words floated back to her tree nest. Could the earl actually be planning to sell his secrets to another spy?

Biting her lip in frustration, she decided to move farther out on a dipping limb. She felt safe among the profuse scattering of leaves and gnarling branches, and confident her movements would not be detected by the spies.

Patience took a deep breath to slow her racing heart and edged closer to the edge, the rough bark poking her sweaty hands. So intent and excited about hearing words of great import, she scarcely noticed the branch trembling beneath her weight.

A loud crack signaled her first sign of trouble before she felt the support give way beneath her. Patience clawed wildly for a lifeline but came up empty.

The pistol-sounding pop alarmed the other forest visitors. They both sensed a trap, and the rider spun around and shot wildly in the direction of the noise, then turned to fire at Bryce.

But the earl had vanished. With a jerk, the stallion and rider leapt back into the satanic folds of the forest.

Bryce watched in anger from the shelter of the rock, his pistol cocked, as his prey flew from his hands. He could hardly prove his loyalty to the spy by shooting at him, although he acknowledged to himself it was probably too late.

What was the noise? The Frenchman certainly would not have shot at his own men. Could it have been Red or Kilkennen following him? After a quick search in the mossy rooted forest, he caught sight of a still figure at the foot of a nearby tree. A trained finger on the trigger, he slowly approached and studied the scene carefully.

The broken branch nearby explained everything but the mysterious intruder's identity. At a glance, Bryce could tell it was not one of his friends. Upon closer inspection, he discerned the figure to be a woman in a common housemaid uniform.

Anxiously, he turned the woman over and felt for a heartbeat. Steady and strong. He let out a sigh of relief. He did not know where she had come from or what she was doing here, but he would glean all of her answers, and soon. First, he must see to her welfare.

A quick examination revealed her left arm had been shot and blood seeped out of the wound. He whipped out a handkerchief to bind her injury, knowing he had to get her back to the house to care for her. He picked up the unconscious woman in his arms, found her spectacles nearby, and mounted Defiance. They managed a slow procession back to the house with Bryce holding the slight form in his arms. What had she been doing out here? Spying? On whom?

Able to slip undetected into the back entrance and then into his room, Bryce laid the stilled woman gently on his bed. He had nowhere else to take her that would not bring on endless questions by the curious. The young woman's countenance was as pale as the white linens on which she lay. He threw off his greatcoat to attend to her. She had not yet awakened, and Bryce thought to have a physician called.

He removed her shoes and cloak before turning to her mobcap which covered much of her face. He reached up and cautiously removed her cap. Deep brown hair spilled across his pillow in a sweep of silky heat. Bryce rose and stepped back, too astonished for words.

It was she. The woman from the fair, the one he had been searching for, Mrs. Grundy. And somehow, he was not surprised.

Chapter 7

The candlewick burned low as Bryce's unwavering gaze remained on the still form lying in his bed. The chair creaked as he rose and walked to the bed, settling gently on the edge. A sigh escaping from the young woman's full parted lips surprised Bryce. He quickly returned to his vigil in the chair.

Only an hour had passed since he had brought her here. After attending to the arm that the French spy's bullet had grazed and finding no indications of lasting head injuries, he had used the time to plan a course of action.

As he leaned back into his chair, he could not tear himself away from the young beauty before him. The candlelight caught reddish hues in tresses lying over one shoulder. He had opened her bodice slightly when he noticed it seemed a trifle snug. Unconscious, her innocence appealed to his protective nature, but he wondered where her true loyalty would lie at dawn's light. Long eyelashes concealed remembered bright hazel eyes.

Ironically, he had Red Tattoo searching over the district, when the woman he sought was in his own home. But why was she here and who was she? And why was he reluctant to call the constable and have her arrested? For what? He didn't quite know the answers yet.

He watched with concern when the young woman turned over on her good side and began to breathe deeply. Although he was no physician, he could tell she had settled into a deep sleep.

He stepped around to the other side of the bed. Her wounded arm stretched out across the sheets as she rested her head on her other arm. In sleep, her movements were graceful, and by the look of the blisters on her hands, unused to hard labor. She was no mere servant, of that he could be sure.

Observing her more closely, Bryce noticed the faint smudges under her eyes. From what? Worry? Fatigue? He painted her soft cheek with the back of his finger.

Shaking his head in bewilderment, he walked back to the chair. By lying on her side, she provided him a lovely view of her charming round backside encased in his linen sheets. Enough. He determined to marshal his wayward thoughts.

He strode to the far side of the room in punishment. Perhaps she was part of the ring of spies sent to watch him. Needing to clear his head and stem his arousal, he opened the casement window and gulped fresh air. What should he do?

Should he confront her or continue to allow her to play this charade? What had she been doing outside his window that night? If she was spying on him, she was obviously not very good at it. But until he knew her purpose, he had to keep her here under his protection and watchful eye.

A painful groan from his attractive and distracting subject arrested him from his thoughts. He turned and found her staring at him, holding the sheet to her chest.

"What am I doing here?" The fogginess in her eyes quickly disappeared as she watched Bryce approach her bedside.

She closed her eyes, remembering her fall out of that blasted tree, and felt a painful burning in her upper left arm.

Patience opened her eyes, focused, and saw the earl watching her with what looked to be deep concern. Taking a minute to peruse her surroundings, she realized she was back in the earl's bedroom. But how? She thought quickly and realized he must have found her in the woods and brought her back to the house. She gently touched the bandage on her arm. He had obviously attended to her injury. Questions about her presence and identity could only be moments away.

What believable story could she conjure to convince this man that she was practically innocent of any wrongdoing? Perhaps amnesia? She simply did not have enough time to invent a plausible story before his lordship's interrogation.

She wet her dry lips and tried to console herself. *Could she be imprisoned for impersonating a maid? She had never heard of such a thing. If he knew she was spying on him, what would he do to her? Perhaps kill her and throw her off a cliff? Hysterical thoughts, to be sure. Perhaps she could throw herself on his mercy? If he had any.*

"How are you feeling?" He leaned over her, concern in his vigilant gaze.

"My arm hurts. What happened?" Her voice was barely a whisper.

"You were shot in the arm. I brought you back to my bedchambers to tend to your wound. Luckily, it only grazed your arm. I can only surmise you hit your head when you fell out of the tree."

She mumbled, "Oh," anxious to look anywhere in the room other than into his intent stare. "I think I should return to my room now. Thank you for assisting me." She started to raise herself up.

He pushed her gently back. "A little longer so I can attest that you are feeling better."

He left her side to return to the shadows near the fireplace. "I must know what you were doing out there tonight, if you are strong enough?"

She faltered under his questioning, then rubbed her forehead, trying to gain time. "I decided to go for a walk and saw the light near the road. With the news about spies, I thought the tree might be a safe place to see what was happening, only I suppose that proved far from the truth," she finished ruefully.

"I see. A simple explanation. You thought you were eavesdropping on spies." The tone of his voice gave explicit doubt to her reasoning. "And, Mrs. Grundy, if that is your name, how came you to be in my home wearing a maid's disguise?"

The moment of defeat had arrived before a thought occurred to her. Suddenly, she found the beautiful designs on the counterpane quite fascinating. "You see, my lord, uh . . . I am, my . . . my brother . . . my brother wants me to marry a man I abhor."

Where had that story come from? She hurriedly continued. "He is at least ten years older than me. I have run away, and since I was afraid my brother would find me, I thought it best to disguise myself." She raised her gaze to him in innocent supplication. "I hope you might reconsider discharging me." Her voice trembled, assuming the worst for her transgressions.

"It is certainly vexing that you must resort to such measures to avoid an unwanted marriage. Nonetheless, you are welcome to stay under my protection as long as you desire it. But you cannot run away from your responsibilities forever," his voice sounding almost kind.

She blinked in astonishment. Was he offering her protection from her fabricated enforced-matrimonial story? *Oh, goodness, why did she seem to keep falling into more lies?*

His next question took her by surprise only by the timing. "What is your real name?" he asked, gazing intently at her.

A little unnerved by his intent stare, she managed a small smile and said, "Patience Simmons, my lord," remembering the surname she had given Mr. Gibbs upon her hire.

A sudden brisk wind issued into the room through the open window. She felt the coolness on her chest, and looked down to find that in her misadventures her bodice had come untied and now the top half of her bosom was displayed more than was prudent. Finding herself almost unclothed and unmasked shocked her into complete wakefulness.

Hoping to distract his lordship, she remembered her earlier endeavor and looked up at him. "Have you seen Gulliver? I am sure he will be better in no time."

He looked taken aback as he rested one hip on the end of the bed, watching his prey, or least she felt like it.

"What about Gulliver? I know nothing of this." He straightened up and waited for her response.

"Lem and I found Gulliver in the woods, his paw having been caught in a rabbit trap. We brought him to the stables and did our best to repair the damage. I believe Lem is with him now."

Bryce stood and walked to her side. "I will check on Gulliver directly. Thank you for seeing to his injuries."

Once more the room remained silent. She felt an utter fool under his watchful stare, and her wounded arm pricked pain at the back of her eyes. She looked away, trying to hide the unshed tears.

His next suggestion flabbergasted her. "I would like you to stay on, as I need assistance with my books. My house steward has left my employ, and I have no one whom I can rely upon. It is a temporary position. That is, of course, assuming you can read and write?"

She lifted her chin. "I am well-versed in many subjects—history, Greek, Latin, and more. I can sew, thread a fishing pole, speak French, and care for sick animals."

He raised his eyebrows. "You neglected to mention playing the pianoforte and singing like an angel," his mouth in a slight smirk.

She avoided his gaze before replying. "Ah, I cannot claim singing or playing the pianoforte. They are virtues, however, my parents believed their children should be well taught in many subjects. Education should be available to all who wish to learn. Do you not agree?"

"True. Perhaps some of your duties could also include tutoring Lem. I daresay he cannot spell his own name, and I do not wish my servants to be ignorant of their basic letters."

Patience stared in shock at the earl. Why should he care whether Lem could read or write, or any of his servants for that matter? His lordship was proving a puzzlement. And why was he not sending her on her way? And not only allowing her to remain but placing her with his books?

She could hardly contain her glee. In no time, she should have the information she sought to convict him. And only a graze to the arm for her sacrifice. Wait until Rupert heard.

"Thank you for permitting me to stay. I know I erred tonight but I shall be more obedient in the future." She hesitated. "May I now leave to return to my room?" she asked, holding her bodice tightly. She fidgeted under his close watch.

The earl tapped his chin. "Not yet. Let me clean up here, and I will help you to your room." He turned from her while continuing, "One more thing: you will need more appropriately fitting clothes than what you have produced so far. I will have Mrs. Knockersmith arrange for new attire." He began to unbutton his shirt.

Patience nodded, the scene before her leaving her speechless. Gathering her courage around her shredded dignity, she asked, "What shall we tell the others?"

Bryce ignored her question as he peeled off the bloodied shirt and threw it into the fire. She watched mesmerized while he emptied the basin water out the window, poured fresh water, and started cleaning off the dried blood.

The shadows of the dancing fire played across the sinewy ridges of his muscular chest and arms. She let her study of him continue down his black breeches, fashionably tight against the lean contours of his waist, thighs, and buttocks. What she would not give to be a lot closer to this magnificent form, forgetting the ache in her arm as heat filled her cheeks and dampened other maidenly places.

Water slurped from the basin as he splashed the liquid over his nearly hairless chest. When she raised her eyes to his face, she saw him watching her with an intrigued look and a smug smile.

"If you continue to look at me in that way, I may be hard-pressed to return you to your room," he told her in amusement.

Patience quickly looked away and gulped. Every time she saw him, she wanted to see more. Much more.

Finally, clothed in his dressing gown, he sat on the side of the bed, careful not to disturb her arm.

"I will inform everyone that you are indisposed for the next few days, until your arm feels better." He cocked his head, watching her closely, his face enigmatic.

"If you will turn your back . . . I shall endeavor . . . to—" She spoke, wanting to vacate his room immediately and restore her senses, alone in her room.

He shook his head. "Although I do enjoy the sight of you in my bed, I fear neither of us would get much sleep." He leaned over and carefully lifted her head and shoulders, wrapping the sheet around her. Then, to her astonishment, he scooped her into his arms, placed her injured arm gently across her body, and easily carried her out the door and up the stairs to her bedroom as she directed him. If she had any energy left, she would not have given in to the temptation to rest her head on his strong shoulder. But the night's events had caught up with her, and she reluctantly embraced Morpheus's dreams, feeling protected and safe in his arms.

When he had laid Patience on the bed, Bryce drew the faded coverlet over her slumbering form, and placed her spectacles on the nearby table. He stared down at her as one creamy breast threatened to slip from its confines from beneath the sheet that had slipped when placing her on the narrow bed. He gently pulled up the sheet to cover her and quietly left her room. He had found his vision, and she had a name. Patience. He vowed soon to uncover all her secrets.

A quiet knock on the door awakened Patience's restless slumber. Judging by the sunlight streaming through her window, she surmised it must be midday. A piercing thread of pain shot through her arm, quickly restoring her memory of the night before.

Her heart beat fast as she called out a greeting. She was definitely not prepared for another encounter with the earl. When she heard Colette's soft-accented reply, she breathed a sigh of relief. "Enter" brought the French maid into the room.

"*Ma chérie,* I was most concerned for you. His lordship explains that you are not well and shall remain in bed a few days. You are ill?" Colette set a tray of food on the opposite bed and turned to inspect Patience for herself.

Patience bore her scrutiny well. She did not quite feel up to answering questions or explaining last night's adventures to anyone. "Thank you for your concern. I injured my arm last night, and his lordship kindly administered relief. He decided I need to rest for a short time."

Colette pursed her lips while leaning over Patience to inspect her bandaged limb atop the counterpane. "His lordship seems quite concerned over your well-being. He asked me to bring you this tray." She hesitated. "Are you sure there is nothing more for you to add, concerning the master and you? I do feel responsible for you here."

Patience's eyes widened in shock at the maid's audacious questioning, and struggled with her good hand into a sitting position. "There is no cause for you to ask me such. His lordship only helped me as a master would a servant. Everything remains the same as before."

Colette listened before smiling. "That is good. His lordship is quite handsome, it would not be difficult to harbor feelings for him other than the hatred you have shared with me. My mistress seeks only a kind word from his lordship, but to no avail. He forgets she is here, and I fear she grows restless. He has not been to her bed since she arrived earlier from Town. I believe she is weary from the chase. The countess and her cousin talk of returning to London, and for me, I must follow."

Suddenly, Patience longed to be finished with her masquerade. Longed for Rupert to be free. Wished to return to her brothers she missed and to her home.

But things had changed; she had changed. She now understood that she wanted something more, yearned deep in her soul for a new life. Perhaps when she returned home, she could persuade Louis to take her to London. Inconceivable to return to her past life.

Colette interrupted her musings. "I have been told Mrs. Knockersmith has arranged for new dresses to be delivered to you later today." The maid rose from Patience's bed and turned to go. "I must return to the countess or she will wonder where I am. I will return later for your tray."

The click of the door reminded Patience how alone she was in a place where she could not be herself and with someone who knew her secret. How could she continue this charade as his lordship had requested—or, rather, commanded? She thrust aside the counterpane and tried to rise from the bed. The sudden movement brought a pounding to her head that forced her to return to a prone position. Exhaustion, worry, and pain caught her consciousness and drew her rapidly into a bearable forgetfulness.

Colette looked up from ironing the countess's morning dress when Captain Kilkennen entered the apartments.

Immediately on her guard, remembering the antagonism between the countess and this man, she asked, "What do you here? This is a ladies' boudoir."

Kilkennen cocked one eyebrow in doubt as he sauntered around the room. "You call the shrew, Countess Isabella, a lady?"

"Captain, you offend me when you dishonor my lady." Although Colette held no love for her employer, perhaps he would leave if she was rude to him.

A wing chair near Colette's table provided Kilkennen a perch from which to watch her.

"The countess is not here. I must ask you to leave. It is not proper." Colette did not tolerate well the idle English. Furthermore, he interfered with her work.

His sharp green eyes assessed her. "Are you ordering me to leave?" he asked with a grin.

Colette hesitated before replying, "No, I would consider it more of a request."

"A request," he repeated to himself softly. "Where is her highness? I mean, the countess?" he asked, ignoring Colette's icy glare.

"I believe she and Mr. Sansouche went visiting."

"Ah, visiting. Perhaps with other French loyalists?" His tone held more than a casual interest.

Colette stopped her ironing and stated emphatically, "Captain, I have no idea of the countess's loyalties. I only know she will be extremely disagreeable if she returns to find I have not finished with my work." She brushed a loose curl from her forehead in disgust.

"Londringham is in need of her. I shall have to report to him that she has flown the coop with the French rooster," Kilkennen remarked flippantly.

"Now that you have accomplished your mission for information, perhaps you might find the door?" Colette petitioned him. This man disturbed her, and she could not afford to be distracted by him. For surely that is all *she* would be to *him,* a distraction. His startling green eyes and sharp, chiseled features in a tan-worn face had diverted many a maiden from her tasks, of which Colette had no doubt.

"I don't believe you like me. Why is that?" Kilkennen asked in a boyish voice.

Colette rolled her eyes in annoyance. "You cannot dally with me as you seem want to do. I work for the countess and those are the only services I offer."

Kilkennen sighed before rising from his chair and walking over to Colette. He shook his head. "Don't you realize the harder you fight, the more challenge you become to me?" Before she had realized what he did, Kilkennen softly kissed her cheek, brushed the errant curl from her forehead, and strolled out the door.

When Patience next awoke, night had drawn its shades on the day. She had slept undisturbed, awakened only by pangs of hunger. Groggily pulling herself up, she glanced at the tray Colette had left hours ago. The food looked even more repellent than it had earlier. While considering a search for food, she noticed the new dresses hanging in the cupboard. Gray. They were all gray. That would certainly make what to wear an easy decision.

A quick knock broke her reverie and blew Lem through the door.

"Livin' a life of ease, I 'ear tell. Cook swears you're only tryin' to avoid work." He jumped on the edge of her bed, sat, crossed his legs, and cocked his head, first one way and then the other. "Ye don't look ill to me. What 'appened? Ye was foine, yestiday. 'ow comes yore 'n bed?"

Patience held up a hand to halt the boy's runaway tongue. "I actually feel fine, except for my arm." She pointed to it for his inspection.

Eyes widened in surprise, Lem gaped at Patience. "You 'ave a wound, just like a soldier. Were you shot at by one of those Frenchies? Can I see? I want me a wound too. I'll show everyone 'ow brave I am with me wound." Lem leaned toward Patience and gently took her arm in his little hands. "Gore, that bandage is a beauty." He looked at it from all angles, then pronounced it a piece of work.

"'ow did you come by that? Ye ain't a soldier, like me." Suspicion mocked his inquiry.

Patience tried not to smile at his inquisitiveness, and diverted his attention. "Lem, I need you for a special mission. I have not eaten anything all day. Could you possibly see if there might be something to eat in the larder? And try not to let anyone see you."

Such a request had Lem beaming ear to ear. He smartly saluted Patience and hurried out the door.

A while later, the two enjoyed cheese and bread and a little whiskey. Lem had found it on the sideboard in the dining room and decided that all wounded soldiers needed whiskey to "fortify their spirits."

Patience coughed down a few draughts, to the delight of the little footboy. He regaled her with stories of Gulliver, who was healing quite well due to her and Lucky's administrations, so said his lordship. Melenroy absentmindedly had just baked bread with sugar instead of yeast. Lem told Patience they wondered whether the cook might be batty.

"And Mr. Gibbs? He has not been too unkind to you? I worry that he has given you too much work to do." When she saw the pain in his eyes, she wanted to bite her lip. Something was just not right between Mr. Gibbs and Lem. The butler acted cruelly toward him, and Patience would discover why.

"I am sorry, I did not think . . ."

A sharp rap on the door froze the friends. Patience did not know whom to expect. Her bedroom was proving to be quite a popular place. Lem leapt into action by throwing her cap and spectacles at her, which Patience awkwardly pulled on. Then the little boy grabbed the tray and stuck it under the bed. Finally, he pulled the covers up to her shoulders with a serious look on his face and, motioning a tree, escaped out the window.

The heat in the room grew oppressive as she fought for air and courage. She managed a squeaky "Enter" and waited with hands clasping the sheets.

Bryce strolled in the door, placed a tray on the bed, kicked the door shut, and turned to examine his patient. He paused, then threw back his head to laugh. She obviously had not been expecting him with the mobcap covering most of her countenance, pushing her spectacles down her nose. Patience looked adorable even as she glared at him with an icy-green blast and higher-than-thou nose for, he assumed, his uninvited presence.

"What do you find so amusing, my lord?" A chill froze her words.

"You were obviously not expecting any guests, and I must say, you will need to find a smaller cap in the future." So saying, he popped the cap from her head and threw it on a chair.

She pursed her lips, in anger or fear, he could not decide. With hands on his hips, he looked around the small room, his study missed nothing. The opened window, dirt on the wooden floor, and a half-hidden whiskey bottle in the folds of Patience's sheets. She had had a recent visitor, but who? His examination took only seconds before he pulled a chair next to her bed and sat down, her narrow cot much too small and close for them both.

Bryce leaned back in his chair, placed his right ankle on his left knee, and folded his arms. He had quite a few questions to ask the young woman but something halted his tongue. He would learn the truth, all of it. But not tonight. For some reason, he found it difficult to remember his purpose here.

The warmth of the room brought a pretty pink flush to her cheeks and her lips were red from biting them as she did now. He noted her small, even white teeth as she chewed her lower lip. And when her tongue darted out to lick her lips, he placed both feet on the floor and admonished himself not to notice her charms and the scent of her rosewater soap.

She was a woman. Hence, untrustworthy, disloyal, and exceedingly dangerous to his well-being.

Her coyness and innocence and unpainted beauty were all part of a calculated game she would use to manipulate him. But perhaps he could seduce her to get the truth? A pleasure he intended for them both.

"Are you planning to guard me all night? Ensure I do not escape into the darkness with the silver?"

Her sarcasm made him smile. Plucky little thing, considering he held all the cards.

"Actually, I am here on a nobler mission. I wanted to rebind your wound to help prevent infection. Is it still paining you?" He kept his tone easy, friendly.

"What? Oh, my arm. Well, I have been sleeping a good

part of the day, but now it is throbbing a bit." She too adopted a casual manner, of surgeon and patient.

"The whiskey has not relieved the pain in any way?" He pointed to the bottle peeping out from the bedclothes, near her leg.

"Ah, I . . . I only had a few swallows, perhaps not enough for medicinal purposes or to cause a drunken stupor," she replied defensively.

A cool April breeze tickled the air with honeysuckle and lilacs. Time for work. He studied her prim muslin nightdress before gesturing to Patience to unbutton it in order to gain access to her bandaged arm.

Heaving a heavy sigh, she turned away from him to present her back while undoing the top buttons and very carefully easing her arm out of one sleeve. He watched in amusement as she clung to her nightdress, obviously not wanting to reveal any more than necessary.

Bryce positioned the tray on his knees and leaned across Patience to gently lift her arm. As he unwrapped the old bandage, dressed the wound, and placed a clean bandage on her arm, he noticed that every time he brushed the front of her nightdress, he could feel her hardened nipple. He seemed to notice everything about her: the way her hair flowed across her shoulders, down her back and curled under her arm, the steady, lovely hazel eyes watching him as he watched her.

"Finished. Perhaps another day in bed should help ease the pain. I will send up some laudanum if it worsens." He commanded no arguments and returned the tray to the other bed.

"I am sure I will be much better tomorrow and am most eager to see to my new duties."

"We shall see," came his vague reply. Bryce was kindling a fond memory of the kiss on the floor the other night. He had not forgotten and wondered if she had. He had no reason to remain but found himself reluctant to leave without tasting her lips again. Medicinal purposes only, to give her something else to think about.

He leaned over her bed, braced himself on one arm, and caught her cheek, all with such speed as to surprise her. He hesitated before capturing her sweet lips beneath his. Her startled little moan vibrated against his mouth. She tasted of whiskey, and gave him a shy answer to his gentle wooing of her lips.

For a moment he broke away from her parted lips. When her tongue came out again, he swept in for victory. Tongues mated, he could not get close enough to the vibrant young woman. His hip settled on the edge of the bed while his hand wandered down from her soft cheek to her waist, to clasp her more tightly to him.

She eagerly welcomed his kiss and embrace, but he had to stop before he joined her in bed, even though he knew that is what they both wanted. He lifted his head and gazed intently into her stunned face, heated from the passion they had shared.

Unable to think of a suitable excuse for his behavior, he swallowed and offered, "I wanted to see if your kiss was as sweet as I remembered it the other night."

She continued to stare at him with wide eyes, perhaps still shaken by his actions.

He nodded. "Mmm, definitely, getting better with practice." How quickly anger stormed into her bright eyes, he thought in amusement.

"I would request that you find another partner to practice with, my lord. I do not need or wish further instruction," Patience told him, with her chin lifted.

"Yes, I do believe you do"—he paused—"need further instruction."

And with that obtuse reply, he quitted the room with his ministering equipment.

Chapter 8

Patience put a hand to her quivering, swollen lips as she watched the earl leave the room. *What have I done? What had he done? Rupert had been right, this man was dangerous, but not in the way either had imagined.*

She still felt his hard lips on hers. It must be wrong. No man kissed like that unless the woman was his wife or his mistress. And she was neither. Was she already on the path to damnation? James would condemn her for responding to his kiss, for allowing misguided passion to rule her head. Confusion reigned because, try as she might to tell herself she was here for Rupert's sake, part of her knew she was also doing this for herself.

Although she had not encouraged his lordship's attentions, she had been the recipient of his soul-taking kisses and tender caresses. She fanned her cheeks, remembering how her good arm had rested on his powerful shoulder, her heart still clipping at a frantic pace.

She took deep breaths to regain her sense and sanity. It did not seem possible to regret what had happened between them, nor did she normally waste time wishing to change the past, reflecting only how the past would affect her future.

Her future. What did it hold? For so long, her history was one of continual love and support for her four brothers and her fiancé, Richard. When he died, a lifelong dream of family and home became obsolete, deemed appropriate for the hopes only of younger girls.

Contentment had been hers in caring for her family. Passion had never played a part in her relationship with Richard, but then, she had not known that there was more emotion and feeling to be realized from a simple touch or a searing look. That in life there is something sweeter than chocolate, more brilliant than rainbow colors, more fragrant than the promising nectar of a blossoming honeysuckle. All for the taking, if only one knew where to find it.

And her teacher had been indeed generous and skillful. There was more, and it was right to want it. Would God think her wicked for wanting to experience something she had never known before? And even though she disliked his lordship's arrogance by insinuating she needed practice, his kisses lit long-dormant timbers of fire in her soul.

Wiggling down into the nest of her bed, she resolved to continue to search for a way to free Rupert and fight for something more which would perhaps bring her greater happiness. But could diverse propositions have hope in a happy reconciliation? She hoped she would not get more than she bargained for.

The next morning, Patience moved slowly down the shiny dark cherry staircase, careful not to move her arm overmuch. She had awakened early this morning with only a dull ache from her wounded limb, her stomach growling. Washing and dressing had proven to be quite a chore, taking over an hour because of her handicap. Oversized mobcap and glasses snug on her nose, she decided to venture out of her small chamber.

Mr. Gibbs, in the kitchen, told her authoritatively, "His lordship has instructed me to show you the account books in his study. He seems to believe you have some knowledge of arithmetic."

A while later, she sat in the earl's chair, safe from all prying eyes, and leaned back, melting into the leather. Tea and a half-eaten biscuit lay nearby. She closed her eyes and all her senses were attuned to his presence. She felt the very fiber of him, with his brandy, sandalwood, and the smell of tobacco permeating her musings.

She jerked herself away from those thoughts, opening her eyes to concentrate on the room. It took only minutes to realize that she could not work in this gloomy atmosphere. She left the large chair and headed to the windows to open the gold-brocade curtains stretched floor to ceiling.

Dust particles flitted through the bold stream of light filling the once-cavelike room. Scrutinizing the furnishings and the condition of the study, to her dismay, she found boxes filled with books piled high in the corner and empty bookshelves lining the walls. But for the desk and a few scattered chairs near the fireplace, the room looked unwelcoming. Actually, she realized, the whole house presented an unloved façade.

As she gazed around the sparse room, she concluded that the house had more of a flavor of an inn than a real home. After reflecting long enough about the earl's manor and his manner of inhabiting it, Patience turned to the books at hand.

The morning stretched into the late afternoon, interrupted only by Lem bringing her a small repast when she had almost finished recording the latest house supplies for the month. She stood up and thought to take the finished tray to the kitchen.

What a sapscull! Why not look in his desk for possible clues to his plans? Her hands trembled with anxiety as she reached for the first knob. A niggling, conscience-grabbing, Methodist-forbidding instant halted her movements. But then she remembered she was on the honorable side of the law and hoped the constable would believe the same thing. Perhaps there was not anything to find, his lordship being far too clever.

Three drawers opened to a slight tug but revealed nothing. The other three remained tightly locked, with no sign of a key. Nothing to condemn the man, except his disturbing kisses and passion-filled bright blue eyes. Frustrating, yes, but perhaps not disappointing.

Who was he, truly? She herself had heard the earl proposing to sell England's secrets. But suppose, imagine, he might not be the guilty party, at fault only for his purposeful seduction that she seemed to fall for time and again. While she might be slightly relieved, it still left two questions: Who had murdered her cousin? And who was the Englishman guilty of treason?

As she gazed at the huge bookcase behind the massive mahogany desk, she remembered Lem telling her a tale about secret passages that led to the shore. Hmmm.

Fifteen minutes later, she had still not found an opening but knew it had to be there somewhere. The mantel clock measured time lost, ticking noisily in her ears. She rubbed her palms against her skirts and tried again, her luck sure to change. Her fingers finally felt a small latch underneath the fourth shelf. She pulled it, and the bookcase opened smoothly, revealing a threshold beckoning the unknown.

Only one way to discover more of the earl's secrets. A little harmless trip down the passageway to see where it led. Before taking a step over the entryway, she remembered to take a weapon, hoping it would not be necessary to use it. She reached over and grabbed a letter opener and candle off the earl's desk. The letter opener fit snugly in her deep pocket. She swiftly lit the wick, hitched her skirts higher, took a deep breath, and stepped into the darkness.

Water drip-dropped and echoed throughout the black corridor. The candle wick in her hand flickered from a faint draft. She placed her right hand on the nearby wall to steady herself down the uneven stones, slick under her feet from condensation. One step, then two. A shiver ran through her from the damp air. In the distance, she could discern running water.

She stopped. Was that a voice she heard? Patience hoped it was not the earl and his friends returning. In an echoing chamber, it was difficult to tell whether sounds were coming from in front of her or behind her. She held her breath for what seemed like hours before proceeding. The voices faded away, and her heart returned almost to its normal beating.

She nearly lost her footing when a small animal ran across her shoe. A shriek escaped her lips. *I don't think I can do this. I don't like the dark, nor the cold, nor an unknown destination, nor mostly anything I can't see.* With a battle of wills arguing in her head, she stubbornly continued her journey farther down into the cave.

Quickly learning to walk on the difficult path, with the candlelight providing only glimpses of what was in front of her, after several slight missteps, she could hear the Channel water slurping the beach. She drew closer to a larger pool of light as she approached the cave's opening. When a mischievous breeze extinguished her candle, she hugged the side of the cave as she made her way to the entrance.

So this passageway did lead to the beach. Easy enough for a French spy like the earl to have a ship waiting to take him back to France. It must not be more than half a mile from Paddock Green.

Patience stopped directly outside the cave and looked down the quiet shoreline marred by a maze of huge rocks and boulders. A glance to the sky above assured her darkness would cover her progress, the full moon stayed hidden behind clouds. While the night might shield her presence, it was also effective in hiding the path the earl might have taken. She closed her eyes and listened to the wind and the water lapping against the smooth sands.

Then she heard them. Voices.

Her mobcap and spectacles stuffed in a pocket, a cool breeze blew a loose strand of hair across her face from her improvised bun.

The sand fell away beneath her sturdy shoes as she made her way slowly across the beach. After about three hundred yards, she stopped and listened again. Only the wind seemed to tease her ear. Without the voices, she lost her compass.

Patience stood with arms akimbo, trying to determine a course of action. Her bottom lip took a savage beating as her teeth chewed a decision.

Forbidding cliffs rose up to the night sky on her left. The ocean hissed its arrival and retreat from land on her other side. Where had they gone? Were they down the shore or had they perhaps climbed the cliffs? And where was the footpath Lem had described?

What was that? There it was again. The faintest light. Something flickered way down along the water surge. It glimmered briefly on the rocks. Then everything went dark.

She concentrated on the spot again to see if her eyes played tricks on her. A few minutes and then a much bolder light swept around an alcove of rocks.

Yes, that was it! She clapped her hands together excitedly and moved swiftly toward the direction of the light.

Confident of her course, and sure to find the French spies and perhaps the earl, Patience continued more slowly toward the spot where she had first noticed the light. Whatever she could learn this night, she would take directly to the constable. Although the brightness did not reappear, she heard the voices again, slight murmurings in time with the constant waves hitting the sands.

As she hugged the rocky embankment, she spied a large, oddly shaped boulder jutting out from the cliffs. A perfect place to hide and listen to spies planning their dark deeds. She crouched down and peered beyond the rock. Two dark figures stood near the shore looking out to sea. *I wonder what they are looking at.* Her brow furrowed, one hand braced in the sand for support, she studied the men. Neither looked like the proud, imposing figure of the earl or his brawny friend, the captain.

She tried to see beyond the rocks out to where the men's gaze held them captive, but frustratingly found her sight hindered by the adjoining rocks. She sank back down on her knees to consider how to get closer to the men. Who were they? And where was the earl?

Patience studied the massive boulder providing her shelter and wondered if it could be ascended. Her hands skimmed the surface and felt small indentations that could allow for toeholds. Carefully, relying more on touch than on sight, she grasped the rough surface for purchase. The first few times proved wearisome, always slipping backward, but finally she pursued another recess with success and pulled herself up slowly by degrees, hampered by her wounded arm. She tried to keep her heaving breaths quiet as she climbed to the top.

I can do this. Do not look down, she encouraged herself. The edge at the top was almost within her grasp. Feeling exultant, she grabbed the slippery sides of the rock and hiked her head up to clear the top.

A weasely, hairy, dirty face stared back at her. And then Patience did a very womanly thing. She screamed as she lost her balance and pitched backward.

Chapter 9

Red Tattoo lay hidden behind the cliff's low hedges, spying on the dark shadows appearing and disappearing near the tall white beacon, Parson's Down, high above. His lordship had mentioned earlier that a small unit of five men who served as sea fencibles kept surveillance for enemy ships crossing the Channel. Rumors abounded that the Frenchmen planned to overtake control of the beacon, but why and when?

His lordship and the captain should arrive any minute. What could be keeping them? A movement from the beach distracted Red from the beacon. He counted two figures by the shore watching the Channel waters. Most likely smugglers.

Perhaps the master and his friend had been delayed, and with this thought Red decided to search for them on the path. It had grown quite late, over an hour since his lordship had sent him up the cliffs. His small, thin figure made no blot on the landscape as he crawled on his belly to a thick copse of trees. Finding the path's hidden entrance, he scurried downward. Halfway down the cliff, the sure-footed Red braked before the surprised earl with the captain right behind him.

"What do you here, Red?" Londringham demanded. "Thought I told you to remain above."

"Yes, what's happening?" Kilkennen chimed in from behind Londringham's tall form.

"Sir, I was . . ."

They heard a sudden, high-pitched woman's scream followed by an animal's bellow.

The commotion froze the men before they leapt into action. Bryce ordered Red back up the cliff to follow anyone that leaves the beacon.

"C'mon, Kilkennen, those sounds came from below!"

"But what about our French spy?" Kilkennen gasped while hurtling himself behind his friend's running form down the twisted path to the shore.

"Our spy could be on the cliffs or below on the shore. But someone is in trouble."

Their conversation could not continue at their frantic pace were they to find the woman whose terror-filled voice had broken the still night.

Patience landed on her side with a thump. The wind knocked out of her, she remained still in order to check injuries she sustained from the fall. She slowly eased into a sitting position, her shaking body throbbed from the jolt. A quick check of her vital parts came up with a suspected sprained wrist and further injury to her still-mending left arm.

Before she could take one step, she found herself scooped up and thrown over a stranger's huge, burly shoulder. The ragged-clothed man, for that was all she could see upside down, rounded the huge rock at a quick pace and proceeded several feet before halting at the side of the cliffs covered with climbing moss and a latticework of branches. The pain in her wrist throbbed in time with her rapidly beating heart.

Oh, why do I have to have such a curious streak? she remonstrated herself.

Breathing heavily and too weak to summon her vocal cords into working order, fear alone kept her silent. *Where was he taking her? Was he one of the spies? Did he plan to do away with her?* She hoped to learn all of the answers soon, except for the question regarding life and death. Perhaps if she appealed to this misguided man, he might have a merciful nature.

The stranger grasped several branches and pulled open a large-enough hole to sidle through with his burden.

"Where'd ye find a woman 'ere, Bear? Bloody trouble. Cover 'er mouth. We don't want 'er screamin' 'er bloody 'ead off and givin' us away." The hard, nasal voice echoed in the small chamber of the dark enclosure.

Her captor, well-named Bear, slipped Patience down from his shoulder and pulled her back against him, smacking a dirty, foul-smelling hand over her mouth. She noticed a smaller man pulling a curtain of heavy branches together at the cave's opening.

She struggled with her captor, anxious to get away from the man's implacable grip and repulsive smell. He obviously had not washed lately, if ever, judging from the strong, putrid odor emanating from his body which threatened to gag her—or else she would surely gag once she was free of his large hand.

Suddenly, another man pulled her roughly out of Bear's clamped embrace. She cried out in pain as a tall, thin man put pressure on her sore wrist, dazedly wondering how many men were in this tiny cave. Slowly closing her eyes, she had an overwhelming feeling that she would either swoon or vomit. Still deciding what to do first, the thin man thankfully released her wrist and stuffed a handkerchief in her mouth, a surprisingly clean one. He made quick work of tying her hands and feet with a slip of frazzled rope before shoving her in a corner. Obviously, this villain had very little practice with tying up hostages, for the loose knots would be easy to untie. Quicker than a sneeze, she could remove the rag and scream—but didn't.

"Keep still, don't move," the tall one ordered in a raspy voice.

Patience, too frightened and shaken, only nodded. She shook her head to remove several long strands of hair which blocked her view. When she could finally look around the small, cramped area, Bear stood on the opposite wall staring at her. His was the face that had terrified her on the rock. Not that his face was utterly gruesome, but he did show more hair than skin on his face, which must have been the reason for his name. Her scream had been more in surprise than fear of this man. His large eyes watched thoughtfully, but she could not guess what lay behind his hairy mask.

The tall, thin man who had tied her up hunkered down near the entrance, peering through a small hole. Yet another man, rather short and energetic, paced up and down in front of her, every few minutes stopping to stare at her and shake his head in disgust.

The guard quickly turned and motioned for everyone to be quiet.

Her heart pounded in her ears. Along with her captors, she heard the sound of footsteps and voices.

The earl and his friend. She recognized them but could not distinguish their conversation. She shivered uncontrollably.

No way out. Even if she wanted to call out to the earl, how would she explain her presence on the beach? And she was not about to let these men know how frightened she was. She had to figure a way out of this mess without the earl's help, nothing else would do.

"She must be here somewhere." Londringham spoke

distinctly from only a few feet away. The cave's occupants heard sand squashed under boots in front of the hidden entrance.

"There is nothing here, Londringham. Besides, with no moon or light, we could not find a tree unless we bumped into it. Let us return tomorrow." Kilkennen's growing frustration was evident.

A few minutes of silence, then farther away, Londringham's response: "By then it may be too late."

Patience lost track of time as she tried to surreptitiously wiggle her hands free. She ignored her wrist throbbing in pain so she could focus on any information she could use to assist in her escape. She heaved a hesitant sigh through the handkerchief when the thin man motioned that they were alone again.

He then beckoned the short man to his side, and the two of them crept from the cave after instructing Bear to watch Patience.

The giant man remained on the opposite wall, only a few feet separating them. Angry, harsh voices sounded outside the cave. *Apparently something had not gone well for these spies. But if they were the French spies, why would they hide from the earl, one of their own? Were they not in league together?* Listening more intently, she heard one of them mention a ship and lost bounty.

Oh, how utterly stupid of me. These men were smugglers, not spies. Will they harm me? Sitting on the dirty pebbly floor of the cave, she had to keep her wits about her. What could she offer them that might help to win her release?

Suddenly, Bear made a move toward her. She stilled her heart and offered many prayers but felt no final blow. With two quick slices, he severed the ropes that bound her legs and pulled her gently to her feet.

She moaned again through the handkerchief, still feeling a

bit woozy as Bear led her outside the cave and onto the beach where his two companions held forth a furious argument.

"'ow could you let this 'appen?" the shorter man remonstrated the tall man sitting on one of the smaller rocks dotting the sands. "'enry, can you 'ear me? This was our first chance with Ledeaux's ship. I promised 'im a safe delivery. What went wrong?"

Tall, thin, pockmarked Henry sat motionless, ignoring the man they called the General, when just then the General caught sight of Bear holding Patience. "And ye." He stalked toward them. "Ye were to watch for trouble. "'ow did you miss 'er? And just what are we to do with 'er? Do I 'ave to do everythin'?" The General then paraded up and down the small strip of beach, berating Bear and Henry at their incompetence to see a plan through. "Remember, I am the brains, yer leader. If ye do as I say, then a little lick of work and we're livin' like Prinny. Perhaps I should search for comrades of higher intelligence."

Bear watched the General continue his tirade, all the while keeping a firm hold on Patience. Finally, the General walked over to them. "Did I tell ye to leave the cave? Did I tell ye to untie her feet? Bear, do ye realize if ye make the rules and not me, then ye see, we 'a' to change the plan. And with ye makin' the decisions, we'll be strung on Tyburn before the next full moon."

If Bear was insulted by the General's last remark, he moved not a muscle nor offered a defense. But then, Patience was becoming accustomed to the idea that he was a man of few or no words.

"I will simply 'a' to locate Ledeaux in the morning and try to explain our little mishap that we were unable to greet 'is ship. Perhaps 'e'll understand, I surely don't."

He turned toward Patience. "And what should be done with ye? And what might ye be doing down 'ere? 'oo do ye work for?" The questions tumbled out of him as he stared at Patience in her plain gray dress.

He waved his hand in indifference. His small, round face scrunched up in consideration. "Of course, we can't take ye with us, and if we let ye go, ye'll report us to the constable. That does not leave us with many alternatives, now, does it, ducky?" He leaned his oily face closer to hers.

Patience decided she had had enough of the little General, as bad as Napoleon, was he! She lifted her tied hands and to the amazement of the onlookers removed her gag.

"Ye could 'a' removed the handkerchief when those men were 'ere, why didn't ye?" asked the General.

"Quite simply, it did not suit my purpose for those men to find me here," she replied tiredly before settling on a nearby stump. "I work at the house, and if the earl were to find me here, I would lose my position."

The three men gathered around Patience looking at her curiously.

She shrugged. "I was taking a walk when I heard noises and thought to investigate." She thought to herself, *I have been taking a lot of walks lately.*

Continuing in her most earnest manner, she assured them, "I will not tell the constable about your presence here tonight, if you do not tell the earl where you found me."

The General considered her bargain. He and his men had never killed anyone before, leastways not a young woman. Truth be told, he became slightly nauseous around blood. He beckoned Henry to the side to discuss a plan of action.

She observed the men for a few minutes as they talked animatedly, looked at her, and then back to each other. So immersed in their conversation, they did not hear her approach. They sprang apart at the sound of her voice.

"Please keep in mind, gentlemen, that since the ship did not land, no smuggling was committed by you. And I have

no proof that would convince a constable of your intent."
She enjoyed explaining that bit of news to them.

Henry scratched his chin as the General weighed her
words. "She does 'a' a point there, 'enry." A pause. "Done.
Yer free. Bear, untie her hands. Little lady, just don't be in-
terferin' in our business, again," the General instructed a
little less harshly.

After Bear cut away the ribbons of rope, she rubbed her
wrists and hands as she studied the men. They actually reminded her a little of her brothers waiting at home. The giant
was like her brother Benjamin, and the General like James.

"Our lookout! We forgot about 'im!" Henry shouted,
pointing to the top of the cliff.

"'enry, signal him to meet us," the General barked as he
walked toward the cave.

Patience started to the entrance of the hidden passage,
and then turned to the would-be smugglers and the General once more. "Have you ever thought of another line of
work? Gainful employment and one with less likelihood of
swinging by the end of a rope? Perhaps you three could
easily find work, in the militia or on a ship? Smuggling
seems a rather dangerous profession."

The General smiled condescendingly to Patience. "'Tis
true, perhaps. But where is the excitement in such jobs as ye
mention? And we 'a' never actually smuggled anything.
This was our first opportunity. And I thought my plan foolproof. I guess it would 'a' been if I didn't 'a' to depend on
a couple of fools." He laughed at his own joke.

When the General had finished snickering, he grew
sober. "Perhaps it ain't smuggling what will bring us fortune. I will have to review our future endeavors." He nodded
thoughtfully while stroking his chin.

Patience shrugged, giving up persuasion for the other

thoughts on her mind. She waved to Bear as she hurried down the beach, and, much to her surprise, he returned the wave.

Meeting with no difficulty in the passageway, she slipped silently through the study and up the stairs. Her hands trembled from exhaustion and fright after her adventure on the beach. She did hope those men would listen to her and pursue more honorable goals than smuggling. She smiled when she thought of Bear. He seemed such a gentle soul for his great strength.

She entered her room exhausted beyond measure, needing to rest and plan how to proceed. Stepping out of her shoes, she fell onto the bed, careful of her wounded arm. Anything else was simply too much trouble.

She felt lost, unsure how to continue. Tonight had been a narrow escape from those smugglers-to-be. Patience needed someone to confide in, someone who could understand. Her thoughts rested briefly on the earl, and she grimaced. Her enemy certainly would not be willing to help her.

But yet when he had held her in his arms on the floor in his room, he did not seem like the enemy, in fact, he seemed very unenemy-like. His arms had felt strong and sure and very comforting. She wanted to feel his warmth again. To taste his lips. *I must stop this playacting,* Patience lectured herself tersely. *If he discovers my true identity, he will have me thrown out of the house, and even worse, perhaps into prison.*

Her hand automatically reached for her silver locket for comfort, a present from her mother. But her fingertips felt nothing. She quickly sat up, all exhaustion banished in fear of her loss. She examined her clothes and the bed, but the locket was missing.

It must have fallen off when Bear carried me to the cave, she thought despondently. *I have lost my precious locket, am nearly killed by smugglers, most likely sprained my wrist, and*

have made no progress uncovering proof of the earl's treason.
What a miserable day. Surely, tomorrow must be better.

In the wee hours of the morning, Londringham, Kilkennen, and Red Tattoo arrived back at the house. Red and Kilkennen went to their rooms, but Bryce had another destination before he could find rest.

He quietly opened the door to Patience's room and found her sleeping soundly. He had thought perhaps the woman's scream he had heard on the beach had been hers, but why, he couldn't say. He shook his head at his fanciful musings and was just about to close the door when he noticed her shoes near the bed. Silently as the moon, he crept into her room and grabbed her shoes for a look.

Muddy, wet, and sandy. He put them back where he had found them, and, annoyed and something more, headed to his bedchamber to find some sleep or peace, probably not both.

Chapter 10

The next day after dinner, Isabella cornered Bryce in the gazebo where he had headed after taking a stroll. The swishing of satin warned him of her approach. He turned to lean his back against a column, watching her enter the sanctuary. The countess smiled coyly at him as she seated herself comfortably on the marble bench, the diamonds sparkling around her neck providing the only light other than the moon's beam.

"Bryce, darling, I missed you at dinner. There was no one to speak to, no one to discuss this weekend's hunt and festivities. And I have spent so much time preparing for it. Where have you been all day?" Her shrill voice startled the quiet night air.

He knew that his answer—avoiding *her*—was not likely to meet with a great reception. Damn, he had forgotten about his promise of a hunt for her friends. Since he had been unable to persuade her to leave, he had hoped that Isabella's friends would convince her to return to London with them, that their endeavors might succeed where his had failed. There had been little gain in keeping his ex-mistress and her French cousin here, especially since Sansouche had been making noise of late about traveling up to Town. Besides, Bryce planned for his new house steward to occupy a lot more of his time.

Isabella prattled on, unaware of Bryce's unresponsiveness. "Everyone has responded to my invitation and have all expressed great enthusiasm over the soiree Saturday night. They all know you have seldom opened your house for any type of affair."

He ignored her words while clinically studying her artfully arranged blond coiffed hair, painted face, and svelte body. Why had he ever been attracted to her? She was considered quite a thing of fashion by the ton, perhaps that was why he had been interested. And Isabella had been persuasive at a time after his brother's death, when he needed an outlet for his grief but had no energy to find it. Isabella had simply pronounced him hers, which he did not feel the need to confirm or deny. But those few times of controlled passion with Isabella had only left him feeling more empty and disconsolate than before.

Now, staring at her beauty in the moonlight brought another face to his mind. Patience. His new house steward whose dark brown tresses promised sensuous pleasures, her luminous hazel eyes passion-filled with innocence, and ripe lips made for kissing. Or for lying, he could not be sure which.

Isabella seductively rose from the bench and moved near Bryce, placing a red finger-tipped hand on his arm. With a little pout, she rejoined, "Can we not have together what there was, once before? I miss you in my bed. I am lonely for your touch and your kisses. Do not tell me you seek another's bed?" she asked, her face a complete picture of sulkiness with an underlay of ire.

He looked down at her arm before gently removing it, and walked to the end of the gazebo before he replied, "Isabella, content yourself that I have not found a replacement for you.

However, in the future, where I care to partake of a woman's company is no longer your affair." Carefully measured words, sure to pour vinegar onto her wounds, but the woman needed firm convincing. His footsteps on the walk heralded no sound in the vacant air he left behind.

Isabella watched him leave, a bitter anger growing inside. After all she had done for him! Well, he would not discard her that easily! She still held a few cards of her own.

The household threw themselves into the tasks at hand, preparing for the countess's visitors. Her guest list included the usual number of fashionable, reputable, and disreputable rakes and ladies normally attending a function outside of Town. Bryce thought wryly of all those who had accepted the invitation simply from curiosity. He could not remember the last time the house had been opened for guests. Society gatherings had always been a duty and never a pleasure for him.

When he thought of his home at Paddock Green, he remembered enjoying outdoor activities with Edward. He was more at home with a fishing pole than with dancing the country dances. Thank goodness he would only have to tolerate the small group of visitors for a few days. Then life and his household would return to some semblance of normalcy. Time was growing short for locating the ring of French spies, and, unfortunately, Sansouche had proven less than helpful.

During the past few days, Bryce rarely caught sight of Patience. She seemed very clever at avoiding him. Mornings she worked on his accounts, and afternoons he spent away from the house working with the constable on Carstairs's murder. The only times he saw her they were not alone. Probably just as well. Bryce could not seem to concentrate when she was near. He remembered her kisses and her heated touch and wanted to experience them again.

Thankfully, Red Tattoo, who watched Patience's movements, could report nothing strange or out of the ordinary to his master. No posted letters, no rendezvous, nothing. But if Patience was not a French spy, then who could she be? And why was she here, in his house? Could her story possibly be true? All evidence was to the contrary.

Although the truth still eluded him, Bryce thought how passionate Patience would be in marriage to a man she truly loved if her actions to avoid marriage to a man she hated were equal. He knew nothing made sense, and he was not a patient man to await the answers he needed. After six months, his brother's murderer still escaped justice and at least one spy resided under his roof.

In time for guests, all bedchambers had been aired and thoroughly cleaned, silverware polished, furniture dusted, downstairs salons opened and freshened. Servants hired from the village had been brought in to help clean as well as provide additional staffing during the visitors' stay. The countess barked orders and harangued the staff as they worked tirelessly, until she was satisfied with the results. When every single floor had been dusted, looking glasses shined clear, silver gleamed pure, and shrubbery nipped and clipped, the countess declared the house and grounds presentable. Most of the staff, including Lem and Melenroy, in addition to the extra hires, professed their dislike of the countess and expressed strong hopes that her ladyship would soon depart.

On the day of the guests' arrival, the occupants of Paddock Green were in a chaotic state as the countess flitted and fussed over last-minute details. Patience, still favoring her wounded arm, escaped to the stables with Lem to find Clara, the goat, to feed her. Gulliver followed behind them with only a slight limp from the rabbit trap incident. They talked of the future, of Patience's return home someday, and of Lem as a soldier in His Majesty's Horse Guards, when he was older, of course.

During their pleasant break from the house, Patience completely forgot about the house books she had had to put away before the guests arrived. She and Lem ran over the daisy-dotted meadows and down the long corridor of green landscape which adjoined the earl's gardens. Returning to the kitchen, they paused to take a breath, and that is where Mr. Gibbs found them, panting and laughing.

His face held no trace of amusement in finding his servants off on a lark. His eyes narrowed to tiny slits and his hands twitched by his side, eager to be put to use. Since Patience had not been a member of the staff very long, she did not recognize these understated signs of his fury.

She approached him apologetically, prepared to defend Lem's absence. "Sir, I fear I took rather long with Lem outside . . ."

But Mr. Gibbs brushed her aside with a slight push to her uninjured arm and turned to Lem. "You, you little blighter. You have caused me trouble for the last time. Come here." The violence in his voice showed in the terror on the little boy's face.

Patience stepped between the butler and Lem. In a voice intended to calm the beast, she continued quietly. "Please, listen to me. Our tardiness is all my fault. We were feeding the goat and lost track of time. It was my idea, let the punishment be on my shoulders."

Sudden shrill laughter from the parlor reminded the three of the newly arrived visitors. Lem darted around Patience, hoping to reach the door to the hallway, but Mr. Gibbs caught him by his collar and hauled the boy in front of him.

Before she could intercede, Lem started a fight of his own—hitting out at Mr. Gibbs and yelling, "Ye ain't gonna touch me! Ye ain't gonna touch me! Ye won't beat me no more! I'm runnin' away from 'ere. Far away, so's ye won't find me!" The footboy's voice echoed in the kitchen, alerting others in the house of trouble.

With one hand on Lem, Mr. Gibbs leaned over and shut the door to the hallway to mute the boy's howlings. Patience suddenly realized what Lem had never been able to tell her. Fury and fear in Patience's heart took over her senses as she stared at the butler's face which was filled with venomous hatred for her and the boy.

Abruptly, Mr. Gibbs raised his fist, aiming to smite his anger at the squirming child.

"No, I won't let you!" she cried and snatched Lem out of his grasp. Mr. Gibbs's hand arched down and knocked her to the floor, her head ringing in pain. She watched as the butler, his face still contorted with hostility, started toward her, but Londringham grabbed him from behind and spun the surprised butler to face him.

"I have been grievously deceived by your nature. You are no longer in my employ."

Patience watched in a cloud of pain as the earl confronted the brutal butler. If she had feared Mr. Gibbs for the cruelty emanating from him, it was nothing compared to the aggressive, lionlike power the earl now displayed. She saw the butler take a step back, fearful of his former employer.

Mr. Gibbs put up a hand to ward off any possible threat and declared defensively, "They were not on duty, I . . . I was only trying to discipline them."

Bryce, his face taut with fury, spat, "I do not happen to like your form of discipline. I should have rid myself of you a long time ago." He hesitated before throwing the first punch, right to the butler's nose. "That was for hitting the young woman," he said succinctly.

Mr. Gibbs landed on his backside, close to the fireplace, his nose a bleeding mess. Before he could rise on his own, Bryce pulled him up by the collar and forcibly hit him in the jaw. "That was for Lem." This time Bryce's fist knocked Mr. Gibbs into the wall, and he slid stupidly to the floor.

When Bryce made another move to the butler, Patience called to him, "Please, my lord, no."

Bryce glanced at Patience and Lem, sitting on the floor, clutching each other and watching the fight in fear. He crossed the few steps in a hurry, anxious to see how they fared. He helped Patience and Lem rise, and, with Lem grasping his coattails, Bryce escorted Patience to the door, but not before Mr. Gibbs had risen unsteadily to his feet.

Bryce told him harshly, "You better be gone before I come back. That is, if you do not want me to finish what I started."

Luckily, none of the countess's guests noticed Bryce slip up the stairs with Patience, Lem at his back. He insisted she retire to rest.

Lem waited outside her door as Bryce escorted Patience into her room and watched her recline on the bed, her black lashes drawn down on her pale face. He whispered consolingly to her, "Would that I could have spared you this pain. I should have realized long ago what he was about. Because I have been occupied with other matters, I have not been sufficiently attending to those under my protection. I promise you this will not happen again."

Her eyes fluttered open as Bryce began to reveal his culpability. She frowned, listening to his self-castigation, and shook her head. "Please, don't worry. I really am fine, just shaken. I shall be ready to return to my duties tomorrow." She comforted him with a smile.

Bryce stood up, once again in control, his mouth grim. "Do not worry about your duties. I want you well. Now I must see to Lem and the rest of the guests." With a curt nod, he left, unable to stop thinking Patience could have been seriously hurt if he had not arrived in time.

And Patience, unable to keep up the façade any longer, broke down and wept heart-wrenching tears that seemed to have no end. For Lem. For Rupert. For the earl, his kindnesses, and for her confusion about who he really was, and how she truly felt about him.

The next morning dawned bright and clear as Patience struggled out of bed. She still felt a twinge of the headache but was anxious to rise and begin the day. Across the hall she heard the servants as they dressed for a busy day of cleaning, cooking, sewing, and pressing for the countess's guests.

As she wandered down into the kitchen for a bit of fortification she realized that with Mr. Gibbs no longer employed, the house staff had no superior. In the bright, airy kitchen, maids and footmen bustled in and around the huge room, their young, shiny faces breathing new life into the once-melancholy place of inedible repasts.

In the center of the room stood a bald man with a gray goatee and a pince-nez, whose short arms did not match his long legs. With arms akimbo, this undistinguished man controlled everyone's movements while enjoying himself like a puppeteer with his puppets. He scolded the two women cooks for scalded hot chocolate, directed the duties of two liveried footmen on handling the guests, and snapped his fingers at the twittering maids, led by the flirtatious Myrtle, smug over her newly increased authority.

Patience spied Melenroy sitting by the fireplace, her cap neatly affixed to a gray bun in starched white apron, a beacon of cleanliness and solitude, and totally overlooked. Hands accustomed to usefulness lay empty in the old cook's lap.

Concerned, Patience walked over to the woman she knew as a dreadful and sullen cook who rarely opened her mouth. She asked, "Is that the new butler?" pointing to the commanding rotund figure in the center of the kitchen.

Melenroy nodded slowly, a lonely sadness in her eyes, and murmured, "Marlow."

"Do you not have duties for this morning?" Patience, confused over the cook's inactivity, felt compassion for the woman who seemed to no longer have a place.

"I am not needed. I will lose my job, and I have no place to go," Melenroy murmured, looking at the floor.

Patience kneeled by her side, the two of them forgotten among the bustling mob of maids, footmen, valets, housemaids, and the commanding presence of the new butler. "Surely you have a place here, no one has dismissed you, have they?" She tried to console the inconsolable.

"It's only a matter of time. The master hired new cooks, so's they shan't be needin' me. The countess wants me gone," Melenroy responded, surprising Patience with her verbosity.

Patience stood before replying, "I shall speak to the earl and ask for Marlow to retain you. Perhaps you could be the new cook's assistant?" she suggested with a smile.

"Would you do that for me?" the cook asked hopefully, amazed at the kindness the younger woman offered.

Patience nodded vigorously, then pulled the older woman to her feet. "Let us first ask Marlow how best you may be employed here in the kitchen, after which, I'll find the earl to discuss your continuing employment."

A short discussion with Marlow and Mrs. Knockersmith followed where they agreed to find a place in the kitchen for the old cook. Patience left Melenroy cutting garlic, and went to work on the house accounts in the earl's study before searching for Lem.

Another of her new responsibilities included schooling Lem in reading and writing. So far, the little scoundrel managed to disappear about the time the learning was to begin. Surprisingly, she found him in the hallway greeting guests. Instruction would have to wait until later, she decided.

Patience also learned that his lordship and the captain were out for an early-morning ride. With the news of the earl's absence, an idea crept into her head. Was it possible that his lordship might keep a key to his desk drawers in his bedchamber? Spying was so terribly difficult when one had no instruction as to how to go about it. Rubbing her lucky stone, she flew up the stairs before losing her initiative.

She stole down the hallway, anxious of the slightest movement, and surreptitiously entered the earl's room, without anyone spotting her.

Patience paused, her back against the closed door while she studied the sparsely decorated room, a room she remembered vividly on a rainy night not in the distant past. Sensibilities warred within her. Although it did seem truly wrong to be in his bedchamber looking for clues that might brand the earl a traitor to his country, especially after his thoughtfulness in caring for her, perhaps she could also find reasons to acquit him of her imagined guilt.

After searching several drawers in the cupboard, heart racing, she came away empty-handed. She could not proceed with her search amongst his personal effects, it seemed too wicked. Patience bit her lip, trying to extricate her warm feelings for his lordship from the confusion over the person she was only beginning to know. And that person could not possibly be a man who would sell secrets to the French or commit murder.

A small box lodged atop the mahogany table beckoned

her interest. She approached the tiny chest and lifted the lid hesitantly, hopefully. Almost empty, except for a silver thread of jewelry in the velvet-covered bottom. She took a closer look and gasped. Her locket—the one she had lost on the beach—His lordship had found it!

But before she could dip her hand into the box to claim her possession, she heard the door swing open.

"What are you doing here?" the shrill voice of Myrtle the maid startled Patience, who quickly turned around, shutting the lid on her necklace.

Patience pushed her glasses farther onto her nose. "I was told to find the master's snuffbox, but it does not appear to be here," she responded, hoping to sound annoyed by being questioned by the saucy maid.

"Coo, it's in the study, I'm sure. I have to prepare the fire, if you might excuse me."

Shoulders back, Patience started for the door, unwillingly leaving behind the one thing she could claim as her own.

It was midafternoon and Patience, intent on her work, had not noticed the lack of sunlight as she sat in the study adding accounts until her vision began to blur. She rose to stretch her sleeping muscles and wandered over to the window, which overlooked the splendid landscaped garden surrounded by many meadowy miles.

The day may have dawned bright but clouds hid the cheerful rays and brought drops of rain, needed by fauna, endured by people. Her face showed complete study, not seeing the rain as she pondered how to return to Winchelsea and find Rupert. She was very concerned about him and truly expected him to impetuously appear at an inopportune time, which would result in a lot of questions and, very probably, his arrest.

All at once, she became aware of the downpour and, wanting to feel the rain on her face, she left the house and walked to the gazebo, a shelter for friends and lovers. She loved this building, painted white with a beautiful carving of Diana, Goddess of the Hunt, on top. She grabbed a column for support and smiled. Even with all her worries about Rupert and her fear that the earl would learn her true reason for working in his household, the rain made her feel like a child again and reminded her of simpler times and long-ago games.

A few minutes later she strolled around the little pavilion, tracing the figurines which lovingly skilled hands had brought to life: Pan playing his flute and a shepherd chasing his love. She rested on a bench before returning to the house.

"Am I interrupting a rendezvous?"

The French accent immediately woke Patience from her daydreams. Countess Isabella's cousin, Alain Sansouche, stood in the entryway, patting his face dry with a lily-white handkerchief.

Patience looked up, and, hiding her fear, adjusted her mobcap and spectacles, her defenses on guard. Sansouche's hard face combined with devil-black eyes and thin mouth would frighten any small child, like the bogeyman. She suppressed a shiver that spelled danger. Out of the rain, he propped one shoulder against a fortifying column and studied her frankly, awaiting a reply.

She opened her mouth to speak and hesitated before saying, "I . . . needed some air while working in the study, I must return. Please excuse me." She rose, prepared to take flight from the evil she sensed within him. Ironically, she had never felt this way about Lord Londringham, even though she judged him guilty of serious crimes.

When Sansouche stepped farther into the small area, Patience took a step back, their movements echoing an ancient predator-prey dance. He raised his arms in askance with a mocking tone, "Why in such a hurry to leave, little one? I believe you and I have much to discuss."

Her eyes blazed open with this unforeseen sentiment. "I am sure, sir, we have nothing to discuss. I must return to my duties." She grasped her skirts to sweep past him, trying to feel more bravado than she felt, when he caught her arm.

Sansouche smiled a smile that chilled her blood. "Are you sure, Patience *Mandeley?*" He drew his eyelids down to watch her squirm with this ace.

But Patience refused to give him any satisfaction. Stiffening her spine, she laughed. "My name is Patience Simmons. You must be confused."

He grinned wickedly. "My dear mademoiselle, I do so enjoy the game you play. Perhaps we could play further in my bedchambers? Shall we say, 11 o'clock?" After he took a pinch of snuff, he rubbed his hands together, almost in glee.

"You, sir, are no gentleman to issue such an unsought, unprovoked, and most unwelcome invitation. I wouldn't come to your room tonight, nor any night after in this lifetime." Her words rang of high-born gentility and not those of a lowly steward. As soon as her thoughts found voice, she wished them silent. Her rejection could only increase his aggressiveness. *Oh, my wayward tongue,* she lamented while biting her lip.

Her consternation only spiraled when the Frenchman's eyes lit in a strange, frightening way. "Haughtiness won't buy your freedom or your brother's."

"To whom do you refer?" Cold fright now flowed in her veins. She needed to escape, to compose herself, before revealing any more.

"I refer to Rupert Mandeley, your brother, wanted for the murder of your cousin Lord Peter Carstairs." He paused menacingly. "Tonight, then."

Courage finally returned to her feet. She jerked her arm out of his hold and flew past the Frenchman toward the house, her heart galloping inside, her hands shaking. Her freedom won but at what future cost? Her identity and Rupert's safety were in the hands of a man determined to do them harm.

Sansouche sat nonchalantly on the pavilion bench waiting for the rain to dissipate, an ugly smile curving his lips. *How she played into my hands,* he thought smugly. *But how best to use her?* Demonic thoughts filled his imagination of Patience in his bed. He wanted to discover what she looked like under the cap and spectacles. His sources had confirmed that she was a beauty, he could not wait to reveal. When the rain began its staccato pattern, the Frenchman strolled cockily toward the house, assured all was proceeding well.

"Is there something out there that has caught your attention, my friend? I have repeated myself several times in the last few minutes with nary a response. The rain seems to hold some enchantment. What, a water sprite?"

Keegan's cheery Irish lilt finally penetrated Bryce's concentration as he stared out the window at the wet landscape. His study windows opened directly onto the garden, with a picture-perfect view of the gazebo.

Bryce stepped away from the window to return to his conversation with Keegan regarding new plans for the capture of the French spy. But a movement outside distracted him. He noticed Patience running toward the house. A few minutes later, Alain Sansouche followed her footsteps from the folly. His evident satisfaction clear to even Bryce's hazy view. *What were they doing together?* he wondered grimly. *Just when I might believe she has no part in this espionage, I find reason to doubt my convictions.*

Turning to his friend with a humorless smile, Bryce replied, "Yes, I thought I saw a vision. But, I was wrong, it was a mistake, a mirage."

The companions continued their discussion before leaving to dress for the small soiree Isabella had planned for the evening.

Chapter 11

Music and women's voices floated in a cacophony up the stairs to where Patience perched on the third-floor landing. From the front parlor a mature soprano voice threatened to bring down the house. In the library overlooking the side terrace, two young dandies played a serious game of Speculation with the captain and the earl. The young men crowed with enthusiasm for the game and an eagerness to fill or let their pockets.

The countess's shrill laughter reminded Patience of the promise issued earlier from Alain Sansouche. A cold worry filled her heart. She was certainly out of her realm in dealing with him. *Oh, if only I could have an opportunity to see Rupert, to know he was safe. Would this Frenchman resort to blackmail or inform the earl of her identity?* If so, her real purpose in the household could be made impossible.

She slowly rose to her feet and leaned over the balcony in contemplation. Weariness had left her, and an excitement sparked in her veins. Probably from considering all afternoon how to retrieve her locket and avoid the Frenchman. *Perhaps I have done too much thinking on it. I must do something.*

She decided to wander down to the second floor and take

a stroll past the earl's rooms. If no one was in sight, and she deemed it safe, she might just slip in, grab the locket, and sneak out before anyone was the wiser.

Her slippers whispered on the smooth stairs as she slowly padded down toward the second floor. Imperturbably, Patience looked from side to side on the landing, to assure herself that her quest went unnoticed. The small crowd of guests in the front parlor continued to enjoy entertainment provided by a duet of soprano and tenor with the music from Mozart's *Die Zauberflöte*.

Although Patience knew she should have returned to bed, she felt rather adventurous in a perfectly safe endeavor. Everyone was downstairs, guests and attending servants. The rest of the staff had long since retired. Entering the room she was beginning to know as well as she did her own little chamber, aided by the moonlight streaming through an open window, Patience quickly rushed to the small wooden box and claimed her locket.

Determining she needed more light, she walked over to the window and opened it. She looked down at the locket. Yes, there it was—*Patience*—engraved on the smooth silver.

A loud click of a door lock frightened her and, not realizing where she stood, she dropped her locket, all the way down to the terrace below. She froze, awaiting the door to open and reveal his lordship's angry face. How could she ever explain to him her presence in his room? What might he do? She simply could not give him the answers he would certainly require.

After a few minutes, Patience released her breath with a sigh. She deduced the noise must have come from next door—in Red Tattoo's room. Luck, and walking as softly as a ghost, would help her escape and not alert the earl's valet. His lordship's doorknob turned silently in her hand, and she slipped through the door.

She scurried to the landing and up to the attic to debate her next plan of action. Patience tied her hair back with a ribbon and, determined to retrieve her locket, tiptoed down the backstairs. After a few minutes of castigating herself for her carelessness, she turned toward the kitchen.

The shadows toward the back of the house helped conceal her presence as she hugged the corridor walls. Once or twice a footman hurried by to obtain more imbibing refreshment, which, from the sounds emanating from the front parlor, they were enjoying to a hearty degree. She listened for any noises from the library where the card games proceeded, but except for the scrapes of chairs and murmuring voices, entertainment for the evening showed no signs of stopping anytime soon.

Outside the house, in a darkened corner of the terrace, she tried to judge approximately where the locket might have fallen. Unfortunately, she realized, as she chewed on her last nail, she would have to leave the safety of the shadows to perform an earnest search. The cheeky moon presented almost a chessboard pattern on the terrace stones through mischievous clouds.

With a quick glance around to assure no one else was about, she crept to the end of the flagstone walkway, judging this to be near the place where her necklace had fallen. On her knees, feeling for a whisper of metal, Patience heard a low whistle. She stopped, her heart pounded in her ears, drowning any other sound.

There it was again. She looked up cautiously to find Rupert, her missing brother, hovering near a large hedgerow, which outlined the flower garden near the terrace.

Her eyes widened in surprise and joy, she jumped to her feet and ran toward Rupert, who pulled her into the moon shade of the hedge. She couldn't believe he was actually here. Patience was delighted to see her brother's beloved familiar face, and they hugged with hasty stolen happiness.

But when she stepped back to stare at her brother, she caught her breath at his haggard appearance. He had not shaved in days, his reeking clothes hung on his thin frame, and he had a new lean look which matched the worried, haunted look in his once-cheerful brown eyes. She tried to halt the tears from seeing him in such a manner.

He had changed, and it frightened her. She still knew well of this stranger.

"Patience, I've been watching this place for a week and have not had the opportunity to talk with you, needing a place to catch you alone and private. I almost spoke to you in the gazebo today but a man walked in to speak to you and then you ran back to the house. I've been worried about you after I heard you had come to Winchelsea to find me." Even his voice sounded faint and tired.

She clutched his arms and steadied her voice before replying, "I'm fine"—intentionally not mentioning the wounded arm, the sprained wrist, the smugglers, a leering and lecherous Frenchman, and a bothersome earl. "I am trying to gain news about our cousin's murder, and I think the earl might know something."

Rupert's face turned somber. "This is madness. You cannot hope to learn anything from Londringham, and as you know, he's quite dangerous. You must return to Susetta Fields on tomorrow's coach. No arguments."

"Rupert, listen to me. You are not the only one to worry. You have not been taking care of yourself. Look at your appearance. I'm worried about you." She paused, looking beyond his shoulder. "And I'm not sure any longer that the earl is guilty."

Rupert raised his eyebrows and shook his head. "Impossible. Our cousin was absolutely positive the earl was guilty of treason. It would not take a large leap from treason to murder. What proof do you have of his innocence?"

Patience smiled. How like Rupert, always thinking, talking, and demanding satisfaction in the same breath. "The earl is trying to find our cousin's murderer. And he has been meeting with the constable to discuss this."

She hesitated, unsure of how much to tell him about her relationship with the earl. "His lordship has been kind to me, and I know before long, I will discover something of import, and we will know without question whom the guilty party or parties are. I just need more time." Patience tried to keep her face in the shadows, avoiding his penetrating stare.

Rupert thrust his hands in his breeches and walked a short distance away. "I cannot tolerate this running. I was convinced the earl was the culprit. Now we seem no closer to solving our dilemma and returning home soon."

Patience went to him and placed a comforting hand on his back. "I do suspect someone. There is a Frenchman here by the name of Alain Sansouche. The earl's mistress, Countess Isabella's cousin. I don't trust him, and I think he might somehow be involved."

Her brother's countenance brightened. "Truly? How?"

How could she reveal that the man was a danger to them both? If she told Rupert about the Frenchman's suggestion, her brother would carry her back home to Susetta Fields.

Hating to lie, she replied, "I'm still working on this idea. The earl also believes our cousin may have been involved in espionage. Perhaps Lord Carstairs played a dangerous game of chance with French spies?"

Rupert shook his head and swore under his breath, forgetting good manners. "Carstairs? I would have sworn—but I don't know what to believe anymore. What are we involved in? I'm running for my life, and you are in the lion's den. Patience, we can't keep on like this. Where will it end?"

He stopped and turned toward her. "I can't leave you here. I'm not convinced you are safe. Come with me. I'll see that you return home safely."

She removed a heavy lock of hair from her brow and squared her shoulders, ready to do battle. "Listen to me, little brother, what harm can befall me? This Frenchman does not know that I suspect him of spying. He only knows me as a house steward. I promise to be careful. I need a little more time."

Rupert looked at her stubborn face and, with a reluctant grin, uneasily agreed. He pulled her close for another reassuring hug. "Only a bit longer. I'm sure Louis and the rest of our brothers are concerned, and we certainly do not want them coming here."

Patience agreed, then paused. "What about your safety? You look all done in," she murmured softly, brushing his cheek with her hand.

"I'm better, now that I have seen you. I've been quite worried when I couldn't reach you. Three strangers I met on the road have taken me in. We keep to ourselves during daylight and only venture out when evening is our cover. They appear to be avoiding the law, as am I."

She gaped at him. "You are living with ruffians?" Ruffians being the only word she knew for criminals.

"Now hush, I know this might sound hard to believe, but I don't think they've actually done anything criminal. If you met them, which I hope to God you never do, you would see, they are harmless and not very bright. I think it a wonder they have not been caught, but they've treated me well and given me a roof and food, so I can't complain of the company I keep." He offered a rueful grin. "I must go. Please be careful, little one. I promise to." With light fingers to her hair, Rupert escaped past the hedgerow and into the trees.

Patience bit her lip thoughtfully as she returned to the edge of the terrace. The soiree's din had grown louder. Laughter and music wafted through the night air, drifting along on a breeze. Before she could continue her search, she caught sight of a masterful presence.

His lordship stood on the Palladian balcony above the lower terrace, transfixed by the night. What did he see? What did he search for? Whatever he was thinking seemed to take him many miles from here.

She waited in the shadows content to study him, almost as if she could determine his character and purpose. It occurred to her that he truly didn't need anyone. This man could take on the whole world and win single-handedly. From his keen observation to his intelligence, broad shoulders, and strong hands, he would be formidable to his enemies.

He had treated her so tenderly when she'd been injured. But that was only because he was trying to weaken her defenses, to get her to admit what she had been doing outside his window or in the tree. *Yes, that's how clever he was.*

And she almost wept with this discovery because she wanted his touch to be real, and she wanted him to need her. Here was a hard man who wore distrust and darkness like a mantle.

Yet, she had seen other sides of him. He seemed to honestly care for Lem and his education. He showed concern over his other servants, and more than once she had heard him mention his land tenants and whether they were receiving enough food and supplies to feed their families.

But where was his reward? His face portrayed a mask of emotions, caught between his own private heaven and hell. His lean, chiseled features captured character and honesty, an honesty he would respect in others. But deception—he would certainly seek to destroy the deceiver.

Weaker men she recognized easily because of having

been surrounded by them all her life. Her brothers and Richard. Louis, strong in character, weak in body. Then there was James, with his constant devout faith and the Bible orchestrating his thoughts of his rewards in Heaven but little help to his family on earth. And, of course, lovable Benjamin. Content to cultivate sustenance from the soil but in great need of nurturing himself. They all needed her.

The strong hands that gripped the smooth stone of the balcony railing knew power and possession. She thought guiltily of wanting to feel that possession and was suddenly envious of anyone who had ever received his attentions. She shook her head. Why did he seem as if he had known more than his share of pain in this world? So many questions swirled in her head, unending.

All this fanciful study of a stranger. Tiredness must have crept upon her after the long day and the excitement of seeing her brother. Right now Rupert would be making his way back to his shelter with those criminals he had mentioned.

"Who's out there? Show me your face." His lordship's orders would not accept delay.

Although she could remain unseen by him and flee without detection, she felt drawn to his mood and had no desire to leave, and every wish to stay, as reckless as it may be. She stepped away from the green garden walls and walked hesitantly toward the house, obeying her heart's impulse, her search for her locket forgotten.

She stood near the garden path and looked up to stare at his lordship's moonlit face, aware that the same light revealed her own identity.

The night seemed made for dreaming and pretending.

"What are you doing out here in the dark, Miss Patience?" his question devoid of any expression of judgment.

"I lost something, and came to retrieve it."

He stared at her intently, perhaps trying to read her face

for duplicity. She wanted nothing more than to be honest with him, but was it possible? If he wasn't guilty of all that she suspected of him, she could ask for his help and seek from him refuge for her brother.

"Perhaps we share the same objective. Have you found what you're missing?" he inquired quietly.

"No, my lord. And you?" she replied, anxious to know his answer. She bowed her head briefly, then returned her gaze to him.

"No, it appears luck is not with us tonight." He hesitated. "The moon adds a shiny luster to your hair," he murmured in amazement.

His comment startled Patience, who self-consciously put a hand to her wayward hair hanging over one shoulder.

"You need bright colors, the gray paints you pale. And so fair. Even by this darkness and a canvas of drab, you are an enchantment. A vision. The night appears to do you justice."

"It would appear, my lord, that we both enjoy the night's companionship."

He leaned his elbows more solidly on the stone balcony railing, seeming to enjoy this moonlit conversation.

"That is so. Although the night spared me from pleasant dreams, that is, until I met you," he told her cryptically. "Am I only dreaming you?"

Patience laughed softly. "No, I am well and truly here before you. A real woman with hopes and fears."

"A beautiful woman like you should fear nothing. I almost believe you. I want to believe you are real."

Until her brother's plight was resolved, she did not know how to make him believe. "Please, my lord—"

Voices from the other side of the house heading in their direction cut short their conversation. Patience identified Sansouche's voice immediately and began to panic. Although she knew he wouldn't insult her in his lordship's presence, she didn't want him to discover her here. She looked around desperately for an escape path. A few of the countess's guests lounged on the side terrace, blocking that exit.

Ignoring the earl's presence, she raced to the door connected to the study and then to the one leading to the back parlor, but found them both locked. Her heart beat fiercely as she sensed her enemy's imminent arrival.

"Patience," the earl leaned down to whisper, "use the trellis and climb up to me," he told her.

She looked at him blankly and then at the old trellis, patterned and cross-stitched with wandering vines and budding roses, then back to his lordship and said, "I can't. With my arm, I don't think I can pull myself up."

"What are you more afraid of? Climbing the trellis or meeting our Frenchman?"

His reasoning brought her straight to the trellis. Studying it doubtfully, she wet her lips and grabbed a high wooden rung. Hitching her skirt to her waist, she began her ascent. She shut her fear of Sansouche out of her mind and concentrated on climbing the fanciful ladder. Any minute the Frenchman would stroll around the corner and catch her climbing the side of the house. *Please let me be in time, God,* she prayed fervently, her heart taking flight.

Her progress was slow with the use of only one hand, and having to use caution because the rungs were wet and slippery beneath her feet. As she grew closer to the top, she remembered her old fear of heights. Her destination actually had not looked that high from the ground. Despairingly, she felt prickly thorns pick at her bodice and further expose her white drawers.

Breathing heavily, she heard Sansouche bid his companion good night, and fear fueled her strength to boost herself the final distance. Looking up, she saw she would need the earl's help to climb over the balcony railing.

He watched her climb with keen interest, admiration in his eyes. When she had almost reached the balcony, she stretched out her hand to him for assistance.

"Can I believe in you?" he asked, his face quite somber.

"What do you mean? Hurry, pull me over, Sansouche will arrive directly."

"Tell me or I will let him find you. Is this a farce or are you not with Sansouche?"

His help was so close. She shook her head, pleading with him, "Please believe in me. I know nothing of this man, only that he frightens me," she admitted. Footsteps rang on the walk around the corner.

Quickly, Londringham leaned over the side of the balcony and, taking Patience by the waist, pulled her over the top. Both stood motionless in each other's arms as they heard the Frenchman stroll along the terrace, keeping to the dark side of the balcony, hidden from the bright moon's gaze. Every few minutes, they heard his footsteps stop, but then he continued around the side of the house, heading toward the party on the side terrace.

She sighed with evident relief when a sudden gust of wind felt close on her legs. Both Patience and Bryce, for different reasons, were drawn to the sight of her drawers fluttering in the wind. Before she could untwine her skirt, they noticed a quite long rip, rending a gaping hole from knee to thigh exposing a pale curved thigh.

Chapter 12

Patience ignored the earl's gaze as she bent awkwardly to join the torn pieces of material together. Ruefully, she shook her head, acknowledging the impossibility of the task. *Why did this have to happen now? I must retain some dignity in this situation,* she thought, feeling a flush warm her face.

Uncomfortable under his scrutiny, she tried to pull down her skirt to hide the tear.

Bryce placed his hand over the hand that wrestled with her skirt and held it lightly in his own. With his other hand, he reached up to gently stroke her cheek.

Patience, captured by his intense blue gaze, could scarcely breathe, so enraptured was she by his spell. When she nervously wet her lips, this tiny, unconscious movement prompted Bryce to groan under his breath before he pulled her into his arms, seeking more of what she wanted to offer him.

His left arm held her comfortably to his side as his right hand carefully cushioned her head while he brought his mouth down on her moist lips, gently at first, then with increasing pressure.

She succumbed to the tender caress of his lips as the blood in her veins whirled and sang in pure delight. No thoughts or conscience disturbed her dream of experiencing his powerful touch. With eyes closed, she gloried in his instruction, wanting to give as much as she received. She eagerly welcomed his seeking tongue, claiming possession with his demanding kiss.

When first one arm, then her other arm wrapped shyly around his neck, Bryce knew soul-saving victory. Her passionate response enveloped him in such pleasure, he determined it would be only the beginning of her secrets he intended to learn tonight. His hand drifted down to her shoulder and rested on her breast. Beneath the thin muslin bodice, he felt her heart pounding with a rhythm that matched his own. Contentment could not end before he claimed the exquisitely rounded breast hidden from his touch.

He enjoyed softly igniting her breast to desire through her covering. But it was not enough. The three top buttons came undone easily, giving him access to the treasure he sought beneath her chemise. He felt a shudder surge through the young woman, which brought his own blood-filling arousal to painful life.

Relieved to find this enchantress as spellbound as he was, he felt her low moan against his lips as her body leaned into his with surprising ardor. He delighted in her shy but ardent embrace as he stroked her lithe buttocks, and continued his assault on the smooth feel of her breast and hardened nipple.

He sought her mouth with a punishing kiss before branding her with his wet-blazing tongue, marking his way slowly and pointedly down to her swelling breast exposed by his fervent hand. She relished his powerful touch and welcomed his hot tongue on her heated skin, her body instinctively arching for more of what only he could give her.

Any coherent thought had fled at his first sweeping touch, his caresses overwhelming her senses. He sought to drain her of her life, her energy, but she quickly grasped the knowledge that instead of taking from her, he was giving—vitality, a renewal of awareness, a teaching of pleasure never known before that would alter her life forever. And she relished each lesson, easily memorizing the senses and images which would always remain a part of her.

He pulled and tugged on her nipple with his mouth, sucking and lathing, as it hardened in response to his driving tongue. When at last he reluctantly dragged his mouth from her breast with a long suck, she whimpered softly in despair. Was this the end? Their passions spiraled her toward the unknown, with no end in sight, his touch hard yet somehow gentle at the same time.

Her hands grasped tightly in his thick hair as his mouth began to wander again. She felt his hands at her waist luring her to the cold balcony floor, welcoming to her heated flesh.

His touch burned her with a fever, sure to set her aflame as she leaned her arm on his shoulder. She lay across the floor, her head pillowed by his muscular arm, her hair sweeping the ground. Trapped in dream heat, his body and skillful hands taught her what to do, how to move, how to feel.

She secretly smiled when she caught the tempest blazing in his blue scrutiny, both of them astonished by their shared passion. Once again he returned to her lips, wanting a refreshment only she could offer him, tasting her honeyed mouth, as a thirsty man seeks a deep well.

She hardly recognized her own body which created a combustion of kaleidoscopic senses. While his mouth teased her sensitive lips, his free hand caressed an aroused nipple again before sliding down to her waist and continuing to the newly opened gap in her drawers. His feather touch on her exposed thigh made her jump in surprise, but he immediately calmed her with soft whispers, gentling her fears.

As tumultuous and confusing feelings tornadoed through her senses, she wondered what would come next, not wanting the embrace to end, ever. All those long years of wonder were unraveling at a dizzying pace. She clutched Bryce tightly, for he was both her sanity and her madness. And he was real.

Bryce felt overwhelmed by her innocent desire and acceptance of his touch. He knew she was innocent, because he wanted to believe tonight that the world was good, and she felt so right in his arms. If this was not true, he didn't want to know, ignoring any rationality for his motives.

Her hair flowed like a dark current over his hand and felt like silk to his touch. He wanted to make her body sing with music to make the angels envious as he watched her soft, undulating body seek a release.

He deftly eased his hand up her thigh to the downy patch of curly hair and moist heat. He heard her gasp and try to block his hand from continuing its search, but issuing a slow breath to control his own fires raging within, he whispered in her ear, "Shh . . . sweet dream. Let me do a good deed tonight. For I need saving. I promise not to hurt you."

She opened her eyes to see if his promise reached his revealing eyes. His somber expression and face taut with passion convinced her, she was safe, here in his arms.

As he slowly stroked her velvety lips, her wet heat helped his fingers slide farther into her warm passage. Again, she jerked in his arms, bewildered by her body's responsiveness to his tender caresses. And she now knew, she must know, where he was so persuasively taking her.

He paused, leaning his brow on hers to catch his breath. He tried desperately to maintain control over his own desires, almost afraid to disappoint her, but it was costing him his power and reasoning. She was so wonderful to touch, he thought as he breathed in her awakening, aroused body.

When he recognized that he could not continue much longer next to this exquisite woman without reaching his own climax, he doubled his efforts to bring her the pleasure she sought by lifting her hips to meet his insistent fingers. He could tell by her breathing that she was almost there. The soft, almost-cooing sighs teased his already-frenzied arousal.

He wanted to be inside her when she found her release, but her desire had overwhelmed him. When she shuddered in his arms with a sweet intensity, he held her captured, feeling her heart pounding, and her breath short.

Quiet in his arms a few minutes later, Patience was reluctant to leave this strange new world of enveloping warmth. She hated to disrupt the tender feelings and pleasures he had taught her and brought her. But she decided to face her fears and him by peeking through her long lashes to discover him watching her intently, his face a smooth mask of tightly controlled emotion.

He leaned down and whispered, "Let's finish our lessons in my bed, lovely lady. For I long to know more of your secrets," his voice husky with promise.

But his invitation abruptly returned Patience to thoughts of the hard balcony, and to confusion and fear about what they had just done and what Bryce wanted to continue. Blimey! How could she have forgotten Rupert and her need to save him from their enemy? Possibly from this man who held her so tightly in his arms?

Quickly, she rolled out of his arms onto the hard stone floor, jerked down her skirts, and hastily buttoned her bodice with shaky fingers. Not daring to look at him, in case she would stand accused of her own seduction in his eyes, with a shaky voice, she murmured, "That is not possible, my lord. I, I, cannot."

Bryce rose slowly on one knee, careful not to place too much pressure on his injured leg, now stiff from staying in one position too long, his body trembling with unspent passion. He walked stiffly to the balcony railing, drawing deep breaths of air to cool his thoughts. Looking at the stars, his back to her, he said, "The night seems to have lost its magic. Perhaps you should return where you came from." He looked over one shoulder as she continued righting her clothing. Disappointment and resignation lined his words.

She knew she had disappointed him, but he didn't seem angry, which was a slight relief. Wanting to offer him comfort, her emotions tore her apart, but her head ruled to make a quick escape. It suddenly occurred to her that she might no longer have employment.

"Do you wish me to leave Paddock Green, my lord?" thinking this his intent and waiting with anxious breath for his reply.

"No, I still need your assistance. This is your home for now," he told her enigmatically.

She nodded and turned toward the doorway, hoping her legs would carry her safely to her room. She took one last look back to find Bryce again watching the darkness as he had done earlier. Recognition dawned on Patience that she was indebted to him for his generosity. No one usually gave her anything, they only took from her. *Oh, why did he have to be my enemy? And why don't I feel something akin to regret?* She fled from the shadow of the man left to the company of the night.

Although Bryce did not see her leave, he knew the moment she was gone. Perhaps it was the perfume in her hair or the sighs she had given to the night air that stayed with him. She couldn't be real, he thought in disillusionment. *She's certainly bewitched me to where I no longer care if she's guilty or innocent. I only know I want to hold her in my arms again.*

To halt these reflections which served merely to strengthen his ardor, he thought of his brother and his mission. Nothing should matter but that before long he would have the French spy in his grasp and discover the identity of the woman who had led his brother to his death.

Late that night, the same dream came to him after his battle with consciousness had won. Even in the throes of a deep sleep, the dream reached out and pulled him in unwillingly, reliving that fateful night.

With the piercing wind at his back, he stepped over black rotted trees encased in stone-hard ground, accustomed to finding his way in the dark, even on enemy soil. The night as his companion had long kept his secrets and since the danger was as much a part of him as breathing, he had never given it a nod before, would not even acknowledge its existence. Until now. His younger brother, Edward, was missing.

The famous English spy, known only as the "Black Ghost," had arrived offshore earlier to discover that his brother, who served as a lieutenant on the HMS Gauntlet, *had mysteriously left the ship an hour before. The Black Ghost had wasted little time arguing with the* Gauntlet's *captain, Keegan Kilkennen, that he could handle the search alone. Their only clue to Edward's whereabouts was from a sailor, who had overheard Edward mentioning the small village of Doume a few miles inland.*

Although the Black Ghost had never been to this corner of France before, slipping in and out underneath the Corsican's nose had become almost like a game to him. His mission was to provide vital information to the Foreign Secretary about Bonaparte's flotilla and his plans for invading England.

As Kilkennen and the Black Ghost stealthily crept over the uneven terrain, they were wary of any sound from the French patrols. The Black Ghost, disguised as a priest—in severe

*black clothes, low-crowned hat, and white neckcloth—
carried a worn prayer book for proper effect. To some the
book promised salvation, but this was a man who had little
need of others' faith. The book's sole purpose was to conceal
false French papers—to be used if he was taken prisoner—
which rested neatly underneath the faded leather cover.*

*The English spy, whose real identity was Bryce Andover,
Earl of Londringham, had long ago determined that his
younger brother would be his heir and continue the long
Saxon line. But Edward had been adamant about sailing the
seas, and Bryce could not stop him.*

*He swore under his breath as tiny white puffs escaped from
his lips. Edward should have been safely back at their home,
Paddock Green. He should never have joined the Royal Navy.*

*As Bryce slipped into the dark lair of the forest, with
Kilkennen a breath away, a chilling thought wormed into
his gut: his younger brother was missing because of him.
Bryce had always felt he would be prepared when the Devil
eventually presented his card. But the wrong man had received it.*

*Now, ironically garbed in a priest's clothing, the spy won-
dered if he knew the words to offer an appeal to God.*

*The two determined men weaved their way among the
silent trees, at times becoming part of the landscape. A mile
inland when the faint lights of a remote village blurred in
the distance, they quickened their steps, still undetected.
Unsure where to look, Bryce planned to leave no stone
unturned in his search. He would not leave France without
his brother.*

*The full moon briefly gleamed silver through the trees'
branches, alighting a tiny abandoned cottage far off to their
right. Quiet since their journey had begun, Bryce called
softly to his friend, "Wait." He thought he heard something.*

He cocked his head, his senses sharpened from the years of playing the game and a strong will to stay alive.

The incautious moan happened again. Definitely human. Definitely in pain.

With catlike grace, Bryce changed direction toward the cottage, approaching warily and looking for signs of a trap. Kilkennen followed him down a winding path, which suddenly veered to the right, and a few steps farther they found a shelter with a half-thatched roof, its broken wooden fence aproned to a tiny clearing. Bryce motioned to his companion that he was going inside and to keep watch. Kilkennen nodded curtly, already reconnoitering the snow-draped trees.

In the frigid November winter, Bryce began to sweat. His right hand swept his waist to check the cold steel in his belt before he lifted and pushed away the rotted door. Unconsciously, his right hand returned to his pistol, and he stepped inside.

Jaw tightened, his heart slowed to a crawl. His keen eyes quickly adjusted to the little light drifting in from the jagged hole in the roof. It was not until he turned to go that he saw him.

Edward. He lay on the damp floor, clutching at the dark stain on the left side of his chest.

Bryce knelt down by his slain brother's side, daring to believe he had made it in time. "Edward, I'm here," his voice hoarse.

Edward's eyes blinked open, glazed from pain and his approaching fate. He struggled to breathe and whispered, "Knew you'd come for me, big brother."

Quickly, Bryce tore off his neckcloth and pressed it to his brother's wound. He replied grimly, "I have come to take you home." His heart denied what his mind understood: he could not save his brother. The smell of death was too close. Eyes damp, Bryce carefully raised Edward's head onto his leg, praying all sorts of forgotten prayers—vengefulness, grief, and loss warring inside of him.

Edward smiled and a spittle of blood slipped from his mouth. "She was . . . beautiful. They called her the 'Dark Angel.'" His pale face looked serene at the remembrance.

Bryce froze at the mention of her name, the very infamous Frenchwoman spy who inspired fear in even the most stalwart of English soldiers. She, with her long mane of black hair and light eyes, claimed many successes at seduction and sometimes murder to get her information. Once she had decided on a target, hope for the hunted was almost futile.

Bryce knew with certainty. He himself had been her next mark.

Time was no longer theirs. Bryce had to know. Anger blazing he exclaimed, "Did she do this? I will find her!"

His brother raised his hand with what little strength he had left. His breathing became more difficult. "She was looking for Londringham. Said . . . said it was important to our country's security. I did not know." A shudder went through him. "I am sorry, my brother."

Bryce nearly wept at his words. "It is I who is sorry, Edward. She wanted me." His words were strained, punctured by knives of grief. "I will not rest until I find the woman responsible, no matter what it takes." His fiercely spoken vow haunted the little hovel.

With a slight shake of his head, Edward managed, "A mistake. She told her friend . . . it was a mistake."

Bryce hugged his brother's cold, snow-shrouded body closer. "Who? Who was this other person?" But his brother could no longer hear him.

"She was so beautiful," remained on his lips with a last sigh.

For once, Bryce had no words, no answers. He was beyond thinking. It hurt so much that he could not believe

*one could feel such savage pain and yet live. He whispered
to his still brother, "Do not go, please Edward, do not go,"
reminding him of a similar plea he had made to his mother
several years ago, when he was a child.*

*She had never returned. Would only it had been him on
this frozen foreign land and not his innocent brother. A part
of Bryce died with his brother, the joy and the love that they
had shared. Guilt and grief lashed at him, until he was sure
the scars would never fade.*

*Kilkennen broke Bryce's mourning as he peered into the
doorway. He murmured urgently, "What is taking so long?"
Seeing Bryce and Edward on the floor, he understood.
"We . . . we have to go."*

*Bryce swallowed hard and harnessed the emotions threat-
ening to engulf him. The spy's survival instincts took over. He
had to get Edward home. He gathered his dead brother's
body in his arms and walked out into the bitter cold.*

"Let's get the hell out of here."

*Heavy-hearted, Bryce followed Kilkennen back to the
shore where they had secured their small boat. Overhead a
lonely nightingale echoed the sad song in Bryce's heart.
He hoped their luck would hold. He had to make it home to
Paddock Green, England's greenest fields, with Edward. He
had to take care of him. One last time.*

*The night began to hum with heightened activity. Every
crack, every snap, meant the French soldiers guarding the
shore could be nearby. Waiting and watching.*

*He heard Kilkennen's sigh of relief at hearing water lap-
ping against the sand. They trudged a few steps farther
before they heard it. The sharp explosion of a pistol.*

*A shout and footsteps thudded behind them, a half mile of
sand stretched before them, their small craft, the only
avenue of escape. Capture or death made them fleet of foot
as the two men pounded down the beach.*

Kilkennen reached the boat first and hastily untied the line to push the vessel out to sea. Not too far behind, Bryce heard another shot whine over his head. He hurried across the dark sands, his burden clasped tightly to him. As soon as he could, he laid his brother's body inside the boat, and, thigh-high in the Channel's cold waters, whipped out his pistol to fire at the line of French soldiers running down the beach like eerie, ghostly shadows.

Shots exploded close by and splintered the bobbing craft's side, propelling fountains of water to douse the Englishmen.

The noisy pop within earshot alerted Bryce too late.

He felt the stinging burn to his thigh, then the warmth of his blood as it seeped down his leg. It was the second shot which grazed his temple and knocked him down into the frigid black waters.

The pain in his head taunted him with unconsciousness, but he fought for air with all his ebbing strength. When he was able to break the water's surface, welcome rushes of hard-won air filled his lungs.

He ignored the throbbing in his thigh which crippled his movement and swam over to the boat's side. With Kilkennen's help, he finally managed to throw himself into the craft. Wasting no time and dripping blood from both wounds, Bryce took up the oars, and together they cleaved through the waters, soon outdistancing the longest French aim.

Drenched and coughing up water, Bryce's heart pumped pain with every beat, but he would not succumb to the blackness which hovered within his vision. Not until they were safely aboard the Gauntlet.

When he looked up from Edward's body, he saw her on the shore. She was smiling and holding out her hand to him as if to help him. He would have recognized her countenance even on a moonless night. Patience.

Chapter 13

The following morning, in another part of the house, Alain Sansouche lay stretched comfortably across Isabella's settee. He watched her through half-closed eyes as she finished her toilette. "They are laughing at you, *ma chérie,*" he told her in French.

Isabella spun around on her chair and spit, "No one laughs at me. Who has cast me as an object of ridicule? How dare you suggest such a thing?" Her long fingernails curled around the arm of the chair.

Sansouche laughed without humor. "Why, my dear, it is obvious you and Londringham have spent very little time together lately. He hardly notices you. Last night while you entertained in the salon, Londringham enjoyed a game of cards before retiring early. Much earlier than you. I must remind you that your intimate friends below are like eager vultures awaiting word that your liaison is dead in order that they may be the first to carry the sweet bits back to Town for the digesting. Perhaps you could return with me and regale your associates with your version of the truth. I would prefer you and Colette to travel with me." He waited for his cousin's response.

Her blue eyes burned a dangerous light as she nodded,

her face pale beneath the bright rouge. "I shall return to London with you as you have suggested. But I swear the earl will not live without comeuppance for the trouble he has caused me. I am not through with him yet." She sighed. "Besides, the country life has bred ennui in me. Have you completed your business here?"

Her question brought Sansouche quickly to his feet, but he answered in a cool voice, "I think it better if we all play our parts more discreetly than some of us have played heretofore. We have decided to meet in Town for the remainder of the time left. But we shall return." At the door, he turned with a sly smile to Isabella and asked, "Who knows? Perhaps it will be with Londringham's head on a pike?"

When her cousin had left the room, Isabella continued to comb, tuck, and touch her appearance into presentability. No one plays her for a fool, she thought to herself. "Colette? Oh, where is the girl? She is more absent than I should allow."

As Sansouche sauntered down the stairs to look for imbibement to start the day, he caught sight of Patience in the study. He watched her from the shadows, a thoughtful expression on his face. She was a bold one. His little maid had failed to appear at the requested time. And he was quite sure he had seen her in the garden last night. But when he had reached the terrace, she was nowhere to be seen.

The necklace in his pocket jingled as he headed down the stairs. It was hers. The engraving distinct in the smooth metal. *All in good time. I wonder if they have found her brother yet. Rupert Mandeley had to be here somewhere.* His men would find him soon enough. And yet another of his crimes would go unpunished. In fact, Sansouche could not fathom why it had taken this long to find the missing Mandeley.

The Frenchman could not linger in the country much

longer, though he would like to stay—if only for the great
pleasure of watching Patience himself to see if she met with
her brother. Sansouche rubbed his hands together. It was
simply a matter of time. Time that was surely on his side.

Bryce paced restlessly in the parlor, the day's events on
his mind. The exercise helped his knee, still stiff from last
night. He was elegantly attired for the hunt in his tan
breeches and tall, black top boots. A white shirt and cravat
under his black riding coat completed his attire.

So much to do, and with no new information, he was
frustrated in being forced to find an alternative plan. The
constable had sent word that they had yet not located
Carstairs's cousin Rupert. Bryce believed the young man
might know the identity of the murderer. However, not only
was Mandeley hiding from the law, but the young man
might also have sensed a threat from the real killer. He must
be found before Carstairs's murderer located him first.

As for the French spies in their midst, unfortunately none
of his local sources had turned up any new information. Red
reported that no unusual operations on the shore, in the
churchyard, or near the bonfires had occurred since that
night on the cliffs. No reason for this inactivity made sense.
But Bryce knew they were still out there, planning the
downfall of England.

With Red following Sansouche to London and Kilkennen
on a trip to France, Bryce reasoned he himself would have
to travel among his land tenants to try to uncover information. There were so few people he could trust.

Patience. Could he trust her? He remembered their first
night at the fair. Was she a Madonna or did she owe loyalty
to England's enemy? By God, he wanted to believe her. Last
night on the balcony he had. She knew how to haunt his

dreams and light his desire, but who was she? What was she really doing here?

He had never known a woman he could have faith in. The women in his life had taught him not to trust anything in skirts.

But what dormant dreams the young woman had stirred in him last night. He smiled when he thought of the artless passion reflected in her lovely hazel eyes. How much would she make him pay, and with what? Currency? Or something less familiar . . . his heart?

Staring into the cold ashes brought him back to the night in the French cottage, holding Edward dead in his arms. A woman had led Edward to his death. Surely his brother's death must have taught him something. What kind of world did they live in, that murderers and spies walked freely among polite society and that trust must be won, not instantly granted?

Kilkennen found him in the front parlor and walked with him out to the stables for the morning hunt.

The weekend finally over, the countess's guests took their leave of Paddock Green. Patience had managed to avoid Sansouche and the others throughout the last day and breathed a sigh of relief when they all prepared to depart.

She rose wearily from her cramped position on the floor having spent several hours organizing Lord Londringham's books and much more work still lay ahead. Although the sun shone yet brightly, a hungry stomach growl and a dusty dryness in her mouth reminded her of a need for tea. She had seen his lordship only at midday, when he was bidding his guests a safe return to Town.

Out the window, she watched with great interest when the countess and her cousin climbed into a hired carriage. .

Before they left, Bryce walked down the steps and handed a long jewel case into the carriage window to the countess. Patience could almost hear the countess's squeal of delight.

The bell clanging frantically disturbed Patience's sleep. She awakened immediately, her heart thumping, and leapt out of bed. After pulling on her gray dress and cap, she flew down the stairs behind the other panicked servants, plaiting her hair as she ran. In the atrium the rest of the servants had gathered, their frightened voices raised in a chorus of noise. Word drifted back to Patience in the back of the hall.

Napoleon had landed. His troops were on British soil.

She grasped her arms tightly, trying to control her shaking. The French were in England! Swallowing her fear, she headed off to find Bryce, working her way into the atrium, where she discovered him talking in hushed tones to the butler. He looked as if he had not been to bed.

Bryce glanced over to her, and their gazes met briefly, his conveying courage. He nodded to her and vanished through the front door.

The butler Marlow commanded everyone's attention by standing on a nearby bench and clapping his hands. He spoke urgently. "We all know what we must do. Lucky has two wagons hitched and waiting outside. Keep calm, this could be a false alarm. I want everyone to get into the wagons immediately. Take as few belongings as possible, there is not much room. We shall take the old Tyler road to Winchelsea where his lordship has instructed he will meet us with further directions. He will have news for us then. And keep quiet, we must exercise the greatest silence."

Before the butler could finish his speech, the anxious servants had already bustled out the door, a few carrying brooms for weapons and most in either working clothes or their bedroom dress, propelled more by fear of the French than by propriety.

Lem. Patience scanned the small area of scurrying servants around her. She could not find him. She saw Myrtle and Melenroy head down the porch but no sign of the little footboy. Patience started for the stables, believing the boy might not have heard the warning bell.

She grabbed Myrtle as she was climbing into the wagon and petitioned her, "Please, do not let them leave without us. I must find Lem. We shall return shortly." Patience did not wait to see if Myrtle did as she bid.

Lem was indeed in the stables, looking for Gulliver. Together they called his name, and finally located the dog by the chicken coop. The little boy grabbed his collar, and they hurried back to the front of the house. Too late. They watched as both wagons rattled and shook down the lane.

Wide-eyed, mouth agape, Lem said, "They left us be'ind. The Frenchies will get us! What will we do?"

Patience took his little hand in hers. "Lem, you must be a brave soldier. We will not let those awful Frenchmen capture us! There are still horses left. We can, umm . . . I know, the gig! We shall harness one of the horses to the gig and follow them."

Anxious to catch up to their companions, they worked feverishly, hampered by the light drizzle of rain that had begun. Lem was quite proficient at hitching Calliope, a calm sorrel, to the little gig, and they were soon pushing Gulliver into the carriage and climbing in after him.

Patience flicked the reins, and off they went in a whirl down the wet lane. She brushed a wet strand of hair from her eyes, her mouth dry from fear. Any moment she expected French soldiers to spring from their forest hiding place and shoot. She had to get them both to safety. Lem looked to her for courage, which she knew she lacked in

great supply. She concentrated on reaching Winchelsea and
sent a prayer to Heaven for Rupert's care as well as for the
safety of her family in Storrington.

The rain began pouring from the night, making it difficult
to see the road or to find the retreating wagons. Gulliver
whimpered from his position on the floor as the carriage
rolled and rocked in their hurried flight.

Patience shouted to Lem, "Do you know where the old
Tyler road is?"

Lem jumped in his seat. "I almost think so."

Farther down the road, Lem bounced up and down. He
tugged on her arm, pointing, "I think that's it!"

"What?" she cried, trying to avoid the deep ruts.

Calliope was becoming increasingly jittery and difficult
to control while rain pelted the carriage roof, making conversation difficult.

"I think there's the Tyler road!" He yelled urgently.

"But how do you know? Are you sure?"

The little boy's head bobbed up and down. Hoping he
knew of which he spoke, she directed the little dogged horse
down the dirt lane.

They turned down Tyler road and a mile along their path,
she bit her lip when the carriage hit a large bump. The reins
almost flew out of her hands as they jerked in their seats.
But they kept going.

Patience shivered from the cold wetness as well as from
fear. She had no idea where they were and worried whether
the next person they met on the road would be friend or foe.

Hoping they'd reach Town soon, Patience, blind to the
moatlike hole on the side, guided the little gig deep into
the molasses mud.

After several attempts to escape their trap, she handed
over the reins to Lem. "Hie Calliope, I shall get behind
and push."

As she jumped away from the carriage, he called after her, "Be careful, miss."

She wiped an offending lock of hair from her forehead and felt a streak of mud trail her fingers across her skin. Within minutes the gushing rain soaked her mantle and dress to the skin. Although more than a little tired and scared, she could not give up.

She slipped at the back of the carriage, trying desperately to gain a foothold. After rocking the coach and falling face-forward several times into the black mire, she finally felt the wheels break free from imprisonment and leap down the road.

Filthy and exhausted she watched in dismay, her mouth agape, as the carriage tore down the path, already merging with the night. She hiked her dress and ran after the carriage, realizing fear ignited her with speed she did not know she had.

Not far down the road, she finally caught up with the runaway coach. Lem tried his best to control the little mare, who continually jerked her head up and down impatiently. After a few attempts, Patience pulled herself into the jolting coach.

"Sorry, miss, I couldn't control 'er. She got away from me!" His earnest expression begged for forgiveness, his white face streaked brown with mud and awash with fright.

Patience took over the reins and smiled wearily, trying to catch her breath, "I know. She is just scared like the rest of us." When she snapped Calliope into motion again, wishing feverishly this night would end, they were once again stopped in their tracks. But not by mud.

Three masked highwaymen blocked their path, each man on the left and right held menacing pistols.

"Please to give us your valuables," the man in the center calmly instructed.

Chapter 14

Patience's heart caught in her throat. She could not speak for the fright whipping through her as her body tensed. *I must be brave. There must be a way.* She studied each man briefly, weighing the dangers before her.

The first man on the left, tall and thin in his saddle, struggled to control his horse with one hand and hold a pistol in the other. The thief leading their little band rode between the other thieves but carried no weapon. The last thief was by far the largest man controlling his skittish horse. He looked uncomfortable both on his horse and at holding a pistol at their carriage.

Something seemed familiar about them.

The thin man to Patience's left snorted. "Ye don't 'ave to ask politely, jes' say, 'Give up yer money and yer jewels or forfeit yer life,'" he told his companion in disgust.

His companion shook his head with such spirit that his handkerchief fell away from his face and floated away into the night. A quick grab came up empty.

"Blast it! Damn the mask!" He hurriedly raised his hand in front of his face, but though Patience peered intently into the dark, she still could not quite make out his features.

She grasped Lem's hand with her right hand, holding the little mare still with her left. For some unknown reason, she believed they would not hurt her or Lem. These men were obviously unskilled robbers. And what was it about them that sparked a hint of recognition?

The voice of the man who had lost his mask—"Begging yer pardon for me language," he surprised them all by saying.

The tall, thin man grew impatient. "Enough of these gentrified pleasantries, General." Looking at Patience and Lem, he told them, "Folks, 'and over yer valuables. We don't want to 'urt ye."

Patience straightened her back and looked determinedly at the trio. The would-be smugglers had apparently decided not to find an honest job. "We have nothing of value," she told them matter-of-factly.

The men stared at her blankly, unprepared for her answer before the thin man told her, "But ye must 'ave something to steal. Per'aps I'll 'ave to take a look inside yer carriage." He must have thought this statement would dampen Patience's bravado.

But she planned to wait them out. "Gentlemen—I may call you that?" Not waiting for them to acknowledge her, she said, "I must needs bring to your attention that we happen to be fleeing from the French who have been sighted and are probably bringing their boats to shore as we speak. We are headed to safety and carry nothing of value. I assure you no trinkets or coins do we possess on our person," she stated succinctly. She heard Gulliver issue a low growl.

The thin man quickly changed his tune. "The Frenchies—'ere? Max, let's get away from 'ere. They'll shoot us for sure."

"Don't ye remember? Ye are to call me General! And yer not supposed to use any names! Can't ye see the lady is bluff'n? Those frog-eat'n Frenchies are too afraid of we brave Englishmen. Now, back to the matter at hand," the General finished.

The thin man and the large man did take a cautious look from side to side, as if expecting unwanted French intruders. In the dim lantern light bumping along the carriage side, the three men turned to each other, talking animatedly. The General forgot to keep his face in the shadows, obviously not too concerned that Patience might recognize him.

Patience decided to continue to press their cause. "Please let us pass. Our enemy will soon be upon us, and *all* our lives will be forfeited."

Just then a rustling noise in the forest bed placed everyone on guard. The thin man jerked his horse anxiously around and accidentally nudged his cocked pistol. The pistol roared in his hand, whistled off the General's hat, and frightened gentle Calliope, who charged toward the thieves, effectively routing them from their blockade.

Patience and Lem left the men far behind on the Tyler road. But not before hearing in the night wind, "Ye almost killed me and made a 'ole in me 'at," shouted a voice.

"Me? You stole the pistol. 'ow was I to know it were loaded? Ye think that was a Frenchie?"

Where was she? Bryce deliberated while swatting his whip against his boot in agitation. Winchelsea's streets were almost empty at this late hour. After racing to Winchelsea's port and conferring with a lieutenant, he had learned that the raging bonfires had been misinterpreted. Men were already dispatched to inform the alerted countryside that British soil was still safe from French invaders. Bryce informed the lieutenant he would make sure everyone from his district found their way safely home.

He had already sent his servants heading back toward Paddock Green. One of the maids told him that Miss Simmons and Lem had stayed behind.

But why? Unless she was meeting with someone. In which case, why was Lem involved? And whom was she meeting? He did not want to believe Patience capable of treason, but why was she not here? Marlow said the wagons had arrived over an hour ago at their arranged meeting place.

He would find her and learn the answers. Barely winded, Bryce's horse pawed the ground, ready for a run. He mounted Defiance and tore off into the night. And he wondered what story she would spin in her defense as a lost goat *baaed* from the side of the road.

Lem looked around at Winchelsea's quiet and deserted streets before turning to Patience, a puzzled look on his countenance. "Where is everyone, miss? Where'd they go? Are we too late?" his voice slightly wavering.

Consternation knitted Patience's brow. She reined the mare next to the inn and flexed her shoulders tiredly. They saw no one. She noted many muddy paths grooved by several carriage and wagon wheels as well as hoofprints.

Where had everyone gone? The tracks, lit by the dim moonlight, seemed to head in all directions, with no deliberate course. As she smelled the damp air and wet animal fur, she contemplated their next step.

Lem jumped down from the gig and volunteered to find someone who could help them, running to the inn steps. She heard the little boy's knock and then his voice in conversation with another, and in her dampened and dirty condition waited impatiently for news.

She watched as Lem returned, his face flushed with a smile. "It were all a mistake as 'e tole me in there." He poured forth his story: that his lordship had arrived over an hour ago and sent everyone home. The bonfires had caught a wind unexpectedly, and a watcher from the tower thought they were meant as a signal that the French flotilla had been spotted.

Patience dropped her head in relief and exhaustion. Every muscle felt cramped in her body and every bone still resounded from the jarring on their perilous flight. Her heart began to beat normally again.

Unbidden, a thought came to her. This might be the time to speak with the constable and discover what he knew about the earl's activities. Then she would know whether he was friend or foe.

Hieing the gig up the street, she located the constable's office next to the gray prison building. Instructing Lem to wait in the carriage and to hang on to Calliope's reins, she slowly climbed down the steps, gingerly holding her wet clothes away from her body.

She found the constable, Cavendish, who was preparing to leave for the night and had just begun blowing out the lanterns.

"Constable, sir, perhaps I could have a moment of your time?" she asked with a hesitant smile on her face.

Cavendish stood behind his desk, his fingers folded over his belly. "Miss, what do you here so late? Should you not be at home in bed? It t'weren't an invasion afterall."

Patience moved to forestall him. "Yes, I understand, but I just wanted to ask you about his lordship, Lord Londringham?"

The constable straightened his back, looking surprised. "Good man, that. What would you know?"

Adjusting her cap, she inquired, "Lord Londringham, is he, does he—"

"Out with it, gel, home is calling and I don't have time to

dawdle, and you look all wore out and wet," obviously noticing for the first time her dishabille.

"Yes, I must get home, but first, I need to know if Lord Londringham could be guilty of treason." The words flew out, and she raised a hand to her mouth too late to halt them. She took a step back, aware that she had just said what she previously had only thought.

His response surprised her. Cavendish squinted at her behind his spectacles, then began laughing, his belly undulating. "Londringham, what, treason?" He chuckled again before replying, "My dear woman, I haven't an idea where you heard such stories. There was never a truer Englishman. He doesn't have a treasonous bone in his body." He collected his coat and walked to the door. "Now, why don't we both go home?"

He showed her out the door and began walking down the street, still shaking his head over Patience's suggestion.

Thankful and relieved, she climbed once more into the gig and wheeled it around, heading back down the Tyler road, with Lem and Gulliver asleep on the floor. Heading home. To Bryce.

Chapter 15

The cook Melenroy greeted Patience at the door after she left Calliope, Gulliver, and Lem to Lucky's sleepy ministrations. Tired, but anxious to remove the grime and filth collected on the hasty trip, Patience helped Melenroy fill a hot, steaming bath. While Patience undressed, Melenroy hunted for soap and a towel, Patience regaling her with a soliloquy on what had transpired after she and Lem were left behind. No one noticed they were missing until the wagons were halfway to Winchelsea, and by that time, no one wanted to turn around. Myrtle had never mentioned waiting for them.

Relaxing in the bone-melting warmth, Patience listened with one ear to the cook's raspy voice as water flowed over and swirled around her body. She could almost envision falling asleep in the soothing bath.

"'is lordship was right worried about you. After he notified everyone we was safe from 'arm and sent us 'ome, 'e went looking for you." Melenroy settled her wizened body in her favorite chair by the fireplace.

Patience sat up quickly when she heard that Bryce had gone looking for her, sending waves of water rushing over the rim. Patience's eyes widened in shock, her heart beat loud enough to drown the rest of Melenroy's report.

He was looking for me? But of course, Lem and I were not in the wagons, and he would be worried about us. In the turmoil of the night, she had been anxious to get to safety and lent no thought to what Bryce might wonder about their disappearance. *He probably realized we became lost on the road and couldn't find the village. But how long would he search for us?*

She bit her lip and sank down into the now-cooling waters. He had to return sometime to get some sleep, and then Marlow could tell him that they had returned safely. Actually, their story was quite amusing, and besides, she and Lem had been trying to save his dog. Of course, at the time they couldn't know that they weren't in any danger.

Melenroy helped Patience wash her hair, and then stoked the fire to warm the kitchen further before leaving to fetch an old robe that Patience could wear to bed.

Finally ready to seek her bed, Patience grasped the edge of the tub and pushed herself up, gasping slightly as a chill swept her body. Quickly grabbing a large warm towel, she patted herself dry, wrapped the towel around herself, then swept thick strands of wet hair out of her face, wrenching the water back into the tub.

The towel gaped open slightly, allowing Bryce a lovely view of her rounded flushed breasts. He stood in the doorway with his hands on his hips, having arrived as she toweled herself by the fire.

"Had an eventful night, my dear?" he asked laconically, trying to check his wandering thoughts, which proved impossible. Slender calves and legs molded superbly underneath shapely buttocks. He had even caught sight of her flat stomach and the dark thatch of curls resting at the top of her thighs.

After an exhausting night of riding, he was now the one who wanted to be ridden, as his hardened manhood pushed against his breeches. Her body surely did not appear innocent, not in any possible way.

She let out a little scream and groped for the ends of her towel to cover herself more completely. He smiled a little as he watched the lovely flush on her face, warmed by the fire and his stare, no doubt.

"My lord, I . . . I . . . you startled me. I know you need an explanation." She hesitated before appealing to him. "Perhaps I can give you the details tomorrow morning when I am more presentable, and you have had a night's rest?" Her voice faded.

He thrust a hand through his hair, disheveled from his journey. He felt more alive than he had ever remembered before.

With hooded eyes, he grabbed a chair, turned it around, and swung a leg over one side, resting his wrists on the chair's back. "I'm not so patient. I would like my answers now," he told her firmly.

Their eyes locked as he awaited the truth, damp tendrils curled over her shoulder by the fire.

Melenroy bustled in without seeing her master. "I 'ope this will do you, dearie. It ain't much to look at but it keeps a body warm," her voice rambling on as she held out the robe for Patience to slip her arms into.

At Patience's nod, the cook turned, caught sight of the earl, and pressed her old body into a stiff curtsy. Patience quickly threw Melenroy's robe around herself, keeping the towel tightly wrapped to her body.

The cook hesitated, unsure whether to stay or leave, but Bryce made the decision for her by dismissing her.

"Now, where were we before we were interrupted?" His voice feigned casual indifference. *And before the robe,* he thought with disappointment. He had rather enjoyed her flushed, warm body, quite a beautiful subject for an artist to paint. Yes, he tried to tell himself, he was interested in her body from a completely aesthetic point of view. The artist's subject hid beneath a rust-colored wool night robe whose tattered edges hung right above graceful ankles and finely arched feet. Then his imagination started to wander, about what lay beneath the clothes she grasped tightly to her chest in protection or shield from him. And he tried to remember.

"My lord, it's all so very innocent. Lem wanted to take your dog with us and was afraid the French would get him. Since he was so worried, he asked me to help find Gulliver, which we did, but by that time, the wagons had left us behind. We followed as soon as we could in the gig."

"Why did they not wait for you? I gave Marlow strict instructions not to leave anyone behind."

She shrugged. "I told Myrtle to wait for us. I guess she forgot to tell someone."

He could believe that. But he wasn't nearly through with her. "Where did you go when you left here?"

She licked her lips. "We had a slight difficulty finding the Tyler road, which Lem said would take us to Winchelsea. And the rain and mud added to our delay.

He nodded thoughtfully. "Did you meet anyone on the road to Winchelsea?"

She hesitated. "Actually, we were stopped by some gentlemen, but they only wanted directions, and we were unable to assist them."

He watched as she shifted uneasily from one foot to the other. *Was there something she had left out of her story? Probably, but nothing more he would learn from her tonight.* He closed his eyes briefly and waved his hand. "Very well, you may retire."

Her eyes flicked around the large kitchen. Her only

escape path lay between his lordship and the servants' door, which led to the backstairs. She hastened across the room, still clutching the robe to her chest. When she drew near him, he caught her right arm.

He felt her tremble like a frightened animal, but the warmth of her touch lightened his next words. "Patience, I want to believe you."

She stared down at him before giving him a brief smile. When he released her arm, she ran out the door and flew up the stairs without a backward glance.

Melenroy watched from her peephole and smiled. "That gel is no servant."

Patience could not sleep. Again and again, she tossed and turned, entangling herself in the bedclothes. He clearly didn't believe her, even though he told her that he did. She thought, despairing, she wouldn't believe her either.

This was not how the night was to have ended. He should be thankful that their efforts saved his dog, in a roundabout way. What could she do or say that would make Bryce trust her, believe in her? She felt he was the kind of man that would accept only complete honesty from someone whom he cared for.

She looked at her locket watch she had brought with her from home. Three o'clock and too early for signs of the sun. She needed to talk to him. Convince him to trust her. But could she trust him about Rupert's predicament?

Although her feelings toward Bryce were in a complete jumble, she no longer wanted to continue this deception. She knew this was the only way.

Calmly, she dressed in a forest green velvet gown by the light of one small candle. Braiding her hair with quick, practiced motions, she smiled at her appearance reflected in the mirror. Pale, but with a pinch to her cheeks to give color, she thought he might find her attractive.

Her plan was simple. She would go to his bedchambers and see if he stirred. If there was no sound, she would continue down the stairs and work in his study until morning. The chances he would be awake were too remote to even contemplate, however, at least it might ease her mind somewhat that she had made the effort.

She had not yet formulated her declaration of innocence, but with palms moist and her heart jumping loud enough in her ears to echo in the unlit long, dark corridor, she walked down the stairs to the second floor. This undertaking would truly not be difficult because, she reasoned with herself, his lordship was sure to be fast asleep. Her slippers slipped along on the dark, glossy stairs.

Down the long hall she slowly walked until she reached his bedchamber. She paused to listen. An early-morning wind shook the hall windows playfully. But the noise spooked Patience, who wondered what sprites were awake at this time of the night.

She paced outside his room, until she decided in relief that she would wait for a conversation with his lordship later in the morning. Meanwhile, she planned to finish cataloguing his library until the sun came up.

As she stepped away from his door, it opened. Bryce stood in the doorway wearing breeches and a fine linen shirt with his sleeves rolled up, his feet bare. His stormy blue eyes caught her gaze, effectively preventing her from moving another step. She twisted her hands in front of her, her mouth too dry to speak.

"Patience, it is approximately three o'clock in the morning. May I ask what you are doing up and about? Or, more specifically, at my door?"

She chewed her lip nervously before opening her mouth to speak. He did not look or sound as if he had just arisen.

"My lord . . . I wanted to explain. That is, about tonight, I mean, last night." Her hesitation allowed him to reply.

"I thought we already had this conversation earlier." He folded his arms across his chest and leaned against the doorjamb. "Surely, what you have to add could wait until the night has broken?"

His reasonable voice relaxed her, slightly. "Yes, you're right, of course. I couldn't sleep, and thought, that is . . . I'll wait for you in your study." She retreated a few steps toward the stairs. "Please forgive me for disturbing you."

"You do disturb me. However, since it is so very important to not wait for full morning to have this discussion, come in." He stepped outside into the corridor and beckoned her in.

She wrung her hands with indecision, and then, thrusting thoughts of repercussions to the back of her mind, slid past his towering frame into his apartments. A fire, which had seen greater glory, now trembled on the brink of extinction on the far side of the room. Sitting on his desk by a large window was a fading candle, which betrayed his late-night activities. She dared not look toward the opened doors to her left. Doors that opened to his bedroom, which reminded her of one dark, wet night.

She took a deep breath, studying a speech mentally, while waiting to see what Bryce would have her do. He stood directly behind her.

"Please. Be comfortable. You can only imagine how interested I am in hearing what you have to say," came his low timbre near her left ear. He ushered her into a wing chair by the fire and stooped to stoke the coals before drawing his chair near hers.

She swallowed hard, noting his sinewy muscles flexing

under his thin shirt as he moved around the room. Perhaps this was not the best idea she had ever had, she thought distantly, growing warm from the nearness of the fire or from his presence, unsure which. In these close quarters, all she could sense were sandalwood and port. She would know the scents blindfolded, it was Bryce.

All her senses grew taut, reminding her of the night on the balcony, when he had set her aflame. Perhaps that is what she had been longing for ever since. She put her hands to her face, feeling her cheeks flush.

His look missed nothing. He leaned forward, resting his forearms on his knees. "Patience, you have my complete attention. Please place my mind at peace, for I am at a total loss to your presence here."

His low voice hummed in her veins. He was infinitely too close for her present state of mind. His strong arms, his large hands, his firm legs flexed beneath his breeches. *You must rein those thoughts in,* she thought firmly. *It just will not do thinking about the other night, especially when his bed is in the next room.*

She fluttered her eyes and smiled shyly. "I couldn't sleep because you see, my lord, it's terribly important to me that you believe me."

He shook his head slightly. "Why is it so important?" The growing flames flickered shadows across his strong visage.

She hesitated and gulped. "Because I thought, now that we were friends"—she hurried on before she lost her courage—"it is important that we trust each other and believe each other, don't you agree?" she asked while twisting her gown beneath her hands.

"Friends," he said softly, almost to himself. "Friends? No, that will simply not do. We cannot be friends." He hesitated, and she jumped into the breach.

"You, you, don't want to be friends?" She held her breath

almost in disbelief. *Then he will surely not help me,* she thought, sensing disaster headed her way.

"No, friendship is definitely *not* what I want from you." He rose and walked over to lean on the fireplace mantel, his gaze unwavering from her face.

Patience, unable to look at him, stood to depart the room. In a thrice he crossed back to her, grabbing her hand in his. With his other hand, he reached out and tenderly stroked her soft cheek. "With all this excitement, I'm surprised that you are not fast asleep in your bed." He continued, "Patience, look at me."

She looked up at him, amazed at the fires blazing in those depthless eyes. "I want something more from you." Holding her gaze, he whispered, "Why are you here? Are you here to tease me or torment me, little sprite?"

Mesmerized by his intent stare, she needed a moment to collect her thoughts. "I'm surely not here to torment you, my lord," her voice quavering slightly. *Escape,* the little voice whispered. *Escape.*

"Ah, then you are here to tease me," he murmured.

"No, not that either." She broke his hold on her and hurried to the door for the safety that lay just beyond from this enigmatic man. He confused her, and his nearness affected her nerves.

He reached the door before her to prevent her from leaving. Gently he turned her around until her back faced her only exit.

"You have nothing to fear, indeed nothing, if you are innocent." The husky whisper in her ear undid her.

What could he mean? Perhaps it was lack of sleep or fear for Rupert's safety, or his lordship's nearness or his gentle touch, but tears sprang to her eyes. She turned away from him, not wanting him to see her cry.

He tenderly turned her head back to him. Tears silently slipped down her cheeks. Bryce swore softly and pulled her into his arms. "Please don't cry. I would not make you sad for the world." He offered her comfort and perhaps a haven, if she was to accept it. With one hand, he tilted her chin to look at him and smoothly wiped away her tears with the back of his hand.

Patience couldn't move, unprepared for his tenderness and the passion she saw in his deep blue eyes. He leaned down and kissed her gently, his one hand nestling the nape of her neck while the other splayed across her back, urging, melting her soft, compliant body into his hardened one.

Stunned by his kiss and caring, she wanted to feel his heat and need. He did need her. She knew it.

She was blind in his arms, instinctively opening her mouth to allow his velvet tongue inside. She wrapped her arms around his shoulders, leaning her body into his on tiptoe.

In no time, Bryce lifted her off the ground, conforming her body more snugly into his. Their lips still met as he captured her mouth in an intense display of the passion he had held in check for so long.

He set her back to the floor before bending down to lift her in his arms, taking her into his bedroom. Laying her gently on the bed, he again claimed her mouth on the way to claiming her cheeks, neck, shoulders, and all the rest he desired to call his.

She didn't want to resist him, but rather show him her own longing. Every time he touched or kissed her, he sparked currents in her heart and washed the sad loneliness from her troubled soul.

"Make me believe in you. Show me the truth," he whispered against her exposed neck.

Words that had haunted her since the night on the balcony. He needs something to believe in. Someone to believe in. She saw how different their worlds had been.

She trusted everyone. He trusted no one. She knew that

to give was to receive, a lesson he needed to learn. Because she loved him, she wanted to show him that another world of goodness, light, and truth did exist. Love? When had that happened? That knowledge wrapped around her heart with unstoppable joy. *Follow me,* she thought. *I will save you.*

All this was answered in his embrace. A home of her own in his arms. She wanted to drown in the senses he awakened in her. Giving back to him came so easily to her.

He slipped her velvet gown off one white shoulder, then the other one. He kissed each shoulder before pulling down the gown farther and farther. Her chemise fluttered open, spilling her full breasts into his waiting hands. He kissed one breast, then turned to give the other attention. Before he continued, he reached behind her back and untied her braid, slipping his hands through her long tresses and spreading them over her shoulders.

"Beautiful," he murmured, looking down to Patience's countenance. He hesitated, almost as if he awaited her permission.

"Please," she cried softly to him, but still he held back.

With obvious effort, he demanded of her, "Say my name."

Hoping her heart showed not in her eyes, she looked up to whisper warmly, "Bryce."

He swept down to possess her lips once more, savoring the taste of her sweet mouth and darting tongue. When he moved his head down her restless body and captured a pliant rosy nipple, he heard her sigh with unspoken delight.

She arched her back to bring her breast more closely to his enveloping heat and matched her body to meet his anywhere she could.

When he finished teasing one breast, he immediately turned his attention to the other. As his tongue lathed her one peaked nipple, his right hand teased and tormented its mate, causing her to moan in pleasure.

Slowly, he removed her dress and chemise, and then her drawers, leaving nothing from his heated gaze. Not able to control himself for much longer, his body tightened, his heart pounded, thinking of her welcoming, moist warmth.

As he drew himself up abruptly to tear off his shirt, she uttered a moan, thinking he was leaving. To assure her of his complete attention, he swooped down to plant another lingering kiss and pressed his chest to her breasts, while easing himself between her legs.

In delight, he heard her purr in satisfaction at his return. He enjoyed her artless sighs and reveled in her satiny body ripe with desire and longing. She belonged to him as no other had held a claim on him.

She was his for now. She wanted him as much as he wanted her. Giving and receiving. He would ensure she would find pleasure with him as he instinctively knew he would find something with her he had never known before.

She marveled at the strength she felt in him. He seemed invincible to her. She thought she would dissolve at the heated passion he inspired in her. But she could not tell if he felt any of the same flames shooting through him.

Her hands slipped down his back to his breeches and she tugged at them, trying to get his attention.

Quickly, he untied his breeches and shoved them over his hips, kicking them off, only pausing a second in the act to kiss her belly. He moved up and over her body, resting all of his weight on one side of her, plying kisses to her red, swollen lips.

His manhood pulsed between her warm thighs. Gently, he reached down and parted her silky curls to find the wetness of her desire.

She moaned deep in her throat, and her body shook at this renewed pleasure. This is what she had been waiting for. He must stop this torture, but she would not let him. Inarticulate cries unknowingly left her, instructing him where to touch her.

He poised his body at the entrance to her slick heat. He found himself hoping she was only his, no matter what her guilt might be.

A sudden movement of her hips and he plunged in, tearing her slightly. He groaned with pleasure and something akin to love that he did not recognize.

He whispered he was sorry he hurt her, but she could not hear him and remembered only his thoughtfulness later.

She didn't allow him to savor his conquest but immediately locked her legs behind his hips, urging him closer and deeper every time he withdrew to make another thrust.

She grasped his face between her hands and brought his lips to meet hers, the aggressor of his lips as she continued to receive his possession of her body. She ardently captured his mouth and thrust her tongue inside, echoing their body's movements.

When she finally let him have his breath, he whispered hoarsely, "So wet, so tight. Only for me. Only for me." Then he sought her taut nipples beneath him.

She sighed again at the exquisite onslaught of emotions and pleasure, and prayed she was satisfying him according to his wordless instructions in lovemaking. She feared disappointing him. So little thought was needed, only touch, and the friction he created in her built to a crescendo that thrilled her.

When he made one last thrust into her, she felt him touch her heart as he climaxed, bringing her to the same exploding threshold.

Slick chests heaved together, he kissed her tenderly before pulling slowly out of her. Immediately, she felt a chill at his leaving, his warmth no longer cloaking her body. But soon he returned and pulled the counterpane over both of them, shifting her against his side. Their exhausted bodies fell asleep as the sun began to wink at the windows.

Bryce woke to a hard knocking on the outer room's door. Although unwilling to leave the lovely woman sleeping beside him, he eased himself out of bed, threw on a dressing gown, and closed the sitting room doors behind him to answer the intruder.

Patience blinked awake and slowly sat up, waiting for a calm to remove her disconcertment over where she found herself. But feeling warm and cocooned and smelling Bryce's scent on her pillow, memories came flooding back, bringing a blush to her cheeks.

She had to return to her room before anyone discovered her. And sort out her confused state. Quickly, she slipped on her discarded chemise and gown. When she stopped briefly, voices in the adjoining room beckoned her closer.

"They captured highwaymen last night?" she heard Bryce ask.

"Yes, one of the men was the one you have been searching for, the young Mandeley," answered a voice which she didn't recognize.

"You have Rupert Mandeley imprisoned?" Bryce queried incredulously.

"Yes, my lord. Just like you wanted. But he isn't talking. I think the boy is frightened."

"I must see him," Bryce told him urgently.

Patience let herself out the other door and fled down the hall and up the stairs to her room, without hearing more.

Chapter 16

Rupert. Imprisoned. The worst had happened. And she had done nothing to help him. And after what had transpired between her and the man who had commanded her brother's capture. What had she done?

Patience reached her bedroom door in the attic, blinded by tears and anger. She closed the door and threw herself on her narrow bed, dismayed and stunned by this dramatic turn of events. But she allowed her cries for only the span of a heartbeat. She had to be strong, she had to find a way to get Rupert out of prison.

Certainly Patience had allowed Bryce's fine looks and charms to captivate her, but no longer. *I must find a way to see Rupert tonight. Talk to him and the constable. Someone would help them.*

How could Bryce have unjustly imprisoned Rupert? And I trusted him, she thought in disgust, punching her pillow and wishing it was his face.

Rising from the bed, Patience dried her tears, looking out the window, her mind numb. She refused to admit how deeply Bryce's betrayal hurt her, and resolved to free Rupert and return home.

She shook her head, wanting to forget this morning. It had only been an action of desire, passion. True, she had felt the scorching flames, but the price she had paid for her heart was too high.

A short while later, Patience heard Lem's young voice through the door. "Miss, you in there? 'is lordship wants you to be ready at quarter of the hour."

She rose to her feet, shoulders back, and slowly opened the door. "Ready for what?" she asked him, testing the strength of her voice.

Lem stared up into Patience's sad face. "What's wrong, miss? Why ye cryin'?" His high-pitched tone reverberated in the deserted hall.

She pulled him into her room where he promptly flounced on the only chair available and cupped his chin in his hands.

"I need your help tonight, and you must promise never to mention this to anyone."

Lem's eyes lit up with excitement. "A special mission? Ye want me to spit in yer eye or draw blood or somethin' to seal our pact?"

"That will not be necessary," Patience told him with a smile. "I must see someone in Winchelsea and will need help hitching the gig to Calliope again, like last night. Will you help me?"

The little boy nodded vigorously, then a puzzled look stole over his chubby face. "But 'oo are ye seein' in Winchelsea?"

"I am visiting a friend who needs my help."

"Oh, very good. Of course I'll help ye. When shall we meet?"

They planned their night's activities before Patience sent the small boy on his way.

* * *

Bryce blinked at the sunlight showering the hall. Since this morning when Myrtle had opened the curtains in the front rooms and washed the windows, the house was beginning to look like a home. Even the front door welcomed in the warm sun's rays peeping in the cracks.

A new day, and he thought everything was slowly falling into place. A special early-morning tête-à-tête with Patience and perhaps later today he would learn from the Mandeley boy who killed Lord Carstairs.

Before he visited his tenants to discuss last night's false invasion, Bryce planned to talk to Rupert Mandeley in prison. Hopefully, Mandeley could fill in some missing pieces and, with a little bit of luck, perhaps help draw a noose around Sansouche's cold-blooded neck.

He shook his head, pondering the young man's role in this drama. *What was the young man doing with highwaymen? And, if the murderer even suspected that Mandeley knew something, the boy's life would be forfeited. Yes, he was assuredly safer behind bars.*

With evidence in hand, he would bet that if he threatened Sansouche, the Frenchman would lead him to the master French spy to save his own wormy hide. The master spy could then lead him to the woman responsible for his brother's death. His eyes clouded at the memory. Once she was captured, and his brother's murder was avenged, then he could contemplate a different future.

Yes, she was like all the rest. Bryce thought he had given her many opportunities to prove her faithfulness, but watching from his vantage point in the stables' shadows late that night, he hated to admit, he was discomfited. He watched as Patience struggled to hitch the gig with Lem's help. Where were they planning to go?

If it had not been for Lucky overhearing Patience and Lem in the stables, Bryce would still be at his desk. Lucky, who was a damn good coachman when not soaked, amazingly had the foresight to spirit Defiance out of his stall and ready him for Bryce. The coachman was due a pint for his work this night.

Not that anyone couldn't have overheard Patience and Lem banging and thumping. Often, Patience would glance warily around the dark corners of the stables as if expecting to be caught in a lie she had not yet told. Bryce watched as the young woman edged toward the wall, a safe distance from the little mare, the gentlest and slowest horse he owned. Apparently, although the woman was able to drive the gig, she wanted to be close to a horse about as much as a live goose would to a cook wielding a sharp axe.

A long black cape enveloped her slender frame, hiding it from view. After an interminable amount of time during which Bryce itched to hitch up the gig himself, Lem declared the little carriage ready. At this distance, Bryce couldn't hear their conversation, but from the look on their faces, the two were having a disagreement. With Lem's dejected face, it was apparent Patience had denied the boy's accompanying her.

Lem opened the stable doors, letting in the cool night wind and the blackest of nights. By the light of her wavering lantern, Bryce saw Patience flick the reins. Escaping out the back, he swiftly mounted Defiance and rounded the stables to silently track her progress.

As he waited in a dark copse of trees to allow Patience enough head, Bryce twisted his lips ruefully. *Things were certainly not dull with Patience. In fact, life had become a whole lot more interesting since that maid had arrived on his doorstep.* Although his leg still pained him at odd times, the blood whirred in his veins and stirred him to action. He had not felt this way in a long time. Then he and his midnight horse blended into the night landscape until they were one.

Patience felt fear stalk her as she drove the gig toward Winchelsea. She should be safe in bed, not venturing out on a night like this. The dancing wind accompanied her, whispering of a cool rain to come, but she hoped there would not be a repeat of the weather from the previous night. She clutched her wool cape closer to her chest with one hand while directing Calliope with her other shaking hand.

What if she met up with real highwaymen and not those bumbling idiots that seemed to keep stumbling across her path? Perhaps she should have allowed Lem to attend her, but although she understood his eagerness to help her, it was too dangerous. She didn't want him to be further involved in her duplicity with Bryce.

That man. He could certainly be a charmer if one didn't look too deep into the well of his character. But now his betrayal stuck in her throat and poisoned her heart against the man she wanted for her own.

She brushed off these thoughts as if shaking raindrops from her cape. Fear followed her in anticipation that the prison officials would not allow her to visit her brother, especially this late at night. But under cover of night was the only way to lessen suspicion at the manor house. Hopefully, Bryce, as well as other night creatures, remained in their lairs while she went about the duty of saving her younger brother.

Luckily, the rattling and creaking of the gig's wheels drowned out many eerie sounds from the nocturnal animals, at home in the oily depths of the forest lining the Winchelsea road. When she spotted the edge of the village, she relaxed her shoulders and flicked Calliope into a faster pace, anxious to leave behind the dark loneliness of her journey.

She drew near the now-familiar inn, where a man stood outside singing a drunken lullaby, urged on by his carousing friends. The small prison stood down the street from the inn, nestled in an obtuse corner. Patience halted Calliope and clambered down, throwing the reins to the ostler sitting on the inn's step. Her head down, she threw the boy a coin and mumbled instructions to care for the carriage in her absence.

With a furtive look in both directions, her hood well covering her face, she hurried toward the dark structure, overshadowed by the large Church of the Redeemer next to it. In front of the prison door, she hesitated. Rubbing the onyx in her pocket for luck, she pushed open the heavy wooden door, prepared with answers to questions she knew were on the other side—keeping bribes, cajolery, and tears in her back pocket for a last-ditch effort. Tears had never worked on her brothers, so that little scheme was by far the least foolproof.

The door opened to reveal a small room, lowly lit by a lone candle halfway to its waxy grave. A small man snored noisily in a chair behind a narrow wooden desk, his feet comfortably propped on top and perilously close to his meager light.

This was too easy. She remembered to close the door behind her before the playful wind could, and thus alert the guard to her presence. She snuck past the sleeping sentry, holding the skirts of her cape and gown which whispered her entrance to the cells.

In the first cell lay Rupert, wide-awake. The jealous moon had finally managed to peek beneath the overshadowing clouds, illuminating Rupert's tiny cell.

Patience flung back her hood and whispered, "Rupert." Her heart was alight at seeing her dearest sibling, but worry still consumed her.

Her brother leapt to his feet from his position on the cold stone floor and rushed to the metal bars. "Patience! What are you doing here? How did you flummox the guard to let you in?" his voice loud in surprise.

Patience put a finger to her lips in warning. "The constable is watching naught in his deep slumber. I slipped past him for I had to see you and find how you are faring. I just learned this morning of your dilemma. How did they catch you?"

Rupert shook his head in disgust. "I was in the woods last night with my friends during the false reports of invasion. They decided to try and rob a few of the folk fleeing to Winchelsea. I had no idea of the plan. We were to go to the coast to scout wrecks. What rotten luck!" He hit the bar with an open palm.

"These are the same men who have taken you in?" Patience asked falteringly, afraid of the answer.

"Yes, they have asked no questions about why I prefer not to be seen in the daylight and given me a place to lay my head at night. One of them calls himself the General and the silent chap is called Bear. Why?"

Patience closed her eyes briefly. "Because they stopped me upon the road to Winchelsea."

Her brother's sunken cheeks hollowed even deeper with his pain. "We became separated when I finally caught up to them, the constable's men not far behind. I can't seem to convince anyone that I had nothing to do with any robbery, but since I am wanted for the murder of our cousin, my words mean less than a preacher without a sinner."

Bitterness came over Patience. "It is all Lord Londringham's doing. He had you arrested, he . . ."

"Wait, Patience. He was here, this morning to see me. He wants to help. His lordship does not believe that I killed Carstairs. Says he suspects a Frenchman. I told him everything I knew about that night. He's the first person that has listened to my story. I gave him the silver buckle I found outside the French doors at Carstairs's estate. Lord Londringham thinks it might lead to something."

Patience stared at her brother in amazement, her mouth dropped in her lap. "Lord Londringham wants to help you?" she asked in an unrecognizable squeaky voice.

"Yes, and unfortunately, he thinks I might be safer in here, especially if the real murderer suspects I have evidence of his guilt. But he thought it wouldn't be too long before the constable would allow me to stay at Lord Londringham's home, while he clears up this fiasco." Rupert's bright smile did nothing to hide his despair.

Patience bent her head to rest on the cell bars, her tired brain trying to assimilate what Rupert had said. Bryce was actually trying to *help* them. Her heart and mood lightened, dispelling the gloom of her brother's cell.

"Did he give you any indication of how long you might be in here?" she queried, almost fearing to hope this nightmare would soon be at an end.

He shook his head with a twist to his lips. "No idea. But at least it's a place where I can rest and no longer have to hide."

She looked at her little brother and patted his arm. "Rupert, I will speak to Lord Londringham to see if we can move you soon to Paddock Green, where you will be more comfortable. Together we will get you out of here."

"Yes, but his lordship still faces the task of clearing my involvement with the robbery during the false alarm. I'm not sure how he will do it."

Determined to be cheerful about the best news she had heard in weeks, Patience encouraged her brother. "Don't despair, little brother. His lordship will fix everything. I know."

Rupert suddenly looked to his right, alert at a strange sound. "Patience, you must get out of here. It's not safe. Did you come all the way to the village by yourself?"

At her quick nod, he frowned. "It's much too dangerous.

There are all sorts of outlaws on the road. You must promise me never to put yourself in such precarious circumstances again."

She smiled. "I think it is you we need to worry about. I can take care of myself," she told him assuredly, remembering the fireplace tongs she had hidden in the gig for protection.

"Have a care, and don't come again at night, unless his lordship is with you."

"Yes, master," she said teasingly. "Oh, and here is a piece of plum cake that I stole from the cook. I wasn't confident they would feed you well."

Rupert hungrily seized the package to smell the contents. "Actually his lordship gave the guard an extra bob to see I was well fed."

Another prisoner called to Rupert. "Is that a woman's voice, boy? Send 'er down here when ye've finished with 'er," the disembodied voice sneered.

"You're not fit to touch her shoe, you jackanapes," he returned.

"Sh . . . Rupert, I must leave before your yelling awakes the guard. Take care, dear brother. We'll be home soon." Then she was gone into the night she knew so well, her hood again covering a face warm from the memory of her beloved brother.

Having retrieved Calliope and the gig from the inn, Patience started her journey home, anxious to see Bryce and reveal her identity to him, and perhaps more. The rain was a missing guest and the wind had died down, leaving the forest's home feeling friendlier and safer.

She felt so happy she decided to hum, confident that all would be well. But her song whispered away as she tried to think how to tell Bryce about her brother and how to address the bigger question: why had she maintained this subterfuge? The answer to that was not quite clear in her mind.

Over a particularly hard bump, a muttered oath broke into her musings. Halting the little mare, Patience turned around and swept back the blanket to discover Lem, smiling brightly at her.

"Lem, what are you doing here? You should be home in bed," she admonished the little fellow, trying to appear displeased at his presence.

Lem climbed over the seat to sit beside her. "After last night, I couldn't let ye go off to the village without protection. Remember, I'm a soldier on a mission to provide safe escort home for a lady," he told her with a proud smile.

After such a pretty speech, Patience couldn't stay angry with him. She hugged him with a free hand and whispered, "I'm glad to see you."

They continued on, Patience hurrying Calliope as fast as the small horse would go. The moon's light led them down the village road when suddenly a huge black horse jumped in front of their gig, scaring the little mare and the carriage's occupants. It took several minutes to calm down the horse.

Patience couldn't determine the rider's identity and hoped it might be Bryce out for a midnight ride. But given Lem's frantic grip on her arm, that didn't appear likely.

"Well, isn't this a charming scene? I've been awaiting an opportunity to gain my revenge, and you've so kindly provided me with one."

She thought she recognized the voice, peering into the dark at the man. "Mr. Gibbs?"

"Yes, it is I. Mr. Gibbs, who has spent the last several days with plans to finish your punishment that I never quite started before his lordship interrupted me. And the same for you, little boy," he cooed in a nasally voice to the terrified boy, shaking beside Patience.

"Let me pass, you monster. I will report you to the constable if you lay a hand on myself or Lem," Patience commanded him, her eyes narrowed in bravado. *He will not hurt Lem, not as long as I am alive.*

A thin, shrill voice came from the left of the carriage. "Mr. Gibbs, ye said I was to have the girl, ye only wanted the boy."

"Shut up, old man, I owe her a few bruises first, then you can have her."

Patience fumbled in the back of the gig for her fireplace tongs and held them up to Mr. Gibbs as he reined in his jittery horse. "If you come near here, I shall brain you with this," she roared, in protection of her cub.

"What a little grappler you are. Quit wasting my time. Get down from the carriage now." To make his point clear, Mr. Gibbs drew a revolver from his cloak and pointed it at Patience's heart.

She hesitated. She had nothing to use against his firearm.

Again he issued an order, not a very patient man. "Now, young woman."

The shot came from nowhere, knocking the revolver from Mr. Gibbs's grasp, which caused him to squeal in agony. Blood spurted from his wound in a water rush. Pounding hooves from behind their carriage in the opposite direction signaled the escape of his associate.

Mr. Gibbs pulled a smaller pistol from his chest pocket, aimed at his assailant and fired. Not waiting to see if he hit his target, he pulled his mount around and spun off into the forest's dark embrace.

The past few minutes had passed so quickly, Patience was afraid to move. Was it another highwayman, intent on harming them? Or was it a friend?

His voice came from the side of the carriage. "Hurry home, you should not be out at this time of night without a proper escort."

She grasped the reins in her hands and took deep breaths

to slow her racing heart. "May . . . May I know the name of our champion to thank him properly?"

"You may thank me later," he told her, before he too left them on the deserted road to home. But she knew their defender would see that they made it home safely.

Bryce rested Defiance in the nightshade of the trees, looking for the gig soon to follow him. Damn, that had been close! If he had been a second late, Patience might—he dashed those thoughts from his mind, realizing that saving Patience from various perils occupied more of his time than he had realized and that perhaps next time he might not be so fortunate.

Mr. Gibbs. He should have known the man wouldn't simply disappear. He would have to guard both Patience and Lem from now on, until the constable's men had a chance to track down the culprit. He wouldn't let Patience out of his sight, a duty made bittersweet.

He had decided not to reveal his identity at the carriage. It was most important that Patience come to him with her confession rather than him questioning her on the open road. She would be bound to give him more lies.

What had she been doing in the prison? Perhaps one of the guards could tell him whom she had seen. He was suddenly very resentful of this unknown man who had beget such loyalty in Patience that she would risk her own life and Lem's to see him. And what kind of ogre did she think he was? She had only to ask him for a favor, and he would be hard-pressed to refuse her lovely entreaties, framed in rosy cheeks with full pink lips and a quivering tongue that he longed to explore.

The gig rattled past him, awakening him from his errant thoughts.

* * *

In the morning, the longcase clock tick-tocking in the hallway deafened the still silence in the study. Bryce deliberated by the fireplace, his arm hung over the marble mantel, as he gazed down into the banked embers as if they would spell answers. Although the parlormaid had opened the shutters earlier in the morning, the grayness outside haunted the room with a misty sadness.

He waited for her. Patience. His appointment with the prison guard had provided some insight. Although the man had not noticed a woman slipping into the building, he did detect small mud prints outside Rupert Mandeley's cell this morning, and another prisoner mentioned as how he had overheard voices near Mandeley's cell. But the young man himself was reluctant to tell him anything.

What was she doing in the prison visiting Mandeley? Why were her movements furtive if she was innocent of any wrongdoing? And, blast it all, why didn't she confide in him? Nothing made sense, but that he knew he had to get her away from here.

She would be safer with him in Town. Safer from Mr. Gibbs. Safer perhaps from the French spies he was confident still hid along the coast. He refused to acknowledge his other purpose was to remove Patience far from this Rupert Mandeley, scoffing at any green thoughts. *If they were not lovers, then what was the connection between Patience, Mandeley, and Sansouche? Or was there? If only she would provide some answers.* Bryce pounded his fist on the mantel.

Yes, he acknowledged silently, given Patience's actions so far, he would need to keep a close watch on her in Town while he met with his compatriots. Everything would be perfect between them—if there was not the little matter of distrust between them.

"My lord, you sent for me?" Her husky voice floated across the room, mixed with the scent of lavender. Bryce spun around to be confronted by a demure picture of Patience in a plain gray gown, her remembered thick dark hair swept neatly behind her. For someone who had quite a full night's activities, Bryce noted she looked so refreshed and guiltless that Admiral Nelson himself would divulge his battle secrets at her slightest honeyed gaze.

Patience broke into his musings with a shy smile. "My lord?"

A smile which lit the room from where he stood. He gestured toward a nearby chair and watched as she sank gracefully onto its upholstered seat.

Bryce relaxed against the mantel while he studied her before beginning. *I wonder if she knows she has been caught. What will she reveal to me?* "I mentioned a few days past that I will be journeying to my town house in London with some of my staff. I will still have need of your services there and request you accompany me."

Her reaction was unanticipated. Patience's face turned slightly ashen as she wet her lips nervously. Bryce thought he detected a shine of tears in her green eyes before she looked away. What the devil! Did this Rupert Mandeley mean so much to her that she couldn't bear to leave him? Who was this man that earned her loyalty and her heart? Bryce pondered in frustration. Would that he could ever know such steadfastness in any woman.

"Is this not to your liking? Most of my staff usually enjoys the change," Bryce mentioned, trying to ease what seemed like a painful blow.

When she returned her gaze to him, her face was composed, all anxiety neatly hidden from him behind her paper mask of duty. "I'm only surprised. I wasn't expecting the change. Yes, of course, I'll go with you," she said falteringly.

"Patience, you know me well enough that I wouldn't force you to attend me. But for many reasons that I cannot divulge at this time, I think it best that you make preparations for Town. And you need not wear the cap and spectacles any longer. You will be safe from discovery by your brother with me."

She nodded her acceptance, then retired from the room with Bryce staring after her. He returned his gaze to the fire, disappointment pumping through his veins. She didn't want to go with him and wanted to stay behind. Since it was his utmost desire not to be separated from her, what persuasion could he offer rather than making it a command that she accompany him?

Bryce now found himself arming his wits for battle with this young woman who had proven many a time to be as distrustful as any of her species. Perhaps his wound had affected more than his leg. His senses, indeed. But surely not his heart.

Patience walked slowly toward the kitchen, trying to collect her scattered thoughts that continued to butterfly around in her head. She was traveling to Town. This was good, she would be with Bryce. This was bad, she was leaving Rupert behind. This was good, she could ask Bryce to go with her to the high court to see about releasing Rupert. This was bad, she had lost her heart to a man who would never allow anyone to look into the window of his soul. To a man that needed no one.

Patience set her chin in determination. By the time she was through with him, Bryce would need her. Would not be able to live without her. How she planned to accomplish this, she hadn't the slightest notion.

Chapter 17

Patience breathed in the warm sunshine after yesterday's moody drizzling rain. No thunderstorms either. She had spent a good part of yesterday packing her trunk as well as assisting in packing the rest of the house for supplies needed in Town. The household appeared in a state of confusion as the servants hurried to ready their belongings and house necessities.

Later that evening in the study, she had hoped to speak with Bryce about Rupert, but she hadn't caught sight of him all day, and now she was out of time.

Very early the next morning, Patience stepped into his lordship's carriage. The coat of arms sparkled like gold dewdrops in the sun, its black surface glossied and polished, shining bright enough for reflections. Lucky looked resplendent in his navy-and-gold livery, as did Lem, sitting beside him on the high coachman's box, aping his movements—flicking an imaginary whip and pretending to spit.

Although Londringham brought Defiance along, he surprised Patience by insisting she join him in his carriage for their journey north. Two other smaller coaches conveying the rest of the staff trunks and household goods fell in line behind them.

Just the two of them. Patience was careful to keep her skirts out of Bryce's way. She shyly stole a glance at the man seated across from her. He neither smiled nor frowned but wore the same expression Patience had viewed many a time before, bored indifference. *How to get the trip started off right? When would be the best time to divulge my identity? Will he throw me out of the carriage when I tell him? And why will he not look at me the way he did that night in his room?*

She ventured a topic of conversation, already knowing the answer but hating the silence stretched between them like an acrobat's wire. "My lord, will our trip be long?"

Opening his vest pocket, he withdrew his watch and flipped it open. "Two full days, depending on the roads and the weather. We shall stop overnight along the way."

"Oh, thank you." *What a stupid thing to say. I must think of more clever words to capture his attention. I need an opening to discuss Rupert.* Patience noticed him rub his left leg gingerly.

"Does your wound pain you overmuch?" *Such a dolt! He would not be rubbing it if it did not hurt.* She could have bitten her tongue. Watching his big hand resting on his muscular thigh reminded Patience of other times when he was rubbing her in the most exquisite places. She squirmed slightly in her seat.

He looked up, startled, unconscious of his gesture. "I am accustomed to it now. Sometimes it is a bit stiff. Who told you about my leg, one of the servants?" His sly blue gaze caught Patience's flush.

She rummaged in her small reticule for her fan to cool her meandering thoughts. *Sometimes stiff, eh?* Coughing first to clear her throat and gainsay nervousness, she said,

"Oh, someone mentioned it in passing. Is there naught one can do to spare you the pain?"

His irritability snapped a reply. "I do not wish to discuss my leg."

"My apologies. I only thought . . ." But she trailed off due to the harsh set of his face. *What have I said? Perhaps he was remembering his brother and the dark night the deed was done.* Patience dug her nails into her palms, wanting to reach for him and offer him comfort, erase the dark lines on his lean face.

Bryce, with almost closed eyes, watched her like a cat watching a mouse, Patience thought.

"It certainly is hot in here. Not much of a breeze." He opened his coat and leaned back in his seat. Spreading his long legs in front of him, Patience could feel his boots touching the edges of her traveling gown.

She glanced down at his feet before lifting her eyes to meet his as she flicked her fan faster.

"Yes, so it is. Not much for it, I suppose." *What sparkling wit!* Patience did not like the way he was grinning at her. She could have sworn he just licked his lips like a hungry wolf, and she was his closest meal for miles around. What was on that man's mind?

"Have you been to Town before?" Bryce asked casually, hooking his hands dangerously near his loins, where Patience was trying desperately not to look.

Patience sighed. "No. Yes. That is, I visited as a child with my parents. But I do not remember much about our trip. It was very damp, very dirty, and the noise hurt my ears."

"Will it be very hard for you to leave the country for a time?" Bryce asked.

Was it my imagination or did he place a little stress on the word "hard"? There was that word again. If only she could keep her imagination in hand. He also seemed to be taking

up more than his share of space. Patience looked down to
find herself neatly pinned between two lean muscular
thighs. When she glanced up and caught him staring again,
she blushed and squeaked, "Oh. No, I look forward to
seeing Town. Can you advise how long you plan to remain
in London?"

"As long as it takes," he answered, his hooded eyes closed
from her. "Do you enjoy keeping my books, working under
my authority?"

Under him. She closed her eyes, and a large bed ignited
her imagination. Patience's pulse quickened. *Yes, I like
being under you.* Her eyes snapped open. *Did I say that out
loud?* One look at Bryce assured her he had not heard anything. "Yes, I like keeping your looks, I mean, your books."

He jerked his head up at her words, watching her closely.
"I have been wondering about you, Patience."

Patience's eyes widened in alarm. "Ah, what could you
possibly be wondering about me, my lord?" Perhaps he
would overlook the anxious twisting of her fan tassel.

"You are a lovely young woman. Surely there have been
other men in your past whose hearts you have broken."

Did he seem to lean toward her ever so slightly, waiting
for her answer? She tossed her fan as if to say, *"what a silly
thought,"* then dropped it into his lap, quite by accident, and
sat and stared at it, wondering how to retrieve it. She quickly
told him, "No, no hearts broken, none I can think of,"
sounding awfully flighty. She watched as he rescued her fan
and handed it back to her.

"Interesting, I thought perhaps you were leaving a loved
one behind," he told her, inquiring eyes meeting hesitant eyes.

Her eyes widened in something akin to surprise. Whatever
could he mean? Did he know about Rupert? Should she—

But Bryce did not wait for a reply, almost as if he didn't

want to hear the answer. "Lucky says it might rain tonight." He lazily opened one eye piratically.

Patience almost jumped, her emotions bubbling over like Melenroy's tea kettle. The dam burst with her words as perspiration beaded her brow. "For heaven's sake, would you please stick to one subject? I swear I cannot follow this conversation, and if I had known you were to plague me with questions I would have ridden with the others." With a snap, her fan broke in two.

Bryce drew in his legs and leaned forward to knock on the roof, a signal to stop. "Miss, you have the manners of a shrew." He hesitated and softened his insult by adding, "But you look lovely when you are angry. Is it not hot in here?" And he slammed the door before Patience could fashion a retort.

A few minutes later she heard a horse thunder past the coach. Out the window she saw Bryce's broad back, but soon he was swallowed up by Defiance's dust, and she realized she had lost the opportunity to inquire about Rupert. Her temper could get her into such trouble sometimes.

A day and a half later, the streets of London came into view, houses lined up together like cards, peddlers shilling their wares, and coaches clogging the thoroughfares. In front of his town house in Mayfair, Bryce climbed out of the carriage, favoring his wounded leg, and ignoring the stares of a few lonely street waifs and vendors wheeling their carts home. After making sure that his other coaches were close behind, he strode up the stairs and disappeared behind the door opened to receive him, knowing Patience and his other staff would soon follow.

Red Tattoo greeted Bryce as he entered the hall. Large and opulent it had a brilliant gold chandelier hanging above and a massive iron staircase with two stairwells in an arch leading to the upper floors. Bryce nodded quickly to the few servants standing at attention in the hallway and addressed the short older man with thinning brown hair, who executed a perfect bow.

"Stone, I believe?"

"Yes, my lord. We welcome your return to Wyndham House. I beg your pardon, my lord, we haven't had much notice to open the house. I—" His thin voice sounded a nervous pitch too high.

Bryce waved his hand as if this news was inconsequential. "My staff from Paddock Green has followed me. I will expect you to show them their quarters and their duties."

When Stone moved his jaw to reply, Bryce, with Red Tattoo a step behind, headed for the stairs and the front parlor. Bryce had forgotten how much he missed the brightly painted rooms, his mother's legacy. Although Paddock Green was where he called home, he had not lived in any one place for several years, that is.

Ever since he had begun work for Prime Minister Addington in the early years of England's first war with Napoleon, his assignments had taken him on many covert operations in Europe, Spain, and the Baltics. Since he spoke French, Spanish, and Italian fluently, his services as a master spy served England in good stead.

A year ago, Londringham had begun his most dangerous mission yet. After the Treaty of Amiens was signed between France and Britain, there was a brief span of a volatile peace before the secretary of war, Lord Hobart, delegated Bryce back to France, distrusting Napoleon to keep the treaty's terms.

In this new mission, Bryce had begun a game of wits with three French spies, two men and one woman, all unknown to each other. Each spy passed on information about the enemy's plans on land or sea. The challenge was to discover what was true and what was false.

And so Bryce had walked a tightrope, working hard and fast to uncover the French army's locations and Napoleon's plans for invading England. His excellent sources were able to prove fairly quickly what information would serve England well. The woman spy was actually British and the most effective transmitter of actual latitudes and longitudes.

After Edward's death the prime minister and the secretary of war called him home. His next assignment was to search for the French spies on the British side of the Channel. Lately, the trail had grown cold, especially after Sansouche went up to Town. Soon after, Bryce had been summoned to London to meet with Addington and Hobart.

In the front parlor, Bryce was pleased to see this was one room that had been cleaned, dusted, and polished. He threw off his coat, dusty from travel, and turned to confront his friend and valet.

"I have missed your skinny hide. How have you done?"

Red Tattoo, his face and whiskers as red as the hair on his head, responded, "I have some news. You were correct m'lord, about the Frenchman. It took me two weeks of playin' his shadow—he spends his time and money a-gamblin' and with women, but I think I might have located where he and his friends are meetin'." His valet smacked his rough hands together.

"That is indeed good news, Red. However the PM requires evidence that they act on Boney's orders. If a host of expatriates wish to meet to recall France's grander days, that is no offense against the Crown." He rolled back his less-than-pristine white sleeves and relaxed against the settee's arm.

"Yes, yes, but I see many what look like foreign gents go into this place, but it's down at the docks in an old tavern. I

think it is owned by a Frenchman. I can't get in." Red
rubbed the knot on his head.

"Good work, my friend. We shall find a way to get Sansouche and the rest of his flock of spies and rout them from
here. I just might have something to make Sansouche talk,"
he told Red, remembering the tarnished silver buckle young
Mandeley had given him in prison.

A soft knock on the door forbid the men continuing their
conversation. With permission curtly granted by Bryce,
Stone braved the parlor, tottering in with a teapot and a
bottle of claret on a tray, unsure which refreshment would
please his master most.

"Something to cool your dry palate, my lord?" Stone
proffered hopefully, cups and saucers noticeably rattling.

"Yes, yes, set it down, man. No cause for distress, Stone,
you're doing fine," Bryce said by way of apology for his
abruptness. "Has my staff arrived yet?" his mind on one particular person.

Stone bobbed his head. "They just arrived and everyone
is helping with unloading. The cooks are in the kitchen, my
maids are showing the others where their stations will be,
yes, all is in order, my lord." His proud smile glowed with
his master's praise.

Bryce started to inquire after Patience but decided to look
for her later, assuring himself she needed to acclimate to her
new surroundings. Then maybe they could have that delayed
talk about Mandeley.

He and Red sat down to enjoy the pot of tea whilst explor-
ing plans to infiltrate the Frenchmen's retreat.

An hour later, intervention by Stone again prohibited
further talk. The butler announced the Marquess and
Marchioness of Avecmore. Red Tattoo hopped up and,
with Bryce's slight nod, slipped out the other door that lead
to the library.

Bryce stood to greet his old friends, quickly rolling down his sleeves, retrieving his discarded coat and shrugging it on.

The marchioness marched into the room like a woman with a purpose, dressed all in black but ablaze with light itself. She made a fashionable habit each year of choosing one color for the Season for her entire wardrobe. Her shiny bombazine pelisse, draped snugly over her large, womanly frame, enhanced her silver hair and sparkling sky blue eyes.

The marchioness launched into Bryce's arms, pecking a kiss on both his cheeks. "I'm so glad you've joined us for the rest of the Season. We've missed you so. You never wrote to prepare us!" Her hands moved in constant motion as if she were waving a horse in to win.

Bryce smiled warmly at the woman he knew as Lady Elverston, an old friend and more of a mother to him than he remembered his own to be.

A tall, slender gentleman with light red hair, expertly wielding a gold-tipped cane, followed Lady Elverston at a more sedate pace to greet Bryce. The man, Lord Elverston, gripped Bryce's hand tightly before releasing it.

"Told Lady Gray to allow you to get settled, but she would not hear of it. If you hadn't come to Town, she planned to visit you and assure herself you had not rotted away." He smiled fondly at his wife, now comfortably draped over the lime baize settee.

Bryce offered a chair to Lord Elverston before saying to the marchioness, "I'm certainly happy, madam, that we did not arrive at such drastic measures." He pulled the bell cord for Stone.

Lady Elverston shrugged gracefully. "I mentioned a visit to Lord Elverston, but he never takes me seriously. However, this Season's been such an awful bore, even the country would have made for a pleasant diversion." She faked a yawn.

Bryce nodded in her direction. "Society indeed would be bereft without the pleasure of your company. I feel I must have done a service to all those who wait at your feet for a moment of your attention," he complimented his friend, knowing a store of peers alike fought for the honor of her company. She was well known for her witty repartee and excellent head for advice. He had often envied Lord Elverston for finding such a companionable, loyal, beautiful woman to share his life with.

Lady Elverston granted him a lovely smile. "You're not out of practice with your gallantry, my dear. Even in the primitive country, I'm happy to see you haven't lost your touch."

After Stone delivered another teapot with cakes, Lady Elverston poured, asking Bryce nonchalantly, "Why ever did we sign the treaty? I'm puzzled, Londringham. This Season, all anyone can talk about is when that vile Napoleon will invade our shores. It simply will not do. We hear many of our friends visiting Paris have returned due to persona non grata over there. Does your appearance here have anything to do with that foul Frenchman?" She leaned back on the settee with a graceful elegance as if not in a hurry for an answer.

Bryce took a long swallow of tea and glanced at Lord Elverston before he replied. "No, a little business, nothing more. Actually, madam, it surely was the promise of your presence along with a desire to meet with a few old friends in Parliament."

Lady Elverston nodded absentmindedly. "Always the clever tongue. However, I daresay you will soon be deluged with invitations to the scene. Not many eligible men this Season, I hear many of the young birds complaining."

He straightened in his chair. "I'm not the marrying sort, as I have mentioned before. And with all due respect, I do not believe the *haut ton* has yet forgiven the transgressions of my family."

"Damn," Lord Elverston said, breaking into the conversation, then, nodding to his wife, "Forgive me, my dear. Now, Londringham, Prinny, and the PM are aware of your service to our country as well as your brother's sacrifice, you should be welcomed with open arms anywhere." His rust-colored mustache bristled in agitation.

Bryce's face turned grim, and he stood up to distance himself from his friends.

Lady Elverston called from her perch, "Londringham, listen to Lord Elverston. Your mother and stepfather returned to France's embrace many years ago, nearly seventeen. And you were not responsible for Edward's death. You must not continue to punish yourself for circumstances beyond your control.

"Besides"—she paused—"isn't it about time you settled down and raised a family? Perhaps one of our young stock may interest you. You would certainly liven things up a bit with your handsome face and substantial coffers."

Bryce shook his head and returned to his chair. "I'm afraid I won't be successful in finding a replica of you. And I'm certainly not in the market for a twittering young lady as a wife."

Lord Elverston interjected, "England needs his services. Plenty of time to think about getting a wife after we deal with the Little Corporal. I envy the peace and quiet he must have without one."

His wife seemed unperturbed by his last remark and, totally ignoring him, continued, "You need someone to make you happy."

"He already has a dog," her husband mumbled to himself.

They heard a soft knock on the parlor doors. When Bryce ordered entry, he was surprised to see Patience in the doorway.

His eyes feasted on her quiet loveliness in dove gray which accented her pale-pink cheeks. He stood to greet her as she shyly crossed the room to his side.

"My lord, please forgive my intrusion, but this note was just delivered by messenger who insisted that it was of the utmost urgency. Mr. Stone is handling a situation in the kitchen." Patience looked up into Bryce's eyes as she relayed her story.

"Very good." He reached out his hand to catch the note and briefly held her soft hand before releasing it. "I will talk with you later," he told her in an undertone.

With a graceful curtsy, Patience quitted the room, leaving behind her lavender scent he knew so well. Obtaining permission from his guests, he broke the seal on the missive, which revealed a request by the prime minister for an immediate appointment tomorrow morning.

Bryce shoved the note into his desk drawer and smiled at his companions, indicating nothing was amiss. After Lord Elverston inquired after Paddock Green's inhabitants and those they shared familiarity with in Kent, Lady Elverston asked, "Who was that lovely woman with the note? I cannot believe she is a servant, for she carries herself as one of the nobility. In fact, she does remind me of someone, but I cannot say who."

Bryce uttered, "She is my house steward."

Lady Elverston surprised Bryce with more interrogation regarding the young woman. "Why does she work for you? Does she not have a home?"

Bryce wearily rubbed his brow, disliking this line of questioning and unwilling to educate his friend about Patience. Never before had Bryce been reluctant to discuss anything with Lady Elverston, except for his work. "My butler hired her at the Mop Fair because she said she needed a job."

Fortunately, his friend dropped the subject, but Bryce had

a feeling this was not the last he would hear about the matter of the lovely Patience.

Patience yawned while unbuttoning her gray cotton gown, silently thanking the butler that she had her own little room at the top of the house. Small though it might be, she was becoming quite accustomed to small bedrooms. Except for delivering the note to him, she had not seen Bryce since arriving at his town house.

How could she get his attention? Mention in passing that she is Patience Mandeley, and that it was her brother Rupert that has been wrongly imprisoned? If Bryce was to ask why she hadn't mentioned this before, it was simply because she had suspected he was the French spy framing her brother. Simple. *At this news,* Patience thought wryly, *he is bound to fall at my feet and promise undying love—or else throw me out of his house and his life.*

"Psst . . . Psst."

She whirled around to find Lem peeping through the bedroom door, and so turned back to quickly button up again. She walked to the door. "What are you doing here? Melenroy is sleeping across the hallway," she whispered.

Lem scooched into the room between the door and doorjamb. "Just thought ye would want to know. 'is lordship is goin' out for the evening." He raised his eyebrows up and down knowingly.

Patience frowned in exasperation. "Whatever are you saying, Lem? His lordship probably plans to visit his club or whatever gentlemen do when they are in Town." Unfortunately, Patience reminded herself, he could also be visiting the countess for auld lang syne. Not wanting to examine the welt of sadness this thought struck, she dismissed it from her mind. *Not now. Not now.*

Lem shook his head impatiently, his brown eyes open
wide. "No, I 'eard Stoney-face ordered a carriage and 'e's
takin' Red Tattoo with 'im."

Patience hesitated, then she let out a long breath of air,
unaware she had been holding it. She wearily rubbed her
brow. It had been quite a long day already. Wherever did his
lordship find the energy to do this spying work? "I do not
suppose you heard where they are headed?" she asked
almost hopefully.

"Nope. But I did 'ear sumthin' about that French fellow
what was with Mrs. Hoity-Toity," Lem told her, referring to
the countess.

Patience knelt down and grabbed Lem's arms gently.
"You mean Sansouche?"

Lem nodded eagerly. "That be 'im. They'r goin' to find
'im," he announced seriously, proud of the information he
could impart.

Patience's exhaustion flew away with the night wind.
They planned to capture Sansouche! And on her first night
in London!

She wanted to be there when they declared Rupert innocent of treason and their cousin's murder. Could she? Dare
she? By St. George, she had every right, after all she had
been through. And she was sure Bryce would have invited
her along if he knew the truth about her identity.

She bit her lip, trying to decide a course of action. "How
much time do I have?"

The little footboy crinkled up his face in thought.
"Lucky's hitching the carriage."

"I must try." She faced Lem and instructed him, "Ten
minutes is all I need. If they look to be leaving sooner, can
you try to stall them?"

Lem squared his shoulders, prepared to do battle for his

lady fair. "Miss, I will do me very best. What is it ye plan'n?"

"I shall go with them, of course," Patience told him confidently, already searching for a pair of her younger brother's old breeches and shirt she had thrown in the trunk she'd brought from Storrington.

Lem pulled on her sleeve. "But ye can't. It's too dangerous."

Patience smiled at her little protector. "No need to worry, Lem. His lordship will make sure no harm comes to me."

He thought hard, then nodded in agreement.

Patience's "Hurry, Lem" sent him on his way to track down the master and his valet.

Dressed in disguise with a low black hat pulled down half-hiding her face and all of her hair, Patience looked back longingly at her bed. Knowing she was infinitely safer in bed, she reflected that if all cowards hid in their beds, the world could never be saved.

Twenty minutes later, the hired coach rumbled down Park Lane in Mayfair, heading toward the docks. The two men inside never noticed the figure slipping onto the back of the carriage on the footman's perch.

Chapter 18

"I shall have Lucky stop at Harrigan's Point. According to my calculations, we'll only be a few blocks from the Lion's Coeur. You are certain, tonight they meet?" Bryce's eyes narrowed in speculation.

Red Tattoo's small head bobbed vigorously as Bryce leaned back against the seat in satisfaction. The evening air blew cool as they passed fewer and fewer night owls the closer they drew to the docks. Bryce's man had never been wrong yet. Flexing his hands encased in black leather gloves, Bryce remarked, "They are an impetuous lot, meeting right underneath the king's nose."

"Aye, and when we find them, they'll wish they never left France!" The valet's enthusiasm broke over his face in a smile missing several teeth.

Bryce appreciated Red's loyalty to a country not his own. Their task to rout the spies had proven as difficult as uncovering Patience's secrets, he thought to himself. He had had every intention of finding Patience today to discuss her situation, but time had slipped away in planning their mission tonight.

She had to know her subterfuge must come to an end.

Only then could she come to no harm, and he would know the truth. She must be sleeping by now, exhausted from their long journey.

He imagined her long, lustrous hair flowing gently down her back as she slept fitfully on her side. Long lashes decorated her milky skin tinted peach. And her full mouth, strawberry red, opened slightly. *"Keep her safe,"* he had demanded, remembering his orders to Stone, his footmen, and even Lem, to maintain a watch on his precious steward.

Bed. A nice thought and where she should be, Patience grumbled to herself as she held tight to the swaying coach. She stared straight ahead, the night air chilling her through her thin coat, her focus committed to Lucky. A backward glance from the groomsman would depose her and greatly anger the man inside the carriage.

Her heart thumping loudly in her ears, she swallowed hard. What was she afraid of as long as Bryce was near? She knew instinctively he would save her if she came into any danger. But then who would save her from his assured wrath if he discovered her presence?

Patience listened to the clicking carriage wheels and the voices of dancers, weary from exertion on the ballroom floor, as the coaches carried them home. Thirty minutes later, Patience began to smell the stench of the docks, the river breeze helping to scatter the vile odors of human waste and garbage.

Where were they headed? As the coach rattled down one narrow lane after another, Patience began to regret her impetuousness. She should have left these matters in his lordship's very capable hands. But she had to do *something* to help Rupert. And that meant capturing the Frenchman. It was the only way.

The carriage came to a rocking stop and Bryce quickly climbed down, instructing Lucky where they'd meet. Tipping his tall hat, Lucky touched the horse's back lightly with the whip. The sound of squeaky carriage springs vanished into the rest of the evening's sounds of stevedores unloading cargo, while sailors and the King's navy enjoyed a bit of frivolity and drinking along the wharf.

Red led the way through a maze of warehouses and taverns lining the busy docks. Bryce's large form overshadowed his smaller companion as they hurried deeper and deeper into the unsavory part of the city, where who knew what sort of culprit watched in the pockets of darkness surrounding them.

Finally, Red halted abruptly and pointed down the cobblestone street to a small, dimly lit doorway. No sign outside announced the tavern, frequent customers did not need directions. The simple wooden entryway connected to a larger stone warehouse.

As they circumnavigated the building to the back, Bryce and Red heard voices but couldn't make out their conversation. Red pointed up, where Bryce noticed a dirty window slightly raised for ventilation. The voices sounded louder but still no words could be discerned.

Bryce told Red in a hushed tone, "The window looks like the only way in." He scanned the rest of the building and devised a plan. He had assumed they would only bring attention to themselves entering the tavern in the normal fashion and would probably not be able to get close enough to hear anything.

He stepped around a huge pile of refuse and to the side of the tavern, where he noticed a ladder leading up to the wooden roof. Bryce motioned to Red to join him, and, one after the other, they climbed the aged ladder. Once on the roof, they crept to the back side of the tavern and peered over the edge. Still not close enough. Bryce decided that the only way to hear was to lower himself down to the window, using a rope anchored to Red's waist.

When his valet untied the rope he carried over his shoulder, Bryce reached for it. But Red danced out of his reach. "I'm lighter, I'll go."

"Nothing doing. I'm going."

Normally, Red would brook no argument with Bryce, but the valet hastened to tie the hemp rope tightly around his waist and handed the end to Bryce.

Bryce thought to change his valet's mind. "How is your French, *mon ami?*"

"*Magnifique.* Better than yours," Red told him with a toothless grin, then climbed onto the wooden ledge.

Bryce looped the rope around the brick chimney for leverage, and pulled it a few feet across so that he could brace his legs against the roof's edge, leveraging his good leg to hold the majority of Red's weight. When he signaled Red to descend, his body jerked with the hard pull of the rope against the demands of Red's body as the tight cord bit into Bryce's gloves.

At intervals, Bryce lengthened the line of rope to assist Red in his descent. When he thought Red close to the window, he leaned over the edge to whisper to his friend dangling in the wind, "Can you hear what they are saying?"

Red looked up into Bryce's face, the starless sky behind him. "Sansouche, I know his voice. He's talking with someone but I can't tell, I think maybe it's a woman." He glanced back at the window. "She's leaving. The Frenchman is now talking with the others. There are maybe twenty men or so." Red returned to staring in the window.

A few minutes passed before Red looked up again. "I hear a little more. The invasion! Soon?"

Bryce gritted his teeth, his valet's weight working on the

muscles in his sore leg. "Where? I need something more. Do you see anyone you recognize? What did the woman look like?"

A door banged closed beneath them just then.

"What's happening?" Bryce asked urgently.

Red frowned, his hands gripped the rope tightly above his head. "They've stopped talking. Someone is pointing to the window. I think someone may have seen me."

"Climb up, we need to move," Bryce called down to him.

Bryce heard only a click of a pistol cocked before a powerful force knocked him down on the roof, and the bullet's whistle pierced the air dangerously close over his head.

Well trained, Bryce pulled his own pistol free and shot at the dark figure across the rooftop. He heard a sharp cry and saw the villain disappear over the roof's ledge.

Red! When Bryce had hit the roof, the rope had unfurled from his hands, snaked free from the chimney, and dropped his friend several feet toward the ground. Bryce limped over to the edge of the roof and was relieved to see Red crawling off a thick pile of smelly refuse at the back of the building. His valet signaled to Bryce he was safe.

Bryce winced as he drew himself up, his knee bruised from the jolt to the hard surface. Who had pushed him and saved his life?

A figure in black lay motionless a few feet away. He inched his way down the roof and turned the body over. Even without the moon's help, he would have recognized the treasured features of Patience. Unconscious, she had probably hit her head when she pushed him out of the way. He breathed a sigh of relief after detecting a slight pulse in her neck and saw the gentle rise and fall of her chest.

He had to get her out of here. Not much time. Already he could hear footsteps underneath him and on the street. Bryce swiftly decided the ladder would take too long and glanced around the rooftop searching for another means of escape. The next building over had a connecting roof.

Bryce carefully lifted Patience in his arms and transferred her to his shoulder. With heart pumping and his leg pulsing in pain, he made his way across to the other building and found a door that led down into another tavern.

He carried her down the stairs until they came to a narrow hall lined with doors. With no one in sight, Bryce pulled Patience off his shoulder and hugged her next to him, holding her up by the waist. He made sure her hat still covered her hair and her features before carrying her down to the public room.

Making his way across the crowded room, Bryce heard an inebriate call out, "What's wrong with your drinking partner? Not used to our hard ale?"

Bryce smiled good-naturedly and nodded. "He's rather young and untried with spirits. His mother will surely box his ears after tonight's adventures. If you'll excuse me, gentlemen, I must get the drunken sot home."

The inebriate, his friends, and the tavern owner bid Bryce and his companion a good night. Outside, Red met them around the corner before Bryce shouldered Patience again in order to better their escape. They waited in a darkened sanctuary while several pairs of feet ran by them and overhead, hearing plenty of swearing, yelling, and huffing, all in French.

Then Bryce did what he did so well, something that had saved his life more than once. He molded his body to become one with the night, carrying the slight weight of Patience's still form. His only thought was to see her to safety. Her reasons for being out at the Frenchmen's retreat he would discover later.

Red followed his master through the anthills of the docks, through boroughs and lanes, which Bryce knew blindfolded after ten years of spying for the British Crown. When they were several blocks away from the wharf, Bryce paused to rest in the darkness and turned to his faithful friend. "Even if I couldn't see you, I can smell you. I hope our enemies do not follow your scent to us," he joked upon noticing spoiled soup remains and rotten eggs decorating Red's ruined black coat.

Red pointed to Patience. "Who might ye got there?"

"Actually, it's my missing house steward and my rescuer."

"The girl? Is she dead?"

"No, I think she must have hit her head. I saw no signs of bleeding, but I must get her home quickly."

Red found Lucky waiting for them at the prearranged spot, and the carriage lumbered away to a safer place for the two men and one brave young woman clasped tightly in Bryce's arms.

When Patience woke the next morning, she blinked away sleep in confusion over finding herself in a half-tester bed in an unfamiliar bedchamber. A nauseating headache pounded her temples as she squinted at the frieze of Grecian figures expertly carved in the cornice of the ceiling. The sun brazened through the slight gap in the curtains, lighting the lovely room of pale blue.

Where am I? She uttered a soft moan. Thinking hurt too much. She heard a chair creak and looked across the bed to find Bryce's deep blue eyes watching her with concern. He looked terrible, as if he had not slept all night.

Suddenly, her adventure from last night flooded back into her consciousness. Her well-intentioned but misguided plan to help Bryce capture Sansouche for her brother. Up on the roof. The man with the pistol, pointed at Bryce. She remembered pushing him out of the way, surprise on her side.

She looked up to see him standing by the bed. "The physician said when you woke, your head would probably still ache," he told her, his voice pleasantly soft.

Patience felt pricking pain behind her eyes. She shook her head. In a husky, thick voice, she asked, "What am I doing here? What is this room?"

Bryce continued to stare down at her. "You saved me from a bullet last night and were rewarded for your efforts with a knock on the head from your fall. You are now in one of the guest chambers. I thought it would be more comfortable for you and offer more privacy."

Patience managed a soft "oh" in reply.

He then added, "The physician left medicine—" But his patient had already slipped back into the welcoming web of sleep.

Something tickled her nose. Soft and fluffy. Patience sighed and rolled over on her back, batting at the offending method of torture which had disturbed her slumber.

It wouldn't go away. She pried open one eye to discover the identity of her torturer. Lem.

He waved a long white feather in front of her nose, then leaned over to whisper loudly in her ear, "Are ye awake yet, miss?"

Both her eyelids reluctantly pushed back the shutters of sleep to find Lem's concerned face hovering inches from her own.

"I am now, you little fiend. How did you get in here?" Patience asked sleepily before pulling herself up into a sitting position. Her head protested only slightly in pain.

Lem climbed onto the big bed, swinging his feet over the side. "I sneaked in when the old lady insisted 'is lordship get some rest. 'e's been in 'ere watching ye for ever so long, even the doc said ye'd be fine. I guess 'e wanted to make sure."

Bryce was here, caring for her? She must look a sight. *Woman thy name is vanity.* Glancing down Patience was horrified to find she still wore her brother's shirt and breeches from her recent escapade. *Not exactly an enticing, fetching appearance,* she thought wryly.

"How long have I been sleeping?"

Lem cocked his head in thought, then replied, "About a day or so, I think. Melenroy an' Lucky 'as been asking about ye. Even Stoney-face seems concerned. It's morning, ye 'aven't eaten in over a day, ain't ye hungry?"

"Yes, I think my appetite has returned, and I'm feeling ever so much better. I shall rise and go to the kitchen to assure Melenroy I am again with the living," Patience jested to the boy. *I wonder if I still have employment with his lordship,* she thought despairingly.

Bryce would want answers. And he deserved them. Branding herself a coward, she feared reprisals upon him learning the truth.

A knock on the door startled them. Lem leapt off the bed to hide behind the door. Patience's heart beat a rapid dance. *Was it he?*

"C-come in," she called faintly, wiping her long knotty hair out of her face and patting it down.

It was the older woman Patience had seen in the parlor with Bryce. Her heart sank, yet she sighed in relief. Out of the corner of her eye, Patience saw Lem scoot around the door after the woman walked over to her bed. Stone followed with a painted teapot and a plate of rolls and toast on a tray, which he placed on a nearby table. He inquired politely after Patience's health, then departed.

Lady Elverston's soft blue eyes brimmed with concern as she studied Patience. Her voice was as pleasant as her graceful demeanor. "I'm glad to see you awake, my dear. I hope you don't think my visit intrusive. I promised Bryce I would look in on you. It was the only way he would get a bit of rest. I thought you might wish for something to eat, if you felt up to it. How are you feeling?"

Patience stared at the woman dressed in fashionable mourning clothes and wet her dry lips. "My head still pains me a bit. I don't believe we have been properly introduced. I'm Patience Simmons. Might I inquire your name?"

The older woman offered a warm smile. "I'm an old friend of Lord Londringham, Lady Elverston. My husband and Londringham have served the House together for several years."

Patience's ears pricked up at this news. This woman knew Bryce. Perhaps she would prove to be an ally for Patience.

Lady Elverston drew up a chair to enfold herself in the welcome glow of Patience's candle. Her bedroom was cozy but dark since the grayness of the morning offered little light through the open curtains. "You're a very brave woman to have saved Bryce's life as you did. He told me how you came to have the bump on your head."

Patience could not hide her astonishment. Bryce had confided in this woman? What else had he told his friend about her? With her kind face, it would certainly be easy to unburden her heart to Lady Elverston.

Accepting a cup of tea, Patience steadied her gaze on the woman. "Hopefully, the blow to my head knocked me sensible, and this logic I shall call upon in the future before attempting any more impulsive acts." The hot tea soared down her throat, a welcome shot of heated energy to her well-being.

Lady Elverston pursed her lips before replying to Patience's self-denigration. "In my years of experience, such impulsive actions as you have described benefit the most noble of causes. I shudder to think what may have happened to his lordship if you had not been there to save him."

Patience gritted her teeth. She had a sinking feeling that she may have been the reason for both the causing and the saving of the almost tragedy, imagining that the pistol-wielding man had caught sight of her climbing the ladder and followed her to the rooftop and thus to Bryce.

Lady Elverston continued, "Dear, we weren't sure how hard you had hit your head, although the physician assured us a few days' rest would make you fit and ready for dancing." She drew off her gloves, prepared for a longer chat.

Patience frowned. "In my position as his lordship's house steward, there is not much call for dancing. I hope I'm not inconveniencing his lordship by my indisposed condition."

"Nonsense," Lady Elverston piped up heartily. "We have him right where we want him."

"We . . . we do?" Patience frowned, wondering what this woman had in mind.

"Yes, I want to speak to you about this adventure of yours. If you feel well enough, I wanted to know what you were doing in the middle of the night following his lordship."

Patience dipped her head to examine the white counterpane more closely. She hadn't expected an inquisition from this quarter. Suddenly she felt very tired and overwhelmed. Tears welled in her eyes and dripped onto the back of her hand. Dimly, she heard Lady Elverston's silky swish of her gown as she rushed to her side.

"My poor girl, please forgive me. I'm simply an awful nuisance! I didn't mean to cause you distress. I don't know what I was thinking." Her weight sank the mattress on one side as she took Patience's cold hand between her warm ones.

"I shall leave, and disturb you no longer. You owe me no explanations. Would you like the medicine for your head?"

Patience practically dissolved into more tears at the warm

sincerity of Lady Elverston's words. When the older woman started to pull away, Patience clung all the more tightly to the lifeline the marchioness had unwittingly given her.

"What can I do?" Her soothing voice floated over Patience like a warm bath perfumed with her favorite bath salts. And the motherly figure simply gathered the weeping Patience into her arms for several minutes, providing the younger woman with a portal in a storm.

Neither noticed the door open quietly nor saw Lord Londringham's face in the shadows as he watched the unfolding scene with interest. It grieved him to note that he was not needed, and that Patience would rather seek solace from a strange woman than come to him. He left as quietly as he had arrived, alone with his thoughts.

Patience sat comfortably against the mountain of pillows at her back, her cup drained, her hunger assuaged. Lady Elverston's exquisitely laced handkerchief was crumpled damply in her hand.

Lady Elverston had ignored Patience's concerns over her rumpled dress. Nothing that a hot iron couldn't fix.

She shook her head in amazement. "So you're Miss Patience Mandeley, the sister of Baronet Mandeley? Do I understand that for the past few weeks you've posed as a maid and steward in the hopes of uncovering your cousin's murderer and setting your brother free?"

Patience nodded hesitantly.

"And you thought his lordship was a French spy?"

Again, Patience nodded, her lips turned down in distress at her errors of misjudgment about the earl's character.

The older woman leaned over to rub Patience's shoulders. "Hmmm. Your shoulders feel rather thin. Certainly not strong enough to take on all these responsibilities. And your other three brothers, they allowed you to play this dangerous charade?"

Plucking at the handkerchief, Patience paused before replying. "Actually, I didn't mention to them about my employment with his lordship. They believed I was staying with our cousin Carstairs while I cleared Rupert's name."

Lady Elverston kept shaking her head in disbelief. "I have never heard of such a story. Such loyalty for your brother. And when did you discover Lord Londringham was not responsible for your brother's troubles?"

"When I spoke to my brother in prison, and he informed me that his lordship was trying to help him by finding the real culprit."

Lady Elverston warmed to the story. "By his lordship's presence in Town can I assume that the real culprit is here in London?"

"Yes, we both believe that the leader of the spy ring and my cousin's murderer is a man called Sansouche, a cousin of his lordship's ex-mistress. We had hoped to catch him the other night."

The marchioness's blue eyes reflected greater understanding. "You followed his lordship because you have a stake in the outcome of this entire affair?"

The two women looked at each other in comprehension before the older woman continued, "And how much does Lord Londringham know about your family and your brother?"

Patience found every place in the room to look other than at her new-found friend, and every reason to prevaricate. "I have been meaning to have a word with Lord Londringham, but the time has not seemed right."

Lady Elverston shook her head. "I think now might be a good time to explain yourself, especially since Lord Londringham is indebted to you for saving his life."

Patience's flushed face hinted disagreement. "I'm not

sure I saved his life. He looked up when the hammer was cocked, he probably would have saved himself."

Lady Elverston patted her hand. "Ah, you're too quick to dismiss your credit. Tell me, what did you think before you pushed a man off his feet who is three times your size?"

"There wasn't time to think or feel. I only had to act and did so out of fear."

"Fear of what?"

Thrusting a bothersome strand of hair from her eyes, Patience replied excitedly, "That Lord Londringham might be killed! I had to help him."

"Listen, my girl. Has it occurred to you that by pushing him out of the way, you could have taken the bullet yourself?"

Patience stared at Lady Elverston in astonishment.

The marchioness continued, leaning against the headboard, "Now, I ask myself, why would someone save another's life at the risk of their own? I suppose there are a number of reasons but one is rather obvious."

Patience stammered, her heart hammered to be free. "Obvious reason?" She stared bewildered at Lady Elverston.

"Could you possibly in the time you have spent with his lordship developed a *tendre* for him?"

Patience was shocked into silence and not ready to divulge the secret of secrets so close to her heart. "I have to admit, at first I thought him a handsome but treasonous blackguard responsible for the death of my cousin and sending the law after Rupert. When I came to spy on him, I learned he wasn't at all what I thought he was. He's been kind to me and my brother. I feel gratitude for him, nothing more."

If the marchioness remained unconvinced, she wisely refrained from disagreeing. "You say you wish to help Lord Londringham find this murderous French spy?"

Patience nodded, anxious to hear what Lady Elverston had to say.

"In order to learn any information, you must travel in certain circles. Your apprenticeship as steward will never do. We must present you in Society as Miss Patience Mandeley. You actually may be able to assist his lordship with his investigation."

Stunned by this announcement Patience's features froze. She even thought she had stopped breathing. She squeaked, "I am to be introduced into Society? But what will Lord Londringham say when he learns of my identity? He'll be angry with me, I know he'll send me home."

Lady Elverston shushed Patience. "It will certainly be entertaining to find out. But first, I don't want you to reveal your true identity or he might not approve of my plan."

Patience's eyes grew round in apprehension. "What plan?"

"We need to buy you a new wardrobe. Perhaps a few dancing lessons. We must have you ready by next week for Lady Leeds's Grand Ball."

Patience furrowed her brow. "I still don't understand."

"We'll surprise Lord Londringham. Right now he thinks of you as a servant, his steward. He needs to see you as one of his own before he notices you."

Ah, he certainly has noticed me, Patience thought, remembering one recent night, but she didn't offer this comment to Lady Elverston.

The older woman gracefully climbed off the bed. "I must get home, dear. I shall return tomorrow. Remember not a peep to you-know-who." She waved her forefinger playfully. "I think I'm forgetting something. Ah, yes, you'll need a chaperone. You cannot stay in this house with an unattached man. Let me see. I know, I will send you Miss Martha Krebs.

A distant cousin of mine. She is a spinster with a delightful furry cat. I am sure you will get on divinely."

"Wait." Patience needed to forestall the woman, her mind spinning with what she'd heard the past few minutes. "But what about my duties as a steward to his lordship?"

Instantly, Lady Elverston paused at the door with a mischievous smile. "You leave the earl to me." Patience could hear the marchioness down the hall talking to herself.

"Now where have I heard the name Mandeley before?"

Bryce watched Lady Elverston's carriage from the front parlor on the first floor drive off with Patience and her new companion, Miss Martha. It had been three days since the disaster on the docks. The prime minister was anxious for news of the French spies' plans for an invasion, and for confirmation that all was safe and quiet along the southeast coast.

News which, at the moment, was impossible to deliver. Bryce had had Red Tattoo following Sansouche again, knowing the spies would be seeking a new meeting place. He gripped the back of his chair, ready to toss it across the room. They couldn't afford many delays. If only Red had learned something more the other night, such as where the invasion was to take place, and when.

England was on the brink of invasion, and a young man was wrongly imprisoned, who would soon be sentenced to hang for murder and treason if Bryce did not catch the real criminal in time.

Then there was Patience. He had barely seen her since that night she had saved his life. Every morning, Lady Elverston's carriage picked up Patience and Martha from the front step, and he didn't see them for the rest of the day.

Bryce kept busy in the House of Lords or with other

members of Parliament or at the secretary of war's offices while continuing to hunt for the spy ring.

Although Bryce was certainly glad of Lady Elverston's interest in Patience, he would have preferred having Patience in the house where he could watch over her and make sure she was safe. At least, that is the reason he gave himself for the disappointment he felt at watching the carriage disappear on a daily basis. He did feel relieved she had suffered no lasting ill effects from their adventure.

And that chaperone Lady Elverston had insisted sending over to stay with them. Miss Martha Krebs. A pleasant yet somber woman with a vicious black cat. Just what Bryce needed if he was superstitious: more bad luck.

If only he could speak with Patience. There was still too much unsaid between them. Perhaps she *wanted* to avoid him.

He couldn't stop thinking about the other night when he had brought her home unconscious. The longest night he could remember. Only one other night in his existence had he felt such helplessness. The night his brother had been killed. His emotions warred between wanting to shake her awake for placing her own life in danger and praying that she would sleep peacefully and suffer no lasting consequences of her impetuous brave act.

He ran a hand over his face. *What was he to do with her? Why had she followed him? Why had she saved him?* Although it was early in the morning, Bryce rang for spirits, wanting to feel fire burn his throat. Perhaps too it would ease the pain in his leg, still aching from the stress of carrying Patience through the streets over his shoulder. As he pulled away from the window, Bryce thought, *It looks like rain.* A mountain of paperwork sat on his desk awaiting his attention.

* * *

Patience followed Lady Elverston and Martha out of the salon owned by Madame Montreax, a modiste renowned for her ability to recreate French fashions expertly, quickly, and discreetly. If Madame Montreax thought it odd that a whole new wardrobe—including pelisses, hats, gloves, gowns, and undergarments—was needed in rather an extreme urgency, she was well paid for keeping her curiosity to herself.

Down the street a brightly colored poster arrested Patience's attention outside the post office, where she stopped in to mail a brief note she had written to her brothers at home. Captain Culhane's "amazing, eye-popping, heart-pounding, a-thrill-a-minute circus" was coming to Town, the same circus that performed at the Mop Fair, where she had first met both his lordship and Sally, whose aunt was a tightrope walker. Patience wondered with a smile whether the child still had Lord Londringham's doll intact.

With the assistance of a footman, Patience climbed into the carriage after Lady Elverston and Martha. Settled comfortably, Patience began, "Lady Elverston, you've been so kind to me these last few days, but I fear I have done nothing to warrant your good will, and I don't know when I can ever repay you for these beautiful things."

Her older friend graciously dismissed Patience's gratitude and concern. "My girl, don't think about repaying me now. It's such a pleasure to watch you turn into a butterfly. Those drab colors you wore before were simply an insult. Now, as for tonight. I think what I should like would be for you to accompany Lord Elverston and me, and, of course, Martha, to Lady Leeds's ball. This will be your first taste of the Season. I mean for you to make your mark." She leaned back against the seat with a satisfied expression on her face.

Patience bit her lower lip in consternation. "Is it not true that young girls have a Season in order to find a husband? I'm certainly not a green girl out of school, and I'm not seeking a husband. I also fear his lordship's wrath when he learns my identity." She finished with a whisper. "I feel my courage deserting me."

Martha sat in the corner of the coach petting her cat, Satan. She looked at Patience in surprise. "You don't wish to marry? Every girl wants to be married and looked after the rest of her life. Have children."

And be loved, Patience thought.

Lady Elverston held up her hand to halt their conversation. "Enough of this talk. Patience, I believe the man you seek will be at the ball tonight, a certain Frenchman? Surely, that should sway your hesitation. Buck up, my girl, you can't quit now. I'm depending on you to save me from dying of boredom for the rest of the Season," she told her young companion with a warm smile. "No more talk of husbands, agreed?"

Chapter 19

Patience kept her eyes closed at Lady Elverston's request until her gown was carefully placed over her coiffed hair and smoothed over her shoulders and hips. Martha, with help from Lady Elverston's maid, Eloise, pulled and tugged everything into place before they shepherded Patience to the looking glass near the dressing table and instructed her to look.

Lady Elverston watched as Patience admired her gown and accoutrements, but then saw a look of bewilderment cross the young woman's face.

Patience put a shaking hand to her neck. "Are you sure there is not a piece to this gown that is missing?"

Eloise smothered a laugh behind her hand and was instantly dismissed. Lady Elverston stood behind Patience to look at the masterpiece she had created. From the tips of her light-pink slippers to the top of her dark hair sparkling with two diamond combs, Patience was beautiful in her sugar-white velvet gown with pink hues. Many women tonight would envy the snowy perfection of her shoulders and that face, which needed no cosmetics to enhance nature. And no artifice could manufacture the innocent excitement shimmering in those lovely hazel eyes heightened by the soft blush of her cheeks.

She was a masterpiece. Now, if only one man would see her as she truly was—and not as a maid or steward but as an equal, worthy of his attention—Lady Elverston would humor Lord Elverston and retire her matchmaking apprenticeship.

"My dear, it's actually less revealing than it seems. Come, we must go," she whispered in Patience's ear.

Patience sighed and turned toward the door, following in Lady Elverston's wake.

Red Tattoo watched his lordship tie his own cravat. Indeed, there was not much call for Red's services as a valet. Red figured the man was used to doing for himself. Truth be told, Red was more a friend and companion than a servant.

Bryce turned to face his man. "I haven't the least notion why I have acquiesced in Lady Elverston's request for me to attend the Leeds's ball tonight. These affairs are such a bloody bore." His expression dark, he remembered days past when he and his brother spent their London evenings frequenting their clubs for late-night card games.

It was at a ball such as this, given by Lady Leeds, where Edward and he first saw Miranda. *A beautiful vision in winter white with impossibly bright golden hair. She looked the part of an angel. Who could tell that frost lay not only on her gown but also in her heart? But that was a long time ago, and I have appreciated the lessons she taught me about the untrustworthiness of the female race.*

"My lord, this night'll be different. Remember, Sansouche will be attend'n with the countess," Red reminded him.

Bryce's eyes narrowed at the thought of seeing his ex-mistress and the French spy at this affair. Unfortunately, Red and he had been unable to discover the French spies' latest meeting place.

Red continued, "You may have luck and learn somethin' from him about Lord Carstairs's murder."

Bryce shrugged into his evening coat. "Perhaps, but at least I'll have him under my scrutiny if he does want to start any trouble. Remember to follow him when he leaves tonight."

Red nodded as Bryce strode out his bedroom door.

Accepting his cane, hat, and gloves from Stone and Lem waiting at the front door, Bryce asked Stone, "Have you seen Miss Simmons anytime today? Should I be concerned over her absence and Miss Martha's, or is she in the company of Lady Elverston?" He raised his eyebrows expectantly, showing a master's concern with his servant's whereabouts.

Stone replied perfunctorily, "I believe the latter to be true, my lord. Enjoy your evening, my lord."

Bryce nodded and swept out the door toward his carriage where Lucky awaited him. If Patience was with Lady Elverston, and Lady Elverston was at the ball, then that would place Patience at the ball. *This evening bodes ill,* he thought, as his carriage rolled down the gleaming wet street and a spring rainfall hushed the night to sleep.

Lord and Lady Elverston, Miss Patience Mandeley, and Miss Martha Krebs waited on the landing for their introductions before proceeding into the ball.

Lady Elverston stroked her black-and-white boa trapped across her neck while she stared at the assembly. She then leaned over to pinch Lord Elverston's arm. "I told you we were much too early. And I don't see any sign of Lord Londringham. Suppose he shan't come?" The pleasure she planned for this evening was on the verge of slipping away.

"Calm down, Lady Gray. If Londringham told you he would be here, then the man will be here. I hear them announcing our names."

After the introductions, Patience followed Lord and Lady Elverston down the stairs in the best imitation of a feather floating on air. Concern still lingered over the unplanned display of more of her feminine charms than she desired.

Her Grace, the Duchess of Leeds, was held in high acclaim by Society, and her soirees were always a crush. She loved to entertain and although her town house could accommodate only a small number in the Great Hall for dancing, no one usually turned down an invitation. The Great Hall bloomed with the rich scent of hot summerhouse lilacs, roses, and pink carnations. Patience welcomed the sight of two sets of French doors that opened onto the balcony. When the dancing started, it would surely be sweltering.

Given their earlier-than-usual arrival, their party easily found seats along the gold wainscoted walls. Her first ball in Society, Patience couldn't believe she was really here. Her heart beat like a bird's wing, and she could feel the moistness in her palms beneath her gloves. Excitement brought a bright glow to her face, but only Bryce consumed her thoughts. *What would he have to say? Will he be willing to help me? Or will he be terribly angry?*

A tall, thin gentleman with hair designed à la Titus materialized at her shoulder with the duchess, who conducted the introductions. He had a pale, poetic face with limpid brown eyes that gazed at Patience as he asked for the honor of a dance.

Although she had secretly hoped to save her first dance for Lord Londringham, anxious glances to the stairs gave no hint to his eagerly anticipated arrival. Perhaps she could use a little practice. She had spent a few hours with a dance instructor this week at Lady Elverston's town house, quickly memorizing the dance steps, to Lady Elverston's great pleasure.

The nervous young man, who seemed younger than she, looked shocked at her acceptance, but his visage immediately beamed. The young man, Gunner Simkins, bowed, and gathered her in his arms to whirl her onto the dance floor for the opening dance of a lively quadrille.

Patience's partner certainly kept her on her toes, literally. Trying to prove light on her feet, Gunner thwarted her efforts with his large, ungraceful steps, landing, more often than not, on her well-shod feet. After their youthful exertion on the dance floor, her partner, unfortunately, apparently wanted to linger next to her chair, as if safeguarding her from other potential suitors.

Patience sent him off in search of a lemonade as she once again scanned the ever-engorging crowd for Lord Londringham. Soon several young men blocked her vision, asking for a dance or one of her smiles. She acquiesced to several more dances before begging for a respite to repair her toilette.

Upon her return, she found the Countess Isabella had arrived on the arm of Alain Sansouche. Patience uncharitably thought the countess looked like a fat sow in her impossibly tight blue gown, adorned with miles of diamonds, probably some of the many rewards given to her by past loves. Sometimes it could be difficult to think good of all people, as her brother James had often schooled her, especially when a particular person had been Lord Londringham's former lover.

When Patience took a few steps into the hall, searching for Lady Elverston and Martha, a new gaggle of young men surged around her, quacking for attention.

Her previous dance partner, Gunner, took charge of the eager young pups and claimed introductions. "Gentlemen, this is the confection of pink and white I told you about.

An angel who flies when she is dancing," he pompously told his agog audience.

Patience tried not to roll her eyes at this sugary compliment. Instantly his acquaintances besieged her for the next dance. To be sure, she had never had this many invitations to dance, due to the scarcity of men back home. Most had joined the service or married their local sweetheart. She usually had to settle for her brother Louis's friend Old Clive Bailey, blind in one eye with a bum leg, or for young Eddie Fishery, who had more hands than a spider.

Lord Bryce Andover, the Earl of Londringham, had arrived a few minutes earlier. His tall, imposing figure striding across the dance floor to his friends astounded more than a few of the gawkers, his presence at the Leeds's ball certainly a surprise, and curiosity-seekers gossiped the reasons why.

More than one had heard numerous stories of his heroism in their war with France, but the latest *on-dit* tantalized the feverish crowd that he may have had a hand in his brother's murder. The rumor had never truly died down, and, for some unexplained reason, people usually believed the worst when the truth held no titillating appeal. And Londringham had no interest in apprising anyone to the contrary.

After Londringham greeted other peers in attendance, he turned to search the room for Lady Elverston and Patience. He soon spotted the countess and Sansouche talking with Lady Leeds and the Marchioness deVillion before he noticed a gathering near the French doors.

Finding Lady Elverston alone on a settee, Bryce gestured toward the group. "What do you suppose is happening over there?"

His friend stood up to have a better view of the commotion and secretly smiled. "I believe several young gentlemen have found a jewel they are interested in acquiring," she responded with a laugh.

The small crowd finally broke apart, allowing Bryce his first glimpse of Patience. His emotions in check, he feasted on the lovely vision in white and shades of pink with a glorious crown of dark brown hair, dazzling in the wealth of candlelight in the hall. *Lady Elverston's machinations, to be sure,* he reflected to himself. Staring at her regal beauty dressed in snow-white finery, could she be the alter ego of his pretty maid and house steward? Anger and disillusionment tasted bitter as he realized Patience had tricked him. *For what gain?*

He spoke through gritted teeth. "Lady Elverston, what is the meaning of my steward in attendance tonight?"

Lady Elverston, with a sly puzzled look, glanced over his shoulder to the swains paying court to her lovely creation. "That, sir, may be your steward, but her given name is Miss Patience Mandeley. Her brother is Baronet Mandeley of Storrington."

"She never mentioned it before." *Mandeley. The name seemed somehow familiar. Of course, the young man imprisoned in Winchelsea, his surname was Mandeley. Could this Mandeley possibly be another brother? If so, that would explain a lot, but not the reason for forestalling the revealing of her identity.* Bryce warred within himself whether to spank her for her subterfuge or taste the honey only he could coax from her sweet lips.

He came out of his reverie to notice the besotted blades fawning over her. His jaw set, he strode determinedly over to the woman that he had overheard the young bucks call the "White Dove." Bryce arrived in time to hear one of them asking her for a dance. He cleaved through the small crowd of worshipers and offered a curt bow to Patience. With one hand wrapped firmly around her svelte waist, he stated firmly, "This dance is mine." His eyes never left her surprised countenance.

Bryce stared down into her softly flushed face, her hazel eyes shining brighter than any star. He asked, "Why didn't you tell me your real identity?"

Patience stared up into his hardened features, dismayed at his clipped words, certainly justified. From the icy blast of his cool blue eyes, she felt her heart freezing over like her flowers in winter. Her hands grew cold beneath her gloves as she tried to follow his lead, her mind numb. *How could I have thought I could make him understand? And where can I start? I should have told him the truth a long time ago.*

"My lord?" she whispered, unsure how to respond.

"You're like the rest of your breed, my girl," he responded sharply.

She felt his disgust crawl onto her skin. Suddenly feeling braver than she usually believed herself to be, Patience faced down this slander of the female race. "I agree that I should have told you sooner," she admitted, lifting a finely arched eyebrow.

But he ignored the beginnings of her apology. "How can I believe you? You are far more clever with lies than you are with the truth." His frozen chips of blue eyes posed a threat to her senses, but no thought could be entertained of fleeing, since he held her tightly around the waist.

She had the temerity to pull away from his stern gaze, her face as pale as her gown.

"Why didn't you tell me what Lady Elverston had planned in launching you tonight? I would have made an effort to be timelier. And all your following? Have you taken a fancy to anyone? They look rather young as playmates."

Patience bristled at this insult, taken aback at his cruelty. Before she could formulate a tart reply, he continued, "And what lies have you told my friend Lady Elverston?"

She shook her head, unable to look away from his uncompromising visage. "None."

His laugh sounded harsh to her ears. "You do possess loyalty afterall to your own sex. You would have thought I had learned my lesson by now."

"I beg of you, my lord, please allow me time to explain later, when we have left here," she pleaded with him. She had wanted to look her best for him tonight. Only him. And now she felt the tears ready to slip through the cracks of her oh-so-thin veneer.

"Please, no tears. That has never worked with me. I cannot believe that Lady Elverston didn't confide in me." Bryce was speaking to himself, paying no heed to her protests.

Another time she would have reveled in his expertise on the dance floor, her other partners long forgotten and wet behind the ears. Anyone watching them dance would never know his leg was still healing. As she contemplated their next confrontation, her head began to ache. Night had fallen on her secret hopes for a new beginning.

So enrapt in their struggle, neither Bryce nor Patience noticed the laughter. It began softly, like the rustling of leaves, weaving through the crush of people until it grew into a crescendo, like an orchestra warming up before the conductor raises his baton.

Everyone stopped dancing and stared at Patience and Bryce before they too soon stopped, and Bryce guided Patience to the steps, his hand at her back and a frown on his face. They knew not what to make of the crowd watching them. Soon, words filtered back to them that sounded like "housemaid" and "master."

Patience bit her lip when she saw Lady Elverston coming toward them, looking like someone out for vengeance. The young woman felt anger directed toward her.

But the older woman had her eyes honed on the earl. "It

appears your former ladylove has created a bother of trouble. Both she and that Frenchman she calls cousin have spread the tale that Patience, your former maid, has been elevated to the grand position of steward . . . or your lover." She flapped her fan rapidly, then snapped it shut with a crack.

"They cannot decide whether she has made a fool of you, or you and I are trying to make a fool of them. No great task, that." She glanced around the room and spied the duchess headed their way.

Patience stepped away from Londringham's shelter and approached Lady Elverston. "Since I'm the one who is found offensive, I will trouble you both no further. I can hire a hack to drive me home. You should not suffer for our acquaintance." She thought her back would break, holding her head so high.

Bryce growled, "You shall leave with me. As Lady Elverston will attest, someone in my family has always provided scuttle for the rabid. Their petty concerns mean nothing to me."

She turned and stared at him in surprise. *Could he actually be protective of her feelings?*

The crowd's mirth reached its climax and had already sunk back to earth as the orchestra got ready to resume, when a child's cry rang out in the din.

"Miss Grundy, Miss Grundy!" The mob in Her Grace's hall parted like the Red Sea as a small child nimbly but haltingly two-stepped down the silvery staircase and ran swiftly to Patience's side. It was Sally, the little girl from the circus with her acrobatic aunt.

Patience sank to the floor to gather the little one up in her arms. Smelling of rain and fire, she wore a faded dress with stockings of light gray. Sally's pink face was wet with tears, and her blond braids shook as she clung to Patience like sealed wax to vellum.

With one hand Patience drew her handkerchief from her gown's shallow pocket. Gently, she wiped Sally's tears while asking softly, "What are you doing here, Sally? And where is your aunt?"

Sally spied Bryce over her shoulder and cried, "Mr. Long. I still 'ave me dolly, the one ye gave me at the fair. See? And I didn't lose 'er head or anythin'." Sally's little fist clasped the wooden shepherdess tightly by the neck, her sorrows forgotten as she awaited his lordship's approval.

"I'm glad to see you, Sally, and your dolly," Bryce told her warmly, stepping closer to Patience.

"I named her Spring 'cause it's me favorite time of year."

Patience smiled as Sally took her handkerchief and dried Spring's tears as well. "Spring is a lovely name for your dolly."

This current state of affairs kept the crowd ogling the little group, murmuring about the child and her relationship to the earl and his now-infamous steward.

A high-pitched voice jarred the crowd as Aunt Bella bustled through in search of her niece. "Let me through. Sally, where is ye? Come back 'ere so's I can take ye to yer father."

Sally clutched Patience even tighter and hid her face in Patience's neck. She whispered, "Don't let her take me— I 'ate 'er." Her voice choked with misery.

"But, child, she is your aunt and worried about you," Patience replied in a low voice.

But the little girl simply shook her head.

Sally's aunt finally erupted on the scene like a black cloud bringing trouble. She wore what was obviously her best gown—rose taffeta, in a fashion many had not seen the likes of in several years. Her appearance in a black shawl, long gaudy earrings, and patched black pumps created a stir.

She honed in on Sally like a wolf after its prey. "So this is where ye be, with yer fancy friends. Did ye not 'ear me callin' ye?" The tightrope walker finally noticed the crowd stunned into silence by her appearance. She sashayed over to Gunner, who stood with the rest of Patience's admirers. "Like what ye see, boy? Ye can see more of me at the circus over in Danskin's Fields," she told him with a wink.

Gunner blushed furiously and turned to punch one friend in the arm for apparently an unamusing jest at the unsought blatant invitation.

Sally's aunt continued to address him. "Do ye 'appen to know how's I may find Viscount Dimton? I was told 'e'd be 'ere."

A tall soldier in the back called, "I just left him in the card room."

Bryce stepped forward and grasped Sally's aunt under her elbow. "I think it's time we settled this matter in private, madam." He escorted her none too gently through the hall with Patience following him, carrying Sally and her doll.

The brazenly dressed woman accompanied him without a single word, apparently honored to be escorted by a gentleman such as his lordship. *Wait till my friends hear about this,* she thought with glee.

The crowd seemed disappointed to see them go, but at the duchess's signal, the orchestra struck up the music, and the circus performer and her niece drifted from their memories, but not before the duchess caught Lady Elverston's sleeve, quietly demanding an audience.

A full fifteen minutes later, the greatly anticipated appearance of Viscount Dimton darkened the library where the little group awaited him. He strolled into the room, slightly weaving to one side, attesting to his consorting deeply with the bottle this evening. Even the anger alight in Bryce's eyes and his intimidating presence by the fireplace failed to draw a response from the besotted man. The viscount tumbled toward a chair and nearly missed falling into his seat.

Then in a slurred voice he asked Bryce, "What is this here all about? Footman tells me you need to see me, and I had to leave the card table, just when my luck was turning."

Wanting to break the man's neck but controlling the outrage that simmered in him, Bryce addressed Dimton. "Do you know this woman?"

Sally's aunt spoke up, jumping from her seat on the sofa. "Of course, 'e do, 'e been payin' me to watch the little brat for four years past. But 'e no longer bothers to send me even a shillin' anymore. I says, pay me what I'm due or have 'is whelp back."

Patience and Sally watched the exchange quite closely. Bryce noted how tightly Patience held the child.

He interrupted the callous woman. "Madam, how can you say these things about your niece?"

The circus performer drew up her full five feet in a huff. "Yer lordship . . ." she began before jerking a finger at the bored viscount. "This one bratted me sister, and then she dies and I 'ave to look after the girl. Well, not no more. I'm bound for Europe, and I can't take 'er with me."

Bryce and Patience looked at each other before he turned to Sally's negligent father. "Is what she says true?"

The mystified viscount seemed to be struggling to recall the past few minutes, let alone the past four years. He scrunched his eyes thoughtfully and burped. "Well, Londringham, I cannot seem to think on the mother, so long ago it was. You know how it is, we cannot take responsibility for every child that calls us Father. Why we would have to care for half of the bastards in England!"

Bryce curled his lips in disgust. "I do look after my

responsibilities, unlike men such as yourself, who disgrace their title and honor." Cold loathing filled every pore in his body at the viscount's dismissal of Sally and her mother.

He looked at Sally's aunt. "Do I understand you correctly that Viscount Dimton did support his daughter?"

The painted woman backed up a step, seeming slightly unnerved by the man's size and penetrating stare. "I can tell ye is a gentlemen, one what listens to a lady." She patted her hair for effect. "Me sister, before she up and died a few years ago, says to me, 'The Viscount Dimton, 'e's the man what you needs to see. 'e'll see to Sally.' Back then, 'e was willin' to spend a few coins to get me and 'is brat off 'is doorstop. But now, like I said, 'e won't sends me no more bob."

Before anyone could reply, Patience approached the alleged father, with Sally's hand in hers. "Lord Dimton, am I to understand you are unwilling to acknowledge your daughter or extend support for her?"

Dimton looked cross at this unfortunate turn of events and at being confronted by such a vision in white. He mumbled, "Never said the girl was mine."

Patience looked at Sally's aunt. "Are you willing to relinquish your guardianship of Sally?"

The woman brightened at the thought. "I can't take 'er with me, and I 'ave no money to feed 'er. Are ye willin' to buy 'er off me 'ands?" Greed shimmered in her cold gleam.

Bryce stepped forward and snarled, "You would sell your own niece?"

"I needs to see to meself," came her defensive reply.

Bryce spared a quick glance at Patience holding Sally before informing Aunt Bella, "Then it is settled. Sally will no longer be in your care, but in mine. It's not necessary to delay our stay in your company any longer. Miss Mandeley, please wait for me down the hall with Sally."

Upon hearing Bryce's instructions, Patience smiled tenderly at Sally hopping up and down. "Let's go home, dear."

Bryce watched Patience lead the little girl from the room, silently proud of his "white angel." Then he turned to Sally's aunt. A pouch of coins landed at her feet. "Neither of you"—he started, including in his glance the viscount, who still blinked in stupor at the events unfolding before him, and the aunt powdering her nose—"will ever lay claim on Sally again." His harsh voice and hard expression forbid any further discussion, and he stalked out of the room.

He caught up with Patience and Sally in the hall. In silence, they walked back to the ballroom where the dancing had resumed, circuited the hall, and walked down the steps to depart. Bryce handed a note to a footman for Lady Elverston. Few took notice of their quick departure, already forgetting the latest *on dit* of the earl and the house steward.

The carriage rocked Sally to sleep on Patience's lap as silence stretched between Patience and Bryce. She stroked Sally's hair, compassion showing in her warm hazel eyes. She looked up, startled, when Bryce addressed her.

"What shall we plan to do with our new charge?" His face was hidden in the darkness of the carriage.

"I . . . I shall raise her myself." Patience surprised herself by that answer. She hadn't given it any clear thought but had only wanted to get the child away from her avaricious aunt and her drunken father. Patience returned her gaze to the sleeping Sally. "The little girl needs a home, something her aunt and father have certainly never been willing to provide for her." Unknowingly, her face glowed with motherly concern.

Her touch light on Sally's golden locks, Bryce found himself jealous of the child, wanting Patience to look with tender love at him. No, with *passionate* love from those hazel eyes, he corrected himself. *She looks so right holding the child,* Bryce thought disconsolately. *How would she look if she held my babe in her arms?*

Spellbound he couldn't look away, but found himself arguing softly so as not to wake Sally. "The child needs a father as well."

Patience glanced across the carriage. "Yes, I agree with you. But I can care for her and my . . ." She hesitated at the word "brothers"—something he still didn't know about.

He ignored her comment. "The girl needs a father," Bryce steadily maintained.

Those were the last words spoken until they reached the town house.

Chapter 20

Shock mapped Melenroy's world-weary face as she watched his lordship walk into the hallway carrying a sleeping child with Miss Patience not far behind in her white finery. She hurried over to the pair where Stone, ever vigilant, joined them.

"Stone, do we have an extra bed where I might place the child?" Bryce inquired of his nonplussed servant.

Patience interjected, "My lord, I would prefer for Sally to sleep with me tonight. I don't want her afraid when she wakes in a strange bed and doesn't recognize anyone."

Immediately understanding her wisdom, Bryce dismissed the servants and carefully shouldered the child up the stairs and down the long hallway to Patience's room. He could hear Patience's skirts rustling behind him.

In her bedchamber, Bryce watched silently by the door as Patience removed Sally's shoes and drew the counterpane over her, tucking Spring underneath the little girl's arm. Anger started burning in him. Why did everyone command Patience's loyalty but not him? Lem, Melenroy, Lady Elverston, young Mandeley, and, now, Sally. He shaded the anger from his face as she made her way over to the door and Bryce.

"Thank you, my lord, for allowing Sally to stay the night," she told him softly.

Bryce nodded, his gaze remained on her sweet face. Since neither could think of a reason for him to linger, he brusquely told her good night and strode down the hallway.

Patience couldn't sleep. She sat by the window, only a friendly wind and Sally's light breathing disturbing the welcomed night. The breeze tickled a strand of hair across her brow, and she swept it back with a sigh. She couldn't sleep knowing she and Bryce had unfinished business between them. Just like before.

If only he was awake, she would go to him and plead her case, remembering with a sharp pain the last time she visited his room. The black night painted with silver stars teased her further awake, accentuating unease and restlessness. She required a good book to take her mind off her troubles.

Her hair beribboned behind her, Patience threw on her blue muslin dressing gown and slippers and tiptoed out the door, the stairs creaking slightly. Only the longcase clock chiming in the hallway knew of her presence. The doors to the little-used library were closed, as usual. Most of the household preferred the light cheeriness of the parlors.

Turning the gold knob, she sidled through the doorway and closed the door quietly, not realizing she held her breath in fear she might disturb someone else's reverie. All quiet. She leaned back against the door and exhaled before a startled peep burst forth.

Bryce was kneeling before the fireplace, stirring the winking ashes to life to warm the drafty room. To her dismay, he wore only his black formal pantaloons. No shirt obscured her view of his broad, sinewy chest, his back and arm muscles flexing easily with his light task. What was *he* doing here? Perhaps he hadn't heard her and she could slip right back out . . .

"It appears that you have trouble sleeping as well." His tone was neither angry nor friendly. Then he turned to face her, his blue eyes slightly chilly. "Do you need help selecting a book?"

"Yes. No . . . I thought a book might help . . ." she trailed off. "But I'm finally feeling sleepy and think I might just—"

"Stay," he ordered.

She gulped and waited patiently, her hands clenched behind her back.

The time of reckoning had arrived.

Bryce briefly stared at her frozen form before he gestured to a nearby chair. "You may sit if you choose. Since we appear to have the time and place alone together, we may as well conduct this interview." He sat down in a chair near the fireplace, seeming informal but poised for attack, or so she imagined.

Patience gulped back the fear lodged in her throat and rubbed her shoulders for warmth. She definitely needed a chair for support and retired to the one closest to the door, already planning her escape. Her heart beat with the flight of a butterfly as she waited for his wrathful explosion.

In a pleasant but deadly soft voice, he told her, "No more charades. I want to know who you really are and why you are here. What lies have you told Lady Elverston about your identity?"

She released a shaky sigh and wet her very dry lips. Where should she start? With that forbidding look on his face, her heart sank, knowing he could never forgive her deceit, no matter the reason.

Straightening her back, she held her chin high until she ached. "I tell you, I have told no lies to your friend Lady Elverston, who has been most kind to me. I am known as Miss Patience Mandeley in Storrington."

"Your parents?"

"Both dead for several years. My brother Louis is Baronet Mandeley of Storrington."

He raised one eyebrow, appearing to contemplate his next move. "What are you doing in Winchelsea? And more specifically why did you become a servant in my house?"

Patience rubbed her sweaty palms, wishing she was anywhere but here. However, she did admit to herself, his questions were reasonable. Her missing onyx would have been of great comfort if she could find it. "It is terribly difficult for one to know where to begin."

Since she looked prepared to give him the entire history of her family beginning with the Saxons, Bryce thought he would assist her in abridging her narrative. "What about the night we met at the Mop Fair?"

She shook her head. "No, my lord, it had begun before that. You see when my brother Rupert . . ."

"The young man in prison wanted for murder and treason?"

Her eyes round as carriage wheels, she nodded quickly.

Bryce felt an unreasonable sense of relief float through him when he saw the confirmation.

"Exactly, which is why I came to Winchelsea, to help Rupert clear these charges. Our solicitor in Storrington told me I needed proof of my brother's innocence, which is the reason for my presence in Winchelsea."

Bryce shook his head, trying to follow her logic. "But why did you decide to pose as my housemaid?"

"It seemed a good idea at the time and my only plan. You see, when I arrived in Winchelsea, I learned my brother was missing. I couldn't return home yet and had nowhere to stay. I thought if I could perhaps gain employment in your household, I could be near Winchelsea and look for my brother." She held her breath, afraid of his next question.

He slumped down on the settee, still trying to fit the

pieces together. He ran a tired hand across his brow. He continued, "You could have found a position practically anywhere, why my household in particular?"

She sank deeper into her chair as the noose slipped even tighter. She couldn't sit there another minute with his probing stare fixed on her. The night stars beckoned Patience through the undraped casement window. She walked over to the window, far from Bryce, to respond to his damning question.

"I . . . I understood through my brother Rupert, who had it on good authority, that . . . that"—she cleared her throat and managed to say—"that you might be a spy selling secrets to the French. Rupert insisted that our cousin, Carstairs, believed you to be the French spy and that you had placed suspicion on Rupert to lead the constable away from you." Her last words tumbled out on top of each other. Patience looked everywhere but at the man she had just accused of treason.

Bryce stared incredulously at Patience. He didn't know whether to be insulted or laugh, so he did neither.

She continued, warming to her story, "You see, I thought if I worked in your household, I would be able to watch you, and when you did your spying, I could report you to the constable and clear my brother's name."

He shook his head. Too fantastical a tale to be believed. And yet he did. He couldn't summon anger with her when he thought of all the things she had done, all for her brother. He had never met anyone with such devoted loyalty, and he admired Patience for it. *Even if she* had *been trying to imprison me.* Only he knew that the constable would have never given her case against him any consideration.

But he had to ask, almost to himself, "Carstairs told your brother I was a French spy?" He didn't see her nod. *It made perfect sense. Since Carstairs had worked for the French,*

Patience's cousin had led the constable to Rupert, while misdirecting Rupert and Patience to him. Very clever.

A thought occurred to him. He leapt from his seat and strode to where Patience stood waiting. He grabbed her shoulders, trying to see behind her frightened stare. "Is that why you came to my room that night? Did you decide perhaps if you made the supreme sacrifice it would be another way to find proof of my guilt?" So far gone in his quick rage, he missed the saddened pain in her big hazel eyes. Her thick hair fell over her shoulders, her ribbon slipping to the floor.

She needed words to lessen his accusation, and closed her eyes against the stark anger lining his face. "No, I had no intention of staying with you. I only wanted to explain my whereabouts during the invasion scare. I knew then that you were incapable of treason or murder and wanted to ask you for help for Rupert, but I couldn't find the words." If she mentioned that she stayed with him that night because she loved him, would it have calmed the beast she saw in him?

He still wouldn't let her go. "When were you planning to tell me about your brother? You have had ample opportunity since that night," his words calculating and accurate.

She examined her clenched hands in front of her. "Afterwards, I determined to tell you the night we arrived in Town. But you know what happened. Later, Lady Elverston chatted with me, and we agreed that you might be more convinced of my identity if I dressed the part." She looked up to catch his shadowed glance. "I ask your forgiveness for the masquerade I played, surely a foolish thing to do. And I'm truly sorry I didn't tell you earlier, reasoning you would have a good excuse for throwing me out on my ear."

She still had one more thing to say. In a faltering voice, Patience told him, "If I have hurt you, then I have only succeeded in hurting myself." A tear slipped down before she could catch it.

The angered lines in his face had smoothed into politeness during her apology. "This evening seemed important to you. Why?" his voice almost gentle.

Fine tears brimmed in her eyes, her heart in a tight lock grip, she hiccuped. "I thought if you could see me as an equal, I might have earned your"—*love, affection,* she wished she could say—"regard."

He stood close enough to her that she could see the blue chips in his eyes melting. "You already had my . . . regard." One more question would ease his mind. His hands lay gently on her shoulders. "Why did you stay when you learned the truth?"

The hardest question of all. Why had she remained with him? What answer did he want to hear? That she couldn't bear to leave him? Taking a deep breath, she said succinctly, "I thought you might help me save my brother. What other reason could there be?"

An enigmatic mask curtained his face with an unknown emotion, his eyes a deeper blue than she had ever seen. "Yes, what other reason?" he murmured.

She paused. "My lord, I'm sorry for the debacle tonight." She thought it best to have done with all her mistakes.

Bryce waved away her apology. "It will be forgotten in a day or two. I'm surprised *you* were not more distraught at your introduction to Society."

She shrugged. "I didn't know them before, and won't in the future, unless they plan to visit my little village of Storrington." She backed away from Bryce a few steps and sighed heavily. "My heart goes out to Lady Elverston. She worked so diligently in preparing for my success tonight. So much time devoted to a plan destroyed in minutes, a plan that never stood a chance of working."

He watched her carefully. No matter what, his estimation of her couldn't have been higher. First her acts of loyalty for her brother and now her solicitousness for Lady Elverston's standing in Society. Did she never stop caring? Possibly not. And when she loved? He knew instinctively her love would be a unique treasure to last a lifetime. Could he ever earn her love? His cynical heart wondered such. At what price?

She waited for what seemed an eternity. Finally, the words tore from her heart. "I shall leave tomorrow to return home. Of course I'll take Sally with me. But my brother still needs your help, and I would hope that you wouldn't punish him because of the trouble I've caused you."

Bryce spanned the distance between them in a heartbeat. "You don't know me at all if you think I wouldn't help your brother out of his troubles," his words harsher than he intended. He finished with a curt order. "You aren't leaving."

She could hardly believe his clipped words. After pouring out her heart and begging his forgiveness, he still wanted her to stay. "I can't stay here, not in my current position, it would never do."

He finally smiled at her. She needed him, oh, how she needed him. "I'll find you a new position. Until then, I will tell you when your services are no longer needed." *Until forever,* but he kept his thoughts quiet. He drew her slowly toward him, wrapping his arms around her before bending down to place a kiss on her surprised lips.

The fire crackled behind him as he expertly plied her mouth with a warm kiss that instantly grew passionate and demanding. He felt her very willing response as she stood on tiptoe to wrap her arms around his shoulders. His hands encircled her waist and pressed her pliant form against his own hard, demanding one, reminding Patience of what they had known before.

She moaned sweetly in protest when he traced her red, swollen lips with his playful tongue. Before he realized it, her tongue swept out to capture his and drew it back into her hot, wet mouth, which caused him to growl in delight at her aggression.

Their erotic play of tongues became a battleground, with him stroking her mouth, giving and taking, leaving little breath for either of them. Her pulse roared in excitement, what power he commanded over her.

He suddenly stopped and drew back. When she frowned in puzzlement, her chest heaving from lack of air, he gently wiped a tear from her cheek that had fallen unbeknownst to her and licked the salty wetness from his finger.

He closed his eyes, leaning his forehead against hers, having difficulty breathing. Then he straightened, once more under control.

"I want you. But not for some misguided gratitude or other noble cause. When we make love, it will be because you want me as much as I want you." He paused, his blue eyes like the stormiest seas, betraying his calm exterior. "And make no mistake, *Miss* Patience Mandeley, that day of reckoning is fast approaching."

He opened the door behind her and stalked out without looking back.

Making her way slowly upstairs, finally drained and sleepy, Patience sat by her bedroom window for a long while, crying with the rain.

Chapter 21

Another gray day, Patience thought dismally, staring out her bedroom window. She had already been summoned to his lordship in the front parlor, probably for a continuation of his inquisition from last night. Sally had left earlier with Lem to go to the kitchen. Wearing a favorite pale-green muslin dress, she walked slowly down the curved staircase and across the marble floor before turning the doorknob, sighing, her hand shaking slightly.

She entered the front parlor to discover Lady Elverston sitting by the fireplace, who smiled encouragingly at her. Were they discussing the disaster last night? She hesitated by the door, her face flushed in anticipation of her reception.

Bryce stood when she entered the room, his face an inscrutable mask, as Lady Elverston rose gracefully from her wing chair to greet Patience.

Sitting next to Patience on the settee, the marchioness began, "Please forgive my early call, but your sudden departure last night troubled me. I told Lord Elverston I must hurry to see Miss Mandeley to see how she does this morning, and, of course, how the little girl was adjusting."

Patience dipped her head in acknowledgment and shyly

responded, "Thank you for your many kindnesses and concern. I'm terribly sorry about last night. Had I known I would create such a scene, I would never have thought . . ."

Lady Elverston held up her hand to forestall any more martyrdom. "I cannot believe the noise the countess started last night. You know, my dear gel, most of the ton cannot abide her awful French manners and most hope she will go back to Boney and be a thorn in his side!" She laughed at her jest.

Lord Londringham had not yet joined their conversation, but Patience felt his strong presence in the bright room.

The marchioness continued, "But that is water under the bridge. My dear, I was simply explaining to Lord Londringham that you must attend me at Vauxhall Gardens tonight."

Patience looked askance, and shook her head no. She couldn't endure to be the cause of further humiliation for either her friend or Lord Londringham.

But Lady Elverston was prepared for any argument. "Hear me out, I beg you. The countess truly did little harm last night that a few whispers in the right ear cannot correct."

Stone interrupted Lady Elverston's persuasions with a silver tray, carrying a calling card to announce Mr. Gunner Simkins.

The energetic young man Patience had danced with last night entered the room, his nervous right hand betraying his confidence. "Lord Londringham, my Lady Elverston, and Miss Mandeley, if I may?" Patience smiled tentatively and with a quick look at Lord Londringham, realized the poor boy entirely missed Bryce's dark look of irritation.

Gunner Simkins addressed himself to Patience. "When you left so suddenly at the ball with the little girl, I was concerned—so much so that I have presented myself here this morning to inquire after your welfare." He bowed slightly to her, unsure of where to stand or what to do next.

Patience's eyes grew rounder, her face pale against the light green of her dress. "Mr. Simkins, I don't know what to say at this unexpected honor. We only danced one dance, and I didn't have the opportunity to bid you good night, so hurried was our departure."

Simkins jumped in, "That is why I am here, I wanted to ask you a rather personal question, if you don't find me impertinent." His face turned slightly red beneath his blond hair.

Bryce interrupted the casual conversation. "Miss Mandeley has no time for questions from you. You have paid your respects, there's the door." His stern voice brooked no issue.

Lady Elverston didn't miss a thing and *tskked* the earl. "Londringham, let us at least hear what the gentleman came here to say. It would be rather rude of us to send him on his way, so quickly."

All three turned to face the intruder, who ran a shaky finger under his cravat. "You see, miss, I was wondering if whether the story is true."

Patience's face turned even paler, and she replied in a husky voice, "What story?" She had been living so many lies, the truth became harder to remember.

With a look Lady Elverston silently prevented Londringham from throwing the young swain out.

Simkins responded, "Word has it that you were Lord Londringham's housemaid." The words rushed from him as he studiously avoided the earl's glare.

Lady Elverston's silvery laugh rippled across the suddenly tomblike room. "How preposterous a suggestion, Mr. Simkins. A baronet's sister, a housemaid?" She rose gracefully and crossed the room to the young man. "Actually, dear boy, the truth of the matter is, Miss Patience and I had a little wager."

She continued parading around the room, drawing his rapt attention. "The country can sometimes become so terribly dull that I wagered Miss Mandeley she could not pass herself off as a housemaid at Londringham's estate. Miss Mandeley performed magnificently, completely fooling everyone, except for Londringham, the clever man who soon discovered our lark. Being the good sport that he is . . ."

Bryce, who had watched the scene from his desk, walked over to Lady Elverston's side. "I decided to give Miss Mandeley a Season since her father was an old friend of the family's," he said, smoothly finishing Lady Elverston's story.

Patience stared blankly at both of them. Oh, bother. Because of her charade, they had both decided to lie on her behalf.

Simkins's eyes looked ready to pop from his head. "A real adventuress?" He turned to Patience with an even more admiring, infatuated glance. "Can you be the real thing?" he asked in awe.

She had the grace to blush under his glowing adoration. "I . . . well," she sputtered, trying to think of a suitable reply. God would never scratch her slate clean if she continued these falsehoods.

Bryce summoned Stone. "Of course she is, young man. Now that you have the answer you sought, you'll want to be on your way."

Simkins hesitated before Patience. "Ah, miss, is it possible you may take a ride in the park this afternoon? With me?"

Bryce answered before Patience had a chance. "This afternoon Miss Mandeley will be busy and for several afternoons after that."

Looking at Bryce's determined face, Patience nodded slightly to Simkins. "Perhaps another time?" She smiled at the shy man who she was convinced had never braved an adversary fiercer than Lord Londringham. She couldn't send him off without some sort of reward for his courage.

The young man turned his hat around in his hands, bedazzled by Patience's winsome smile and warm regard. "Ah, miss, I almost forgot. You dropped this at the ball. I came to return it." He shyly proffered a freshly pressed handkerchief into her hand.

His chivalry surprised Patience. "Sally must have dropped it before we left. It's a favorite of mine, I promise not to be so careless in the future."

Her sweet gratitude was more than he could bear. He stammered, "It would be an honor to . . . to return all your handkerchiefs to you." A sudden blush reached his hairline.

Bryce opened the parlor door while informing the young swain that he must spend his time more wisely than erranding handkerchiefs to ladies.

Stone arrived to usher the besotted young man out the door, but before Simkins left he remembered his manners. "Adieu, Miss Mandeley, until later. Lord Londringham and Lady Elverston, it has been the greatest of pleasures." One more adoring look at Patience, and he was gone.

Bryce threw himself on the settee, looking over at Patience with raised eyebrows. "What a simpering fool and how could you encourage him?" His voice sounded harsher in his address to her than he realized.

She stared down his irrational ire. "Was that what I was doing? I had no idea a simple thank you would allow the young man to think he could pay court to me."

"You were flirting with him, and you know it," Bryce growled.

Lady Elverston thought it best to intercede. "La, would you look at you two? I would say you are two lovers quarreling, if ever I saw it, but I know that not to be true. Patience, would you allow me a moment alone with his lordship? I have some matters to discuss with him. Until tonight." She smiled at Patience.

Patience drew up her shoulders squarely, set to vacate the room. "We are certainly not lovers!" she cried, disagreeing almost too vehemently with Bryce. And then, directing her last comment to Bryce before sweeping from the room: "And I was not flirting!"

Bryce ignored Patience, pondering his old friend's words.

An hour later, Bryce found Patience in the kitchen with Sally, Martha, and Melenroy. Flour covered the big wooden table, the floor, and the laughing women. Sally stood on a chair giggling while Melenroy, Martha, and Patience paraded around the chair pretending the little girl was the Fairy Queen. Flour became fairy dust, which rose in a cloud to the ceiling.

When Patience sneezed after throwing a fistful of flour, Bryce, leaning against the doorjamb responded, "Gesundheit."

She whirled around in surprise, catching Martha's and Melenroy's attention. Their noisy song in tribute to the Fairy Queen stalled, drifting like the flour onto the floor.

Melenroy hurried into action, grabbing a broom and viciously swiping at the uncooperative flour dust. Martha scooped Sally from her "throne" and into her arms, murmuring something about cleaning her up as she passed by Patience.

Bryce lifted one eyebrow with barely a hint of a smile. Patience saw him staring at her dress, and following his downward glance, she saw her once-green frock, now whiter in appearance. She raised her head and began, "My lord, Martha and I found Sally with Melenroy, and she seemed rather sad. We were trying to cheer her up," she whispered lamely.

"No explanation needed. We must discuss Sally's welfare. However, there is something more pressing I must share with you. Would you please attend me in the parlor?"

"May I first make myself more presentable?"

Bryce hesitated. "What I have to say you'll not wish to wait."

His words struck a chill in her heart. Something had happened to Rupert. What else could it be? She followed him silently down the hall and up the stairs, wringing her hands behind her.

They entered the smaller back parlor, Patience's favorite. The soft rose color of the wallpaper matched the fabric on the settee. Sunlight streamed through the light-pink curtains onto the Oriental carpet, splendid beneath her neat green slippers. She sank onto the nearest chair, awaiting Bryce's news with trepidation.

Anxiously she waited as he stared at her, trying to stick a curl back into her knot. Most of the flour adorned her green gown, which she could see left a faint trail behind her as she walked.

She interrupted the silence. "What did you wish to tell me?" she asked, her voice slightly shaky.

Bryce rested one hip on the desk as she waited and held her breath.

"My news concerns your brother Rupert." Before she could react, he hurriedly added, "He is unharmed that we know of. He has escaped from prison, we believe with the help of his former comrades."

Patience leapt from the settee and cried, "How could this be? Rupert would do no such thing. He was waiting for you to clear his name. He told me so." She looked at him with accusing eyes.

He held up his hand. "Wait, things are not as bleak as they may seem. From the constable's note I just received, the escape happened two days ago conspired by three men wanted for smuggling and thieving. Witnesses claim that your brother went unwillingly."

Her face turned even paler under the smudges of white

powder. She couldn't think of anything to say but shook her head and walked to the window, the sun momentarily blinding her.

Bryce watched her slim back. She seemed so fragile, how could she possibly take care of her brother as well as Sally and all the rest of the people that depended on her? She bore the weight of so many others. Bryce wished he could relieve her burden but didn't have the ability to do so just yet. *Lady Elverston already believes I'm half in love with the woman. Could this be so?* He supposed it was not impossible. But not now, with so much to do. *Have I not already learned my lesson too well about the wasted emotion of love?*

He went to her and stood behind her and waited for a gesture from her, something that told him that she needed him and his help.

When she turned to face him, her hazel eyes were sad but held no tears. She took a deep breath and smiled a tiny smile. With shoulders back, she addressed him. "I must return to Winchelsea and locate my brother. Rupert has concerns that the person who killed our cousin, Lord Carstairs, might indeed be after him. I must find him and take him home where he'll be safe." Her bottom lip quivered, belying her resolution.

Bryce's strong arms reached out to grab her shoulders. "That won't be necessary. The constable's men are looking for him. They know not to hurt him, and I've asked that he be returned to Paddock Green under the watchful eye of Marlow, who will keep him safe. There is nothing you can do in Winchelsea. You must remain here where I can protect you."

His firm words relieved her, and she gave up this battle. She had to plan. She tilted her head back to look into his face. "I have your word that you will do everything in your power to ensure my brother's safety?"

His gaze held hers. "I will not allow any harm to come to him."

As if she couldn't bear any more time in his company, Patience broke away from him and whispered, "I must see how Martha is doing with Sally. And prepare for the Gardens tonight. I don't wish to disappoint Lady Elverston a second night in a row. Please excuse me."

Bryce watched her go and couldn't put a name to the desolation and frustration he felt when she left.

"*Ye* look like a Fairy Queen," Sally told Patience sweetly as she helped the little girl into bed.

Patience had dressed for Vauxhall Gardens in a celestial blue silk gown that Lady Elverston had insisted enhanced her dazzling deep brown hair.

Martha and one of the housemaids had swept Patience's hair into a high knot with sweet wispy curls surrounding her face. Lady Elverston even sent over a sapphire necklace with matching combs for Patience.

Patience smiled down at the little girl, safely tucked in her own bed. She did feel like a Fairy Queen tonight, and terribly afraid she would wake from this dream. She couldn't help but feel a sadness and frustration, not knowing how to help Rupert, but content with Bryce's promise to her.

She turned to look around at the little bedchamber they had made for Sally. The housemaids had helped Patience and Martha turn a third-floor room into a cozy place where Sally could be comfortable and unafraid. The small bed's counterpane of bright blue brightened the chamber, as did the white curtains at the window. One of the maids had even borrowed a few stuffed animals to cheer the little girl.

A normally affectionate child, Sally had everyone wrapped around her little finger, except for Lem. He felt the girl received entirely too much attention, especially since Sally was an orphan, just like him.

Sally looked up at Patience, who was tucking Spring under the covers.

The little one's smile of gratitude lit the tiny room. "Do ye have time to read me a story? Lem says you read to him sometimes and no one ever reads to me."

Patience smiled, hoping Bryce, Martha, and Lady Elverston wouldn't mind waiting for a few minutes. She brought a small chair next to Sally's bed and began the story of Sleeping Beauty, a favorite story that her father had read to her a long time ago. Since Sally didn't know the story, Patience felt sure she could tell a shortened version, but the little girl kept interrupting her with so many questions that Patience spent more time than she had anticipated.

Neither one noticed the dark shadow at the door nor how long Bryce stood there watching them. When Patience finished, Sally's long eyelashes caressed her tiny face.

He called softly to Patience, who looked up in surprise. She nodded and rose to move her chair when Sally's voice halted her. "And they lived happily ever after?" she asked sleepily.

"Yes, darling, they lived happily ever after. I must go, and you must go to sleep," Patience whispered. She bent to kiss the little girl's brow, but Sally shot straight up when she saw Lord Londringham at the door.

"Mr. Long, you 'ave a story to tell me, just like Miss Patience?" All traces of tiredness had fled from her chipper voice.

Lord Londringham came into the room with his head slightly bent. His tall form not easily adjusting to the shorter ceiling, he was elegantly attired in a black dress coat, his white shirt shining in the darkness.

Patience, wary of his nearness, remained rooted to her spot.

Lord Londringham crouched by her bed. "Sally, Miss Patience and I have an appointment for tonight. May I promise you a story for tomorrow night?" His low baritone voice reverberated around the room, striking nervous cords dangerously near Patience's heart.

The little girl wrinkled her face as if trying to make a decision. "I guess so. Good night." She fell back down to her pillows, grabbing her doll close to her chest, eyes shut tight.

Relieved to be able to vacate the room, Bryce had difficulty breathing in this small room, with Patience's perfume floating over him, every crinkle of her gown firing all his senses.

He escorted Patience down the stairs and helped her into the waiting carriage, sweeping the ends of her cloak behind her. She settled herself next to Martha, who had been reading Mrs. Radcliff's latest novel while she waited for Miss Patience and Lord Londringham.

Martha gazed at Lord Londringham seated across from her and considered him from a writer's perspective. He certainly fit the picture of one of Mrs. Radcliffe's heroes: tall, strong, handsome in a darkly sinister manner. The way his sharp eyes pinned Miss Patience to the seat, Martha could sense the tension in the carriage and thanked the heavens above she was not his target.

She knew that if Miss Patience and Lord Londringham were to have a happy ending, like in any good novel, they would need to overcome great danger. She smiled at her fancifulness. This was not one of Mrs. Radcliffe's page-turners, but real. Martha wondered what the next "chapter" would bring.

She felt Patience fidgeting beside her. These two were in love if ever she saw it. And how was she supposed to keep them apart? Lord Londringham looked ready to pounce on Patience and devour her whole. Now that would surely make things interesting.

What if she failed in this assignment? She knew Lady Elverston despaired that she would ever find a secure position and would be a burden indefinitely. But Martha would not let that happen. No, something would turn up. It must.

Bryce knew he was being obvious and unrestrained by staring so openly at Patience's loveliness. Her cheeks blushed with the bloom of England's roses and the way she gnawed on her lower lip made him insane to taste those sweet red lips again. But he had vowed that he would touch her again only if she asked him.

Hmmm, what was that little mark on her neck? He leaned forward to stare at a small brown spot on the left side of her neck. Could it be a smear of chocolate?

"What is that spot?" he asked, pointing to her neck.

Her gaze shot nervously to his. "What, where?"

"There on your neck. "Wait a minute." He deftly produced a pristine handkerchief, wetted the tip with his tongue, and reached out his hand to dab at her neck to remove the spot. Martha looked on in avid interest until Bryce shot her a black look, at which point she suddenly found something fascinating outside the window.

Patience's voice sounded husky in his ear. "I . . . I carried Sally . . . Sally to bed and she must have had a piece of chocolate when she rubbed her face . . . um . . ." Her voice faded in explanation because she couldn't remember what came next. She watched him bent over her breast, completely absorbed in his task. "Thank you, my lord. I am sure you have it," she told him, trying to get his attention.

Bryce looked up, his eyes guiltless. "What? One more moment." He leaned forward off his seat as if to whisper something in her ear, his mind only on the now-clean spot at her neck. He quickly pressed his lips to her neck, snaking his tongue out to taste any lingering chocolate.

She jumped and uttered a little cry as he returned to his

seat, calmly replacing his handkerchief. Martha turned and looked first at Patience, whose face was bright red, and then to Lord Londringham, who had acquired a rather bored expression on his face. His feigned indifferent mask proved difficult to continue with Martha staring him down in silent accusation.

He shouldn't have touched her. Touching her sweet skin had nearly undone him, and now, before they had even arrived at the Gardens, he was as hard as the Handel Statue.

At last, to almost everyone's profound relief, the carriage rolled to a stop outside the entrance to Vauxhall that led to the central gardens, supper-boxes, and orchestra. Bryce assisted the ladies from the carriage with the help of the footman, and escorted them into the gardens where Lady Elverston and a circle of her friends awaited them. They found Lady Elverston in one of the supper-boxes sitting in front of one of the famous beautiful engravings depicting children playing.

Patience sat beside Martha, who gaped at the exquisite colorful gowns of the ladies present and admired all the sparkling jewelry shimmering on so many white necks and hands. But it was Lady Elverston's fantastic ruby-and-diamond necklace that caught Patience's attention.

"I've never seen anything like it, Lady Elverston. It is truly magnificent."

Lady Elverston smiled and inclined her head in acknowledgment. "These jewels have been in Lord Elverston's family for generations." With a twinkle in her eye, she added, "If rumors are to be believed, his great-great-great-grandfather was a pirate who fell in love with a viscount's daughter. He bestowed these jewels to her as proof of his love and that one day he would return to marry her, even against her family's wishes."

Martha leaned forward, enthralled by this tale of true love. "And did he return?"

Lady Elverston shook her head. "No, I believe he died at sea, and she died giving birth to his only son and heir. On her deathbed, she showed a devoted friend their marriage license. Her child was named heir and called Henry Charles Elverston."

Patience's wistful expression attracted Bryce, who stood next to Lord Elverston and his friends. "How very sad that he was never able to return to her. But, at least she loved and was loved in return."

Lady Elverston made a clucking sound. "You and Martha are such romantic ones! I'm sure this tale is a fable. The true story probably did not match the magnificence of these jewels and someone in the family decided to create a little fiction to do them justice."

The orchestra had begun to play as fine ladies paraded past their box, intent on a table near the orchestra or a walk to enjoy the rest of the gardens.

Lady Elverston's party watched the blaze of gown colors as they listened to Haydn's popular *The Seasons,* when a tall gentleman, rather distinguished-looking with a handsome black moustache, intruded.

"Does this party contain a certain lady who posed as a maid in Lord Londringham's employ? The story must be too fantastic to be true."

"La, sir," replied Lady Elverston, "the story certainly is true and there the lady sits," pointing to Patience.

Patience felt a slow blush rising, trying not to roll her eyes at yet another admirer.

The gentleman nodded formally, addressing Lady Elverston and Patience. "Allow me to introduce myself. I am Lord Ralingford of York and am delightfully intrigued by this enchanting story. Might I impose upon the young lady for a dance?"

Patience opened her mouth to refuse his invitation but saw Lady Elverston's slight shake of her head. Puzzled, she rose and accompanied Lord Ralingford to the dance floor.

Lord Ralingford held her comfortably during the country dance, his admiration bold enough to take her breath away. If only Bryce would look at her in that way. He asked a few questions about her tenure as a maid, and laughed delightedly when she told him about deceiving the countess and her French cousin, and about surprising the other household staff.

As he led her back to the supper-box, Lord Ralingford requested a second dance later in the evening, but she hesitated to commit herself and instead withheld an answer until he obtained a glass of refreshment for her.

She started toward the ladies lounge when she caught sight of someone familiar. Rupert? Here in London? It had to be he! She would recognize that profile anywhere. But where was he headed? Was he looking for her? She hurried after him as he left the pavilion, walking toward the Rural Downs. Did he not realize the danger he was in?

Although she saw a few couples on the dark walkways, and heard a few whispers and tinsel laughs, Patience ignored them, intent on the figure twenty yards ahead of her. She called after him, but he acted as if he hadn't heard her.

A few drops of rain made her wish she had picked up her cloak before hurrying outside. Why didn't he answer her? He actually looked to be running *from* her.

"Rupert, it's me, Patience. Please stop. Why are you running?" she cried. But he disappeared down the maze of paths, leaving her breathing heavily by an ivy-covered gazebo. When rain began to fall, she rushed into the shelter to avoid a soaking.

She gazed anxiously back at the bright lights of the

orchestra building and wondered if anyone missed her, knowing she would have to wait out the storm just overhead. Crashesof thunder and blinding lightning had everyone scouringfor cover.

There he was again. Rupert headed back to the Grove and turned when she called, looking directly at her. She saw at once it was not Rupert after all, but someone that could be his mirror image. The man smiled at her before running toward the building, pulling his coat around his head.

"Well, *ma chérie,* what are you doing out here? Meeting with a lover? You know, we still have some unfinished business."

Chapter 22

The poisonous tones of Sansouche bit into Patience as she spun around to confront this dangerous man. His dark shadow leaned against the edge of the gazebo while lightning flashed behind him, creating a more eerie and sinister edge to his overwhelming presence.

She swallowed her fear and bravely confronted Sansouche, her shaking hands behind her back. "I thought I saw someone I knew, but I was wrong. I'm merely waiting for the rain to cease to rejoin my party. Perhaps there is another gazebo nearby where you can wait?" she mentioned pointedly.

Sansouche abruptly started toward her. "Possibly, mademoiselle, but, I think, none with your charms." His words and presence frightened her beyond measure. With his company, the storm in all its harsh elements offered more of a sanctuary than did the gazebo.

She turned to run, but the Frenchman, sensing her flight, caught her arm and brought her up against one of the wooden columns. "I've been planning this since the day I discovered your identity. I'll not disappoint you, like other men."

His moist, foul breath threatened to gag her. One of his hands captured both of hers behind her back, bringing her damp bosom closer to his wet greatcoat. Sansouche reached his other hand up to grasp her breast while she turned her head to avoid his wet lips, summoning the strength to wrench herself away from him.

Her movement only served to tear her thin gown at the shoulder, revealing even more of her breast, which the Frenchman eyed hungrily.

She couldn't breathe, her fear all-consuming, seeing the mania in his eyes.

Then she was free. The Frenchman fell to the floor at her feet. Patience stared in horror at the still form. What had happened? She glanced around frantically to see who had saved her, but there was no one. Deciding this was her *only* chance to find safety, she ran down the path, quickly becoming drenched, her gown soaked through. She could feel her hair falling around her shoulders. Perhaps if she could gain Martha's attention, she would be able to repair the damage and hide her wet gown underneath her cloak.

And, of course, then there was the body. She had to tell someone about the body. Bryce. She fervently hoped he would believe her.

Blinded by the rain, she felt strong hands reach out to grab her from behind, halting her flight. She fought to free herself, when she heard Bryce's voice.

"Patience, it's me. What's the matter? Where have you been? Everyone is searching for you."

She caught the concern in his voice as she felt the smooth, warm silk of his coat across her back. Shaking in his arms, she allowed him to lead her to a small shelter in a copse of trees. He stared down into her ashen face with large eyes, her fear still quite evident.

"Tell me what has happened." His voice warmed her like his hands and coat.

Patience gulped and tried to catch her breath, determined

to hold back the tears. "I . . . I thought I saw Rupert near the entrance and followed him. But . . . but it wasn't him. It was someone else. When the . . . the rains began, I found a gazebo that provided shelter, only he showed up." She gulped and began to shiver again.

He held her firmly in the protection of his arms. "My dear, who is he?"

"The . . . the countess's cousin, Sansouche. He grabbed me." When Bryce's coat slipped down from her shoulders, he noticed her torn dress and the smudged bruises beginning to form on her pale arms.

"Where is he?" He cast his eyes quickly over what he could view of Patience, assuring himself she had suffered no further harm.

"I think he may be dead. Someone came from behind him and then he dropped to the floor." Her voice barely rose above a whisper.

"Did you see anyone?" Bryce had difficulty following her story.

"No." She looked up at him, her face flush and damp from the rain. "Do you suppose perhaps he had a heart condition?"

He shook his head. "Doubtful. Can you show me where you last saw him, if you feel you are able? I'll be with you. You have no reason to fear him anymore."

She nodded and led him back to the gazebo where she had left the Frenchman. She was cold, shaken, tired, and only wanted to go home. They rounded the ivy-covered walls and entered the little shelter. Empty.

He turned to inquire, "You're sure this is the place?"

She nodded, frowning. "Yes, I know this is it." She spied an article of clothing on the gazebo floor and recognized it as part of her torn dress.

"Look over there," she told him, pointing.

Bryce walked over, leaned down and picked up the ragged-edged silk cloth and stared at it before he crumbled it in his hands.

She walked over to him, still trying to put the pieces of the puzzle together, feeling much braver with Bryce by her side. "Who could have moved his body? He was right here. I know he was." She sneezed.

"This certainly is strange, but I intend to find out what happened to him, and when he and I meet, he will regret ever touching you. Now I think I should get you home before you catch a chill." He adjusted his coat to fit more snugly over her slender frame. "I think it would be better to send a note with a footman to inform Lady Elverston to bring Miss Krebs home and not to worry about you. The fewer questions asked, the better." He stopped to think for a moment and said to her humorlessly, "This habit of leaving early and sending a message to Lady Elverston appears to becoming a habit with us."

In no time, Bryce had Patience safely ensconced in his carriage. He sat beside her with her nestled in his arms for the entire journey home and wondered if she wanted his comforting—something that would pleasure him greatly. It had been a very long time since anyone had needed him.

He had been quite concerned fearing for her safety and felt great relief in finding her on one of the paths. He burned with a hatred that knew no bounds at the man that had touched Patience in violence. Sansouche would pay, he vowed, as she fell asleep against his shoulder.

Upon reaching home, he carried her out of the carriage and up the stairs to her bedroom, asking Verna, one of the new maids, to follow and assist Miss Patience.

Bryce laid her gently on the bed and removed his coat. He heard the little maid gasp at the sight of Patience's torn gown gaping open and her bruised arms. Silently, he drew the edges of her gown together, then, before quitting the room, requested Verna to oblige the young woman in whatever she needed.

He finally left the room, assured Patience would be well looked after, his face set with promised retribution.

As soon as the guards he had sent for arrived at the house, he would return to the Gardens with the Runners to learn more about what had happened in the gazebo and to try to find the missing Frenchman.

Patience struggled out of her deep sleep. What was that noise? Something wouldn't allow her to return to the welcoming darkness of forgetfulness. She brushed a lock of hair over her shoulder and slowly sat up in bed, wondering what had awakened her.

She listened for a moment. All still. The storm, which earlier had thundered over the house, had settled into a gentle rain. She heard the drops tapping at her window, but that wasn't the same noise.

Wait.

There it was again.

She closed her eyes to listen more clearly. A faint sound of an animal. Yes, a meow. A cat's sad cry. If it indeed was an animal, it must be in trouble. She pushed away the blankets with her feet and slowly rolled out of bed. At first she felt a little light-headed, but the cold floor beneath her bare feet soon repaired her senses.

Her dressing gown missing, she grabbed a thin blanket and wrapped it around her shoulders while walking toward the door. Cautiously, she opened it and peered around the edge, wondering if anyone else had heard the crying and planned to investigate. Silence, except for the cat.

She padded down the hall, stopping every now and again to listen for the cat and to follow the noise. The longcase clock downstairs in the hallway chimed one o'clock in the morning, scaring her heart into a race. What was she so afraid of? Bryce discovering her in her present condition in a nightdress and blanket?

Earlier tonight, when his hot tongue had touched her, she knew she would never be free from him—his smile, his warmth, his strength, his touch, his kiss. Not even long after she had returned home to Storrington. Sansouche's touch was already a nightmare locked away from remembrance.

The third squeak on the stairs halted Patience in her tracks, surely her thundering heart would wake the household. The quiet held, no doors swung open, no light shined on the stairs revealing Patience to be the intruder she felt.

On the first landing, she heard the cat's plaintive cry from outside. She raised the sash, slowly revealing the night filled with a thousand dewdrops, a thousand stars, and one big, fat black cat sitting in a wet tree.

Martha's Satan.

She called softly to him. "Come here, little kitty. Come to Patience."

The stubborn cat sat in the tree, glad to have an audience but not willing to budge one inch. Judging the distance between the window ledge and the tree, she thought she might be able reach out and grab the cat. She looked down, then wished she hadn't. Even one floor off the ground looked a great distance.

She wrapped the blanket around her waist, took a deep breath, and leaned across the wet window ledge. The cat remained just beyond her reach. A few more inches and she could grab the fat cat. Edging out farther, her waist now across the sill, one arm holding onto the window sash and one hand outstretched to Satan.

So concentrated in her efforts to save the cat, she didn't feel her feet leave the landing or her blanket slide farther

down her body. Satan almost in her grasp, the playful cat
batted away her hand with his paw.

"You stupid cat, I'm trying to save you. You should be
more cooperative," she told Satan in agitation, but he sat
there and continued his mewing. "All right, then."

She made one last attempt and lunged for the cat.

And began to fall out the window.

Someone roughly grabbed her legs in time and pulled her
to safety. Patience shuddered in her rescuer's arms, grateful
for the assistance and forgetting the thin nightgown that
kept her decently covered.

It could only be Bryce.

"Patience, what were you doing out the window? I left
you asleep in your bed."

She looked up at Bryce. Here he was, saving her again. *Is
it possible I may have as many lives as a cat?* Flicking her
damp hair out of her face, she gestured toward the window.

"Martha's cat, Satan. He's caught in the tree. I heard him
meowing from my bedroom and tried to save him, except he
wanted no part of my help."

They both leaned out the window to discover the black
cat had ventured even higher in the tree, obviously seeking
safety from any troublesome humans, and blending into the
night, his gold eyes their only target.

She stared in dismay before turning a beseeching look on
Bryce. "Can you help him? I'm rather afraid of heights."

He grimaced, knowing bed would have to wait. Remembering how her wet and warm body felt in his arms, it was
going to be a long night.

To keep his thoughts off her very desirable body, he bent
to pick up her forgotten blanket and wrapped it around her
before leaning his head out the window to plan his cat-
saving mission.

No other windows on this side of the house would enable

him to reach the troublesome cat, who no doubt would eventually come down on his own accord. But one look at Patience's countenance ensnared him: the hero-worship look. He sighed. Did she never take a respite from saving children or animals? He pulled his head in from the window, closed the sash, and started down the stairs.

"Where are you going?"

He stopped and turned to look at her, trying to ignore her bare feet and shapely calves showing below her nightdress, but it was too Herculean an effort. Once again, her body wielded control over a certain part of his body, almost as if his member had a life of its own. He wished the rain could help cool his passion, but he knew nothing ever would.

"I plan to save that damn cat. The only clear way is to climb the tree," he told her succinctly.

"Oh, but is that the only way? You might fall out of the tree and hurt yourself." She followed him down the stairs.

"My lady, you disappoint me with an obvious lack of faith in my abilities. I've climbed that tree many times in my youth. I think I can save one miserable cat." He stalked away, leaving the house, clad only in his white shirt and black breeches.

Patience rushed back up the stairs to watch him out the window. She saw him nimbly climb the lower branches of the tree, seeming to know which ones would hold his weight. She chewed her lips, fearing for his safety and afraid to look and watch him fall.

But up and up he went until he finally reached the cat's resting place. He reached over and managed to grasp the black cat, who appeared quite unwilling to accompany his champion. But Bryce had a firm grip on him and slowly, methodically, rerouted himself down the tree.

Once he slipped and nearly dropped the ungrateful animal. When Satan dug his claws well into Bryce's shoulder for salvation, he concentrated harder on descending the tree and not on the sharp, throbbing pain delivered by Satan himself. Irony abounded.

Reliving the miserable evening, he could not wait for this night to end: Patience looking so damn fetching yet he couldn't touch her, her attack in the gardens by that scum Frenchman, and now climbing down a wet, slippery tree with a cat making mincemeat out of his shoulder. All for Patience.

She opened the kitchen door and watched Satan leap from Bryce's shoulder onto the wooden floor and calmly make his way toward the hall. Bryce was wet through and through and obviously not in the mood for her gratitude. He brushed by her, intent on having a stiff draught of whiskey and retiring to bed with the bottle. Maybe then he could forget her wet curves and her warm mouth. Or was it her warm curves and her wet mouth?

"My lord?"

Bryce turned around and faced her, wondering what more she could possibly want from him.

She warily approached him, sensing the tension in him and thinking he looked like he could explode. Although she greatly feared the fierce expression on his face and the wild, dark look in his eyes, she reached up to touch his shoulder where blood had seeped through his shirt from the cat's claws.

"Your shoulder needs to be seen to. It looks quite painful." Her soft voice and concerned lovely face penetrated his anger.

"Yes," he told her abruptly, suddenly not wanting to let her out of his sight. "Bring some bandages to the library."

A few minutes later she joined him in the library, now cozy with the beginnings of a fire. Bryce sat by the hearth, slumped in his chair, a whiskey bottle in his hand. He had yet to take a sip and couldn't for the life of him discover why he hesitated.

Patience approached him, still clad in her nightdress and

her thin blanket for protection. She set a basin of water behind him on a small table, along with her bandages and scissors. Her nervous tongue ran over her dry lips as she carefully pulled the ripped shirt from his bloodied shoulder and concentrated on avoiding Bryce's heated gaze.

She knew what she was doing. Or did she? Did she realize she was playing with fire, playing with a hungry tiger and looking more and more like his meal? Instead of frightening her, his look only caused molten lava to heat her skin wherever he looked, while a thin perspiration formed on her skin.

Suddenly, Patience felt like the inside of Melenroy's large kettle bubbling over the fire. She wiped her brow and returned his gaze with more assurance than she felt. "I . . . I think"—she cleared her throat—"I believe this will work better if you remove your shirt."

Bryce shrugged and placed his whiskey bottle on the table before unbuttoning his shirt. Standing over his half-naked body brought their one night of passion thundering back to her, unless the sound was actually her heart beating, fast. She felt her nipples harden in response to the expanse of firm, muscled chest revealed before her.

He threw the shirt on the floor and settled once more back into the chair. She leaned over him to reach the table, and her muslin-clad breast accidentally brushed his shoulder, causing them both to jump.

"I'm sorry, I'll try to be more careful."

He didn't bother to reassure her that she hadn't hurt his shoulder but merely scorched his skin with her innocent touch.

Patience studiously cleaned the wound and wrapped it with a clean bandage, admitting to herself he handled the pain admirably, with no need for spirits. She stepped back to admire her handiwork.

"There, did he hurt you anywhere else?" She faltered

under his intense gaze, most anxious to quit the room before she threw herself onto his lap and wrapped her arms around his inviting masculine chest.

"Ah, as a matter of fact, he scratched my hand in several places," he suddenly remembered and held out his hands for inspection.

She studied his firm, strong hands but could not find any scratches.

"See, right there." He pointed to a small scratch on his little finger.

Patience had to bend quite close to see the scratch, then looked back at Bryce, as if to judge whether he was bamboozling her or not. Only innocence etched that fine face she had learned to care so much about.

With a sigh, she cleaned the little scratch as well, then gathered up her nursing tools, prepared to leave. He watched her carefully, and Patience prayed he would not see her intense longing, which she tried to hide. But if he had, he said nothing. She stepped back to see his face by the firelight, wondering what he was thinking, and with a smile to him, turned to go.

His eyes were shut, avoiding her gaze. She started to back away, but he grabbed her nearest hand, holding it lightly in his, brushing his thumb over her smooth skin.

He murmured softly, yet harshly, "What do you want from me, Patience? I can't go on like this. Tell me you want my touch. I need to hear you say it."

His eyes still closed, he wanted to hear the truth in her words, if he couldn't read it on her face.

Patience bit her lip. What did she want? What did he want to hear? That she wanted his love? That she wanted to be his wife and bear his children? That she wanted never to leave him because it would break her heart and her spirit? What truth did he want to hear?

She found herself drawn to him in a spell and whispered, "Yes, I want you to touch me. I want you to kiss me. Make me feel as I did before."

He finally opened his eyes and her breath caught in her throat at his heated blue eyes blazing with passion. She told him softly, "I want what we had before. I want you."

He savored his victory of her acquiescence only briefly before giving his lady what she wanted.

Chapter 23

Stretched comfortably on his chair, Bryce drew Patience onto his lap and tenderly wrapped his hands around her narrow waist, her nightdress and his breeches still between them, her instruments of mercy fallen forgotten to the floor. Each stared mesmerized at the other as Patience placed her arms around his neck, waiting for his kiss.

He slowly tilted her chin up, brushing the side of her soft, warm cheek with his hand. His mouth hovered over hers briefly before kissing her slowly and gently, almost as if this was the first time they kissed. An unexpected spark surged between them. Something was different this time. Something more forever.

Patience's hands in his thick hair, she rubbed her wet nightgown against his very warm chest, as Bryce deepened the kiss. He groaned, feeling her body touching him in all the right places.

They were both on fire. He swept his tongue into her mouth, seeking possession and her sweetness. She gave back willingly and ardently, wanting him as much as he wanted her.

Bryce unwillingly ended their tongue play to gain his breath and the upper hand, which Patience seemed to be taking from him unknowingly. He wanted to make the night last and shower her with such passion that she would never forget that she was a part of him.

He lifted her from his lap to stand and held her lightly in his arms. He couldn't take his eyes off her. In front of him, her full breasts begged for his touch. He easily captured one nipple in his mouth through her thin white nightdress, causing Patience's sweet moan at the sensuous feel of his hot tongue on her breast. His right hand slid up from her waist to grasp her other breast, kneading and stroking the lovely fullness at his whim.

She placed her hands on his shoulders for support, arching her back for his pleasuring mouth. When one breast became a taut wetness, he turned his attention to her other nipple, laving and sucking the tip to her delight and his immense pleasure.

She thought she would expire from the flame in his touch. Her senses drowned in this wet fire, lit higher when he grasped her hips and pulled her back on the chair with him, her legs on either side of his legs and centered to his swollen member tight in his breeches.

He slowly rubbed his length at the juncture of her thighs, as Patience caught her breath and uttered a soft cry. He stroked her legs, pushing her nightdress up to her waist. She shivered at his touch as he kissed her again with such intensity, all thought and reason swept away. There was only him and her and this night.

Bryce pulled her reluctantly away from him and looked up into her face warm with passion. His hardened maleness pulsed achingly when he saw her hazel eyes darkened in desire, desire that he had created in her, and only he. He allowed himself a small smile before rising to stand with her, still holding on to her, her legs now wrapped around his waist. After a few more punishing kisses, he set her gently down.

Patience watched him with wonder and trust in her eyes, which made his heart swell. Without losing any time, Bryce quickly arranged her blanket on the floor before the fire with a pillow for her head.

He turned to her while kneeling on the floor and outstretched his hand for her. He saw her shy smile as she brushed her wispy hair from her cheek and knelt down before him. Bryce captured her face in his hands and claimed her ripe mouth in a soft kiss, which instantly became demanding.

Patience, wrapping her arms around his shoulders, eagerly returned his kiss before they slowly pulled apart. She feathered tiny kisses along his solid jaw, then mischievously painted his lips with her tongue, before delving into his mouth to mate with his tongue.

He started slightly at her boldness, he was not sure how much longer he could last until he had to press inside her to relieve his aching need.

He gently pushed her to the floor, until they were both stretched out along the blanket. He slid one leg between hers to rub his knee against her quivering form while he resumed his searching kisses, branding her with the passion she inspired in him.

He leaned up and away from her, trying to gain control of the raging heat inside of him from just the taste of her lips and the passion-filled gaze in her hazel eyes. Bryce slowly traveled down her body, planting kisses on her nightdress, causing the little shivers that shook her body.

She moaned in protest the farther he moved away from her, but he looked up and whispered softly to her, "The pleasure can sometimes be had in the waiting." Kissing her at the center of her womanhood brought her head up in surprise. She leaned her weight back on her elbows, never taking her eyes off his face as he totally concentrated on bringing her pleasure.

Bryce reached for the ends of her nightdress and slowly, torturing himself, raised the garment up past her lovely white calves to reveal slender thighs, trembling beneath his hard stare, kiss by kiss up each warm limb. And he pushed her garment still farther up, revealing the soft dark curls at her thighs' juncture.

He hesitated before continuing to slide the thin material past her smooth waist to her full breasts waiting for his touch. Slowly, wanting the sensations to last, he caressed her stomach and then her breasts, drawing a soft moan from her—his woman. For that was who she was and would always be.

As he drew closer, Patience reclined on the blanket, then her arms reached up to grasp his shoulders. He paused to unbutton the few buttons at the top of her nightdress before pulling it over her head. Bryce stopped and stared at the lovely vision before him gilded in golden firelight. Shadows danced across her enticing curves and hidden valleys, a wondrous land he fully intended to explore this night. But her entrancement lay in the beautiful dark innocence of her warm stare.

Bryce thought perhaps Patience would allow him to touch her soul tonight, at least he would make every effort to try.

She continued stretching toward him, imploring him in silence to return to her but he shook his head. He was determined to give her what she wanted and even what she didn't know she wanted.

Grasping her waist between his hands, he leaned down and attended to the pert rosy nipple posed next to his mouth. Again and again he laved the tip with his hot tongue before taking it into his mouth and plucking at the bud between his teeth.

She writhed uncontrollably underneath him, caught by the tidal wave of passion lashing over her. "Please, I want . . . I want . . ."

He looked up into her flushed face and asked quietly, "What do you want?"

But she shook her head wordlessly. "Do it again, like before. How long will this go on?" she implored him.

He smiled a secret smile. "As long as you command, my lady." Then he turned to her other peak and coaxed it to pliancy beneath his expert mouth. Bryce's member pulsed inside his breeches, needing to be free. He took a deep breath, knowing the end for him was not yet in sight.

But he realized he would have to speed his progress slightly for both to find fulfillment together. As he kissed the valley of her flat stomach, he slipped a hand down to open Patience's thighs in preparation.

He stroked the soft insides of her legs before gliding a finger up to her womanly heat and easing inside of her. He heard her soft cry, and he shuddered, warmly stunned at her burning dew enveloping him. He couldn't wait any longer and, placing her round buttocks in his hands, brought her wet heat to his mouth.

Before she could protest, a sob choked back, he had already found the sweet bud of Patience's femininity and claimed it for his own. He nibbled and tickled her blossoming flower, then took the tiny nubbin in his mouth and stroked Patience until her body quivered and climaxed.

He held her shaking body, enveloped in passion's embrace, her hands with a death grip on her blanket. Then he looked down her body to pin his brand on her, knowing that her honeyed pleasures belonged to him, till the end of forever.

Giving Patience and himself time to catch their breath, Bryce leaned up to sweep a kiss on her surprised lips. He quickly discarded his breeches and stood before her, his rampant manhood ready to besiege her welcoming wet fortress.

He knelt again between her parted legs and then hesitated. He looked up into her green gaze and asked her anew, "What do you want of me, Patience?"

She looked startled at his query and shook her head in confusion.

"You must tell me." *And soon,* he thought, because he could delay his passion for her no longer.

"I . . . I want"—she cleared her throat and spoke falteringly—"I want you . . . inside me, please, Bryce."

That was the request he needed to hear. His only words: "As you desire."

Her arms wrapped around him tightly, he gritted his teeth to control his surging passion as he probed gently at her entrance before pushing himself into her tight chamber. He pulled out slightly, then thrust in again, this time farther and deeper.

She cried out, her voice heavy with desire.

Bryce clenched his teeth, stifling a moan. She felt so good and so very tight. Every time he brought his member to the edge of her heat, with legs wrapped around his hips, she voraciously pulled him back inside, her hips bucking beneath his hands.

He guided her to a rhythm she impatiently matched, her soft, inarticulate cries echoed in the room and in his heart. It was soon time. His thrusts increased, their speed as fast as the beating of their hearts. At the zenith of their loving, he reached up and laid his lips against hers in an unspoken promise before he growled deep in her throat and caught her passion-filled sob in his mouth when he poured his release into her haven.

Time stood still as he stayed nestled inside of her, before withdrawing from her wet heat. Lying down beside her, he wrapped one arm around her shoulders and with his other brought her to his chest, his arm holding her tight to his side. He held her tenderly in love's comforting aftermath.

For a long while, neither moved. He didn't want to leave her side, and she had no wish for him to leave.

"There you are, you bad kitty. How did you get so wet, Satan? Were you outside in the storm?" Martha asked her pet affectionately when she found him near the library. The black ball of fur rubbed his damp coat against his mistress's face, seeking forgiveness. "Satan," she cooed to him, "you are my one faithful companion, albeit a very naughty one."

Noises from inside the library drew a frown on Martha's brow. Still holding Satan in her arms, she walked silently to the doors, easily discerning the voices of Miss Patience and his lordship. She shook her head in defeat. Lady Elverston would not like this one bit. Again, she had failed in her duties to her sponsor.

Suddenly, she straightened up and marched to her room. Perhaps it was not wrong that the earl and Patience were together before the sanctity of marriage. Any fool could see how much they were in love.

She pulled her worn white nightgown over her head and crawled sleepily into bed. *Would that a man looked at me in such a fashion.* Martha quickly gathered sleep around her like a blanket. With slumber, she could forget, and her tears would be safe.

With only the embers left of their once-blazing fire, Patience suddenly felt chilled, even though Bryce's hard length heated her side. She must get to bed. Alone. She needed time to think. Where do they go from here?

She slowly drew herself up and reached for her nightdress in a ball at their feet and slipped it on.

"Why would you want to cover such lovely charms?"

Bryce had raised himself on one elbow, casually watching her, his face almost in the shadows of the dimly lit room.

Patience could barely breathe. "I must return to my room, my lord, before we are discovered, like this . . . uh . . . together."

Bryce held up his hand to object, but she had already risen and crossed to the door. She turned to look at him, sadness and pain wetting her lashes. *He must not see my tears.* Taking a deep breath, she told him, "Please wait a few minutes until leaving after me." She practically ran down the hall, leaving him in stunned confusion.

Patience climbed the stairs, whisked her door open and shut, and flew to her bed. Flinging herself prostrate across her half tester, only then did she allow her tears to fall. Would they, could they, have a future together? She cried for Rupert and the peck of trouble he was in. And she cried for Sally because the little girl had no home and a father who didn't want her. Finally, she cried for the sadness she often caught in Bryce's eyes that he didn't realize showed.

Her cries silenced by her pillow, Patience jumped when she heard a soft knock and saw the door opening. She wiped her tears on the back of her hands and watched as Bryce, dressed in his breeches, stared enigmatically at her.

She took a deep breath and then another one. What was he doing in here? She uttered a startled whisper and felt the bed dip as Bryce sat on the edge. He gathered her into his arms, whispering comforting sounds in her ear.

Hushing. Hushing.

Causing a torrent of tears to melt down his solid warm chest. Several minutes passed before she lifted her head, unable to meet his gaze which she knew sought answers. He pushed his handkerchief into her hand, which she used to dry her face.

Not quite finished, Patience choked back a few more

sighs and gulped a few breaths. Bryce remained by her side
and stroked her hair and rocked her back against his chest,
seeming to understand her unexpressed need for solace
without words.

Finally, feeling more composed, she drew into a sitting
position and smiled abashedly. "Crying is such a silly waste
of time, is it not?"

He frowned. "Why would you think such a thing?"

She shrugged. "My elder brother James is always telling
me not to behave like a silly female, and tears, he says, are
only used for womanly wiles and not at all proper or godlike."

Bryce shook his head with a wry smile. "If we are made
in his image, then surely tears are godlike. I do not deem all
tears as stratagems that women use on men—well, actually
I did, until I met you." He paused and tilted her head with a
gentle finger beneath her chin, staring into her eyes as if
trying to learn her secrets.

He asked the question that had hung on his lips since
hearing her cries outside her door. "Were you crying because we made love?" he asked, his voice low and urgent.

She looked in shy surprise at him. "No, my lord. I wanted
to be with you." Then she hung her head, unable to respond
to the demanding stare. Silence. She knew he was waiting
for an explanation and would not leave without one.

Patience settled back against the bed's bolster and sighed.
"I'm worried about my brother. Will he ever be free to go
home?" That part was certainly true. "And I'm afraid someone will try to kill him. Perhaps one of the constable's men
or one of the French spies."

Bryce leaned back on his elbow to watch her and shook
his head slightly. "No, the constable wants him alive to
answer questions about his cousin's death, and the spies
are much too busy with plans of their own to warrant interest in Rupert."

Patience blinked in astonishment. "Do you think my brother is guilty of treason?"

His lips twisted. "Patience." He reached out a hand to stroke her exposed arm. "I do believe in your brother's innocence. Unfortunately, what I believe and what the constable believes are not necessarily the same. It is only his opinion that counts."

"You can convince the constable to let him go free." She unknowingly grabbed his hand to her breast in her ardent plea.

Bryce liked the feel of his hand against her heart. "If there is anything in my power to liberate your brother, I will certainly do so. I have my staff at Paddock Green keeping a watch for your brother, but so far, no one has seen a sign of him. At this uncertain time, we're all on alert for a possible invasion. We need to learn what the French spies are planning."

"Do you think Sansouche is dead?" she whispered.

His gaze never left her countenance. "As of yet, no trace has been found of his body. That could mean a number of things."

She nodded absently, exhausted by the events of the entire evening, still clinging to his strong hand.

"Patience?" Bryce asked her quietly. He had a question that needed answering, one he had thought of often.

She glanced at him, patting her wayward hair behind her. "Yes, my lord?"

"Why did your brothers send you to Winchelsea to help Rupert? It seems to me unconscionable to send a lone woman to a strange town to find her brother and free him from treason charges. Ludicrous, even." Traces of anger fed his words.

She wasn't insulted at his lack of confidence in female ingenuity. Smiling tremulously, she leaned back against her throne of pillows, his hand released. "My eldest brother,

Louis, Baronet Mandeley, is rather sickly. All his life he has suffered from a weakness in his lungs. We have had to watch him very closely, and we are quite lucky his health has slowly improved."

She sank farther into the bed's depths, engrossed in her story. "My second eldest brother, James, is our parish's cleric and has been the unwanted family conscience for years."

Bryce lazily blinked, his lips thinned wryly. "Oh, yes, our brother James who detests a woman's tears."

She sent him a censured look. "James has a good heart and works very hard for his parish. He couldn't leave his people for any length of time, and we were unsure how long this would take."

He reached for her nearby calf crossed beneath her and caressed the velvety white skin, closing his eyes to listen to her story.

"Then there is dear Benjamin. He works with our land tenants, enjoys tilling the fields and talking with the farmers. For any matter other than agriculture, Benjamin is unknowledgeable. Out of the field, he is, shall I say, out of his depth?"

She sighed. "Ever since our parents were killed in an overturned coach accident when I was fifteen, I have been taking care of my brothers. Ensuring Louis took his medicine, that James did not become too pompous and overbearing, and assisting Benjamin in keeping his records have kept me quite busy, with little time for anything else." She stopped her soliloquy, remembering and missing home.

"Then there is of course, Rupert, a rather a wild one. Always getting into scrapes." She smiled sadly. "When this latest trouble arose, I made the decision to come to Winchelsea to help Rupert. None of my elder brothers were entirely convinced it was a good idea or even that I would succeed.

However, no argument could persuade me not to attempt the trip." She trailed off miserably.

Bryce slowly sat up, frowning. "While you were busy taking care of your brothers and every wounded animal or lonely child, who looked after you?" his question almost rhetorical.

Patience shrugged, a little amazed at his question. "I've always taken care of myself."

"Was there never anyone in your past? A beau? Someone who would look after you? Even now, I'm sure your brothers are managing admirably in your absence." His heart stilled awaiting a reply.

Her enchanting green gaze drifted past him to a forgotten memory. "There was a friend of Louis's. His name was Richard, a widower, several years older than I. He proposed marriage one summer and then left for a trip to the Continent." Her voice had lowered to a hush that required him to bend forward to catch her words. "He was gone for over a year and a half. I kept waiting and hoping. But word finally reached us that he had been killed in a skirmish with French soldiers. Apparently, Richard happened to be in the wrong place at the wrong time."

He struggled to speak his next words. "Did you love him?"

Patience's gaze came back to linger on his shadowed face, missing the concerned tone and the apprehension in his eyes.

"I loved him . . . as a brother. He reminded me of Louis, only in stronger form. Our time spent together was in quiet appreciation of literature, a good game of chess, or his indulgence in my hours in the garden." She would have wondered at his question if she was not so lost in the past.

Her eyelids began to drift to her cheeks. "Perhaps, you should leave now," she murmured, reaching for his hand and clutching it to her chest.

Bryce had no recourse but to mold his body along hers,

feeling her rounded bottom above his groin. She held his hand snugly between her breasts, nestling back against his hard form.

Almost asleep, she whispered, "I never knew real love until I met you."

Her curly hair tickled his nose. He allowed himself the pleasure of stroking the silky strands, reflecting on the silken strands of Patience's web she had spun around him. A strange feeling slowly stole over him, at first unrecognizable.

It was fear. Cold, irrational fear. Sweeping long loops from her ear, Bryce leaned down and breathed quietly to her, "Please don't love me . . . It will only hurt all the more when you leave." But Patience was already in Morpheus's arms.

Chapter 24

Patience woke languidly and stretched her toes beneath the covers. A perfume of lilacs assailed her senses. She sat up in bed and discovered three branches of lilacs lying next to her. Brushing away the cobwebs of sleep, she picked up the flowers and wandered over to the window, drawing the curtains to allow sunlight to shower the room.

Today felt wonderful. She loved Bryce and planned to tell him. She suddenly wanted to be free of all the lies and traps she had made for herself.

Together they would write their own happy ending, just like Sally's Sleeping Beauty. The rumble in her stomach intruded on her carefree thoughts as she prepared to head down to the dining room for her repast. She dressed hurriedly in a sky blue muslin dress with white pinafore and fichu, not wanting to call a maid for assistance. A ribbon to corral her thick curls completed her toilette, and with her heart in her hands she ran lightly down the stairs in hopes of finding Bryce still in the house.

She slowed her progress on the last few stairs. The cavernous hallway bloomed with flowers—lavender, pink and yellow lilacs, roses, gardenias, and hydrangeas tinted the long entryway, a beautiful indoor garden. The sight of all those flowers made her heart smile.

Sally watched one of the housemaids place yellow roses in a tall white vase near the door when she heard the sound of Patience's footsteps.

The little girl ran to Patience, yelling, "Miss Patience, we 'ave a garden growing in the 'ouse! Are the flowers not beautiful?"

Patience smiled down at the child. "Yes, they are lovely. These flowers certainly brighten up the vestibule, and their perfume is absolutely wonderful." She noticed Stone standing nearby. Have you seen his lordship this morning?"

"Miss Mandeley, Lord Londringham left a short time ago, advising he would return with a surprise for you," his tone cool and judgmental.

"I wonder what it could be. Thank you, Stone. I think I shall have something to eat. Want to come along, Sally?"

The two entwined hands and walked down the hallway to the dining room together.

Later in Patience's bedchamber, Martha caught Patience's gaze in the mirror and grinned in amusement. Patience nervously tried to button the white cotton shirt of Martha's riding habit, with little luck.

"It appears that you are a bit more amply endowed than I am in this area," Martha told her, smiling.

Patience grinned. "It does appear so," she answered as she looked nervously into the looking glass. She tried not to think about Bryce's proposition, and had thought of every excuse she could to dissuade him from teaching her to ride. But finally she agreed after he assured her that her horse would be as docile as one of James's congregation. She must somehow overcome her fear of horses, to please

Bryce. Without time to have a riding habit made, she had to borrow Martha's.

She pulled on the short dove-gray basque and noted the buttons did not quite meet across her bosom. "It will simply have to do, Martha. Thank you kindly for allowing me to borrow it." She carefully placed the matching gray hat with its fashionable feathers atop her hair, the only piece of the ensemble that did fit, and turned to face her friend for approval.

"I have seldom had occasion to wear it myself. Perhaps tonight I can alter it for you."

Patience hugged Martha. "I am so glad Lady Elverson thought to send you to me as my chaperone. I'm indeed so lucky," she told her friend as they walked down to the vestibule together, where Martha watched her depart from the steps.

Late afternoon, Lucky and a groom drove Patience to Hyde Park in the earl's carriage while Bryce rode behind on Defiance with Red Tattoo beside him. Patience's mare, Apples, followed behind their carriage, newly purchased at Tattersalls this morning, after her previous owner assured Bryce the mare would handle perfectly for a novice rider. With a tame name like Apples, Bryce thought she might be perfect for Patience.

The little white mare paraded proudly, her silky tail bobbing nobly with her even gait, keeping pace with the other two larger horses beside her.

After reaching Hyde Park, Red Tattoo untied Apples while Patience climbed down from the carriage. She struggled to jerk her basque down over her cramped breasts, not noticing the light in Bryce's eyes. She nervously rearranged her little hat while awaiting instruction from Bryce.

"Would you rather take a ride in the carriage?" In fact, he

thought, the way her breasts threatened to burst from their containment, that might indeed be a better idea.

Patience straightened her shoulders, chin high, and replied, "No, I need to try. I'm sure that with your assistance, I will manage admirably." Courage ringed her words, no coward she.

Bryce smiled approvingly. "Good. First, let me introduce you to the lady who will be providing your ride."

They walked in front of Apples, who stood at attention, watchfulness in her big brown eyes. As Patience pet the little mare's nose, Bryce pulled off one of her gloves, and placed a shiny red apple in the palm of her hand, his hand warm on hers.

"Since she loves apples, this seems an appropriate gesture of friendship. Keep your hand very flat, like this," he said, demonstrating by straightening her fingers, each touch a caress. Patience shivered in the sunlight from his heat, having to remind herself to pay attention to his instruction, his *riding* instruction. Oh, bother.

Together, they fed Apples before returning to the horse's side. While Bryce prepared to lift Patience into the saddle, he watched as she wet her lips and hesitantly reached out to stroke Apples's fine white coat, calling, "Easy, girl. Be gentle and stay still."

She placed her foot in the stirrup and with Bryce's help, raised herself into the saddle, swinging her right leg over the pommel. She sat still, adjusting to the feel of the mare beneath her as the horse grew accustomed to her. With his hand still on her calves, he looked up at her and asked, "How does she feel?"

"Good, I . . . I think," her smile a bit confident and a bit shaky.

"Right then." He leaned over to capture the reins and handed them to her. "Hold them here, but not too tight.

Allow her some head. But not too much, show her who is in charge," he told her in a calm fashion.

"Yes, not too tight and not too much. I shall try to remember." She became a little frantic when the groom came to lead Patience and her mount around in a circle. She held her breath as Apples moved slowly and passively, following the lead. Bryce and his valet reseated themselves on their mounts with Bryce keeping a careful eye on his pupil.

After several circles, he called to her, "Do you think you can walk Apples on your own?"

She glanced at Bryce, and her excited expression captured his breath. With her lovely hazel eyes shining and the sun glinting red-gold on her hair, she was a vision. He allowed himself a moment of contentment and pride. She was truly his.

Single riders and carriages mobbed Hyde Park. More than one male rider stopped to admire Patience's form on her little mare, but it only took a glare from Bryce to send them on their way.

Finally, at a signal from Bryce, the groom released the reins, and Patience nudged Apples toward Bryce and Defiance.

"How am I doing?" she asked brightly.

"Beautifully, as if you were born to ride," he said, chuckling to himself about his double entendre.

"Shall we venture further afield, my lord?"

"With pleasure."

As they walked their horses along the stone path, Patience explained, "When my father tried to teach me to ride astride, the horse spooked, and I fell off the horse. In the fall, I broke my leg and swore I would never mount another one of those beasts. You have disavowed my oath, my lord." She turned to bestow another dazzling smile to the man beside her.

"Would you like to learn to ride astride? Perhaps when we return home to Paddock Green we can continue our instruction. Here in London, I fear, that unladylike behavior would cause too much gossip." The way she looked at him made him want to promise her anything, as long as she never withheld from him that same warm smile.

Patience looked at him curiously but didn't respond. Home, to Paddock Green? He planned to take her back with him? What did this mean? He had not yet mentioned love or marriage. Her heart tightened in a silent ache. What she wanted was to be with him, even forever would not be long enough. What about Rupert and her brothers? They needed her, and she knew they would find it difficult to live without her.

A loud sound snapped her out of her reverie. A gunshot blasted from a nearby copse of woods, frightening Apples. A woman screamed as the little mare took off with Patience clinging to the pommel, the reins dragging uselessly on the ground. Patience heard shouting behind her but could only hold on for dear life. She felt herself falling to the left, and fear seized her, remembering the broken leg years ago and knowing the pain would be much worse.

Several horses started out of her way as Apples swerved around other riders and carriages. The yelling from behind was deafened by the loud and rapid beat of her heart and the mare's heavy pounding hooves. The pommel slipped beneath her gloved grasp, and she closed her eyes, her body tensed for the hard ground.

Just then Bryce brought Defiance beside her and made a grab for her as she slipped from the saddle. With great strength, he pulled her from Apples and lifted her onto his lap. A slow ripping sound accompanied his movements.

She clung to him, shaking at her near fall. He stroked her back while reining his stallion to a halt. He had to catch his breath, lost in fear when he saw the little white mare charge off down the path. Patience could have been seriously hurt, and he felt responsible. He held her tightly, noting one of the grooms had captured the runaway mare and brought her under control. Red Tattoo rode up beside him and shook his head.

Bryce's mouth turned thin and grim. He nodded, turning Defiance to trot back up the path toward their coach. By the time they had reached his carriage, Patience's breathing had returned to normal. She had lost her hat, and no amount of patting and puffing could undo her wayward hair. Her face pinched white, she gladly welcomed assistance dismounting from Bryce's horse, still needing his steady hand when she reached the ground.

Throwing the reins to the groom, he assisted her into his carriage before turning briefly to Red Tattoo. Out of Patience's hearing, his valet told him, "No sign of whoever it was shootin'. I think he was on foot and is probably lost in the crowd."

Bryce's face was a mask of controlled anger, a look Red had seen only a few times before. His lordship planned to do battle, and woe to his enemies unknowing of his reprisal.

"Do you think that bullet was meant for Patience?"

"It was terribly close to her mare," Red at last told his master.

"Red, I've been careless where Patience's safety is concerned and have no idea why someone would want to harm her. Now that I've been warned, I shall safeguard her with everything I have." An avowal made from his heart. That part of him he had long forgotten after Edwards's death. He could finally feel again.

Bryce climbed into the carriage and signaled Lucky to take them home. Surprisingly, Patience sat dry-eyed, staring dismally at her riding habit, more concerned over the habit than over her close chance with danger. The torn white shirt left a gaping hole to expose the tops of her creamy-white breasts. A tear in the basque's shoulder revealed further damage.

When Bryce dropped onto the seat beside her, she sighed. "This is Martha's. I don't know if it can be repaired." Her voice sounded so sad, she seemed on the verge of tears. Over a torn riding habit?

Puzzled, he did the only think he could think of, he drew her onto his lap and into his arms. She melted against him and all tension seemed to flow out of her body. They remained like this as Bryce tried to offer comfort to Patience and keep his body under control, obviously becoming increasingly difficult to do. The sight of her exposed skin aroused him most painfully. Surely she could feel his hardened member beneath her bottom. He willed his mind to put his own needs aside and concentrate on hers.

What was that? A warm mouth found the bottom of his jaw. In fact, Patience feathered the edge of his face with tiny kisses. He groaned, then turned to meet her seeking lips. She met him with an utmost urgency, her tongue sweeping into his mouth, probing, hot, and wet. She softly bit his lower lip before her teasing tongue came out to assuage the pleasure-pain. He reluctantly tore his lips from hers and sought the whiteness of her breasts, planting wet kisses along the warm mounds, swelling under his careful ministration.

His hands came up alongside each breast underneath her jacket to ply her hardened nipples. She sighed, willing his touch to continue.

Suddenly he broke away, carefully placing her on the leather seat and moving to the opposite side of the carriage. He should be more concerned about the disaster that had almost befallen Patience instead of pawing her beautiful form.

"How are you feeling? You must have been terrified when Apples took off with you. This experience may have only redoubled your fear of horses." His concerned gaze captured her unfocused one.

Patience frowned in sweet confusion. What did he say? Something about apples and horses. Conversation for another time. She held out her arms to him, wanting him to return to her, offering a muted passionate plea.

But Bryce kept ahold of his gallantry and other senses, and held up his hand to forestall her with a smile. "No more. You must be in shock. You could have been killed." He was trying to tell her something, but she resolutely closed her eyes, determined not to think about her near miss with death, only to dwell on that sinful mouth of his.

"You saved me," she told him sweetly. "You always save me." She smiled a little smile.

Bryce shook his head and leaned across to tip her face to his to gain her attention. "Little one, I hope I do not need to continue to rescue you. After all, how many lives do you have?" He knew he would come to her rescue whenever she needed him and refused to think about a possible time when he would not be there for her.

With great green eyes, she stared him down until he absolutely had to reclaim her mouth again.

The lovers reluctantly dragged themselves apart upon reaching his lordship's town house. Stone met their carriage with an urgent message for Bryce from the PM demanding his presence immediately. Patience assured him she would be fine while climbing down from the carriage and thanked him very prettily for the flowers in the hallway.

With a gleam in his eye, Bryce told her, "Their beauty fades in comparison to your own, my dear."

Martha hurried to inform Patience that Lady Elverston was waiting. Although Patience would have preferred time for a more thorough washing, a quick towel bath would have to suffice.

Patience changed into her lemon day gown after ruefully explaining to Martha how her riding habit had been torn. Her chaperone was horrified to hear what had happened, but relieved that no harm had come to the young lady, and assured Patience not to concern herself about the clothes.

Afterward, one of the maids, handy with comb and pins, artfully fashioned her hair in a lovely style of tendril curls around her face with the rest pulled back to the side with a silver comb. Patience patted her cheeks, pleased to see her natural color had returned.

Lady Elverston waited in the first-floor drawing room visiting with Martha. A large bow window offered a panoramic view of the street. Stone followed Patience with a tea tray while she greeted her guest. While Martha relaxed on the window seat, Patience poured tea.

Accepting a cup from her hostess, Lady Elverston mentioned, "I was extremely concerned over the earl's and your disappearance last night at the Gardens. A slip of a note from a footman in apology certainly did not set my mind at rest. However, you appear to have suffered no ill affects. Might I inquire what exactly happened to the two of you?" her tone friendly but inquisitive.

Patience quickly decided to tell Lady Elverston almost the whole truth, leaving a few insignificant details—like the Frenchman—out of her story.

With eyes shining bright, her face slightly warm, she explained lightly, "I must confess to a lack of sensibility on my part. When my partner left to procure a refreshment, I thought I saw someone I knew outside. I followed him and got caught in the rain, destroying my gown. I fear I looked a sight. Lord Londringham found me in the Gardens and thought he should take me home, lest I catch a cold. There was nothing to it more than that."

She leaned warily back in her chair, tensed to see how Lady Elverston would accept this abridged version of last night's events.

The marchioness nodded thoughtfully but did not immediately reply. Speaking in a low voice so as not to alert Martha, engrossed in her book, Lady Elverston pinned a direct stare at Patience and asked, "You do have affection for Londringham, do you not?"

Patience stifled a startled gasp, unprepared for this direct assault. "I . . . I . . . yes, I do have affection for his lordship, who has been very kind to myself and others. I sense in him deep depths where no one really knows him." She looked puzzled, wondering what more Lady Elverston wanted.

The older woman leaned forward and prompted, "And?"

"I respect his intelligence and wit. I marvel at his generosity and depth of understanding, and I wish I could take the sadness away that I see sometimes in his eyes when he thinks no one else has noticed.

"Without him, it is almost like I am missing a piece of my soul and that my life has stopped and cannot continue until he is with me again. My heart loses a beat when I see his tall form and his warm blue eyes that notice everything and everyone.

"He has the ability to make my heart smile with a touch of his hand or a soft word in my ear. He can also wound my spirit with the melancholy I sense in him. Then I only want to share his pain, but he won't allow me close to him. Something tells me he has lived in darkness for a long time. I only wish to brighten his world." She let her impassioned words fall softly around her. Her soliloquy convinced Lady Elverston and enraptured romantic Martha.

"That, my dear girl, is not affection," Lady Elverston told Patience quite adamantly.

Patience raised her troubled eyes in shock at this suggestion. "It isn't?"

"No, Patience that which you have just described is love, the very lasting kind." She added thoughtfully, "I wonder how his lordship feels about you?"

Stone entered the room, intruding on their quiet conversation, carrying a silver tray with a calling card. "A gentleman to see you, Miss Patience." He stared directly ahead.

Patience picked up the card. "Lord Ralingford. From the Gardens? Whatever do you suppose he could want?"

All three women drew to their feet when Lord Ralingford entered the room. Over one arm he carried Patience's cape.

She fluttered a hand to her breast in amazement. "My lord, this is an unexpected pleasure," her smile welcoming the immaculately-dressed older man.

He acknowledged Lady Elverston and Martha before accepting a cup of tea from Patience and resting on the brocade sofa. His dark brown eyes lingered on Patience's warm face.

His baritone voice echoed in the room: "My apologies for interrupting your tête-à-tête. I was anxious over your sudden disappearance last night and needed to assure myself that no harm had come to you. Also, the return of your cape gave me reason to hope for admittance."

Patience blushed slightly, wondering what Lady Elverston thought of this older man coming to call. "I'm certainly overwhelmed and grateful for your thoughtfulness and for returning my cape, Lord Ralingford. As I mentioned to Lady Elverston, I thought I saw someone I knew and ran outside to confirm my suspicions, however the person disappeared and I became caught in the downpour. Fortunately, Lord Londringham found me and we returned home. No more of an adventure than that," Patience tossed off with a laugh.

Lord Ralingford acknowledged her story with a nod. "Please believe me, my lady, when I say that I am completely restored by the sight of your good health. May you continue to bloom as the flowers I saw in the hallway."

Patience chewed indelicately on a nail, unsure how to prompt his retreat.

"I wish not to overstay my welcome since I have accomplished my mission. If I may be allowed to call on you, perhaps in the future?" Lord Ralingford bent over her hand and placed a soft kiss on it.

Biting her lip nervously, she wondered in dismay, was this man making love to her? And if so, how to refuse him gently? Although not engaged, she did belong to another man. And always would.

She stood up and walked him to the door. Taking a deep breath for confidence, Patience smiled brightly. "Thank you very kindly for the return of my cape. You will always be welcome here as a friend."

Lord Ralingford smiled in understanding. "I am content with your offer, hope ever strong in my breast that we will one day know each other better." He silently departed.

"Whew!" Patience sighed, then returned to her chair upon Lord Ralingford's departure. "Such a nice gentleman. Did you not think so, Martha?"

Martha didn't respond—watching their visitor walking down the steps and into his carriage, she never heard the question.

Patience turned her attention once again to Lady Elverston. "My lady, knowing how I feel about his lordship, I wondered, I hope . . . that is, I would that you would tell me more about him."

The older woman's eyes grew distant, and Patience thought she had intruded too much on their friendship.

"Please believe me when I say that I want to make him

happy. But I can't, if I don't know the cause of his pain. Can you help me? I know that you care a great deal about him."

The marchioness nodded. "What little there is to tell has brought Londringham more pain than happiness for his years. His father died after Edward was born and Londringham was ten. His mother remarried a French nobleman, and soon they returned to France.

"Londringham and Edward were raised by tutors with a distant cousin as guardian until it was time for Eton. They had no real father figure for most of their lives, they really only had each other."

Patience asked hesitantly, "And their mother and stepfather. Did they never return?"

Lady Elverston's face hardened. "They never came back. You see, they were French loyalists and later were killed in the Revolution. Their perfidy caused a great scandal years ago and not many in Society would open their doors to the orphaned boys of French loyalists."

Patience's mouth dropped in shock. "How awful for the boys."

Lady Elverston continued, "Bryce taught himself early how to take care of himself and his brother. All his life he had something to prove. He has served our country for a long time, while caring for his tenants and his estate."

Lady Elverston sighed softly. "You see, he felt that because of his mother's betrayal of her country, he must make amends. His service to England has more than compensated for his mother's disloyal actions. However, not many people know of his contributions and service to his country because of his vocation. I don't know all the details, other than his work is quite dangerous."

"What about his brother, Edward?" Patience had to know.

Silence reigned in the room for several minutes. Wearily, the marchioness replied with her eyes closed, "He was killed several months ago somewhere along the coast of France. He served as a lieutenant on Captain Kilkennen's ship. Bryce has not shared the story of his brother's death with me. I only know that Londringham found his brother dead and brought him home. Folks whispered that Londringham was responsible for his brother's death, because he locked himself up in Paddock Green and refused to see anyone.

"Not many knew that he had been injured in retrieving his brother. Only time could heal his spirit and his leg." She paused and opened her eyes. "You, my dear, have saved him. He only needs more time to come around."

All of this was simply too much for Patience to absorb. She didn't hear Lady Elverston's last words. Gazing at her friend in anguish, she asked simply, "What can I do?"

The marchioness answered in her gentle manner. "Love him. It is as simple and as difficult as that. There is no stronger healing medicine than love."

Patience smiled wryly. "That's true, I suppose. However, what happens when the patient is not even aware that he needs 'medicine'?"

Lady Elverston poured herself another cup of tea before replying. "He will know soon enough if you are no longer here. You should know that he has vowed to find his brother's murderer. I am afraid you will be unable to find happiness together until this happens."

The unflappable Stone knocked and entered, once again interrupting. "Miss Patience, at the present count, three gentlemen who saw you riding in the park this morning have left their cards inquiring after your health. There are also five gentlemen in the vestibule that insist this is where the adventurous lady maid lives, and they demand an audience. Oh, and the gentleman from yesterday is paying you a return call. Shall I send them in?"

Patience blinked in chagrin, aghast at all of her would-be

suitors, but common sense prevailed. "Stone, would you please inform these gentlemen that I am under the weather and will be for an undetermined amount of time?" She hated another lie, but she felt a bit exhausted after the morning's events and Lady Elverston's story.

Martha and Patience waited dinner for Bryce until it was quite late, and Melenroy had assured them that the goose was overcooked and the potatoes dry enough to serve as kindling for a fire. Alone in the dining room, Martha tried to have a conversation with Patience, but the young woman seemed quite preoccupied.

She had dressed in her loveliest gown which had just arrived from the matisse-maker's. Her simple, white silk gown accented her dark brown hair, a simple silver chain with an angel charm that her mother had given her hung around her neck.

"Please, Miss Patience, could you stop that tapping? It is making me nervous," Martha asked Patience not unpleasantly.

"I'm sorry. I have such on my mind that I don't what I'm doing. I think I shall retire to bed. It has been a very long day." Patience smiled at Martha absentmindedly and quietly left the dining room, whereupon she bumped into Bryce.

He swiftly claimed her with a kiss, then unromantically mentioned his need for food.

Patience rushed to the kitchen to see what they could salvage of dinner for Bryce. She watched him tenderly as he ate, concerned over the weariness she read in his eyes. He surprised her by mentioning he had to go out again.

He shrugged. "Unfinished business." With that firm statement, Patience knew not to ask for details. "But first," he said, grinning at her, "I have an appointment with a lady."

Her ire rose just slightly. What was he up to? Trying to

sound indifferent, she smiled and asked, "May I know the name of the lady?"

"Yes, Lady Sally. I believe she is waiting impatiently for a story which I promised her last night." With a kiss to the top of Patience's sheepish head, Bryce headed for the little girl's room.

Patience remained behind to read in the drawing room in order to bid Bryce a good night. The candle had sunk to half its height before she heard the door quietly open.

She turned to beam at Bryce, but the light slowly left her face when she saw his angered expression.

"Is something the matter, my lord? Is it Sally?" She rose to stand next to her chair.

"No, nothing is wrong with Sally. Although I went to tell her a story, she told me a quite interesting one of her own. It appears that this house has been extremely busy today welcoming your myriad admirers. Since I know Sally tends to exaggerate, I presume the number of hundreds of suitors is slightly high?" He leaned back against the door with arms folded across his chest.

Patience wet her lips nervously, fingering her angel charm for comfort. Clearing her throat, she told him succinctly, "I was entertaining Lady Elverston and Martha when a few gentlemen came to call. They stopped only to leave their cards and inquire after my health."

"I see, a few. That number is certainly more reasonable. And do you also have the habit of leaving articles of clothing behind in order for gentlemen to have an excuse to call on you?"

She peered at his shadowed face by the door, confused by his strange behavior and accusing questions. Could he possibly be jealous?

"Whatever happened in the parlor today was quite civilized and proper. It is only a coincidence that my handkerchief and

cloak were left behind on the two occasions I have had to
see Society's amusements." Her back up, she bristled, "If I am
to be accused of something, I would like to know the charge."

Bryce rubbed his forehead tiredly. "I am not in the mood
to trade barbs with you this evening. We shall save it for another time."

Before he was finished, she had marched over to him and
jabbed a finger in his chest. "It *has* been an extremely tedious day, and as soon as I could, I sent them on their way,
giving them absolutely no encouragement to their suit. Lady
Elverston and Martha shall support me in this."

She was close enough to see the amused light in his eyes
and wanted to hit him for not trusting her. He didn't give her
the chance but caught her slender waist in his strong hands
and tugged her into his arms.

He kissed her once and murmured in her ear. "Your kisses
are like a bottomless well from which I will never have my
thirst quenched." One last lingering kiss and then he simply
hugged her to him in silent need, and swept out the door.

She was speechless and felt a great happiness shining in
her heart. He was so close to saying that word "love."

Chapter 25

Ever the efficient butler, Stone waited at the door when Bryce finally arrived home at half-past two in the morning. Thoughts of his recent meeting with the prime minister and the secretary of war still consumed him as he wearily climbed the stairs to his bedroom. He damned the fates for the bad luck of not learning the spies' plans that night on the docks.

Everyone tonight had thought it likely that the French invasion would probably happen within the week. All agreed the only practical landing for the French was along the southeast coast. Now, if they could only discover where and when. Easy to find the questions, not so easy to find the answers.

He lingered by Patience's bedchamber door but didn't want to disturb her, although he yearned for her healing warmth. His hand reached out to touch the door and slid down to the knob. Then dropped away.

Bryce tapped lightly at Red Tattoo's room near his and the door immediately opened, the valet's dark face watchful. He was still dressed.

Red Tattoo shook his head, his mouth a grim line. "He has completely disappeared. No one has located any unidentified body in the river or elsewhere."

Bryce sighed, pursing his lips. "Damn!" He hit the door-jamb with his hand. "He must still be alive. We must find him, he is our only source. I have the bait but where do we lay the trail?" He paused. "We shall continue our search tomorrow." He made his way down the hall to his bedchamber, annoyed with himself. There was something he was missing, a piece of the puzzle teasingly so close, but he was too exhausted to think more on it.

"Why is Stone sending all the gentlemen callers away, Aunt Patience?" Sally asked from her vigil by the window. She patted Spring's neatly combed hair absentmindedly, then turned to face Patience, who sat comfortably in a blue damask wing chair mending Martha's torn riding habit.

In another corner of the parlor, Martha played a Haydn sonata, the haunting notes spinning smoothly off the walls. They were enjoying a quiet afternoon together. His lordship had disappeared before breakfast and had not yet returned.

Patience looked up when Sally called her name. "What did you say, sweetheart?" She pushed away a wayward curl from her forehead, her gaze softening on the precious child she had come to love so easily.

"The butler is sending our visitors away. I thought ye liked having gentlemen to see ye." Sally's round face frowned in confusion as she went to stand beside Patience.

Patience put her handiwork to the side and lifted Sally onto her lap. "I do not feel like entertaining guests today and asked Stone if he would kindly thank our guests for their visit and to call another day."

Martha quietly finished Haydn with a graceful lift of her fingers and walked over to where Patience and Sally sat, kneeling beside them.

"Aunt Martha?" The child had taken many relatives upon herself.

Martha's gray eyes shone warmly on Sally. "Yes, dear?"

"I was just thinkin' that ye are like me."

Martha met Patience's confused gaze with a slight smile, wondering what the child meant by that remark.

"Yer nice so people are kind to ye, like Aunt Patience, and she give ye a 'ome, just like they did to me."

Martha's face grew pinched, and she uttered a slight choking sound while rising from her position on the floor. She obviously didn't know how to respond to the wound Sally had inadvertently caused.

Patience rushed to comfort both of her dear ones. "Sally, I say that it doesn't matter where you live, as long as you are surrounded by people who love and care about you. Although this house is a place where Lord Londringham has generously allowed us to stay, it need not be this grand. It may only have four walls and a ceiling. It's the place where you have found your heart."

Martha murmured by the window, "What a pretty speech."

Her remark surprised Patience, who had not realized her chaperone a cynic.

But Sally was not through her inquiry with Patience. "But 'ow long will this be our 'ome?" Her blue eyes held a hint of sadness.

That was a question Patience could not answer. She was suddenly afraid for Sally, because she could certainly not give her assurances that any of them would have a home with his lordship. And what about Martha? Patience's heart went out to her kind friend, who depended on others for their charity and generosity. Patience knew Martha longed to be married and have a home of her own. But at the age of eight-and-twenty, it had been a long time since Martha had received any gentlemen callers interested in pursuing matrimony, she remembered her friend telling her.

Sally interrupted her musings by reaching out her little hand to turn Patience's head to her. "Lem says we have guards that won't allow anyone in the house. Why do we have guards, Aunt Patience?"

"I believe his lordship is concerned over everyone's safety, and since he is not here to protect us, those men will." Merely thinking of Bryce made her smile. She could still smell the bough of honeysuckle he had left on her pillow this morning. Patience put Sally down and called to Martha, "Shall we have more tea?"

Her friend glanced up from studying the scene on the street. "Did we not have tea this past hour?"

"Umm . . . I know, but right now another cup of hot tea sounds wonderful." Patience closed her eyes and leaned back in her chair.

Martha allowed Sally to ring for Stone, but after several minutes, no one came to their request.

Patience frowned. "How unlike Stone. What could be keeping him?"

Martha grinned. "He is probably turning away your suitors looking for the adventuress. I shall walk down to the kitchen myself and see. Want to come, Sally?" Martha offered, standing by the doorway with her hand outstretched. Sally eagerly skipped over to Martha. They promised to return soon with a hot pot of tea and perhaps something sweet to eat.

A few minutes later, Patience heard a knock on the door and stood up when Stone entered the room.

"Martha and Sally left to find our refreshment. We do not need your help after all."

His face an impenetrable mask, as always, Stone handed

Patience a note. "I just received this missive from a street urchin who bid tell you it was urgent."

She looked curiously at the vellum paper, puzzled by the mysterious note. "Thank you, Stone. Have you heard anything from his lordship?"

"No, miss," he said, and then bowed and took leave of the room with stiff dignity.

After seeing he was indeed gone, Patience hurriedly cracked the seal and opened the slip of paper with spidery writing. Glancing at the signature, she saw it was from Colette. Strange, she had not heard from her friend since they were together at Paddock Green. She had assumed the French maid had returned to her home country with her mistress.

Patience slowly sat down again in a nearby chair, immersed in the letter. Colette was in great trouble and urgently needed her help. She did not detail her worries, asking only that Patience meet her in Puffins Lane, a few blocks from Covent Garden, where she was staying with the countess. A glance at the ormolu clock on the mantelpiece showed half-past six. With Colette expecting her at seven o'clock, Patience didn't have much time to make a decision.

If only Bryce was here, he could accompany her, but then she scoffed at the idea. *After all that has happened in the last few weeks, I should surely be able to help Colette in her time of need.*

Perhaps the countess had dismissed her? If so, what could she doing at a house in Puffins Lane, and how could Patience help her friend? As she ran down the hallway to grab her light brown pelisse and matching bonnet she speculated on what possible trouble the French maid could have.

Since the daylight was fading, Patience knew she had to hurry. She jammed the note into her pocket and rushed down the stairs, bumping into Stone. An immovable force, he effectively blocked her path to the front door.

"Miss, I cannot have you leave without first speaking with his lordship," he told her, his face an impassive mask.

"Stone, I appreciate your concern. But, truly, an old friend wishes to see me and needs my help. I assure you I will only be gone a short while." She smiled her most beguiling smile, hoping to persuade him.

Stone hesitated before moving out of the way. He intoned, "Please advise Lord Londringham that I did instruct you not to leave this house."

Patience jammed on her silk brown bonnet and ran out the door, calling, "Yes, yes, of course."

Fortunately, she had sent Lem ahead to find a hack, and within the better part of fifteen minutes of receiving the note Patience was on her way.

Later, as Stone passed the stairs on the way to the kitchen, he saw a white piece of paper. When he stooped to retrieve it, he discovered it was the very same note he had delivered into Miss Patience's hands earlier. Concerned over her safety, he scanned the letter before rolling his eyes heavenward. His lordship would not like this one bit. Not one bit.

Bryce climbed out of his carriage, noting that his injured leg felt somewhat better, and hurried up the steps, nodding to a tall stranger in the shadows of the corner of the house, one of his men responsible for security. It had been a lovely spring day, one he wished he could have spent with Patience.

He tossed Stone his coat and asked his venerable butler, "Where is Miss Patience?" Patting his breast pocket assured Bryce his present was safe. So anxious to see Patience, he had totally missed the paler-than-normal look on his butler's face.

"Ah . . . she has gone out to meet a friend . . ." Stone fiddled with his watch chain. He never fiddled with anything.

Bryce's cheerful mood quickly vanished. He stalked over to Stone and demanded an explanation.

Stone's hand shook when he handed his lordship the note. Bryce rapidly skimmed the note, then crumpled it in his hand. It could be nothing and yet again, he couldn't stop the feeling of foreboding sweeping over him. His well-honed instincts told him something was at odds here. Patience was in danger, he knew it as well as he knew his own name. He had met Colette previously but didn't remember her well. What could the countess's abigail want with Patience?

"How could you let her leave?" he demanded, his voice deadly soft.

Bryce heard fear in his butler's voice. "I did try to persuade her not to go, but she paid no heed. I understood she was visiting a friend." His words became stronger as Stone convinced himself he had done nothing wrong.

Bryce worked his hands by his side, frowning, feeling his body tense, harnessing his power and senses, like a beast ready for the hunt. Only a day ago, someone had taken a shot at Patience in Hyde Park. "Miss Patience should not have left this house without me. You better pray no harm comes to her." Bryce's eyes scorched Stone all the way to Hell.

"How much time is she ahead of me?" Bryce glanced at the longcase clock. Seven o'clock.

"Perhaps thirty minutes, my lord," Stone informed him while helping his lordship back into his discarded creased coat.

Bryce swore under his breath. Time was of the essence. Every minute he was losing light. With the address memorized, he headed for the door.

Stone cleared his throat. "I hope you can forgive me someday, my lord, for allowing Miss Patience to leave. Please bring her back safely."

Bryce stared in surprise at his ordinarily calm and collected servant. He had never seen Stone show such humility. Bryce nodded determinedly. "I shall."

No one would have doubted the look of resolve on his lordship's face as Stone shut the door behind him. Certainly not his butler, who sank down on the nearest chair in the hallway, mopping his brow and whispering prayers for the safe return of his master and Miss Patience.

"Where is this place?" Patience continually peered out the window of her carriage, searching for Puffins Lane. Unfortunately, her driver, being unfamiliar with this part of London, slowed his ancient horse, calling back to Patience that he was confident he would soon find it.

She jerked back from the open window when a black-sooted face materialized in front of her with a toothless grin. Glancing at her locket watch, beads of perspiration dotted her brow. Quarter past seven. She was late. What if she did not reach Colette in time?

She dabbed her face with her lucky pink handkerchief. Would Colette wait for her? What kind of trouble was she in? Perhaps she should have brought a weapon with her. Planning a course of action, she opened her reticule and pecked around, finding a change purse, powder, a comb, and walnuts.

Walnuts? No wonder her reticule felt heavy. The bottom of it bulged with various sizes of nuts. Even her cloak pockets felt bumpy. Reaching her hand into a pocket, she discovered more nuts. She could not help but smile when she remembered that she had promised to take Sally to the park to feed the squirrels. The child had offered to gather the animals' dinner and apparently decided to use Patience's reticule and cloak for a satchel. She weighed one small walnut in her hand and wondered if she could pelt someone with it.

No, it would definitely cause no damage. She sighed and leaned back against the carriage seat.

"There it is, miss." Patience nearly jumped off of her seat. "I knowed I would find it," he shouted exultantly. Her hand shook as she reached for the door handle, her heart thumping out of control in her ears, her courage deserting her. Was it too late to return to the town house?

Out the window, she saw a busy sidewalk filled with ragtag urchins pushing each other in the street, ladies of unknown reputation sauntering by twos, and several filthy men loitering about, eyeing her carriage suspiciously.

She frowned at noting the sunset creeping toward night. Unsteadily, she climbed down from the coach, clutching her reticule tightly to her chest. She remembered feeling much braver earlier about this adventure.

I must help Colette. She needs me, Patience thought over and over again, trying to draw courage from her empty well of confidence.

The driver agreed to wait for her after she paid him an extra bob. Her eyes focused on the house in front of her, Patience studied the brick three-storied building. It looked like it had not been lived in for quite some time. Carriage wheels creaked down the cobbled streets while a putrid smell of heated garbage assailed her senses.

Surreptitiously, she glanced around her before walking hurriedly up the stairs, leaving the unkind streets behind her. At the front door, she rang the doorbell, her hands clasped in front of her, wishing, wishing, wishing the door would open quickly. What could Colette be doing here? The sooner she found her and learned of her difficulties, the sooner she could help her friend and return home.

Hardly daring to breathe, afraid of what she might find, she grasped the doorknob and turned. The door opened to reveal a large vestibule, rather dusty and dirty.

"Colette? Are you here?" Cautiously, she stepped inside onto the broken-tiled floor, careful to watch her step. Gray light through mottled windows checkered the black-and-white hallway.

Strange, Colette must not be here, perhaps I have the wrong address. She felt in her pocket for the maid's note but came away empty-handed. Contemplating leaving, she noticed the fragile-looking wooden staircase. If Colette was hurt, she would never forgive herself for at least making sure her friend was not in the house, even if her courage now rested at the bottom of her shoes.

Wetting her lips and blinking three times for luck, she firmly grasped the handrail and pulled herself up, wary by wary step. At the top, she noticed two closed doors on each side of a short hallway. They looked to be old abandoned apartments, judging by her peek inside the doors to the right.

The other doors led to rooms facing the back of the house. One bedchamber was completely empty. Wishing she had thought to bring a candle, Patience decided to check the last room and then bid a hasty retreat.

The last room was not empty. She peeked in to find a wooden chair, a broken bed frame, torn mattresses, and a person sleeping. A person not moving. A person . . . dead?

Chapter 26

Patience could not make it down the stairs fast enough, nearly falling through a hole in the boards. At the bottom of the steps, she heard someone call her name.

Bryce. She called him over to her as she neared the bottom of the stairs. When Patience saw his concerned face, she launched herself into his arms, clutching him tightly to her.

He held her shaking form closely. "Are you hurt?" he asked her urgently.

She shook her head into his chest and mumbled something about a body.

He pulled her slightly away so that he could see her face. "What about a body?"

Her eyes opened wide in terror. She pointed up the stairs and whispered in a quivering voice, "Up there. In the last bedroom, I saw a man. He's not moving. He looks rather dead." Her last words were barely discernible.

Although Bryce's main desire was to take Patience from this place and get her safely home, first he wanted to investigate to see if she had actually seen a body. Perhaps it was an inebriated sop sleeping off whiskey spirits, but it could be someone hurt and needing assistance.

He gripped her shoulders firmly. "You stay here, do not move. I shall go see what has happened. I need to take the lantern but there is still light from the vestibule foyer. I'll be back shortly."

Patience reluctantly parted with his greatcoat beneath her nails and watched as he climbed two steps before starting after him. She wasn't staying alone in the dark and wasn't afraid to show her cowardly side.

Following him up the stairs and down the hall, their steps echoed in the stillness. When they reached the room with the body, Patience remained outside the door when Bryce entered. He crossed the room and looked down at the prone figure that had gone to his maker and shook his head. He began to turn around when he noticed something shiny on the floor. Stooping to pick it up, he turned on his heel and left the room, grabbing Patience's arm as he walked by and ushering her down the hallway and stairs. His lantern swung wildly with the effort of stepping over broken boards.

Confronted with his back, she asked, "Is he very dead?" Her voice was not as strong as she thought.

When Bryce stopped to answer her, she plowed into the back of him, holding on to his waist. He held her hands as he turned to face her, concerned what the news would bring. "Exceedingly so. It is, or was, Sansouche."

Her jaw dropped as she suppressed a shiver. "So this is where they put the body. I *told* you they killed him."

He stared past her head. "Someone certainly did kill him, but not at the Gardens. The blood leaking on the floor is fresh, indicating he has not been dead for long." The terrified look on her face showed him that this had not been a good time to mention the fact.

Patience began quaking. "You mean his killer may still be here?" Every word an effort.

He rubbed her back and led her down the rest of the stairs

to the front door, ignoring her question. "We need to get you home."

They both heard the shouts at the same time.

And the footsteps. He efficiently doused the lantern, looking about quickly for an exit. From a nearby window, he thought he recognized the scarlet waistcoats of the Bow Street Runners. Soon, loud voices and boots pounding on the steps cut their goal short.

"Hurry, in here." Although he hadn't deciphered what exactly was going on, he didn't want to be in the position of the Runners finding him and Patience in an empty house with the dead body of a French spy. There would be too many questions.

He pushed her down the hallway on the first floor and into a dark back parlor where the closed curtains hid the light. Her hand grasped in his, he crept along the back wall near the darkened windows looking for a way out. They didn't have much time. She could only follow his lead, not able to breathe in the dusty stuffiness and because fear had crawled into her throat.

Finally, behind a long black curtain, Bryce felt a window without its glass. He stopped to listen outside to see if the Runners had rounded the house but only heard steps on the stairs.

For what purpose had someone led Patience here? Were the Runners to have found two bodies? Sansouche's and Patience's? He nearly choked on the thought. What if he had not been here in time? Or was the plan to find Patience alone with the murdered man? Would she not have been accused of the deed? He would get to the bottom of this.

With agility and strength, he quickly but carefully lowered Patience out of the window before following suit. Not giving her a chance to catch her breath, he snatched her hand and started running down the alleyway. Lucky and the waiting carriage were only a few blocks away.

"Stop, you there!"

The loud command only made them run faster. Thinking quickly, Patience opened her reticule, and while still running behind Bryce, turned it upside down, dropping the contents behind her, and throwing more walnuts out of her pockets. Several paces away, she was pleased to hear a thump and a groan. Those walnuts had proven useful afterall.

They finally reached Lucky, and, jumping into the carriage, the coachman struck the horses and made their escape. Surely the darkness would hide their identities and the carriage's coat of arms.

Melenroy, Sally, Lem, Martha, Stone, and the other servants waited eagerly at the door for their master's return. They breathed a collective sigh of relief when his lordship finally escorted a dazed and dusty Patience through the door.

Cobwebs hung from Patience's bonnet, dust covered her chin, and her lace petticoat that had torn on the window trailed miserably after her. Bryce was not in much better shape. Filmy black soot covered him from head to toe, and his coat was torn at the shoulders where Patience had grabbed him.

After convincing everyone that they were safe and no harm had befallen them, Bryce swept Patience up into his arms. He could tell she had not much strength to go farther. Her head resting on his mussed once-white shirt and with her arms wrapped around his chest, he carefully climbed the stairs to her bedchamber, his look never leaving her sleepy countenance. Melenroy and Stone hurried into the kitchen seeking hot water and spirits. Martha and Verna followed Bryce, and after he left her room, Verna helped Patience undress, bathe, and prepare for bed.

Several hours later, Bryce came to Patience's bedchamber, telling himself it was only because he was concerned over her near hysteria earlier. But truthfully, he wanted to hold her in his arms, to protect any future danger.

Certainly Sansouche could never hurt her again. Bryce's eyes narrowed in anger when he remembered the other night. He would be unable to avenge Patience.

His fury swiftly evaporated when he slipped into her bedchamber as quiet as the moonlight showering through her opened window. He stood staring at her for a long while. He liked the way her full lips were slightly parted, and the way her dark brown hair flowed in a silky pattern down her back. He liked her thick winged brown eyebrows on the lovely canvas of her face. And he liked the way she curled her legs up to her chest. Hell's teeth, he liked everything about her. Her way with children. Her smile that lit a darkened room. Her loyalty to her brother. Her dangerous trip to save her friend tonight. The way she needed him, which bespoke of an indefinable power he had never experienced before.

She brought out his protective side, and he understood more than anyone that Patience needed someone to look after her. And Bryce had assigned himself the task. For life. He whispered a finger down her soft cheek and heard her moan softly. Hell, he loved her. He was caught more securely in her trap than a fly in a spider's web. He smiled. Exactly where he wanted to be.

He discarded his robe on the floor, anxious to feel her warm body close to him, and crawled in beside her. She instinctively rolled toward him.

As he lay on his back, Patience, sweet-smelling and fresh, curled into him welcoming the feel of his hard form. After a few minutes he looked at the ceiling. Hmmm, this might be a challenge. Just smelling her unique fragrance of lavender and peppermint incited his thirst for her and other parts of her sweet body. Surely it was a small price to pay for the pleasure of being with the woman he loved. He felt her hand sweep lightly across his chest, and he bit back a moan. This was proving more difficult that he had originally thought.

She was exhausted and needed her rest after this latest episode. Her silken strands between their connecting bodies teased his skin and set his senses on fire. A sweat broke upon his brow. If only she would stop moving, he could control his desire and go to sleep.

When she nudged her face into his chest, he smoothed her tangled hair from her pale cheek and kissed her softly on her brow. Looking down at her sleeping countenance, he sighed. He wanted to tell her that he loved her, but he would simply have to wait, and take every opportunity to show her when she was awake. Drawing her closer, knowing she was safe, Bryce finally nodded off into a deep slumber.

Chapter 27

Captain Keegan Kilkennen relaxed against the carriage seat, the torn leather padding and bumpy ride not disturbing his concentration. So much had happened in the fortnight while he was at sea. His ship had nearly been sunk off Bologne, hence their return to Winchelsea Harbor for more repairs. His eyes narrowed angrily. Someone had known of their plans, for the French had been waiting for them. Only Keegan and Admiral Nelson had known the *Valiant*'s mission.

Several men had been lost or wounded from gunfire, the *Valiant* barely managing to limp home. Keegan stared grimly down at his tightly bandaged left hand, missing two fingers from cannon blast. He had spent the last week recuperating from the attack. At St. Josephine's Hospital outside of Bristol doctors tended to his wounds along with those of other injured members of his crew.

Keegan also reflected grimly on his upcoming reunion with Londringham tomorrow morning. It would go hard on Londringham, the news he had to share, but he would be there to support his friend.

As the carriage jounced on, he was surprised to still feel pain in his missing fingers. He knew Colette would be shocked to see him, but he couldn't wait any longer to see her. He had to hold her in his arms again. Keegan finally smiled. That French girl could certainly tie a man in knots and make him hard as a cannon ready to shoot.

By the time he arrived in Charing Cross night had fallen. The countess had taken a small town house painted black with blue shutters, a rather unremarkable dwelling off the main thoroughfare. Colette had written him with the address but told him that the countess and she soon would be departing for France.

Keegan climbed carefully down from the carriage, paid the driver, and sent him on his way. Feeling like a shy young man paying court for the first time to his sweetheart, he held his cocked hat in his injured hand and wished he had some small token of affection to present to Colette.

His tap on the front door brought a sullen, frail-looking housekeeper with black eyes peering through the crack. Before he could introduce himself, the servant informed him in a nasty tone that the countess already had a gentleman caller and please to leave.

This announcement did not faze Keegan, since his interest was in the countess's lady's maid.

He hurriedly put a foot through the door opening. "Madam, I am here to see Colette. I believe she is her ladyship's maid?"

The cautious black eyes blinked at him with distrust, giving Keegan time to worry, until she finally took pity on him, seeing his bandaged hand, and opened the door.

"Thank you for permitting me to enter. I know it is rather late, but it is urgent that I speak to Colette. Is she home?"

The housekeeper still eyed him with suspicion, then turned away to creep down the hallway, her thin back hunched in protection. He thought he heard her mutter, "Like mistress, like servant."

After twenty minutes of standing in the hall, Keegan decided to have a look around the countess's rented town house. The door to his right opened to a small front parlor, which, by the looks of its dusty contents, and furniture coverings, was rarely used. Sauntering down the corridor, his patience wearing thin, he entered the library. Mahogany bookcases stretched floor to ceiling on all four walls as moonlight streamed silvery rivers on the gaudy Oriental rug through openings in the drawn curtains of the bay window across the room. Thinking the moonbeams lovely but miserly, Keegan lit a lamp that he found on the sideboard.

A noise behind him announced he had company. He turned and started at the lovely picture Colette presented in the doorway, where the light from the hallway emphasized her slender form. Only she could affect him like this. He could not contain his eagerness to speak with her, touch her, his gaze devouring the very sight of her.

He crossed the room in a thrice and gripped her hands clasped lightly in front of her, ready to pull her into his arms. But Colette gently disengaged herself to skirt around his large, commanding figure. He couldn't take his eyes from her.

After she had arranged herself comfortably on the settee, the only piece of furniture in the room for sitting, Colette asked Keegan to close the doors, in a manner to suggest she wasn't happy to see him. Still puzzled, he obeyed. This is not the Colette that wrote to him, told him that she cared for him. His injured hand shook as he crossed the room to reach for spirits and poured the glass of brandy he had been promising himself. She had wounded him more deeply than the cannon blast.

With his emotions under control, he faced the maid. Dressed in a lovely black gown, she looked ready for an evening event. God, but she was beautiful with her dark

brown curls arrayed stylishly around her perfectly oval face
with dark eyes. Surely her coldness was due to his unforeseen arrival.

Colette broke the awkward silence. "I'm surprised to see
you. I had not expected you. Why are you here?" Her voice
was soft and sounded pleasant, as if she were talking to her
lace-maker, not her lover.

Keegan propped one shoulder on the wall closest to the
liquor, already regretting his hasty decision to see Colette
when he had not fully recovered from his injuries. He stared
at her, bewildered, trying to find the woman he had fallen
in love with.

"It is quite late," she continued easily. "I do not wish for
the countess to find you here. She would not like it."

The mantelpiece clock struck midnight. He took a long
draught of brandy, his steady gaze never leaving her face.
His voice low and devoid of sentiment, Keegan replied, "I
came to see you because I believed you would care to see
me. That you would actually welcome my call, no matter
what the time of day."

He drained his glass, enjoying the liquid burning down
his throat. "I must have been mistaken about you." His features harder than the marble mantelpiece, he finished, "It is
a mistake unlikely to happen again." He pushed away from
the wall and bent to leave his empty glass.

"Wait." Colette jumped off the settee and rushed over to
him, tenderly taking his bandaged hand in her own. "*Mon
amour,* what have you done?" Her feather touch stroked the
injured hand before bringing it to her lips for a kiss. "Why
did you not tell me you were hurt?" she asked with an
almost accusing manner.

Keegan's eyes widened at this chameleon of a woman
standing in front of him. Why was she playing such games
with him? His eyes dark with anger, he told her, "What of

my injury? I am still the same man when I walked in the door and was greeted with your frosty reception. Please spare me your pity."

But Colette clutched his arm in dismay, her touch penetrating him through his wool evening coat. With tears streaming down her achingly beautiful face, she begged for his forgiveness. "You must know, I am pleased you are here to see me. I was afraid the housekeeper might be listening. She may tell the countess I had a gentleman caller this late and my mistress would be very angry," her apology laced in a seductive whisper.

His hooded green eyes prevented Colette from seeing his forgiveness. His only response was an order. "Kiss me."

Colette gently wrapped her arms around Keegan's stiff shoulders and pulled herself up to his waiting lips. She brushed her lips against his, teasingly, lingering with a promise of more. But when he went to capture more of her sweetness, she danced from his arms and back to the settee, watching him, eyes lit in amusement. She had other plans for him. "Please, sir, not so hasty," she told him teasingly. "Let us talk first," she said, patting a place next to her.

Patience felt the glorious sun upon her face the next morning, feeling happy until she remembered the events of the previous night. Surely finding a dead body would unnerve any person. But Bryce had saved her yet again. And no more Sansouche to be concerned about, although she would not have wished him departed to the next life. Prison would have done just as well.

But nothing could intrude on her warm thoughts of the man determined to save her from herself. Although he still had not mentioned the words "love" and "marriage," she knew he would, he only needed time. Time, what her brother Rupert did not have. She must dress and see Bryce about returning to Winchelsea to find her brother.

She sent two little prayers up to Heaven, one in supplication for Rupert, the other in thanksgiving. Her gratitude was for the man she had found and loved, for Patience had secretly despaired after Richard had left, never to return, that he had been her only hope for marriage and companionship.

But fate had something else planned for Patience—in the form of a handsome, naturally, English spy, who seemed to fear little, except for the safety of those whom he loved.

Patience threw back the covers, anxious for the day to begin, knowing each morning she awakened, she would be impatient to see Bryce.

A sparkle caught her eye. On the pillow next to her lay a beautiful emerald necklace entwined with diamonds in a dainty gold chain.

She stared at it.

First, in delight.

Then, in wonder.

Then in curiosity.

Then, in horror. Suddenly remembering the morning when Bryce had given the countess just such a jewelry box and said farewell—and meant good riddance to his once-mistress. Patience leaned over the bed and promptly retched.

Bryce leaned back against the comfortable, well-padded chair in Lady Elverston's parlor. He had planned several errands for this morning, including one last stop at Whitehall to finalize their strategies to stop the French spies. Prime Minister Addington had just received urgent news to share with him and word was making its way around the city that Napoleon planned to declare war in the very near future. They had to fortify the southern coast and gain any advantage by capturing the spies in their midst.

Even with a possible impending war with France, Bryce thought of Patience. He was anxious to return home and discover whether she had liked the little present he had left her. Instead of more honeysuckle like he had left the day before, he had placed the diamond and emerald necklace, a family heirloom, on her pillow. He rubbed his hands in anticipation of the ways she was probably planning to thank him. But first, he would confess how he felt about her.

"Bryce, I am truly concerned over Patience," Lady Elverston said, her anxious voice finally biting into his woolgathering, something he never before realized he did.

Bryce leaned forward in his chair, resting his forearms on his thighs. "Why?" He frowned, wondering if his friend could have learned about their escapade last night.

Lady Elverston waved a graceful hand. "I know she is worried about her brother, whom, she tells me, has disappeared from prison, and she is worried about you and your injury."

Bryce scowled darkly when she mentioned his wound, almost healed. That was his concern and none other's.

She did not see his dark look but continued, "That girl has taken on the problems of the whole world, and she simply does not look strong enough to carry the burden. I want to see her happy, she deserves to be happy." Lady Elverston eyed him pointedly.

He rose, avoiding her gaze, and placed his empty teacup on the table. "Yes, she does," he agreed softly.

With Bryce pacing the room like a caged lion, Lady Elverston quietly proceeded with her attack. "Yes, and since she is not getting any younger, I do not know if we can wait another Season."

He stopped in his tracks, spinning around to stare in puzzlement at the woman. "Wait another Season for what?"

She merely laughed at his expression. "Well, for a proposal, of course. Martha has informed me that she has received many gentlemen callers, I think perhaps even the Duke of Grensham has made an appearance?"

Arms crossed in front of him, he told her arrogantly, "There will not be a proposal accepted from the duke or any of the rest of her callers."

Lady Elverston watched him in false disbelief. "And why ever not? Her lineage is good, she is certainly lovely to look at, she keeps your accounts remarkably straight, and those around her are truly blessed with her boundless supply of love." She paused markedly. "Have I missed anything?" Her smile bright, she seemed to be seeking his assistance in ticking off Patience's marriageable attributes.

Bryce pulled a chair around and sat while resting his arms on the chair rack, looking at ease, only the slight twitching in his jaw telling Lady Elverston their conversation was having the desired affect. "Yes, she cannot sit a horse, she's superstitious, and she's constantly putting herself in danger in order to help those around her."

Lady Elverston nodded in agreement. "I see what you mean. Having a good seat certainly keeps up appearances with the genteel folk in Society. Superstitious beliefs reflect a rather flighty humor, hmmm . . . even an unstable character. As for placing herself in danger for others, well, that is simply ludicrous, lunacy. After all, the first instinct all humans have is for survival. Imagine a selfish girl like that, thinking of others and not herself." She rose to conclude their conversation.

"I am certainly glad you have apprised me of Patience's shortcomings. I see now that I have been wrong about her character, and finding a husband for her will be more difficult than I originally had surmised."

Bryce rose from his chair to confront his longtime friend.

With a distinct twinkle in his eye, he added, "And if you would allow me to finish . . . Appearances in Society do not mean a fig to me, or Patience, for that matter, so if she never wants to ride again, that suits me fine. I find her peculiar superstitious beliefs charming, and she needs me, for when Patience is looking out for everyone else, she needs someone to look after her. And it certainly pleases me to oblige.

"Her compassion and loyalty are equaled by none other of my acquaintance. She has taught me about hope, belief in the goodness of people, when I was convinced otherwise. And about the truly frightening, overwhelmingly foreign emotion called love. I am her apt pupil and have much to learn.

"Before Patience, I had vowed not to marry until Edward's death had been avenged." His face shadowed as he recalled the night he had made his vow. "But I find myself more impatient than ever to make her mine." He fell silent, suddenly realizing this was the first time that he had ever revealed his vulnerability either to himself or to his friend.

Lady Elverston waved her hand as if to swat him. "Why, you liar, you flummoxed me! I asked you here to convince you that in your right mind, you should marry the girl."

Bryce patted his breast pocket. "Marriage license in hand," he told her with a grin.

He had finally shocked Lady Elverston speechless. She could only stare at him, shaking her head in bewilderment. Fully recovered, she raised a fine eyebrow.

"Have you told Patience how you feel?"

"Not in so many words, but my intentions have been fairly clear. If she has any doubts, I will clarify them for her tonight." *By word or deed,* Bryce thought. His manhood stirred in anticipation. He paused significantly. "Would you and Lord Elverston join us for a surprise announcement this evening at 75 Courtyard Lane?"

Lady Elverston returned, "It would be our singular pleasure. This calls for a celebration. I know she will make you very happy."

His amused expression beamed. "Of that, madam, I have no doubt."

Sally peered through the crack in the front parlor door. Aunt Patience was crying again. This time she didn't make any noise, the tears just slipped down her cheeks, and every now and then she would wipe them away with her handkerchief.

The little girl held her doll, Spring, by the neck, at her side, wondering whether she should go find Aunt Martha or Aunt Melenroy, perhaps they would know how to cheer Aunt Patience.

"Let me see," Lem whispered urgently in her ear, pushing her away from the door. The little footboy squinted through the crack, then sighed as he frowned at Sally, who watched him avidly. "She's still cryin'."

"I know. I was watch'n before you pushed me," Sally retorted.

"Why do girls cry all the time?" Lem muttered almost to himself.

Sally's little shoulders straightened back. "We don't cry all the time, just when we'r sad, like when I lost my doll." Spring hung forgotten by her side.

Lem's eyes widened in concern. "Why is Miss Patience sad? Someone should tell the master."

Sally shook her head sadly. "But 'e isn't 'ere to 'elp Aunt Patience."

Lem stared beyond Sally's small blond head. What would a soldier in the King's army do to comfort a lady? His little face furrowed with heavy thinking. Then he remembered that Miss Patience liked Miss Martha's cat, Satan. He would find Satan and bring him to Miss Patience. He was sure that would cheer Miss Patience right up.

He ordered Sally to stand vigil outside the parlor door, in case Miss Patience needed her.

Sally's tiny mouth pouted slightly. "But I'm too little to stand forever by the door." Spring's dress dusted the floor.

"Ah, ye can't do anythin', yer such a baby. Then sit on the floor," Lem's impatience with the little girl obvious.

Before she could tell him she wasn't a baby, he had lifted her in his arms and sat her down with a plop on the soft carpet. He pointed his finger at her. "Ye stay 'ere and I'll be back to get ye." He marched off on his mission, leaving Sally staring forlornly after him.

It sure was lonely here in the hall. Sally heard the housemaids in the dining room, and through the nearby open window heard merchants calling their wares. The little girl wandered over to the window nearest the front door. Pushing aside the white linen curtains, on tiptoes she could see the busy street below her, the beautiful carriages wheeling by with shiny coachmen driving the lovely shiny horses. Was that the pudding man?

Sally bit her lip. Standing guard sure could be hungry work. Perhaps if she left Spring to watch over Aunt Patience, she could find Aunt Martha and they could buy a pudding. Carefully placing Spring by the gap in the French doors, the little girl skipped down the hallway and down the stairs. She would return before Lem did, so he would not know she had left her post.

Patience dropped the necklace she had been worrying on the fireplace mantel and turned in stunned amazement at Colette waiting in the doorway. Her last tears had dried after she had decided she would confront Bryce about the necklace. He surely did not think it would be that easy to get rid of her.

She swept across the room and pulled her friend into the room, shutting the door behind them. After seating Colette comfortably on the sofa, Patience sat down beside her, concern etched gravely on her face. "How are you? Where have you been?" It was amazing how someone else's troubles could make your own fly right out the window. "I have been so worried about you."

Colette blinked her long dark lashes in surprise. "But why? There is nothing wrong with me."

Patience shook her head, grasping the maid's arm. "But the note. I was to meet you at Puffins Lane last night. You were in trouble." She could not control the dismay and confusion in her shaky voice.

The maid's green eyes grew wider, her mouth slightly open as she listened to Patience. "I sent you no note. What did the note say?"

Patience rubbed her brow and collapsed against the back cushion of the sofa. "None of this makes any sense." She paused and drew a deep breath. "Late yesterday, I received a missive with your signature claiming you were in trouble and needed my help. When I arrived at the specified place in Puffins Lane, I . . . found the countess's cousin, Sansouche. He was dead." Patience still had not fully recovered from the previous night's shock.

Colette looked down at her hands in her lap. With a voice barely above a whisper, she told Patience, "We learned this morning. The constable visited with the countess, who is distraught over his death. I must help her with arrangements to return to France immediately."

Patience turned to her friend. "Does anyone know who might have wanted him dead and why?" She hesitated before telling Colette, "I think someone sent me there to find his body, and they knew I would come when I heard you were in trouble, but why?"

Colette shrugged and rose to walk to the bay window, looking outside. "I do not know. All this trouble, it makes me anxious to return to my home."

She paused, then turned to face Patience, still mulling over this mystery. "I am here this morning because I *do* need your help."

Patience sat at attention at this unexpected announcement. She raised her eyebrows in query. "But what is it? You *are* in some type of trouble? What can I do for you?"

Returning to her side, Colette took Patience's hands in her own. "As I said, I must leave England."

Patience offered her friend a smile of support. "I'm sorry to see you go. What will you do on your return to France?"

The maid looked down before replying. Quietly, she told Patience, "I have learned of my uncle's malaise. He needs me and has asked for me."

Placing a comforting arm around Colette's shoulders, Patience commiserated with her. "I understand about the needs of family. You should return."

The room remained still, each woman consumed with her own thoughts. Then Colette turned an anxious face to Patience. "That is why I am here."

Patience stared curiously at her friend. "If it is within my power, I shall do whatever I can to assist you."

The maid's face brightened a little. *"Mon ami."*

Just then Stone entered without knocking, part of his nature, with a tray of tea.

Before continuing, Colette watched Stone until he had vacated the room. "You see, it is the Captain Kilkennen, his lordship's friend. The man fancies himself in love with me, but I do not return his affection. I am asking you to help me write a letter to him, to tell him I am leaving and to not follow me. My English lettering is not so good, so I thought perhaps you could write it for me."

Patience listened in rapt silence, her eyes widened in surprise. She had had no idea that Colette and Bryce's friend had a liaison. Although she did not know the captain well, Patience thought the news would cause a tremendous blow.

"Are you positive that he loves you? Perhaps you are mistaken?"

The maid, with a cold, determined look in her eyes, shook her head. "No, he thinks to promise me marriage but I want nothing from him. Please will you help me?"

"Perhaps I might be able to handle this gently, to save his feelings," she told Colette, then she rose from the sofa and walked to the escritoire by the window. The last thing Patience wanted was to be involved in the dissolution of their affair. However, if she could word the letter carefully, she might be able to salvage the Captain's pride.

She wrote "*Sir,*" then looked expectantly at Colette across the room, waiting for the maid's suggestions. "Can you offer me any lexis to use?"

"*Oui,* I have thought on this, and I would like to say that 'honored as I am at your attentions, I cannot reciprocate your affections. I do not love you.'"

Patience's head was bent as she wrote the letter, her heart constricted for the man who would suffer such pain at this, knowing she was part of the instrument that caused it.

Colette's train of thought resurfaced. "'After I am gone, you will know this was for the best. You understand in war, the innocent are always hurt. But you are not innocent and neither am I. What I have done and am about to do, I did for my country.'"

Patience's jaw dropped as the quill fell from her fingers. "Colette, what are you talking about? What have you done?"

Colette pursed her lips, her deep-green eyes hiding many

secrets. "Let us finish writing the letter, and I will explain these things to you."

Lately, everything concerning Colette was an enigma, a complete tangle that had no beginning or ending. Patience shook her head, then resumed transcribing.

"'I return to France, my home. Someday you will learn the truth and be surprised. I will have surprised everyone at my success.'" Addressing Patience, she ordered, "Let us end the letter with, "'Do not follow me, for I cannot be found. Be content that in time I am sure I will pay for my sins.'" Her voice was becoming raspier, her breathing harsher. She had walked over to the desk and stood behind Patience, watching her as she wrote.

Patience looked up to observe Colette more closely. Her face was pale as she leaned against the desk to inspect Patience's work. She was ill, that much was certain.

Uneasily, Patience scratched the last few words, her friend from Storrington seeming more a stranger than ever.

She started up from the desk. "You are ill. I shall send for Stone, he will know what to do." All thoughts of uncovering the mystery surrounding Colette halted temporarily. She helped the weak woman into a nearby chair and asked her, "What can I do? Perhaps some water?"

Colette put a hand to her brow, her face compressed in pain. "I simply need to rest for a moment."

With a distressed backward glance as she left the parlor, Patience hurried to procure some water for her tormented friend.

She didn't see Sally hiding behind the door. Sally was looking for Spring. She had enjoyed her treat and returned to collect her doll, but Spring was nowhere to be found. The little girl watched as Aunt Patience ran from the room, and decided to see why she was in such a hurry.

She peeked inside the room and saw a strange woman

bending over the desk, writing with a quill. Sally shivered when she saw the wicked look on the woman's face. It was like the face of the witches Aunt Patience had described in Sally's fairy-tale books. Yes, the witch had frightened Aunt Patience, but she had escaped.

Sally quickly realized that if the witch caught her spying, something awful might happen to her. She hoped Spring was safe somewhere else, and Sally ran with the wind behind her as fast as her little legs would carry her, away from the witch with the evil eyes.

Patience bustled into the room with a glass and smelling salts in her hand and halted. Colette was no longer on the chair. She started to glance around the room, when she heard Colette speaking over her shoulder. "I will not be needing the water. But I would like you to come with me." In a suddenly regained strong voice, the request was more like a command.

Slowly, Patience pivoted to confront a completely healed Colette holding a very menacing-looking pistol. "Colette, what has happened? What are you doing? I don't understand." Her voice shook with fear.

Colette's eyes were as cold as a storm-tossed winter sea. "You'll get your answers in due time. I just need you to sign your letter to Lord Londringham and then we shall depart."

Patience stared aghast at her once-friend. "*My* letter?" she managed to squeak.

"*Oui.* His lordship will return and read the letter and know it was you who are the French spy. He will know your betrayal and will not pursue us." Colette nudged the pistol in the direction of the desk. "Please finish, we have little time."

Patience stared in disbelief. "You, you are the French spy Lord Londringham seeks?"

The other woman shrugged, her secret could now be told. "Yes, I have fooled everyone, including his lordship and many others. They seek a man, when it is a woman who has trumped them!" Her bold words rang in the room. She pointed the pistol at Patience's heart, waiting.

Patience walked slowly toward the escritoire, her heart thumping with dismay and pain. She slowly signed her name "Patience Grundy."

"Please to let me see it." When Patience proffered the letter to Colette, the woman nodded quickly. *"Magnifique."*

Colette propped the letter on the mantelpiece and instructed Patience. "I want you to walk out this door, get your cloak, lead me out the front door and down to the carriage I have waiting. Tell the butler that you and I are going for a carriage ride and should return in an hour. If you give my little secret away," she warned Patience, indicating the pistol, "then I shall not be responsible for any injured or dead parties. They will be on your conscience if you did not do as I say. Have I made myself clear?" Her face held almost a friendly, companionable expression with a very dark smile.

Patience knew she would do whatever she had to do to get Colette out of the town house before she hurt anyone. She nodded to the woman. "No need to use that thing. I assure you I will cooperate. Please do not hurt anyone. They have done nothing," she pleaded with Colette, who looked as if she had bloodless veins.

"Do you not remember? You wrote my words. The innocent are always hurt. It is the price of war and victory." Colette's voice was calm and distant.

Patience placed her trembling hands behind her back. She must keep her composure. With a blank look on her face, she disagreed with Colette's statement. "No, it is the price of hatred they pay with their blood." Perhaps if she could keep Colette talking, Bryce would return. But then Colette might kill him.

Colette waved her pistol in the direction of the door. "We have a long journey ahead of us. We should get started."

That was when Patience noticed the cold, unfeeling light in the depths of Colette's eyes trained apathetically on her. She had never noticed it before.

Patience would go with Colette, but somehow she would find a way to return to Bryce. Her former fury with him seemed insignificant compared with the danger she faced now.

Chapter 28

Standing on the stoop Lem, Sally, and Stone all watched in silence as Patience waved farewell from her friend's carriage, her face pale white but still smiling. Stone went about his business, but the children lingered on the stoop.

Sally's eyes filled with tears. "Is Aunt Patience coming back to us?"

Lem looked worried. "I dunno. I thought I 'eard the coachman mention Winchelsea, yet Patience said they were only going for a drive."

Sally tugged on the older boy's sleeve. "Lem, would you help me find Spring, my dolly? I put 'er outside the parlor, but she isn't there."

Lem sighed, knowing if he didn't help the girl, she would have another reason to cry.

But even though the children scoured the ground floor and first floor, Spring had simply disappeared. Sally crumpled into a tiny ball on the floor of the parlor, losing two loved ones in a day was too much for the child. Lem was thankful when Martha returned from her shopping expedition. Perhaps she would know what to do.

* * *

Had there ever been a more glorious day? Bryce could hardly contain himself in his eagerness to see Patience and hold her in his arms. He wondered what she thought of his present from this morning, and wanted to shower her with more gifts only to see her lovely smile. The urgent meeting with the PM and the secretary had lasted far longer than any of them had planned, but there was no help for it when the security of their country was at stake.

The next few weeks would be difficult for them. He envisioned sending Patience to Lady Elverston to stay before their wedding. This, he told himself, would be as soon as earthly possible. Knowing Patience was to be his brought a certain lightness to his step and a grin that stopped most of the lords and MPs in their shoes, unaccustomed as they were to seeing the Earl of Londringham with anything but a dark, shadowed look on his face.

Was it his imagination or was his carriage slowing down even though he had instructed the driver to hurry? He knocked his cane on the roof and called out to Lucky in his impatience. His coachman replied that there was too much traffic on the roads, and he could do naught to speed their journey. Bryce resigned himself good-humoredly and leaned comfortably back against his seat.

He wondered what her answer would be to his marriage proposal. Hell, Patience better respond in the affirmative. He smiled, too overwhelmed with his euphoric feeling to contemplate any obstacles in their way because he knew Patience loved him. Perhaps her words had only been whispered in her sleep, but it was enough to plant hope where only despair had once lain.

Finally the carriage drew abreast of his town house. Up the steps he went and through the door. Had he ever been this close to happiness before? Stone greeted him at the door and relieved him of his hat, coat, and cane. Bryce's warm greeting jolted his butler's formal composure until he asked, "Would you happen to know where I might find Miss Mandeley?"

Stone hesitated, then cleared his throat. "My lord, ah . . . she is not at home at present."

Bryce remained evenly calm, not yet concerned. "I suppose Miss Mandeley left with Miss Krebs for calling or shopping. Any notion on when we might expect their return?" He patted his left pocket, gratified to hear the crackle of the marriage license. He was already briskly walking up the stairs to the parlor for his port when Stone's reply brought him to an abrupt halt.

"Miss Krebs is in the parlor waiting for you, my lord. Miss Mandeley left earlier this morning with, I believe she said an old friend, a woman by the name of Colette d'Acoeur." Stone watched his master dash back down the stairs.

How could this be? This was presumably the same woman that Patience had gone to help last night. What more could she want with Patience? Remembering what transpired the night prior, Bryce flinched. He walked over to the butler. With his hands on his hips, his voice composed, he asked, "How long ago did you say they left?"

"This morning, around ten o'clock."

Bryce stood silent, thinking quickly. Where could they have gone and why had Patience left with the maid? His brow furrowed, he glanced at his watch. "It is nearly twelve. Why has no one searched for them? Was no one alarmed? Why was I not notified?"

Stone nary blinked, his lordship's anger justified. "Miss Mandeley accompanied her friend, and we saw no cause for concern. We have been expecting her imminent return."

His butler was right, of course. Perhaps he worried needlessly, something Bryce never did. He nodded briefly at

Stone's explanation, then headed for the stairs with the hope that Martha might be able to enlighten him further.

The parlor doors flew open, causing the woman sitting on the settee to jump to her feet. Nervously, she stood waiting for his lordship to enter the room.

"Miss Krebs, do you know anything about Miss Mandeley's disappearance?" He hoped the concern he felt didn't reflect in his voice, for he didn't want to frighten the poor woman. He stood in the middle of the room, waiting for answers, hoping for answers, praying for good news, if he could remember how to pray.

"I . . . we don't know, my lord. Miss Mandeley had already left with her friend when I returned home from my errands. We are all very worried, even Sally and Lem. This is so unlike Miss Mandeley."

Bryce could easily detect the distress in Patience's companion and wanted to comfort her but knew not how. With a calmness he was far from feeling, he motioned to the settee. "Please sit down. Perhaps there is no reason for my apprehension. I'm only anxious to see her. Do you have any clue as to where she went?"

A voice from the opened doorway drew their startled attention. "Perhaps planning the denouement of England," drawled Keegan dramatically from the edge of the room.

Bryce jumped up and crossed the room to his friend and welcomed him in. "I had not learned of your return. What has happened to you and what say you about Miss Mandeley?"

Keegan slumped into a nearby wing chair and brushed his forehead wearily. "I have been one step behind you all day, trying to find you. A most difficult task I am relieved to see completed." He looked up at Bryce standing near the settee, watching him closely. "We need to talk. Alone." He pointedly stared in Martha's direction.

"Miss Krebs, would you please have Stone send up some brandy?"

The solemn woman nodded to Bryce before quickly quitting the room, silent across the Oriental rug.

After she had closed the doors, enveloping the men in privacy, Bryce turned his attention on his friend. "We were not expecting you for some time. You have a lot of explaining to do. I don't care where you start, just make it brief, and tell me what has happened to you and what you know about Miss Mandeley." He began pacing the room as Keegan delved into his tale.

With a sigh, the captain told Bryce, "To begin with, when I stayed at Paddock Green earlier this summer, I received my latest orders, coded, of course, for my next run on the *Valiant*. It was not until I had made it to port that I discovered my papers were missing. I wasn't too alarmed, thinking I had thrown them in the fire with other documents that needed to be destroyed. Also, like a sapscull, I believed that if anyone did happen on these papers, that the code was virtually unbreakable. To my gravest shock, I learned differently." He held up his bandaged hand.

Bryce stared in shock. "What happened?"

"After a week of sailing along the coast, we were in position near Bologne. We hoped to learn more about Napoleon's flotilla and a possible timeframe of his invasion. Suddenly, we were bombarded with cannon fire as if they were anticipating our arrival. Although we returned their gunfire, we were easily outgunned by the French ships. We managed to escape in the dark hours before morning, but not until after we had sustained many losses, and I injured my hand."

Bryce's eyes darkened hearing his friend's misfortune, and he shook his head. Unfortunately, his experience in the earlier war with France had prepared him for this type of news.

"You think someone at Paddock Green obtained your papers, broke the code, and warned the French?"

Keegan nodded slowly and moved uncomfortably in his seat. "I do."

"Who?" his tone quiet and authoritative.

A brief pause. "Someone who calls herself Miss Patience Mandeley." Bryce froze, his features hardened into a statue, his breath held, his heart barely beating.

He shook his head. "I don't believe you."

"I knew you wouldn't. But I discovered, while on this last mission, that the French woman spy you had dealings with, the one you suspect lured your brother to his death, left France several months ago. In fact, not long after the incident last November. My sources told me that she had traveled to Storrington before arriving at the Mop Fair in Winchelsea seeking a position in a certain Englishman's household."

Bryce collapsed onto the settee. "I simply don't believe it. You must have made a mistake. Your sources must have made an error. I tell you it is not the same woman." He thrust his fingers through his hair, grief showing clearly on his face.

"Who of your acquaintances may I speak to? Something is terribly wrong. I am telling you that the French spy who killed my brother is *not* Miss Mandeley, who should be home directly. I prefer to hear from her before I make my judgment."

Stone entered the room carrying glasses and a brandy decanter on a silver tray, which he placed on the sideboard before he was dismissed.

Bryce rose and strode across the room to pour himself and Keegan each a glass of brandy. After handing Keegan his glass, Bryce walked over to the fireplace, staring at the dying embers. When he looked up, he discovered the letter on the mantelpiece addressed to him, and quickly broke the seal. After skimming the few lines, he let the vellum drop to the floor. Gone was the renewed hope he had known ever so briefly. What further proof did he need of Patience's clever duplicity and his own imprudence?

My Dear,

Honored as I am at your attentions, I cannot recip-rocate your affections. I do not love you. After I am gone, you will know this was for the best. You under-stand in war, the innocent are always hurt. But you are not innocent and neither am I. What I have done and am about to do, I did for my country. I return to France, my home. Someday you will learn the truth and be sur-prised. I will have surprised everyone at my success. Do not follow me, for I cannot be found. Be content that in time I am sure I will pay for my sins.

Patience Grundy

His face pale, he felt the grave wound to his heart, greater than his mother's betrayal and even more than his brother's death. A few words had consigned him to a hell of his own making. This damnation seared the remembrance in his heart that it would always be a dark, interminable winter. He would never again know the warming light that once saved his soul in surrender or the healing cure of love. His once-treasured marriage license now burned swiftly among the greedy flames.

He threw himself into a nearby chair, trying to make sense of these latest events, knowing he had to put aside his emotions. But—something didn't quite fit. Why had she signed herself "Patience Grundy"? She knew that he knew her real name to be Patience Mandeley.

Before he could think more on it, Keegan rose from his chair and retrieved the discarded piece of paper. He could only shake his head. It was obvious Bryce was in love with the girl and her treachery had been a terrible blow.

"What do we do now?" he asked Bryce, after silence had reigned for several minutes.

Bryce told his friend quietly and determinedly, "We find her. We find *them*."

A gentle knock on the door broke the tension between the two friends. When Bryce granted permission, both men had to wait until Sally slowly swung open the door, and then remained standing in the doorway, looking lost and forlorn. Bryce beckoned her into the room, hoping this would not take long. His only thought was to find Patience.

She stared at the captain for a moment, before braving the storm and toddled over to Bryce, now sitting on the settee. She climbed into his lap, unaware of the swirling emotions filling the room like a blustery wind, and took Bryce's chin in her little hand so that he would look at her.

"When is me Aunt Patience coming 'ome?" Her little voice was filled with anguish.

Bryce started, not ready to disappoint the child about yet another person in her young life deserting her. "Soon, I hope."

Sally shook her head. "But ye sent her away. I heard 'er."

Startled, he placed his big hands lightly on Sally's thin arms and looked warmly on the child. "What did she tell you?" he asked, trying not to frighten the child with his anxiousness.

Sally stared solemnly into Bryce's face. "She was crying this morning, all morning until the witch came."

He sighed, knowing he would have to be patient to hear and fully understand what the child had to tell him. What was that part about the witch? "Did the witch make her cry?"

Sally shook her head, her little mouth in a frown, growing a little impatient with her newly christened uncle.

"No, she was cryin' because ye gave 'er the necklace."
She paused thoughtfully. "If ye give me a present, will I 'ave
to leave?"

"You will never have to leave here." He hugged her little
form tightly against his, offering the child his assurance. Patience had cried over the necklace, obviously not in joy, as
he would have believed. He tried a different tact with the
child. "Who is the witch?"

Sally's blue eyes grew round as saucers. "She is the one
who took Aunt Patience away. Will ye bring Aunt Patience
back? Lem and Aunt Melenroy and me misses her."

He patted her hand. "Yes, I'll bring her back for all of
you." *And for myself,* he added silently.

Keegan cleared his throat. "We have other rather urgent
things to discuss."

Bryce ushered Sally out the door as Keegan stood to
stretch his legs. Keegan said, "I think her note means that
the invasion is happening quite soon. How long does it take
to get to Winchelsea from here?"

Thoughtful, Bryce replied, "Probably close to eight
hours. I shall have Lucky bring the carriage and the horses
around, expediency is a must. If we start now, we might be
able to catch up to them on the road to Winchelsea." He
headed for the door but stopped at Keegan's next words.

"What makes you think the invasion is planned for
Winchelsea? It could be anywhere along the southeast coast
from Dover to Hastings."

Bryce smiled thinly. "With a rash of spy activity lately
in Winchelsea, I've a strong suspicion that is their point
of landing. We shall go directly to the fencibles and seek
their help."

Keegan fell silent in agreement and followed his friend
out the door.

A short while later waiting in the drawing room for their

carriage to be brought around, Bryce and Keegan heard urgent voices at the front door, which then echoed in the vestibule.

They hurried down to the entryway to discover three men arguing with Stone, the butler insisting that "she is not here."

Bryce walked over to Stone and the gentlemen dressed in country tweeds. "What is this business about? Who are they looking for?"

Stone answered, after the tall, thin man had stopped talking. "These gentlemen insist on seeing their sister, Miss Mandeley.

"Bryce didn't know how many surprises he would need to endure this day. "You are Miss Mandeley's brothers?"

Keegan stepped next to Bryce and sneered, "Why are you not with the spy, helping to plan the invasion?"

The tall, thin man introduced himself with a sneeze. "I am Baronet Louis Mandeley. Who are you calling a spy? And where is my sister?" He drew himself up in a huff.

Bryce raised his hand to forestall Keegan and an ensuing argument, a strange feeling sweeping over him. "What are you doing here?"

A smaller man in cleric frock broke into the conversation. "We have decided to fetch her home. Her letter said we would find her here."

The gentleman who called himself the baronet looked at the cleric brother. "I told you this was all a mistake. Is Colette here? Perhaps she might offer some assistance."

Bryce and Keegan started at the name. "No, why?" Bryce inquired.

"She accompanied Patience to Winchelsea to help her find our brother Rupert. I knew this was a bad idea when Patience suggested it. I should have stopped her. Now we have a sister *and* a brother missing," the baronet stated dismally to his other brothers. He turned to Bryce. "Do you know where we might find her?" Louis asked hopefully.

Bryce flexed his shoulders. "No, but we believe we know where to start looking. We think she may have returned to Winchelsea with Colette this morning."

Louis stared in astonishment at the earl. "But why would she return to Winchelsea?"

"That is exactly what I intend to find out," he told Patience's eldest brother. He grabbed his coat, hat, and cane from Stone, and headed out the door, followed by Kilkennen and the three brothers.

As he made his way down the front steps, Keegan kept trying to forget what he had just heard. He didn't want to think what he was thinking. If Patience was innocent, as her brothers seemed to think she was, then the only person that could possibly be the spy was . . . Colette.

On the sidewalk, Louis caught Bryce's arm. "Why the speed? Is Patience in some kind of trouble?"

Bryce measured the man with a hard glance. "Yes, I believe she may be in danger."

The other brothers stepped forward. "We shall do our best to not be far behind."

Bryce nodded curtly and stalked down the stairs where Lucky waited with the coach and horses.

They set off south for the coast, hoping to find the women safe and prevent an invasion, a tall order. Each man was lost in his thoughts, Keegan refusing to believe what had transpired in the past few minutes. One minute he is convincing Bryce that Miss Mandeley is the spy, the next, everyone is thinking but not saying that Colette is the culprit. *But it couldn't be. It simply couldn't.* After all, he was one and thirty. He knew women. He knew Colette couldn't have the deaths of so many people on her hands. He knew her, didn't he?

In the fast-moving, bumpy carriage, Bryce felt a huge burden lift. Although there were still some pieces missing, like the crumpled note in his pocket, he knew deep in his soul Patience was a true-blooded Englishwoman, incapable of harming anyone.

It had to be Colette. If he was right, he thought grimly, his blood running cold, Patience was indeed in serious danger. Where was she? He wouldn't even consider the possibility that he wouldn't make it in time.

Chapter 29

Patience leaned her head wearily against the hard wall of the coach. Every bumpy mile they traveled took her farther and farther from Bryce. If her heart wept tears of despair, she was determined not to show any sign of weakness. Colette and Patience had occupied the same space for over four hours, pausing only once to change horses.

Strangely enough, Colette appeared unwilling to discuss the kidnapping or what her plans were. The woman's cold silence stilled Patience's impulse to question her. After Colette had partaken of refreshment at the inn, she had sent one of her men out to the carriage to give Patience water and bread, which Patience choked down, realizing hunger would weaken her body, making escape harder.

She sighed dismally. Escape. Her chances looked bleak. Colette travelled with five men: two coachmen on top and three on horseback. All were French and spoke little English, hurrying to do Colette's bidding. She commanded them easily with her poise of power and her threats of retribution for those who dared oppose her. And all the while, either she or one of her minions kept a pistol trained at Patience's heart.

Somehow, someway, Patience would find a way to escape

and return to Bryce. She still burned with the need to knock
Bryce in the head for trying to dispose of her in a similar
fashion to his old mistress. Since she had no idea where they
were headed, she didn't know much longer their journey
would take. Her hopes and prayers rested on the belief that
Bryce could be fast approaching.

The sun had long dimmed day into night when Colette
nudged her awake. "We're almost there."

"Where?" Patience drew herself away from the carriage's
side, massaging her sore neck muscles resulting from her
awkward sleeping position. She blinked and squinted into
the darkness of the coach with only a shallow lamp for light,
trying to read Colette's face. She drew back at the poison
that blazed from the woman's cold eyes.

Patience had never seen such a look before on a woman's
face, and her blood ran colder than a December morn at the
hate unveiled in Colette's eyes. It reminded her of the
enemy, known and unknown, and evil, like Jesus' once-
friend Judas. And of Sansouche. And of the dirty, cruel
deeds men performed under the cover of darkness for greed,
revenge, or for simply no reason at all. What were Colette's
dark secrets? And who had stolen her womanly nature and
replaced it with merciless hatred?

"You think you're innocent, but you're not. None of the
English are. Our noble leader will overcome your despica-
ble English country and people, and you will all kneel at the
superiority of French society," Colette mocked.

"Why do you pursue this mission of destruction?" Patience felt a chill crawl up her spine. She needed to know
these answers. Any information might help her situation.

Colette's short smile did not reach her half-hidden eyes.
She shrugged, as if realizing how little difference it would
make in the end if her plans were known. Nothing could stop

her. Perhaps she wanted someone to know her success, her final triumph.

"I am the Dark Angel. This is what has been planned for me since I was thirteen, when English soldiers attacked me on the road back from Town. They raped and bruised my body so much that for many months, I couldn't speak of their heinous crime. I only wanted to die—until a man came to see me. He took me from my parents, assuring them that he would care for me, raise me well, and return my voice to me." She hesitated, the only sign the story affected her emotions.

"The man kept his promise. In only a few months, he had found the key to unlock my voice. It was the word *'vengeance.'* She smiled. "Revenge. He taught me, and three boys of similar age who had also lost their childhood, that we could be taught to use our bodies and our minds to best serve France. He pounded the word *'vengeance'* into our heads, until it was branded on our souls. Until we slept dreaming of retribution, wielded a weapon with deadly force, and felt nothing, tasting only of the rewards of honor to come."

Patience leaned slightly forward in fascination of Colette's story, reminded of the cruelty of the world she had little experience with, until now.

"When we were old enough, we realized how little value our own lives held to our master. We were only his instrument of war. Our successes would please him, our punishment harsh if we failed. We learned quickly not to fail."

A self-assured smile sprung to Colette's lips, and Patience stared in awe at this transformation.

"I was the master's best. He never thought I would be better than the boys, because you see I am only a woman. He had to only underestimate me once, before he learned his lesson. He still bears my scar on his face."

But Colette's story grew long, and Patience still had no idea what was happening to her. "What does all this have to do with me?" Her question almost brought Colette out of the past.

"For over a year, I've been playing a tune in the ear of a certain English spy, giving him just the right amount of information to convince him I was loyal to his country. We played a dangerous game—he would tell me something, I would tell him something. But we never knew what the truth was." Her eyes lost their harsh look and turned slightly warm. "He was a most handsome man, Lord Londringham."

Patience's gasp turned Colette's gaze on the woman across from her. "Yes, *his lordship*. Last November, I had decided he was too dangerous and had to be dealt with. Remember, I had been skillfully taught that killing for the right reasons alleviated remorse." She scoffed, "We were to meet in our usual place. Sansouche had sent word to Kilkennen's ship, for Lord Londringham. His brother, Edward, happened to be on board, and came in his place."

Patience's heart sounded like thunder in her ears, horrified as Bryce's history unfolded, scarcely able to breathe in the enclosed carriage and fearful of what would come next.

Colette shrugged indifferently. "I had to kill him. He was in my way. I even waited for Londringham to show up to claim his brother, but his lordship and his men escaped our French bullets, except for the one to his leg."

Patience found her voice, shaky though it was. "You . . . you killed Bryce's brother?"

Colette looked at her with disappointment. "Have you not heard anything I have said? The innocent are sometimes hurt in war. No one is safe. My only regret is that Londringham did not die on our French shores. Still, here or there, he cannot stop this."

Patience clenched her hands at her side, ever aware of the pistol unwavering in Colette's hands. She almost leapt from her seat to attack the Frenchwoman, but knew she would be dead before her hands had touched the spy's throat. How could anyone that had caused so much pain talk so cavalierly about her actions?

This woman was the Devil's wife. She had been stripped of her humanity and only the shell of wickedness kept her alive.

"The master sent Sansouche and I to England. We were to pay well any Englishmen willing to sell your country's secrets, such as Lord Peter Carstairs."

Patience raised her eyebrows at this turn of events. "You killed our cousin?"

"*Non,* Sansouche had to kill him because although he had given us vital information on the barracks and fencibles governing the coast from Dover to Hastings, Carstairs became terribly greedy and had outlasted his purpose. Fortunately, your brother played right into our hands, a good piece of luck. He happened to find his cousin's cold body after Sansouche had killed him. With the constable and his men searching for Rupert Mandeley as a murderer and traitor, we were left to pursue our strategy."

Colette glanced out the window, then returned to her story. "When I saw you in Storrington on our way to Winchelsea, with our similar traits, I thought you might come in handy. We became . . . friends, and while you sought a position with the earl, I already had a position as a lady's maid with the help of the countess and her cousin, Sansouche. His lordship never suspected I am the Dark Angel because he was still too consumed with grief over his brother's death, and I made a concerted effort to stay out of his way."

She sent Patience daggered looks. "You, my dear, kept getting in the way. Insisting Bryce was the spy and not Carstairs. At a midnight rendezvous, I tried to kill Bryce but someone was watching us and interfered. You had Mr.

Gibbs fired, another man of mine, and then Sansouche followed you like a female dog in heat, causing him to become careless. However, despite your untimely interventions, all our plans were coming together, especially when your brother was arrested. We left for London to meet with the rest of our men to finalize the details for our invasion."

Patience reclined slightly in her seat, and certainly with more bravado than she felt, said, "As soon as Bryce and Keegan find your note, they will be after us. They will stop you."

If Patience thought her words would put a scare into this mad woman bent on destroying England, she was sorely disappointed and vaguely surprised to hear Colette peal off a laugh.

"My poor girl, with your note, you've destroyed Lord Londringham's hopes. You've broken his heart, and I can assure you he'll have no interest in finding you."

Patience felt the blood slowly drain from her face. She didn't think she could bleed any more from the sharp thrusts to her heart than she had already in the past several hours. She then actually did contemplate assaulting Colette. Perhaps she had no way of winning, but death seemed almost welcome at the moment. Her death.

"Bryce will find me, and he will stop you. He will save England from this invasion, of that I have no doubt."

"There you are wrong. He won't find you and our plans for the invasion will proceed accordingly."

Patience had one more question for the madwoman. "Why did you kill Sansouche?"

Colette snorted. "It was a beauty of a plan that came to me after he attacked you in the Gardens. I knocked him on the head, so he wouldn't hurt you. You were too valuable to me. I decided to kill him and send you a note. You were to be there when the Runners discovered his dead body. They would have accused you of his murder."

"Only," she spat, "Londringham got in the way of my plans and removed you before the Runners arrived. Damn the man!" Her venom filled the stagnant coach air, causing Patience's stomach to churn disagreeably.

"And what about Captain Kilkennen? Did you love him?" The bewilderment of using another human was evident in her query.

"Another innocent, even if he is a good captain. I easily stole his papers one afternoon and sent the information across the Channel so my compatriots were ready for his ship. He almost died too, but he, like his friend, seems to be very clever at escaping death."

Patience forced the words from her tight throat. "And me? What are your plans for me?"

"You'll learn soon enough. If Londringham is not persuaded by your letter, he and his men will be searching for you; and keep away from the coast, where tonight we have planned a little surprise for your fellow countrymen."

Patience's mouth dropped open. "Tonight is the invasion?" she asked in a faint, horrified whisper.

Colette nodded. "It really doesn't matter if you know the truth, because you won't be there to see it. Such a pity."

Patience turned her eyes away from Colette's triumphant, sick gaze. Nothing would stand in this woman's way. She was determined to destroy everyone, and no compassion made her indeed a dangerous adversary.

No, Patience suddenly determined, with her back straight. She wasn't going to die with Bryce thinking her a traitor. She would escape and find him. She wiped her damp hands along her muslin dress. Something would come to her, a plan of sorts. Perhaps she didn't have Colette's diabolic training, but her brother James had taught her that good does triumph over evil, and Patience knew she had good on her side.

Four hours later, Bryce and Keegan changed their horses for ones obtained at the inn in New Folke. After speaking with the innkeeper, Bryce was sure they were on the women's trail and only two hours behind them. He was disturbed to learn that the innkeeper had seen only one woman, but Bryce refused to believe any harm had befallen Patience, until he had seen it with his own eyes. He nodded grimly to Kilkennen, who had yet to betray his own thoughts concerning his lover, Colette. Both knew the name of the villain who sought to lead the invasion on English shores.

Patience and Colette jerked to attention when they heard a knock on the top of their carriage.

"Soon, I shall be back in France. Your part of the journey has come to an end," Colette told her in a very businesslike manner, glancing out the carriage window.

Patience's senses heightened in deadly awareness. "My part of the journey? You're leaving me somewhere along the London road?" not bothering to control the tremor of hope in her voice.

With lips pursed, Colette responded, "It's not as simple as that. I've acquaintances waiting for you near Winchelsea." She rubbed her gloved hands together in anticipation of the night to come.

Patience swallowed hard. Who did Colette have waiting for her? She knew these acquaintances spelled danger. In her best composed manner, she asked, "Since I am being left out of the festivities tonight, might I inquire where your ships will be landing?" She wasn't ready to surrender.

Colette's eyes narrowed slightly before replying. "Although I've never made it a practice to reveal pertinent information, especially to the enemy, soon you won't be in any position to sabotage my plans. Tonight should be a fine calm night for sailing. In a few hours, my men will have taken control of several bonfires along the coast between Winchelsea and Dungeness, from where we will signal our ships for landing at Hastings. Some of your fine Englishmen have already revealed where your infantry's positions are along this stretch of land.

"Since we control the 'signals,' no one will be alerted to our invasion, until it is too late." Her manner was light and easy, belying the seriousness of their conversation.

Patience studied the Frenchwoman for several minutes before asking softly, "When will your revenge be complete? When will you stop this madness? Will there ever be too much blood on your hands or your conscience?"

Colette could only laugh at Patience's naïve questions and shake her head. "You are indeed an innocent. I was very lucky when early in my life someone taught me to live for a purpose. Take that purpose away, and I shall die."

Patience could think of no reply, and thought Colette's justification insane. Perhaps James could have taught this wronged woman about forgiveness and a grander destiny than the evil and harshness of a dark world learned at the knees of her satanic master.

The carriage continued to rattle on into the night, but the road grew more rocky and bumpy, alerting Patience that they were off the main road. Several miles later, the coachmen brought their horses to a heaving halt. Colette quickly swept out of the coach with a warning for Patience not to move or she would be shot.

A meaningless threat, Patience thought, considering her death was imminent. Slowly the tears she had held back slipped down her cheeks. In her distress, she bit her lip to keep her anguish silent, afraid to alert the guards outside. Her whole body shook with an invisible pain, her arms wrapped tightly around her body as if to hold in her grief.

She cried because she would never see her brothers again, or Sally or Lem or Martha or Melenroy, all her friends. But mostly she saved her anguish for Bryce, at the thought of never seeing him again. Never feeling his lips caress hers, never again knowing his touch that had branded her heart, body, and soul. "Unfair," she whispered in a litany. How could evil win? This wasn't supposed to happen.

Then her chills started. She couldn't get warm, covered only by her thin pelisse. As her breathing became more labored she leaned back against the carriage seat, eyes now dry, and tried to compose herself.

The door at last opened, and a deep, harsh voice instructed her to climb down. She slid awkwardly to the ground, her feet unsteady beneath her after their long ride. She balanced on the carriage door while she gained her perspective and gasped in horror.

They were in a graveyard. Old gravestones dotted the ground like the sticks in her tomato patch. A slight breeze amplified the silence of the night, marred by low talking among the Frenchmen and restless horses. The graveyard sprawled before her, with modest and magnificent stones alike, in an eerie, silent, forgotten resting place with high weeds their only keepers.

Not far away, she could hear the Channel waters meeting the shore, but the night blurred the separation between sea and sky. The five men that had accompanied the carriage stood in a small circle, ever watching the play about to begin.

Her eyes widened at the mounds of dirt on either side of a large hole and at the wooden coffin that lay next to it. Could this be Colette's plan? Would this be her gravesite?

She felt nauseated and gripped the carriage door handle until it marked her tender skin. With only a few moments left to live, Patience was determined not to make it easy for any of them. Stoically she turned to the small group of men and asked, "So, on whose conscience will be my death?"

No one moved, no one answered her. The quiet was deafening, even the forest animals quit their activities when they realized humans were nearby.

Colette's men only looked over to their leader, who called to Patience, "Come over here."

But Patience remained stubbornly where she was and missed Colette nodding to one of her men because suddenly she felt another hard pistol in her back, pushing her toward the grave where Colette and Lord Londringham's former butler, Mr. Gibbs, and another awaited her.

There was something to be said that in her last moments on earth, Patience was to see the very people she hated most in this world. And hate was a word foreign to her vocabulary.

Colette watched her approach the open grave. When Patience was a few feet away, she announced, "We must be leaving. Mr. Gibbs and Snively will see to you." She almost hesitated. "I wish I could be sorry that an innocent like you must die, but it simply is not in the plans for you to live. You have served your purpose."

She started to walk away but Patience's words stopped her midstride. "Your plans will fail because Lord Londringham will stop you, like he has done before. And, Colette, I have it on good authority that you will pay dearly for your sins—in Hell."

Colette turned and looked at Patience with almost admiration in her eyes. "Good and evil, could it be that simple?"

The carriage and riders soon were on their way back to the main road.

Patience quickly turned back to the two men when Mr.

Gibbs sneered, his bulbous face red with the effort, his own gun unsteady with joyous emotion. "See how the mighty have fallen. We have you all to ourselves. No one can save you, not even his lordship himself. No one knows where to find you."

His friend Snively chuckled in glee, and spit near Patience's skirts.

She twitched not a hair, nor altered her expression after hearing his ugly, ominous words. They certainly didn't deserve the satisfaction of seeing her cower. She was going to be brave when she went to meet her maker, at least that was her plan before she hitched her skirts, turned, and ran in the other direction, surprising her captors. Bullets pocked the ground as she ran but her enterprise proved short-lived.

Unfortunately, the small, wiry Snively managed to dive for her skirts, pulling her down with him to the ground. She fought with the little man determinedly, aiming to claw his face or give him a swift, hard kick, especially when she saw that distinctive leer in the small eyes peering so close to her face.

"Snively, this chit is too much trouble. The sooner we bury her, the sooner we can join the others," Gibbs told his friend, while throwing his companion off Patience and pulling the young woman to her feet. In short shrift, he had her hands tied behind her back and around her waist. They hauled Patience kicking and pulling across the graveyard, screaming to wake the ground's residents.

They finally managed to tie her feet but not before Snively had received a grand kick in the eye and Mr. Gibbs a knee in the groin. Unfortunately, her efforts were rewarded by their calloused, harsh hands dumping her into the open coffin. Patience continued to plead for mercy, but they ignored her, both men intent on finishing their ugly task. They pushed her prone into the coffin before placing the lid on top. Nails pounded into the wooden sides and top, and sealed her fate.

Patience couldn't fight the panic. It was her nightmare, and it was coming true. She was being buried alive. She couldn't breathe. She needed air. There was no escape. Her thoughts were soon drowned out by the loud *thud, thud, plop, dribble, dribble* of dirt raining on her wooden eternal bed. Patience began her last prayers, asking God to forgive her sins and asking him to take her gently from this world into his. And to watch over Bryce and her brothers, and Lem, and Sally, and . . .

Chapter 30

The General watched the proceedings with great interest. He and his other two companions had just arrived in the cemetery, ready to begin work, when the activity at the far end of the plots caught his attention. He motioned to Harry. "Our first one. This should be easy. We need to 'urry them away, so we won't 'ave to do all that undiggin'."

Henry nodded, his broken teeth in a grin, for he had followed the General's thoughts. "Perhaps we can scare them away?"

The General chuckled at the idea. From their vantage point behind an elaborate statue of the Greek god Mercury, they could see two men, one husky, medium height and the other a scrawny, short fellow flinging dirt on some poor sod's last resting place.

"Oooooooooooo Waaaaaaaaaaaaaaaaaaaa." Together, their voices rose in a ghostly, hallowed moan, sure to raise the hackles of any mortals nearby.

The grave diggers stopped and listened. All was quiet. They resumed their work.

Louder. *"Oooooooooooooooooooooo Ohhhhhhhhhhhhhhh."*

The grave robbers sent up even more ferocious howls as

vengeful ghosts prepared to walk the earth. The prospect of meeting immortals hastened the grave diggers' departure.

The General clapped his hands together delightedly. "'urry, boys, lots of useless gold teeth to be found tonight. Useless to their owner." He chuckled merrily at his own small wit. They scurried like the rats they were to the open grave. Henry and Louis lifted the light coffin easily out of the grave and brushed the remnants of inhibiting dirt from the oblong box.

The General snapped his teeth together, always excited in the moment of his success. With a cool breeze behind them, they made short work of the lid using a crowbar.

A woman. They collectively sighed, hesitant to disturb a female's grave.

That was before she moved.

Her eyes fluttered open and all three would-be grave robbers screamed and jumped back.

Alive! Was she a ghost? Henry and Bear sank to their knees and watched in amazement as Patience hauled herself with difficulty into a sitting position, staring incredulously and jubilantly at her rescuers. The General had fainted dead away.

Patience sat comfortably next to Bear in the sparse grass, their shallow lamp providing a warming light to the night. And life. She held a whiskey bottle in her hand, generously offered by the big man. All three comrades, the General having regained consciousness, continued to stare at Patience as if she had just risen from the dead. Which is exactly how she felt. Over and over she praised them and called them her saviors. This, of course, after sending several prayers to God thanking him that he didn't need her quite yet.

She shook her head in amazement. "How came you to be

here? Were you following our carriage? Did you intend to rob me again?"

The men looked slightly confused at this reference.

"Well, never mind. It matters not. The important thing is that I'll be forever in your debt and that you saved me even when performing your nefarious little work." She unsteadily rose to her feet, breathing deeply several times, unable to get enough of the fresh air back into her lungs.

"Much better, I'm definitely feeling stronger. I must still ask for your assistance." She cocked her head to look expectantly at the pale men who had hastily risen to their feet. "Is your carriage nearby? I should like to borrow it. You see, I must stop the invasion," she told them matter-of-factly.

The General stepped up to her when he heard this, looking at her queerly. "Ye were the one on Winchelsea road that night, claim'n the French were com'n, just as we were about to light'n yer valuables. Why is it that ye are always on about the French invad'n? We 'aven't seen 'em yet, 'ave we, boys?" He smirked to his cohorts, who watched this little scene.

Patience hesitated, pondering how best to convince them she spoke the truth. "I know this is rather hard to believe, but truly, the woman who brought me here is a French spy. She's preparing to signal to the French ships that it's safe to land on English soil. I must try and stop her."

From the looks on the faces of the General and Henry, her words rang false.

But Bear stepped forward and told her, "No carriage, miss, but you may have my horse."

She tried to control her shudder of revulsion at the news of her only form of transportation and hope. "Ah, thank you, that is very kind of you. If you will show me to your horse and point me to the Winchelsea road, I would greatly appreciate it."

Bear held the reins with one big hand and boosted

Patience up with the other. His mare shifted nervously with the new light weight on top of her. Patience patted the pretty mare's neck, leaning over to coo assurances in the horse's ear. The reins tense in her hands, she listened carefully to Bear's directions, then turned the mare, strangely named Kitten, toward the road. One tap of her heels sent the mare flying, and Patience hung on for dear life. Surely God had not saved her in order that she might break her neck on the back of a horse?

At the gallop of her mighty hooves, Patience thought, *"Kitten" was a misnomer if ever I've heard one.* Soon Patience found the rhythm in Kitten's gait, and their reckless ride became a bit more tolerable as the wind whipped at her hair and skirts.

She had to find help. She headed in what she hoped was a southerly direction, where she remembered something about barracks outside of Winchelsea. Perhaps someone there would believe her story.

The night mocked her journey, giving up no secrets of her whereabouts. When she reached the main road, hoping she headed due south, she pushed her mare faster. Patience marveled at staying the ride and not lying in a ditch.

Riding astride was infinitely safer even if her petticoats were on display. The cool night air did little to diminish the dampness from her exertions and fear that she might be too late. She didn't know if she had any prayers left that would be answered.

After several miles, cottages began appearing along the dusty road. The village must be near.

When she noticed the church tower in Winchelsea, she breathed a sigh of relief that she was almost there. She continued to race through Town, hoping to find the soldiers' barracks directly beyond.

She finally slowed Kitten, sawing hard on the reins, both

mare and woman breathing hard. Immediately she heard shouts and footsteps running. With the small reservoir of energy left, she lifted her right leg over the mare's flank and slid all the way to the ground, landing in the dust on her bottom. Someone close behind her grabbed her under the armpits and hauled her unceremoniously to her feet.

A young man in a uniform with a rifle wielded expertly strode forward between the small gathering of soldiers surrounding Patience in curiosity. A woman in their midst with dark hair swirling in knotted curls around her shoulders must have caught their interest.

In an urgent, breathless voice, she told them, "I must speak to your commander at once. For the security of our country." She heard the collective hushed intake of breath at her words.

The young soldier regarded her closely. "What's your name and what business do you have here?"

Patience put a hand to her chest, ineffectively trying to calm her nerves. "I'm Patience Mandeley and the French are planning to land near Hastings tonight."

The leering loitering soldiers nearby immediately straightened their backs, their weapons poised for action. The attaché barked an order and they immediately disappeared back into their barracks.

The lone officer told her, "It's close to midnight. We've already had one mistake this month over false reports of an invasion. I hope you know of which you speak. The commander does not like being awakened."

Patience shuddered at his choice of words.

Several minutes later, in the dimly lit room of Commander Rightner's office, both men listened incredulously to her story of Colette, her men, and the devastating plans to invade England.

Patience's confidence began to build. Perhaps it wasn't

too late. Infantry number 79 immediately came alive with sounds of weapons being loaded, low men's voices, and the jingling of horse's harnesses.

Patience had remounted, ignoring the commander's orders to stay behind. There was no way he or anyone else could keep her from finding Colette.

They rode single file through Winchelsea, heading for Hastings, when they came to a sudden halt by a larger contingent of militia, led by Bryce and Keegan.

Patience saw him before he saw her, and thirstily drank in the sight of his tall form and beloved visage. All her anger fled as quickly as Kitten's flying hooves. She wanted only to dive into his arms and remain there forever. Coming close to dying does strange things to your soul, she had discovered.

Bryce, Captain Kilkennen, and a uniformed officer approached Commander Rightner.

Bryce spoke first. "We have reason to believe the French will try and land tonight, somewhere between Winchelsea and Hastings. We've just come from London and my orders are from the secretary of war. We secure all lighthouses and bonfires, all infantry on alert."

Commander Rightner listened intently before replying, "I have information that the French will strike at Hastings."

Bryce studied the man before him, his face etched in stone. "Who is your source?"

A lieutenant motioned for his men to send Patience to the front of their columns. She walked her mare cautiously toward the commander, Bryce, and Keegan, her eyes trained on Bryce. She thought she glimpsed relief, surprise, and something else in his stormy blue eyes before he turned away.

"What proof does she offer you?" his question directed to Commander Rightner.

"The truth," Patience called over to him, daring Bryce to look at her again.

He steadied his gaze at her and hesitated.

Patience watched in horror at the emotions that played across his face. If she wanted evidence that Bryce had believed the note, he had confirmed it with his dark look and clenched jaw.

Horror switched to astonishment when he said to Commander Rightner, "Let us onward to Hastings." He reined his horse around, then back again to point to Patience. "She is to come with us." Bryce and his mount became a blur as they leapt down the road in a hard gallop with the troops and Keegan following behind.

Patience clutched Kitten's reins, bending low over the animal's neck. Soldiers surrounded her, making sure she couldn't escape. But she paid no notice. She was trying to keep sight of Bryce's broad back.

The ocean gleamed silently and still, the moonlight winking in the roving waters. Only a few stars peppered the late-spring night that was cool and breezy. As they travelled along the coast road, Commander Rightner sent men to cover the lighthouses and bonfires, first warning them there might be Frenchmen waiting for them.

Patience tasted the salty night air while clinging to Kitten's back, her whole body fraught with fear of what the next few hours would bring. Worrying about the safety of Bryce and England her sore muscles tensed.

She saw the cliffs in the distance and the lighthouse but none of the bonfires was lit.

Something was wrong. She could feel it in her tired bones. She reached up a gloved hand to push away a lashing strand of hair obstructing her sight.

At the front of the dark-colored columns of riders, one group broke away and headed farther south, the other group, including Bryce, left the coast road to begin the slow, arduous climb up the steep road leading to the top of the cliffs.

Pesky thorns and branches pulled and picked at her hair, scratching her stockinged legs to shreds. Still, she climbed on with the soldiers.

By the time the last riders and Patience reached the top, Bryce, Keegan, and Commander Rightner had vanished. After nudging Kitten forward through the wall of heaving horseflesh, Patience came upon a group of men near a dead bonfire, the sound of bullets reporting perhaps two miles away.

Where were Bryce and Captain Kilkennen? Where was Colette? Perhaps she was someplace else along the coast.

She halted her horse and slipped off Kitten's back, handing the reins to a soldier nearby. He tried to prevent her from leaving, but she easily evaded his reach while he tried to control both horses.

Patience ran across the cliff top toward the lighthouse, stumbling down the shallow valleyed green in the dark. Picking herself up, she crept closer and closer, unsure of what she might find. She leaned against the lighthouse wall to catch her breath and heard the pounding, lashing crash of the waves against the rocks below and shivered with the implication.

She had to reach Bryce and Kilkennen or Colette might try again to implicate Patience in her revolting plans. Feeling the raspy rough wall beneath her hands, she slowly rounded the lighthouse.

There they were, behind the lighthouse, near the edge of the cliffs. A line of soldiers, the lieutenant, Commander Rightner, Bryce, and Kilkennen with weapons at the ready stood near the lighthouse as Colette and her line of men faced them with their backs to the cliffs.

She edged closer to hear their conversation, and her eyes

widened in surprise as Colette fabricated a story that she
and her men were on the watch for the French spies and had
just arrived to light the bonfires. She insisted that they had
done nothing wrong. Although Colette's men did carry
weapons, they had as of yet committed no crime.

Patience ran out into the clearing between Bryce and
Colette. She turned an impassioned plea to Bryce. "She lies.
This woman tried to kill me. She had me buried alive. She
calls herself the 'Dark Angel.' She is a French spy who is responsible for the Frenchman Sansouche's death. They are
planning to invade tonight, she confessed this to me on our
journey from London. It was Sansouche, not my brother,
who killed my cousin, Lord Carstairs."

Too late, in the cover of darkness, Colette had snaked up
behind Patience and grabbed her, the ever-present pistol
cocked sickeningly against Patience's forehead. Bryce and
Keegan stood like statues transfixed at this sudden attack.
Patience's eyes remained fixed on Bryce as the blood
drained from her face.

Colette had her again and perhaps this time she would be
successful in causing Patience's death.

"I want a clear route to the sea or else she dies, gentlemen, what shall it be?"

Colette ignored Keegan's indignant snort of disbelief, her
sight leveled on Bryce. They stared at each other for several
long minutes, both knowing they held Patience's fate between them.

Bryce kept his pistol cocked, his finger on the trigger. He
burned with rage at the danger Patience was in and blamed
himself for not better protecting her. With passionate eyes,
pale face, and a cloak of dark tangled curls over her shoulders, Patience was alive, and he intended that she remain so.
For his very love, his very life, was also held in the balance.
He knew that Patience's death would savagely wound him

deeper than Edward's had. A fate he would never have thought possible.

His jaw clenched and unclenched. He had faced his own death before, but the pain and fear gnawing in his gut was unfamiliar to him. If only he had a distraction, one second, and he could shoot the French bitch.

Patience closed her eyes, summoning her strength. After seeing her death once tonight, this second time seemed almost easier. If she was going to die, she could still give one last present to Bryce, his brother's murderer. Releasing her breath, she said loudly to Colette, "Tell Lord Londringham how you killed his brother, Edward, when you meant to kill him. That you were waiting for Lord Londringham in the cottage to kill him."

Colette uttered a sharp laugh. This news would surely prick at Londringham's pride. "Yes, I was the one who sent you the note, but your brother came in your stead. He tried to escape, and I shot him."

She underestimated Bryce's skill at hiding his feelings. His stare would have made a lesser man or woman back down.

Not Colette. They were at an impasse.

Bryce finally earned his second. Keegan, not able to stand the wicked laugh from the woman he once loved, vaulted forward in anger toward Colette.

In seemingly slow motion, Colette turned and shot her once-lover as Patience tumbled to the ground, free. Bryce shot the Frenchwoman below her left shoulder.

Colette dropped her pistol, amazement stretched her features as a tiny sliver of blood leaked from her mouth. Her hands flailed as she fell backward toward the cliff, her mouth open to argue her fate.

Patience tried to crawl to Kilkennen, lying motionless on the hard ground, when she felt a strong pull on her skirts.

Suddenly, she found herself being dragged to the

edge, and looked down to find it was Colette with life still beating in her eyes clutching her clothing.

Patience clawed the earth frantically as Colette yanked her toward the abyss. In a fevered litany, Patience called for Bryce over and over. Then he was there in front of her, grabbing her arms and shoulders, his heels dug into the crumbled ground for leverage.

He tried to draw both women onto safer soil but Colette's grasp was tenuous. When her eyes glazed over in death, her grip lost its potency, and she freed Patience's skirts, falling backward and down, down, down to the black waiting sea below.

Bryce hauled Patience into his arms, both of them shaken from her near death over the cliff. She gloried in the sheltering warmth of his arms but couldn't stop shivering, knowing she would never forget Colette's last look of desperation.

Bryce tilted her chin so that he could look into her eyes. "You're safe now, she can no longer hurt you," he whispered against her forehead before they rose and walked over to where Kilkennen was receiving treatment from one of the soldiers. They learned he had been shot in the shoulder, high above the heart, but was losing blood rapidly. Plans were made to immediately carry him into Hastings for a physician.

Commander Rightner's soldiers seized the last of Colette's band of mercenaries and poor English farmers who had been promised French riches for their services. As Bryce and Patience rounded the lighthouse to return to their horses, she caught sight of her four brothers, Louis, Benjamin, and James with Rupert in tow. She flew down the path and into their arms, joyful to see them and curious as to their presence.

Satisfied that Patience was safe for the time being with her brothers, Bryce followed Keegan's man-made stretcher down the road.

She kissed them all and kept clutching Rupert's hand while listening in astonishment to her younger brother's derring-do. While she and Bryce were saving England from being invaded, Rupert had assisted in capturing Frenchmen trying to land in a longboat near the shore a few miles away. They were actually smugglers and now safely ensconced in a welcoming prison cell.

"Excuse me, miss. I found this lying on the ground and this hanging out of it," a solder told Patience, handing her Sally's doll, Spring. The gift of the emerald necklace splayed dark in her hands. Colette must have found the doll and hidden the necklace in it. At least Patience could return Sally's doll and his lordship's necklace. She grimaced.

The Mandeley family rode down the foothill and heard Patience's horrid tale of being abducted by Colette and her brush with death. She had no time to tell them more about her stay at Paddock Green or London, and needed to think more about what she wanted to tell her older brothers about Bryce.

Relaxed in a safe public room in Hasting's only inn, the family chattered away as they caught Patience up on news back home. They had obtained rooms at the inn while they awaited Bryce's report on the captain's condition.

Bryce finally left the physician's cottage after speaking to Keegan and reassuring himself that his friend had not suffered any permanent harm. He arranged to have Keegan moved, when able, to recuperate at Paddock Green. If he knew Patience, she would want to take complete charge of his friend's convalescence.

He quickly wrote a note to Patience, explaining his urgent need to see Secretary Hobart to report the failed French invasion. He said he would meet her at Paddock Green within a week, and they could discuss their future.

Patience. He had to see her, talk to her. There was so much he wanted to say to her.

But he had to start preparing for his trip to London. Soon he would come home to Patience. He would send his house staff and Sally back to wait for him at home. Home, a place where he wanted to be.

The first breeze of the morning awakened Patience to the bold sunlight. Although her body and mind still begged for sleep, Patience had to find Bryce.

The innkeeper directed her to the only physician's house. Patience walked quickly, anxious to find Bryce and concerned over the captain's health. She met a soldier on the path striding from the physician's direction, who assured her Captain Kilkennen's condition had improved considerably over the night.

Patience breathed a sigh of relief, realizing she would not have his death on her conscience. But she would have to find a way to make it up to him after his sacrifice.

She stopped for a moment to get her bearings. Right at this corner and straight up the hill until she saw the low cottage. Inside, Patience found the captain sleeping peacefully but learned to her surprise that Bryce had left for Town.

Unbeknownst to Patience, the letter from Bryce had arrived at the physician's home, but then had fallen to the floor and was forgotten.

Why would he not have stopped for her? Then she remembered the necklace he had left her. Was there still time for them? She slowly walked back to the inn, lost in her thoughts.

Benjamin and James assisted Patience into their coach, her solemn expression forbidding any questions as to their early departure. As the coach carried them down the coast road, Patience thought she heard the dirt plunking suffocatingly on top of her coffin.

Chapter 31

It had been two weeks since the eventful night in Hastings. Long weeks as they collected suspects in the failed invasion attempt and heard depositions. He had finally obtained a reprieve after attending several long conferences and seeing to the demands of the PM and the secretary of war. He knew he would have to return to London soon, but, God willing, with his new bride by his side.

His town house was empty except for Stone and a few other staff. Bryce had occupied the lonely wee hours of the morning by writing letters to Patience—telling her how much he missed her, and holding on to his promise of a quick return, which perversely made every day seem that much longer.

Now, after a long carriage journey and his hard ride on Defiance the last several miles in anxious desire to see Patience, he ran up the steps to Paddock Green.

As he entered the hallway, he noticed a stack of his letters to her sitting on a table.

"She is not here, my lord."

Bryce stared in confusion at his butler.

Furthermore, Marlow informed him, Patience had not been at Paddock Green since their first departure for London.

Exhausted from his journey, Bryce wanted only to sit down and rest his leg, drink a stiff glass of port, and ponder over Patience's absence. With a fire crackling by his side on this early May night and a full bottle of the finest spirits this side of the Channel untouched, he was no closer to understanding the truth about Patience's whereabouts.

Of course it didn't help matters when Sally, Lem, Melenroy, Martha, and even Kilkennen all wanted to know where Patience was and when she would return home. Presenting Sally with yet another new doll did help pacify the child somewhat, however.

Always one to think matters through thoroughly, that is what Bryce set about doing. He considered the possibility that having been put through such an ordeal, she had wanted to rest in her own home. He frowned, then dismissed the thought. Not likely. Perhaps her brothers had not been keen on her returning to Paddock Green alone, and had persuaded her to wait in Storrington for him to come and formally ask for her hand in marriage. Yes, good.

His features hardened into stone upon contemplating the more bleak possibilities. Why had she written that traitorous letter? Had Colette forced her hand? Why—as Sally had asked him, that morning—had she been crying? He refused to consider that her lovemaking had been out of gratitude for helping her brother. She didn't have a dishonest bone in her body, he knew that about her.

He had to put the pieces together, but it was impossible without consulting Patience. Bryce determined to sleep off the effects of his exhausting trip, promising himself he would leave for Storrington in the morning to find her. He feared not the consequences of what he might learn there, but only what would happen if he didn't make the effort to find the truth.

* * *

Patience was angry, furious, even. After all she had done to save Bryce and their country, and almost losing her own life many times, albeit most of the time her own fault, but still. She determined she would go to Paddock Green and confront Bryce and tell him that she loved him. And he would just have to accept that because he couldn't send her away. Not ever again.

With a quick note to her brothers, she grabbed a few necessities in a carpet bag, and ran to the stables where the groomsman, Mr. Grundy, hitched up their little gig. She was going home.

Mr. Grundy left her in Storrington to wait for the coach that would take her to Winchelsea and Bryce.

It was near to ten o'clock in the evening, when she saw the familiar sight of the tree-lined drive, just barely visible in the dark.

Patience was impatient. Finally, the driver pulled the coach up to the front steps, and she jumped from the carriage, launching up the steps. Lem opened the door for her. She hugged the little boy, trying to control the sweep of happiness enfolding her, then reprimanded him for staying awake this late, then hugged him again. Was she really home?

Unable to contain her excitement, she asked Lem where his lordship was.

Martha, from the drawing room door, answered her. "He arrived home today, rather exhausted. I believe he has turned in for the night." Patience's London companion walked across the marble floor to greet her friend. They shared a warm embrace, Patience slightly dazed at seeing Martha at Paddock Green.

Martha explained, "Bryce has retained me to look after Sally as governess, and my other duties have included nursing

Captain Kilkennen back to health. Surely, no woman on earth has had to endure a more cantankerous patient. But he is on the mend, thank the Lord."

Did Martha blush slightly at the captain's name? Patience would have to look more into that reaction.

Patience heard a shout of glee from the top of the staircase. "Aunt Patience, yer back!" Sally, holding tightly to the railing, maneuvered down the stairs and jumped into Patience's waiting arms.

She clutched the small child to her chest and hugged her tightly. She whispered in Sally's ear, "I've missed you, sweetheart."

Sally planted a big, wet kiss on her cheek. "I told Mr. Long you would come back to us."

Patience smiled at the wise child. "And so you were right."

"Ruff, ruff." Everyone watched as a little black-and-white puppy scampered down the glossy hallway floor, slipping and sliding.

They adjourned to the kitchen where Melenroy delighted in seeing her. And Lem introduced Patience to Falstaff, the newest addition to the family, that he had found on the road to Winchelsea.

Over a cup of tea, Patience learned about the events of the past two weeks. But since the earl had sent them here when he returned to Town, they could offer little news of him, for which Patience was famished.

Now that she was back at Paddock Green, she couldn't wait to surprise Bryce. But she was afraid she would be the one surprised at his reception. She couldn't know for sure what it would be.

On her journey across country, she had planned what to say to convince the hard-hearted man that he needed her, and that he might as well marry her. She shook her head. *No, I can't make those demands of him. I shall be loving and*

*patient and especially humble and offer him my heart and
pray desperately he has no cause to reject it. I will assure
him, no, promise him, that I will seek his advice on matters
beyond my knowledge and try to restrain my impulses, and
that I will simply be a good and faithful wife. No, none of
this sounded right or even sincere.*

Since she couldn't sleep, she decided to wander outside.
Everyone else had settled in for the night and a blanket of
silence had swept over the house. Standing on the stone terrace Patience gazed up at the midnight sky, awash with
bright stars, and drew her nightdress and wrap a little closer.
Assured Bryce slept, she would simply have to wait until
morning to see him. Footsteps sounded above her. Her
heart slowed to a crawl, and she rubbed her arms with a
sudden chill.

It could only be Bryce. As sleepless as she? Silence.

Patience stepped forward and looked up to find Bryce
leaning on the balcony's stone wall. She simply stared in
sweet imagination at his curly brown hair and beloved face.
He stood and gazed up at the sky, almost like a statue of a
Greek god in the faint moonlight.

A dismayed sigh escaped her when he began to walk
away. She ran out into the light. She had to stop him. What
could she say?

"What are you wishing for?" her slightly out of breath
voice called up to him.

Silence. Perhaps he had not heard her.

Then the footsteps again, closer. He peered over the railing, his face too dark to read.

"Patience?" he called softly. "Are you real? Is that you?"

Her silvery laughter floated on a cloud up to him. "Yes, I
have returned to do you a good deed. What do you wish?"
Her voice filled the night air between them.

He placed his hands on his hips. "Are you here to stay?"

He paused meaningfully and asked, "Why have you returned to Paddock Green?"

Patience licked her lips. "I . . . I left something behind. Please make a wish for me," she pleaded with him.

"What did you leave behind?" his voice low and disturbing, his dark eyes shadowed.

Patience hesitated. "My heart." She stretched out her arms in supplication. "Please, make a wish."

"You," he replied, his voice ragged with emotion, "I want you in my arms for tonight and for every night darkness covers the earth. I want you with me every day from the moment the sun wakes till it falls asleep at night." Bryce paused, finding the words in his heart. "I wish you never to leave me. You have given me all the stars in the sky and the richest treasure known to man. You alone have brought me the light of hope I never knew existed and taught me the love and faith of an eternity."

Patience stared up at him, the force of her love shining blindingly bright in her eyes. "Your wish has come true, I'm only a mere mortal who stands here wishing for your touch."

"A wish easily granted."

In no time at all, Bryce climbed down the wooden trellis that Patience had once used, and strode over to her. Two steps each brought them together.

Bryce groaned at the completeness he felt deep in his soul when he clasped Patience in his arms, the loneliness and despondency which earlier had imprisoned his spirit freed at last. He swept down to claim her lips, the kiss first gentle with wonder, then deepened with desire.

Patience wrapped her arms around his broad shoulders, but even standing on tiptoe, she couldn't get close enough to him. She demanded and took all that he could give her and yet it was not enough. Bryce urgently bent down and clasped her buttocks in both hands, lifting her off the cold stone. She never lost touch with his lips, her legs now locked around his waist, her arms tight around his neck.

He entwined his fingers in her hair, finally lifting his lips from hers, and leaned down to taste the long length of her white delicate neck, gratified to hear a low moan from his lady. He carried her into the side door and up to his bed-chamber with never a thought for his weariness or the ever-present ache in his injured leg. There were more important things on his mind.

Bryce and Patience kissed unabated as they tore off her robe and the nightdress beneath it. He stepped away only briefly and hurriedly to remove his shirt and boots before re-joining his naked nymph waiting for him. She had been waiting all her life for him.

Their bodies stretched and meshed perfectly on his high soft bed. Patience, with the dark glow of passion deep in her eyes, tore at the strings on his breeches and, before long, her soft, undulating body matched his hard, rigid form, seeking, searching, wanting.

She closed her eyes, letting the sensations wash over her as he caressed her breasts until they throbbed with pleasure and she panted beneath him. She gasped and her eyes flew open when she felt him probing at the entrance to her wet heat. When he thrust into her, his stormy blue eyes captured her passion-drenched green gaze and sealed their bond.

The rhythm of desire called to them, and they answered it with the hard, insistent, unstoppable force of their love for each other. Their lips clung to each other, tasting and teas-ing. She captured his tongue, pulling it farther into her mouth, and he responded in kind.

She heard him whisper, "Sweetness, only for me," against her ear.

She felt her heart jumping inside of her, in awe of the

power of his body and of his love. The power of his love almost frightened her before she realized she would never have anything to fear again.

Again and again, he slaked his hunger for her, a hunger which he knew would never be truly appeased. Then he looked deep into her soul and increased his rhythm until she shattered into a million pieces and took her soul with him. They remained entwined for a very long while, not willing to relinquish their real dream.

Patience knew Bryce wasn't sleeping but only play-acting with those loud snores. It was the other side of midnight, and she still needed answers. Answers which couldn't wait until morning. She lay with her back against his strong chest and her bottom against his groin, one strong hand draped over her breast. Patience tapped him on the thigh. Nothing. She rolled over onto her back, creating a slight gap in their bodies. That did it.

Bryce's eyes flickered open. "Where do you think you are going?" he asked lazily.

Patience, dazzled by the look of possession in his eyes, knew it matched her own. She thought for a moment. "I was trying to get your attention."

He leaned down to plant a long, slow, wet kiss on her lips. "There are other ways of getting my attention without leaving my side. In fact, I can think of . . ."

Patience attempted to be serious. "Bryce, I'm trying to hold a conversation with you."

He reached a hand around her waist and pulled her tight against his aroused body. "Sweetheart, the only talking I am willing to do right now needs no words."

"Please, Bryce. I need to tell you something."

He nuzzled her throat, then sighed and propped himself

up on his elbow, willing to grant this woman anything, but she had better make it fast. "You have my attention."

"About the necklace . . ." She held her breath, wondering what he was going to say.

His eyes widened. "The locket?" He reached for his coat lying on the floor, fished inside, and dropped her locket on her belly. "I believe this is yours."

Patience sat up, her white body gleaming in the warmth of the candlelight. "You found my locket my mother had given me! Where did you find it?" The joy in her eyes was unmistakable.

Bryce hesitated, then shrugged. "I found it on the floor next to Sansouche's body at the house on Puffins Lane. I meant to say something earlier to you, but I forgot."

Patience leaned over and kissed her thanks to Bryce. "I don't know how that man got ahold of my necklace, but I was distraught that I would never find it again."

Bryce pulled her back against his warm side. "Now that that matter is taken care of, how about . . . ?"

Patience held him off another minute. "But it was not my locket to which I was referring. You left an emerald-and-diamond necklace on my pillow our last morning in London together. Did you want to get rid of me?"

This immediately riled Bryce, who pulled himself into a sitting position next to Patience. "What the devil are you talking about? That necklace was a family heirloom. I was trying to tell you that I loved you and that I was going to ask you to marry me when I returned," his angry tones filled with disbelief that Patience would have thought of such a thing.

"But, you gave the countess jewelry when you wanted her out of your life. I thought you wanted me gone too." Her explanation ended in a sad whisper. He pulled her into his arms to comfort her, his right hand naturally finding and caressing her soft pink nipple till it crested with his gentle ministrations.

"Never. I had a talk that morning with Lady Elverston who insisted that I marry you. I already had the marriage license in hand."

Patience licked her way along his solid jaw, then something else occurred to her. "Colette tricked me into writing that note. She told me it was for the captain."

Bryce raised his eyebrows in consternation. "I thought that might be the answer."

As Patience, eager to share her part of the story, elaborated about Colette leaving the note for the captain, Bryce's features grew troubled, empathizing with the pain his friend must have felt. He held her even more closely when she told him how the three grave robbers saved her from being buried alive. Bryce told her that the constable had informed him that those same three men had been caught by a press-gang and were on a ship, heading to Spain.

"I never knew she could be so evil. I'm never letting you out of my sight again." Bryce didn't care how protective he sounded. He drew her back down onto the bed, anxious to show her how much she meant to him, but the worry in her eyes halted his motions.

"What is it, Patience?" he asked, wanting to see the happiness back in her eyes.

"What was that part you said earlier? That part where you explained the necklace's origin. I was wondering if I might hear it again."

Bryce grinned. "You mean about the part where I say, 'I love you, and I want to marry you'?"

Patience smiled at her only love. Her heart full, she could barely breathe. "Yes, that was the part."

First, he had to kiss her when she did that thing with her tongue. Then he looked into those hazel eyes alight with love and professed his own. "Patience Mandeley, I love you. Will you do me the great honor of becoming my wife?" his heart in his hands and a most serious look on his face.

"Oh, yes, yes, yes. Those same words of love I return to you a thousandfold."

Bryce sealed their vow with a mountain-moving kiss before beginning to pay homage to her body.

"Bryce?"

He looked up expectantly from the valley of her breasts. "I thought we were through with the talking part."

All he got for his efforts was a cuff to his shoulder. "There's something else."

"Mmmm . . ." he mumbled as he nuzzled her arm.

Thud. Thud. Two small sacks landed on his chest.

Bryce sat up and looked suspiciously at the brown bags. "What in Heaven's name . . . ?" he began.

Patience sat up beside him. "They are seeds from home. I want to start my own garden, here at Paddock Green."

Bryce actually shivered from the powerful emotion running through him. She was never going to leave. Her love had broken the pattern of his loved ones leaving him.

She closed her eyes, a beautiful smile decorating her lips.

"Patience?"

"Not now, Bryce, can you not see? I'm trying to fall asleep." She sounded more awake than sleepy, with laughter lacing her words.

She opened her eyes when he kissed her with such urgency, then whispered to him, "If only all of England would learn what we have been through since our marriage, I think they would call you 'The Notorious Bridegroom.'" Patience fell asleep listening to Bryce's husky laughter.

Author's Note

England's Sea Fencibles

The Sea Fencibles were first formed in the 1790s to watch the southeastern coast of England for an invasion. These Sea Fencibles were composed of volunteers and the militia who were trained to watch and signal towers and operate available gun-boats. They were the first line of defense in case of an invasion, and they were also needed to alert nearby villages to escape further inland. In May 1803, renewed hostilities with France began after a tenuous two-year peace. From 1803–1805, the threat of an invasion from France was at its highest. The southeast coast has the narrowest Channel passage, and at some points, those on watch could actually see the flotillas France was building for their plan to invade. The Royal Navy's victory at Trafalgar in 1805 secured the seas at home and abroad.

Romantic Suspense from
Lisa Jackson

See How She Dies	0-8217-7605-3	$6.99US/$9.99CAN
Final Scream	0-8217-7712-2	$7.99US/$10.99CAN
Wishes	0-8217-6309-1	$5.99US/$7.99CAN
Whispers	0-8217-7603-7	$6.99US/$9.99CAN
Twice Kissed	0-8217-6038-6	$5.99US/$7.99CAN
Unspoken	0-8217-6402-0	$6.50US/$8.50CAN
If She Only Knew	0-8217-6708-9	$6.50US/$8.50CAN
Hot Blooded	0-8217-6841-7	$6.99US/$9.99CAN
Cold Blooded	0-8217-6934-0	$6.99US/$9.99CAN
The Night Before	0-8217-6936-7	$6.99US/$9.99CAN
The Morning After	0-8217-7295-3	$6.99US/$9.99CAN
Deep Freeze	0-8217-7296-1	$7.99US/$10.99CAN
Fatal Burn	0-8217-7577-4	$7.99US/$10.99CAN
Shiver	0-8217-7578-2	$7.99US/$10.99CAN
Most Likely to Die	0-8217-7576-6	$7.99US/$10.99CAN
Absolute Fear	0-8217-7936-2	$7.99US/$9.49CAN
Almost Dead	0-8217-7579-0	$7.99US/$10.99CAN
Lost Souls	0-8217-7938-9	$7.99US/$10.99CAN
Left to Die	1-4201-0276-1	$7.99US/$10.99CAN
Wicked Game	1-4201-0338-5	$7.99US/$9.99CAN
Malice	0-8217-7940-0	$7.99US/$9.49CAN